THE RACE TO RAINHILL: A DAWN OF THE RAILWAYS ROMANCE

A TRADITIONAL GEORGIAN ROMANCE

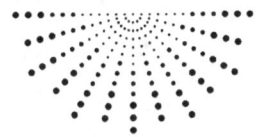

SUZETTE HOLLINGSWORTH

ABOUT THIS NOVEL

The romance of the rail ignites Irish immigrant Sorcha O'Shea's personal romance in 'The Race to Rainhill".

Sorcha O'Shea is a poor factory artisan who has the opportunity to be present at an event which changes the course of history: the race for dominance of the first passenger steam locomotive. The winner of the Rainhill Trials will build the steam locomotives for the Manchester-Liverpool line, the first passenger rail line in history.

While Sorcha is at the Rainhill Trials watching history unfold, she meets Robert Stephenson, the engineer who built the entry *Rocket*, as well as Thaddeus Fulbright, a newspaper reporter for *The Liverpool Mercury* who annoyingly turns up at every corner.

Lawrence Davenport, Sorcha's employer, has less than honorable designs on Sorcha, whose family depends on her income. Lawrence holds Sorcha's family's survival over her head.

Still living in an historical period containing all the elements of a Regency romance, "The Race to Rainhill" has carriages, horses, ball gowns, theatre, class hierarchy and aristocrats while on the cusp of the next phase of British life: the rail, which transformed travel, work, leisure, and even home life.

Experience the romance of the rail as history unfolds and Sorcha finds true love.

A traditional Georgian Romance.

THE GEORGIAN, REGENCY, AND VICTORIAN ERAS

"The Race to Rainhill" opens in 1829. The Regency era of British history is commonly applied to the years **1795 - 1837**, although the official Regency for which the era is named only spanned the years **1811 - 1820**, the reign of the Prince Regent George IV.

Technically "The Race to Rainhill" commences in 1829 in the Georgian Era (1714-1830) which includes the Regency era, though this novel certainly had its beginnings in the Regency era.

The Georgian era was named after the Hanoverian kings George I, George II, George III and George IV. Technically George IV was the **Prince Regent 1811-1820** (hence "The Regency") and the **King 1820-1830**. The third son of mad king George III, **William IV, was the king 1830-1837**, reigning alongside Queen Adelaide. The definition of the **Georgian era** is often extended to include the relatively short reign of William IV, which ended with his death in **1837**.

The Victorian era began 1837 with the coronation of Queen Victoria. When William IV died, Victoria became queen, and thus began the Victorian era in 1837. Adelaide was the dowager queen until her death in 1849.

"Cranford" by Elizabeth Gaskell, staring Judi Dench in the movie version, is an early railways classic book set in the early 1840s. Also "North and South" by Elizabeth Gaskell set 1851, movie version starring Richard Armitage and Daniela Denby-Ashe. "North and South" is a heart-wrenching portrayal of the interaction of those still living in the Regency with those moving into the Industrial Age.

So one minute we have a slow-paced agricultural society with carriages and horses in the style of Jane Austen and, not nine years later, we have the steam locomotive transporting both goods and humans.

One must not think that the only interesting or romantic era is the Regency era. In a sense, time stood still during the Regency era and life was much as it had been for centuries. Not so with the advent of the steam locomotive. Time went blazing into the future! Paradoxically, socially and culturally the Regency was known as a time of loose morals among high society (following George IV's example). With the reign of Queen Victoria came more traditional and family-focused values.

If everyone had wanted to stay in the Regency, that's where they would have stayed: but the future called with more opportunities for the working person: the railways expanded job and education opportunities as well as extending the areas where people could live. To be sure, there were some tragic developments with industrialization, but industrialization was also part of the movement towards universal education, voting rights, women's rights, racial equality, and a higher standard of living for the masses.

An interesting fact is that many of the early players in British rail were Quakers (e.g., Edward Pease) and men of God with high ethical standards. There is the common belief that a businessman must be ruthless and unethical to succeed. There are those who did not fit this mold and yet were very financially successful.

The time period of "The Rainhill Trials" on the cusp of both the Regency and Victorian eras is a fascinating era. There were people who lived through the Regency, the Georgian, and the Victorian eras.

These were not set periods of time in which people immediately transitioned into in one or the other with the corresponding personality type. Life was continually transitioning and there were electric forces at work impacting the social, economic, and legal structures of the day.

Welcome Aboard!

ACKNOWLEDGMENTS

I want to thank my wonderful husband Clint Hollingsworth for creating my beautiful cover (and also helping me with some of the more violent scenes. I'm not actually known for my fighting skills). I am blessed to have Clint, who is a black belt in karate and an exceptional editor/artist/writer and award-winning author of thrillers (the Mac Crow series), sci fi (the Seeker series), and apocalyptic (Wandering Ones). My husband, Clint, is the light of my life.

I based this novel on the real-life story of one of my friends, Michele Martin Kelly, **whose Italian great-grandmother brought her entire family to America** (New York) from Italy, supporting them all with her artistic endeavors! I was astonished to learn that *a woman* could support her family before women could even vote! I had always read that the majority of women could not make anything but dirt poor wages outside of prostitution or inheritance (read Charles Dickens and Henry Mayhew, among many others). It is no doubt true that social, legal, political, and economic conditions were terrible for women (and workers) in general in the industrial age, but there are always exceptions. Read on to discover Michele's great-grandmother's profession (and my heroine's), which will astonish you! I'm still astonished.

In Michael Portillo's "**Great British Railway Journeys**" he retraced the journeys taken by early train travelers. Portillo carried his 130-year-old Bradshaw's Railway Guide, the first book of railway time tables. I learned about the Rainhill Trials and the development of the railways, along with many fascinating train journeys, watching this show.

Another great reference and fascinating documentary is "**Full Steam Ahead**" with historians Ruth Goodman, Alex Langlands, and Peter Ginn. Well worth watching and quite entertaining! You can catch it on Youtube.

An excellent book and resource specific to my topic is "**The Rainhill Trials: The Birth of Commercial Rail**" by Christopher McGowan, which delves deep into George Stephenson's character and antics as well as into the politics of the time. I was shocked to learn that some things never change in terms of human behavior where there is a contest and power and money to be had. There is a great deal of fascinating behind-the-scenes information in McGowan's book.

And I want to thank my dear friends **Charlsie Sterry** and **Kem Chambers** who have supported me in my writing career and in all things and have truly helped boost my mood and kept me positive about myself and my life. Kem Chambers is the author of an inspiring, uplifting devotional/NDE recounting "My Journey with the Holy Spirit" which has helped me to listen to my inner guidance. I respect all world religions and most spirituality practices.

I remember all friends and the fascinating people I have met who have enriched my life and gotten me to this point. I am actually a relatively solitary person, but they are all precious to me.

PRAISE FOR SUZETTE HOLLINGSWORTH'S NOVELS

An experience

"She offers an incredibly varied experience. It's more than well written and the amount of information given in the story is rich and plentiful without clutter. You will emerge from the story feeling as if you truly journeyed somewhere real and at the same time imagined. It's a beautiful mixture and balance of history and fantasy....and such epic passion. The characters stay with you well after the story 's conclusion. I love it."

– Kindle customer

A Different Take on Historical Romance

"I've been reading HR books for 40 years. It's a welcome thing to find an author who can write a love story, based in history, yet have a novel approach. Ms. Hollingsworth is a delightful find, not the same retreads found in many HR books. I will gladly look for another book of hers to try, as she managed to keep my interest from page to page." – Elizabeth C.

A Pure Delight

"Mrs. Hollingsworth has an elegant writing style with a talent for providing ample amounts of detail without it being overbearing. A clear picture of the setting is painted perfectly each and every time. I never once wondered which character was talking, presenting themselves, or where the characters were. The story line progressed smoothly with plenty of humorous moments added in along with some bits of action. Overall a perfect blend of romance, clairvoyance, humor, history, and action. It is always a delight and pleasure to read Mrs. Hollingsworth work." – Nicole Yobbe

A most engaging read

"I love a good historical romance book that actually teaches the reader parts of history we don't normally know. I was thoroughly engaged from beginning to end, not sure how it would end. I loved the Hero and heroine for their depths of character. It seemed their love was an impossible probability, with perfect sexual tension all the way through. If you like an in depth love story, you will not be disappointed." – Elizabeth C.

"The Great Detective in Love" series is a finalist in the Chanticleer Mystery & Mayhem awards, Goethe Awards for Historical Fiction, International Book Awards, and Readers' Choice Book Awards.

"This is an excellent, gifted writer, with a true future ahead of her." – **CHARLOTTE CARTER**

"**A Sherlock tale with Hepburn and Tracy flair** . . . It had the feel of a classic old Hollywood mismatched romantic comedy to me.... Hepburn and Tracy. It was charming and would really appeal to people who love the idea of a kind of Jane Austen meets Conan Doyle mash-up." - Rayna-Red, Audible reviewer

"Very well done **watch out Johnny Lee Miller and J. Brett and B. Cumberbatch and Robert Downey Jr., this is the real deal**" – Byron, Amazon reviewer, 5 stars

"I'm truly enjoying Suzette Hollingsworth's The Great Detective In Love series. I love the actor for the audiobooks as well. . . She keeps the integrity of Sir Conan Doyle's original characterization of Detective

Sherlock Holmes and Dr. John H. Watson, while shaping a strong, confident, feminine, and loveable character in Miss Mirabella Hudson. The cases are dark and suspenseful enough without being stab-you-in-the-face scary, while providing scenes of well rounded characters. I hope she continues writing more, as they add a layer and depth to Sherlock Holmes that I've always wanted and hoped for with him. **As a massive Sherlock Holmes fan, this series warms my heart, gets it racing, and makes it sing.**" – KF, Amazon reviewer, 5 stars

The Race to Rainhill:
A Dawn of the Railways Romance

Romancing the Rails #1

A Traditional Georgian Romance

DEDICATION

To Kem Chambers
My dear friend who always has time to talk!
She's always there for her friends

To Charlsie Sterry
Who has supported and encouraged me since day 1
And who shares in my Scottish ancestry
Maybe that is where the mischief comes from?

To my mother Mary Denison
Who has had a lifelong love of trains and train travel
And has taken me on a few!

THE RAILWAYS CHANGED THE WORLD

"Internet? Bah! It had nothing like the impact of the railways!"

- Ruth Goodman, historian
"How The Steam Train Changed The World ", PBS video series

"The experiments at Liverpool will give a greater impulse to civilization than it has ever received from any single cause since the press first opened the gates of knowledge to the human species at large." – *"**The Scotsman**"* on The Rainhill Trials, October 1829

RAINHILL: BIRTHPLACE OF THE RAILWAY

"There is no precedent to the spectacular race known as 'The Rainhill Trials'. The crowd is a mix of every walk of life—and, shockingly, everyone is welcome. High society nobs, parliamentarians, railroad officials, sporting men, constables, engineers, scientists, food merchants, shop girls, domestic staff, grandmothers in their shawls, coal-heavers, dustmen, Gandy Dancers, Navies, the soiled doves, pickpockets, grand ladies in their gargantuan hats and balloon sleeves, servants attending to their masters' horses and carriages, and, need I say it, even the news men are welcome.

The old and the young. All having an equally good time and happy enough to share the platform on this one occasion. Today and only at Rainhill everyone is equal on this stage.

Children are beside themselves with glee; the adults are as well, but some of the more self-conscious make an effort to hide their delight so as not to be thought improper and vulgar. Which is a waste of time since no one can see anything but the steam locomotives stealing the show.

Being cast out of the limelight by the iron horses and their race, all spectators are both equal and frivolous.

The rail is the great equalizer." – Thaddeus Fulbright, The Liverpool Mercury

***

Rainhill is a village and civil parish in the county borough of St Helens, in the county of Merseyside, England.

Rainhill Trials is the first steam locomotive race
Changing the course of history
The beginning of commercial steam travel

CHAPTER ONE

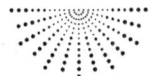

"*It was a time of enormous change, innovation, and creation. It was a time when we were all on the cusp of something great and magnificent—and no one knew what it was.*

It was as if we were looking through a window into the future but the window was blackened.

But we could feel it even if we could not see it. In some ways it felt as if we were living through the creation of the world again, the energy was so electric. It was both thrilling and terrifying, as change always is." – Thaddeus Fulbright, *The Liverpool Mercury*

April 13, 1829
Darlington, England

"FIE ON THE EXPERTS!" exclaimed George Stephenson, Chief Engineer of the Darlington-Stockton Railway, jumping out of his chair to face Edward Pease, principal owner. "The so-called 'experts' don't know what the hell they are talking about!"

"That is a brash statement, George!" Pease objected.

"You're damn right it is!" Stephenson sputtered. "And also true!"

"The conclusions of an extensive study by the top engineers in the field are here." Pease thumped a large mound of paperwork on his desk as he faced the other owners seated around him. "The engineering experts have done a thorough review of both the proposed steam locomotive, supported by Mr. Stephenson"—here he tipped his head to George Stephenson—"and the rope and pulley system of rail. It is their expert opinion that the rope and pulley system is the rail of the future."

"They're idiots if that's what they think. If they *do* think, of which I ain't seen no evidence." George roared. "They want an engine off-site to control the locomotives instead of putting the engine aboard the train! What do they have for brains? Mincemeat? And you're idiots for believing them."

Michael Longdridge raised his eyebrow at the Darlington line's Chief Engineer. "You're speaking to your bosses, Stephenson, take another tone."

"You talk sense to me and I'll change me tone!" George retorted.

"They must know something. They all have degrees from Oxford and Eton," said Mr. Craggy, no doubt alluding to the fact that the self-taught George Stephenson had not even gone to grade school. At the age of six, he began working. George went down the pit to mine coal at the age of ten. At fourteen years of age he became an assistant fireman, later manning the winding machine which pulled the cages of miners up from the pit face.

Stephenson's family was extremely poor, both his parents illiterate, and George had to go to work to support the family.

Which he did with gusto. George used his spare time to take apart and rebuild engines. While other men were drinking, smoking, and gambling, George used every second of his time to increase his knowledge. At the age of eighteen, George went to night school to learn how to read and write, progressing slowly and painstakingly.

But, in the eyes of the world, George Stephenson, with his northern brogue and lack of town polish, never had the same authority as college-educated engineers.

Longdridge pointed to the paperwork which would have proven laborious for Stephenson to read. "George, The *experts* did an extensive study."

"Balderdash! That's all they know how to do! They don't know how to build or fix anything! If any one of them had an idea, it would die of loneliness!" objected Stephenson, whose broad Northumberland accent the London engineers poked fun at, George not speaking the 'language of Parliament'.

"Nor do they know how to invent anything for that matter." George added. "Their *expert* opinion is that wagons moved along rails by a fixed steam engine utilizing a pulley system will work better and faster than a steam locomotive with the engine on board!" Stephenson stared back at his bosses, laughing, never inclined to suffer fools. "Don't you see the foolishness in it all? Dammit, use your common sense. You don't need a degree to tell you it is idiocy! Proof that him what's got credentials and fancy words can make you believe anythin'. Next you'll be tellin' me we can live without air if the Eton boys say it is so!"

Stephenson directed his attention to Pease. "Didn't I say when you had the intention of setting up the Darlington rail utilizing horses that a steam engine could pull 50 times the load horses could? And wasn't I *right*?"

Pease nodded. "Yes. And I agreed and hired you as the Stockton and Darlington Railway's chief engineer."

"And haven't I done a good job?"

"Excellent job."

"And still you turn to the fancy school boys."

"The rope and pulley system still proposes to utilize a steam engine," Longdridge considered. The remaining owners watched the argument escalate with interest.

George shook his head. "It will take double the locomotives to do the same job with a rope-and-pulley system. Not only that, but the Stockton & Darlington utilizes a one-way railway: coal is hauled from the collieries in the west to the wharves in the east. Then the wagons return empty to the collieries."

"How does that impact the conclusions of the study?" Longdridge asked.

"Damn it!" George threw his hat against the table, frustrated at the stupidity of everyone around him while labeling him uninformed. "The Liverpool & Manchester will be a two-way traffic hauling the same tonnage both ways instead of a light load on the return trip. These so-called experts have based their conclusions on a one-way system when we're talkin' about a two-way system. They've underestimated the number of locomotives needed with a rope-and-pulley system."

"I'm sure this weight difference has been accounted for," Mr. Craggy said.

"Whoever says that has only got one oar in the water! And did you read the report?" George thumped on the mountain of paperwork.

"Well...yes...of course I mainly went to the conclusions..."

"I ain't talkin' 'bout it no more!" exclaimed Stephenson, heading for the door. "I can see no one here has the brains fer it."

"Where are you going, George?" Fear gripped Pease as he realized he might lose the smartest employee he'd ever had. "You've not been dismissed from the meeting."

Stephenson turned, fire emanating from his eyes. Several of the owners scooted back in their chairs.

In an instant George's expression calmed, as if he'd had an idea. "If my word ain't good enough for you, fine, no point in talkin' about it. You have to see for yerselves."

Pease wrinkled his brow. "How would we do that?"

"Have a contest. See whose system works better. See whose vehicle is faster and carries more weight."

"A contest between your locomotive and the rope and pulley system?" asked Longdridge.

"No. A contest between steam locomotives." George laughed out loud. "The numbers for the worst entry will be better than the best rope and pulley data. Make it open to everyone. You already know how the rope and pulley system works. You can compare those numbers to each of the steam locomotives—*including mine!*"

As it so happened, George had been building steam locomotives for fifteen years. He and his son Robert formed the first company in the world created specifically to build railway engines, *Robert Stephenson and Company Ltd.*, commonly called the "Forth Street Works", as the company was located on Forth Street in Newcastle upon Tyne.

But nepotism was not the reason for George's enthusiasm. He believed the steam locomotive was not only the future, but the solution to transport.

He believed in the steam locomotive.

4

"Hmmm," Pease considered. "Trevithick built the first steam locomotive. He might have a fine entry."

"He very well might." George smiled broadly, as if he knew something none of the other men knew. "But will it be the best one? You'll find out just how the steam locomotives compare and who builds the best one." George muttered under his breath, "If you still want the rope and pulley after that, then there's no hope for you."

"What did you say, George?" asked Pease.

"I said 'all my employees are dopes, I need to fix the flue,'" Stephenson continued, "Don't have much more time to waste. I actually have to work for a living." George added under his breath. "They can't be told nothin', whether short or tall. They have to see it fer themselves."

"What was that George?" Mr. Craggy asked. "Please speak up. You're not really one to speak quietly, now what's got into you?"

"I said 'the circumference of the flue is too small, it's like it was built by elves.' Now, if you don' mind—it's going to blow..."

"We'll have to give a good cash prize to attract the best entrants," Longdridge considered, warming to the idea.

"But it will be worth it." Pease was decisive. "We'll have completed laying the groundwork for the Liverpool and Manchester line."

"Damn straight," Stephenson said, turning on his heel. "The cash prize is good, but it don't make no difference. The real prize is the winner will get the contract for the Liverpool and Manchester railway."

"If the steam locomotive outperforms the rope and pulley system," another owner objected.

"Ha! Ha! Ha!" Stephenson broke out into a gale of laughter. "*If.* Oh, these guys are as dimwitted as they are funny," he added under his breath.

"What did you say George?" Henry Booth, the company treasurer who was taking notes, asked.

"I said, 'The skies the limit, if you have the money.'"

"Right. Right." Longdridge nodded.

"Where will the contest be held?" Booth asked.

"Rainhill has a purpose-built line," Stephenson suggested.

"Hmmm...Rainhill...outside of Liverpool," Pease considered. "We could call the contest 'The Rainhill Trials.'"

"I hope we have some entries," Longdridge mused. "Outside of George's that is."

Stephenson shook his head and walked outside the door, slamming the door behind him. "See you there!" he yelled on the other side of the door, adding under his breath, "Eejit!"

* * *

"STEPHENSON SURE CAN BE difficult to work with," another of the owners said.

"Yes." Agreed Pease. "And also the best to work with. And he's made us all wealthy."

"Let's hope he doesn't lose it all for us," Longdridge muttered.

Edward Pease was a Quaker and a member of the "Anti-Slavery Society" who knew his obligation to God and country.

Pease happened to have a gift for making money as well. He shook his head. "Don't you remember the new mine at Killingworth where London's top engineers installed a Newcomen atmospheric engine to pump out the water? In six months, they couldn't get the mine drained. Then George stepped in and accomplished the feat in four days."

"Right off, he saw where the problem was," Longdridge agreed.

"If only we had a swamp which needs draining," Mr. Craggy muttered.

Pease raised his eyebrows. "We very well may."

In short order, the owners agreed to the proposed race, open to all entries.

And so the Rainhill Trials was set in motion to determine who was right: the experts or the self-taught engineer of the Darlington Railway, a man who never went to grade school and who had outperformed men of formal education, solving baffling engineering problems which had all but George Stephenson scratching their heads.

The prize of the Rainhill Trials was to be 500 pounds, a tidy sum of money. But more importantly, the winner won the contract to produce the first passenger steam locomotive for the tracks.

The winner would be a wealthy man indeed.

* * *

TEN VEHICLES WERE ENTERED. The organizers of the Rainhill Trials were surprised at the interest in the contest, both in entrants and in observers: thousands of people made plans to attend the multiple races over several days. Three hundred constables alone were hired to keep the crowds in check.

The Rainhill Trials had all the trappings of a grand race—and a turning point in history.

CHAPTER TWO

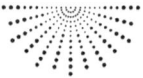

Above *Gorski's Butcher Shop*
12 Scotland Road, Vauxhall
Liverpool, England

*W*ANTED. – *A Smart active girl who can cook, clean dishes, and get up fine linen to do the general housework of a large family . No Irish need apply.* – London Times Newspaper

SORCHA, her mother, and her grandmother sat in their kitchen and did their needlework and mending while a stew cooked in a pot over the fire. The scent of meat, potatoes, tomatoes, carrots, and cabbage filled the room while the fire warmed the small home. The kitchen was also the living area and they felt fortunate to have it—and food.

"Before we moved to Liverpool the O'Sheas were never hungry and never lived in filthy conditions," Mrs. O'Shea said.

"Then came Hockenhall Alley," Grandmother Oonagh muttered.

"We'll never go back," Sorcha pronounced defiantly. "You need not worry, Mum, we have left that place forever."

"We still live in Vauxhall," Mrs. O'Shea said, as if Hockenhall Alley could reach out its octopus' arms and recapture them.

"But on Scotland Road in a much better apartment, right over Gorski's Butcher Shop," Sorcha reminded her mother.

"Mr. Gorski is a saint among men." Cecelia O'Shae wiped her brow. "He gives us leftover cuts at reduced prices."

"Stanimir Gorski is a Polish immigrant who appreciated our plight and rented to us." Sorcha nodded her agreement. "And you are a master at turning scraps into good meals, Mum."

Mrs. O'Shea sighed. "I always thought...you know, Sean did so well in the Royal Irish Constabulary, and they had a better reputation than the British police force even...well, I thought he might get a job with the Peelers or the Bobbies...*Ouch!*" Cecelia inadvertently jabbed herself with her needle. "But the Irish are 2nd class citizens here. I should have known."

"Yes. Considered part of the 'disorderly problem,'" Sorcha said, taking a sip of her tea.

The Irish were maligned in England. Sorcha O'Shea didn't dare misbehave—or breathe—for fear of appearing immoral. In this town an Irish woman putting one foot in front of the other was wicked.

I would like to not worry about what other people think of me for just one day.

I know who I am. I know I am a good person. I know right from wrong and I try to do the right thing. But sometimes when people stared at Sorcha she felt as if there was something wrong with her.

What are other people seeing that I don't see when I look in the mirror?

But she had nothing to complain about. Sorcha's heart ached for her father. All he ever wanted to do was police work—but he wanted to do it where he believed in the law; where "criminals" were actually criminals instead of his countrymen desiring independence.

"Turns out Sean doesn't have a country," Cecelia added. "Ireland doesn't want him, and neither does England."

"Doesn't want any of us," Grandmother Oonagh said matter-of-factly. "And yet here we are. God is greater than all of that foolishness."

"I never thought to see my husband working as a bartender and playing his fiddle on the side," Cecelia reminisced.

"He's a good musician. My boy can do anything he sets his mind to,"

Grandmother Oonagh remarked. She looked up from her sewing to lift her eyebrows at her daughter-in-law in a disparaging manner, as if her son had married beneath him.

"But Da is an even better lawman, Grandmother," Sorcha reflected. "And that's what he wants to do."

"What you want and what you get in this life is two different things," Grandmother Oonagh pronounced. "And it's no never mind neither."

Sorcha couldn't agree. An exciting and wonderful opportunity had come Sorcha's way and, more than anything, she'd like to say 'yes'. But she had to obtain her parents' permission first.

I'd like to have just one adventure to remember for the rest of my life.

And this might be her only chance.

Sorcha worked hard, contributing her earnings to her family's survival, and she was proud to do so. But she longed for a holiday.

Grandmother Oonagh handed Sorcha a sock. "Here, you can darn this while you're jabbering away."

Sorcha sighed heavily, setting down her teacup. "I need to ask Mother something. It's important."

"No reason why you can't work while you talk," Grandmother Oonagh said. "That's important too."

Sorcha picked up her needle and the sock.

"Sean has broken up his share of fights in the bar. So many knife wounds." Cecelia shook her head.

"It's what he was born to do Ma-ma," Sorcha said. She understood her mother's worry, but there was no stopping Sean O'Shea.

Cecelia O'Shea tightened her lips. "I wish he would quit that job as a bartender."

"You know he won't, Mum. It pays and they say Da is the best bouncer they've ever had at the pub," Sorcha said. "We have a nice home here on Scotland Road and we have food to eat. Da isn't constantly being threatened like he was in Ireland."

"Only for a few hours a day," Mrs. O'Shea muttered.

"And Papa would be down-and-out without employment: the pub was the only job he could get," Sorcha added.

"Except working the docks," Grandmother Oonagh offered.

"Hanging about at the wharfs, one is likely to go missing," Sorcha said. Many men were 'enlisted' into the Royal Navy against their will.

Sorcha paused her sewing momentarily to pick up the book she had gotten at the lending library.

"What is that book, Sorcha?" Mrs. O'Shea demanded.

"'The Last Day of a Condemned Man' by Victor Hugo," Sorcha replied.

Mrs. O'Shea raised her eyebrows. "What is that about?"

It means I am condemned to work until I die and never have a pleasure outing whatsoever.

"The book expresses Victor Hugo's criticism of the death penalty," Sorcha explained.

"Oh. Doesn't he think there should be a death penalty?" Mrs. O'Shea asked.

"No, he doesn't," Sorcha answered, returning to her sewing. "Hugo doesn't think any man should be put to death, whatever his offence."

"My father might still be alive if that was the law," Mrs. O'Shea whispered.

"He shouldn't have been executed anyway. His only offence was patriotism," Sorcha replied.

"Hush, Sorcha! Don't let anyone hear you say that!" There was genuine fear in her eyes.

"I would never say it in public, Ma-ma."

"I wish you had never learned to read, Sorcha. I never know what might slip from your lips, endangering us all." Mrs. O'Shea shook her head.

"The girl has no control of her mouth," Grandmother Oonagh nodded, for once agreeing with her daughter-in-law.

"I wonder where I get that from," Sorcha murmured, raising her eyebrows at her grandmother.

It was a point of contention that Sean insisted all his children learn to read and write. And now that he could no longer afford to educate them, he was glad he had put his foot down. The older taught the younger. For Sorcha, reading was not only a path to improvement, but reading opened up a whole new world to her. And yet Mr. O'Shea labored to read and write and Cecelia not at all.

"How do I know what you are readin' in them books?" Cecelia demanded. "A Mother should know what her daughter is filling her head with."

Clearly Cecelia didn't like the idea that her daughter could communicate in ways she was unable to monitor.

"Papa could teach you to read and write now that he has more time on his hands." Sorcha suggested, attempting to reduce her mother's frustration. *It would be difficult to feel helpless where one's children are concerned.*

"When do I have time for schooling, Sorcha? I work all day as a chair bottomer and you and Papa play in the pub some evenings." Cecelia O'Shea muttered under her breath. "Disgraceful."

"Oh, for goodness sake, Ma-ma, I play in the pub for the music. Where else am I going to play? In the streets? I do play in church sometimes."

There was nothing Sorcha loved more than playing her mandolin and singing. And Papa was quite good on the fiddle. Playing in the pub—Ye Olde Hole in the Wall at 4 Hackins Hey—was the most enjoyment she had. Papa relented and allowed Sorcha to play when he was there and able to keep an eye on her, for which she was eternally grateful.

"And Papa is chaperoning me the entire time," Sorcha added carefully.

"Sean never held to girls working before we left Ireland," she muttered. "And certainly not playing in pubs!"

"Everyone is so nice there, Ma-ma. And it's a respectable establishment. No low-lifes. Not like the Slaughterhouse." Especially now that her father was there.

Mrs. O'Shea raised her eyebrows. "No one is nice to the Irish in England. Particularly not the English." Cecelia didn't ordinarily let her bitterness show—it served no purpose.

"If someone is nice in this God forsaken place, they are up to something," Grandmother Oonagh pronounced.

But her mother had reason for resentment, Sorcha knew. Beginning with Cromwell's invasion of Ireland in 1649, crushing all resistance with extreme brutality and confiscating lands. Many Irish lords lost their lands and hereditary titles, suddenly becoming English tenants. Irish culture, laws and language were replaced. Under the Penal Laws of 1695, Catholics could not hold a commission in the army or enter a profession. It wasn't until the "Catholic Emancipation of 1829"—this year!—that Catholics were allowed to enter various professions.

"I lost my father in the 1798 Irish Rebellion," Cecelia said somberly.

"Yes. We know." Grandmother Oonagh said, "They hung him."

The British did not treat the Irish fighting for independence as prisoners of war, but, instead, executed them, generally by hanging. They regarded the Irish rebels as traitors to the crown. Tens of thousands of Irish died.

"True, the Irish have no reason to love the English, but I have fared well in Liverpool," Sorcha said. She felt guilty to love the life created by her mother's enemy who murdered her grandfather—it seemed a betrayal of sorts—but it also seemed better to be happy than resentful. "Indeed, I have to work hard, but I have a job. And a good job at that."

Sorcha knew her mother had a constant feeling of living among the enemy. *What a horrible way to live.* Cecelia was constantly on edge, even in her sleep.

But for Sorcha, life was better than it had been in Ireland. And, if truth be told, it was better for her mother too. But Cecelia was still tormented by the horror of her childhood.

"Yes, because you are young, pretty, and talented, doors have been opened to you, Sorcha." Cecelia frowned, her fear for her daughter apparent. "And yet, being young and pretty can be a disadvantage too."

Sorcha thought immediately of Lawrence Davenport, her boss' son, who had ulterior motives, but she didn't want to worry her mother. There were unscrupulous people everywhere. Sorcha had to learn to deal with them and to stay out of their way.

Maybe going to the Rainhill races wasn't the best way to do that.

I need to ask Ma-ma's approval to go and I'm having difficulty finding the right time.

Sorcha was desperate to go to Rainhill, she had been given the means to do so, and now she just had to obtain her parents approval.

Just that.

"I wish we had gone to America instead," Cecelia O'Shea said, placing her needlework in her lap. "I think there would be more opportunity for your father there."

"Perhaps. But the move to Liverpool has turned out so much better than I ever imagined," Sorcha considered. "I am happy here."

"I suppose you're thinking of marrying that young singer from the pub?" Cecelia shook her head. "He would not make you a good husband, Sorcha."

"Do you mean Enoch? He is perfectly nice." *And so dreamy.*

"A little too nice. And he definitely knows how handsome he is, mark my words, he knows when the girls are looking at him."

Which is all of the time.

"How could he not? He'd have to be an idiot not to know, and I can't abide idiots."

"Enoch is a little too free and easy with his favors," Mrs. O'Shea added. "I don't like you going down there and playing at the pub. It's no place for a young lady."

"I love playing music Ma-ma."

"Enjoy it because it has ruined your reputation. You have no chance of receiving a marriage proposal from a boy with a good reputation once he finds out you play at a pub."

"I don't play very often, Ma-ma. And if you know I'm not doing anything I shouldn't, and I know I'm not, why should we care what others think?"

"Because it closes doors for you, Sorcha. And you're such a beautiful, talented girl. I feel you should have the world..." Mrs. O'Shea dabbed her eyes with her handkerchief.

Sorcha put her arms around her mother. "Don't cry Ma-ma. I am happy. The children are doing well."

"I can't bear the looks: Others looking down on my wonderful family," Mrs. O'Shea sobbed.

"Please don't be sad, Ma-ma. You know I loved Ireland, but you have to admit it's a much better life for us in Liverpool."

"It is now." Mrs. O'Shea shuddered. "When we first lived in that cellar in Hockenhall Alley with no air, no light, no water." She closed her eyes briefly, releasing a sob. "Danny died. It was horrible. And Jamie almost died it was so unclean."

Sorcha held her mother at the memory of her brother's demise. "It's not your fault, Ma-ma. It's better now. I wish we could have saved Danny, but at least we all had each other to help us through our grief." As her mother attempted to control her tears, softly Sorcha added, "I wish you could stop being afraid and sad, Ma-ma."

"You're not afraid because you haven't seen what I have seen, Sorcha. That's exactly what I would want for you, love. It's better to have a pure and open heart and to have confidence. The world treats you better."

Cecelia shook her head. "The world hasn't beaten you down yet, Sorcha. I try to forgive, and I go to church, but I keep me eye on me back."

"Yes, Ma-ma. We all must."

Cecelia sobbed. "How could God have let Danny die?"

"God didn't kill Danny, Ma-ma. The greed of men did."

"Danny was so good."

"Yes, Ma-ma." Sorcha nodded. "Maybe too good for this world."

"I know God didn't kill Danny. But why didn't he stop Danny from dying? He knew how much I loved that little boy. How could he let my heart break like that?"

"I don't know Ma-ma." Sorcha put her arm around her mother. "But I do believe we will see him again. I feel that in my heart."

"I know why Danny died," Grandmother Oonagh interjected. "It's because of the Garden of Eden. The sin of man. Ain't got nothin' to do with God."

"I'm sure Danny didn't take the apple," Mrs. O'Shea murmured.

"We were in paradise, and now we're not. It's not that hard to understand, Cecelia," Grandmother Oonagh explained.

"Ma-ma, there is something I need to talk to you about," Sorcha posed.

There is never going to be a right time.

"Yes?" Mrs. O'Shea looked up from her needlework.

"I've been asked to go to the Rainhill Races. I want to go."

"The what?" Mrs. O'Shea exclaimed.

"It's a trial of the steam locomotives. Mr. Davenport asked me to go."

"Mr. Davenport? Your boss?" Mrs. O'Shea's revulsion and utter confusion was apparent.

"Calm down, Ma-ma, there is nothing wicked about this!"

Mrs. O'Shea began to swoon, as if she were going to faint. Grandmother Oonagh jumped up out of her chair and obtained the smelling salts.

Sorcha rolled her eyes. She was losing her patience. She understood that if bad things keep happening, then one expects it, but she was ready to leave it behind.

I am tired of always being distrusted when I contribute so much to the family, handing over most of my funds like a dutiful daughter. And she was nineteen years old, old enough to leave home!

Why does everything around here have to be such a Cheltenham Tragedy? You would think the angel of death had just passed through the house and foretold the death of all it's inhabitants.

"Oh, Mother! This is a ridiculous reaction to a proposed journey—a wonderful opportunity for me! Have I ever done anything to disappoint you? I am the most responsible daughter. Why am I always being treated as if I'm up to no good?"

"I would never allow a daughter of mine to go to a race! Put that entire idea out of your mind. I hope I raised you to be a lady, Sorcha O'Shea!" pronounced Mrs. O'Shea.

CHAPTER THREE

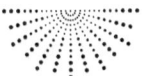

Newspaper offices of *The Liverpool Mercury*
May 1829

*T*he Reverend James MacGowan's **Preparatory and Finishing Classical and Commercial Academy** *was re-opened on Thursday, the 6ᵗʰ of May, 1829.*

The terms of instruction, in all or any of the languages, arts, and sciences, is eight guineas a year, depending on the age of the pupil.

'But what price can be placed on the acquiring of refinement and education to a marriageable lady desiring an eligible match?' asks Reverend MacGowan, an educated and respectable man of God by all accounts.

Apparently a price of eight guineas a year. Thaddeus Fulbright, junior reporter, thought to himself.

If I am bored to death reading this 'news', how will the general public respond? Thaddeus shook his head. *How will I ever make a name for myself if I must report this drivel?*

I need a big story. Finishing schools for young ladies? Bah!

Murdered prostitutes, bribes in Parliament, respectable people being thrown into debtor's prison, spies hung as traitors to the crown, the detestable sin of sodomy, the terrible influence of the Irish upon society.

That's what I need.

Indecency and Misdeeds, that's my ticket to success. Sensationalism, and the channeling of hatred and fear.

Thaddeus placed his illuminating reporting of MacGowan's Finishing Academy in his out-basket and picked up the second typed article for review.

Sometimes the ladies in the typing pool made an outrageous error and it was his job to catch the error.

Not that it would make that much difference. Possibly an error would improve the article.

CHAPTER FOUR

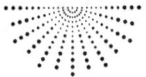

Above *Gorski's Butcher Shop*
12 Scotland Road, Vauxhall
Liverpool, England

"We may not be rich but we're not riffraff whatever anyone may say. We're as good as anyone and never forget it!" exclaimed Mrs. O'Shea.

"I'm sure we are," Sorcha agreed. But sometimes she wasn't so sure. She had seen ladies hold their noses up in her direction after taking one look at her strawberry blonde hair and green eyes.

"Reputation is everything, Sorcha Fae," Mrs. O'Shea added. "You must always protect it."

"Why should I try to impress people who will never like me whatever I do?" Sorcha asked.

"Impress me then, Sorcha Fae. You know I care about you and want the best for you," Mrs. O'Shea added with finality. "What is this talk of a race?"

"Mr. Davenport told me about it," Sorcha said.

"Your boss? Mr. Davenport wouldn't give you time off work to go anyway." Mrs. O'Shea was astonished. "There is no such thing as a holiday for the poor."

"You don't need no holiday," Grandmother Oonagh interjected as she sat in her chair doing needlework. "Idleness is the Devil's work."

"But Ma-ma," Sorcha objected, "Mr. Davenport is the one who told me about the Rainhill Trials. He says the trials are going to be one of the biggest events of the century."

"Why would Mr. Davenport be talking to you about races?" Cecelia O'Shea asked with suspicion. "Is that right conversation for a man to have with a young lady?"

"A young lady shouldn't be having no conversation with any man but her father or her husband," Grandmother Oonagh declared decisively.

"And her boss who pays the bills," Sorcha added. "Oh, Mr. Davenport talks to me about all kinds of things. You know how men of a certain age are. I'll just be sitting there working and he'll rattle on."

Mrs. O'Shea raised her eyebrows. "Such foolish talk must distract you from your work."

"Not at all. I keep painting, as his ramblings don't require much conversation from me. I don't mind. I find his stories amusing and maybe our brief interaction helps keep Mr. Davenport from being lonely." Sorcha shrugged. "You know he lost his wife last year."

"Has Mr. Davenport ever made improper advances toward you, Sorcha?" Mrs. O'Shea was nothing if not direct.

"Of course not, Ma-ma, I'm so grateful to Mr. Davenport for giving me a job when no one else would!" *But his son Lawrence, on the other hand...*

"We all are! And Mr. Davenport may talk about the races—as men are prone to do, though I must says I don't think it a right conversation a gentleman would 'ave with a young girl—but Mr. Davenport won't let you leave work to go. As if the *Davenport Textile and Mercantile* would let you off work to go schmoozing with the race crowd. And even if Mr. Davenport will, I certainly won't!"

"Thousands of people are going, Ma-ma. It's going to be like a world fair—only bigger. Can you imagine?"

"Precisely. Filled with criminals and pickpockets."

"I don't have anything in my pocket. What do I have to steal?" Sorcha considered. "Most of my money goes into the family jar." If there was any left after rent and food, her parents gave her a small amount back to save, which she hid in the floorboard.

Mrs. O'Shea looked down, ashamed that her daughter largely supported the family, but she was resolved on one point. "Then how are you going to pay for such a journey as that? Rainhill must be a full fifteen miles away."

"True. It is a world away. That's why it sounds delightful." Sorcha sighed happily.

"There is no such thing as a holiday for the working class only for the rich folk."

"Well it's not *exactly* a holiday, Ma-ma." *Even if it might feel like one.* "Mr. Davenport—"

"Where would you stay in Rainhill, Sorcha?" Mrs. O'Shea asked. "Did you think to stay in the saloons in downtown Rainhill? It would take a rich man's fine carriage at least four hours to get to Rainhill and very likely more. Sorcha, love, have you lost your mind?"

"I'd stay with my Aunt Hannah, of course. I'll write her and tell her I'm coming."

"You certainly won't do that!"

Mrs. O'Shea dotted her eyes with her handkerchief, attempting to regain her calm. "We owe you so much, Sorcha. You got the job at *Davenport's* and we moved to a decent house on Scotland Road." Her lips formed a trembling smile.

"It is lovely here, isn't it?" Sorcha remarked.

Looking about her home Cecelia sighed happily. "It is a comfortable room. You girls and your grandmother have your own bedroom. Sean and I have ours."

"And the boys love sleeping by the fire." It was a supreme luxury to have separate rooms. For a working family, often the entire family lived, slept, and cooked in the same room.

"Jamie and Colin are quite happy by the fire. And I'm happy to have a fireplace, as well as food in the cupboard." Mrs. O'Shea smiled contentedly.

It was a small house, nothing fancy, (but bigger than the damp cellar was), with lots of light coming in, and they only shared two walls with any other dwellings in this row house. They weren't completely boxed in. That was almost unheard of for the Irish.

The home was not luxurious, and they weren't rich, but they were *safe*. Sometimes the smells were unpleasant, but they were *always* unpleasant in Hockenhall Alley.

Of course, all the adults had to work diligently to keep their home. Everyone in the family worked, even the children, but there were three major bread earners, and five bringing in pennies. It all added up.

All four of the younger children contributed—Colin, Jamie, Molly, and Felicity—as well as Grandmother Oonagh. Jamie, who was eight, had a musical gift and he sometimes played for pennies. Colin, ten, sold newspapers in the street. Molly, fourteen, and Felicity, twelve, did very skilled needlework, which they sold.

"I'm relieved the children don't have to work in factories or coal mines, or become chimney sweeps or domestic servants," Sorcha said. None of the children worked full-time.

"Yes, Grandmother Oonagh takes in laundry and the girls help with that. It is all hard work, but nothing to the 12-hour factory days." Mrs. O'Shea sighed.

"But I wish we could send them to school," Sorcha added. She was sorry the family could not afford to send the children to the parish school at St. Andrew's Catholic Parish, besides the fact that they couldn't afford to lose the children's income. So the children were educated at home with what time Mr. O'Shea had, which was a fair amount.

"Phhtttt!" Grandmother Oonagh sputtered. "They don' need to go to school, they need to work."

"Don't you want the children to improve their situation in life, Grandmother?" Sorcha asked. "If they get an education they'll have better jobs later."

"It's sinful not to be satisfied with the station in which God has placed you," Grandmother Oonagh said.

By the pained expression on her mother's face, Sorcha could see that her mother tended to agree with Grandmother Oonagh. But Cecelia was torn as she wished the best for her children.

"No, Grandmother. God did not place us in Hockenhall Alley, nor did He wish us to stay there. That I know." Sorcha said. "Any God who would wish that does not love His children. And I won't worship such a God."

"Sorcha Fae!" Mrs. O'Shea exclaimed, making the sign of the cross. "That is blasphemy! Never say such a thing!"

"She has become the most uppity girl since she learned to read," Grandmother Oonagh muttered. "Thinks she makes the rules."

"I also read the Bible, Grandmother. And I won't take it back. That is not our God and not the God I worship. How could He not wish us to better ourselves? Or wish us to not have food on the table? Why did Jesus feed the four thousand then?"

"Because they were hungry," Mrs. O'Shea said.

"Exactly! It is not God who makes us poor but the greed of men. God has provided more than enough." Sorcha said.

"Hmph!" Grandmother Oonagh muttered. "It is dangerous to hate your betters."

"True, it might be, if they're actually better," Sorcha considered. "But I'm sure I don't hate anyone. I hate their actions sometimes." Sorcha touched her mother's hand. "I am sorry you work so hard Ma-ma."

"Well, at least Mr. Davenport doesn't work you to death and ruin your gift, love."

"Mr. Davenport gave you a chance when no one else would," Grandmother Oonagh said. "It's God's work."

"I do appreciate Mr. Davenport, but I assure you my boss is entirely motivated by self-interest and not by altruism." Sorcha knew very well she wouldn't have any clout at all if she weren't Davenport's best artist.

"What does 'altruism' mean?" Grandmother Oonagh asked with displeasure.

"Charitable acts," Sorcha replied.

Grandmother Oonagh shook her head in disapproval. "Sorcha reads so much she don't sound like the rest of the family."

"The Lending Library is free entertainment, Grandmother," Sorcha replied. "That must be better than drinking gin and whore-ing about."

Cecelia O'Shea clutched her chest and moaned while Grandmother Oonagh bowed her head, exclaiming, "The Saints preserve us!"

"And this is what education does for a girl!" Cecelia shook her head in dismay. "Such language!"

"When God smites down Sorcha take care you ain't sittin' too close to her," Grandmother Oonagh advised.

"I didn't read that at the lending library," Sorcha objected. "I might have heard it at the dinner table."

"Not from me, you didn't!"

"I'm sorry Ma-ma, I didn't mean to upset you. I was merely stating the truth."

"Watch your mouth, Sorcha, and refrain from 'the truth'," Mrs. O'Shea commanded.

"Yes, Ma-ma."

"We ought to wash her mouth out with soap if it weren't so dear." Grandmother Oonagh looked at Sorcha suspiciously. "You keep talkin' of the races and Mr. Davenport. Is he expecting you to express your gratitude for your job in a way which ain't fitting or proper?"

"Oh, no, Grandmother! Nothing of the sort!" Sorcha exclaimed. "And I can't believe you think I would ever agree to such a thing!"

Mrs. O'Shea shook her head. "I won't have you putting on airs, Sorcha. Just because you have a fancy job and you've learned to read, don't forget your place. And don't think you're better than everyone else in the family."

"Why should my wishing to improve myself mean I'm putting on airs?" Sorcha didn't mention that she gave her brothers and sisters reading and writing lessons too.

Who do you think you are? Her mother's expression seemed to say. Sorcha knew 'knowing one's place' was deeply rooted in fear, but that didn't make it any less important in her mother's eyes.

"Not at all." Mrs. O'Shea cleared her throat. "I worry about your safety and reputation, Sorcha." Sorcha shook her head.

"Sorcha, I know I get upset about your readin' sometimes," Cecelia added. "But I just feel left behind. Like I'm not part of your life anymore." Cecelia dabbed her eyes with her handkerchief. "I love you so much and I want you to be safe and to have a good life."

"You'll always be a part of my life, Ma-ma. I love you." Sorcha hugged her mother. "I'm doing very well. I'm happy. I don't know why you worry so much."

"It's not you who've done anything to worry me, Sorcha. You're a wonderful daughter." Cecelia sighed. "I'm not worried about what you might do, Sorcha. I'm worried about what others might do *to you.*"

"Sorcha is nineteen years old, after all. She could get married and

leave this house and you would have nothing to say to it, Cecelia."
Grandmother Oonagh muttered under her breath, "Then she would be
somebody else's problem."

"That is true. I am full grown." Sorcha agreed. "And I want to go to
the Rainhill races."

"A race is not a fit place for a lady. And how would you get to Rainhill, Sorcha? With no money you can't even go by the mail coach."

"I have a little money, Ma-ma," Sorcha replied indignantly.

"It's not right for Sorcha to support the family," Grandmother
Oonagh said. "That's the man's job."

Cecelia ignored this slight on her husband. "If it was just a matter of
the money, I would approve your trip to Rainhill since you earned it, but
it is impossible, Sorcha. You might as well ask if you can attend a prize
fight."

"The Lord doesn't like selfish and uppity women. Look at Eve,"
Grandmother Oonagh added.

Sorcha barely contained her laughter. *Who is uppity, if not you,
Grandmother?*

Sorcha remembered a sermon at St. Anthony's: women weren't
supposed to think of themselves and they weren't supposed to have
dreams—unless those dreams involved marriage and children. Anything
else was selfish.

Am I never to enjoy myself? Certainly the wealthy were pleasure bent
all the time. Sorcha had never been on a holiday. And she worked hard.

The way of life for the poor was to work six days per week with
never a holiday until one died. This was the only option for the poor.

"This trip is something I want. I rarely ask for anything for myself,"
Sorcha said. "It's not a regular race. It's about the future of our town, Mr.
Davenport says."

Cecelia O'Shea raised her eyebrows. "What does that mean?"

"The winner gets to build the steam locomotives for the Manchester
to Liverpool railway which is almost completed."

"There will be an iron horse going from Manchester to Liverpool?"
Mrs. O'Shea appeared shocked.

"Yes, the train always carried coal, but now it is going to carry people
as well."

"I won't be riding it!" insisted Mrs. O'Shea.

"Maybe not, but lots of people will."

"Well, they're crazy then," Grandmother Oonagh chimed in, if she had ever chimed out.

"Mr. Davenport says the completion of the line will greatly affect his business, the textile and mercantile. Which will, in turn, affect me and our family."

Mrs. O'Shea appeared to soften. "What do you mean, Sorcha?"

"Because textiles can be brought more easily and cheaply from Manchester to Liverpool."

"That may be so, but you still aren't going to the Rainhill races, Sorcha Fae O'Shea. Not as long as I live and breathe!"

CHAPTER FIVE

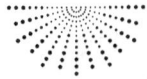

Newspaper offices of *The Liverpool Mercury*
June 18, 1829

*his evening's entertainment will commence with the ascension and
dissension of an inflated balloon, grand and magnificent: designed,
painted, and splendidly decorated, in honor of the Victory of Waterloo June 18,
1815.*

*Only fourteen years ago the Duke of Wellington and General von Blücher
put a decisive end to the French attempt to dominate Europe, destroying
Napoleon's imperial power forever.*

*Certainly a day to be celebrated and remembered. How close the world came
to domination after twenty-three years of war but not for the Iron Duke and the
Prussian General!*

*For tonight's commemorative event, the young gentleman acrobat will,
during the balloon's ascension and dissension from the back of the stage to the
pit, perpendicularly exhibit HIMSELF ON HIS HEAD, maintaining equilib-
rium (it is hoped!) during the whole of this unprecedented feat of agile exertion.*

*But—can it be believed?—this breathtaking exhibit is not the finale! Made-
moiselle Nina Ferzi will then balance a pyramid of forty lighted candles!*

Finally, the two acrobats will be enveloped in a shower of fireworks to ensure the delight of everyone present.

Could there be a more poignant remembrance of the critically important Battle of Waterloo which secured freedom from tyranny for the British isles?

WHAT COULD BE A MORE appropriate nod to the Battle of Waterloo and the brave men who died than a man standing on his head and a woman balancing forty candles?

Thaddeus shook his head in disgust.

And, ideally, going up in flames.

Thaddeus had no objection to sensationalism—in fact, he placed his life and his success in its hands. But it should be meaningful, inspiring, *somewhat* true sensationalism.

Nothing worse than fabricated drama. It's an offense to thinking individuals to make a circus of such a significant battle to freedom-loving patriots as the Battle of Waterloo.

I used to be a fun sort of person always ready for a good joke. Now I'm a bitter twenty-five-year-old desperate for content. For advancement.

It's difficult to advance without content. Where are the wars, the maniacal dictators, the corrupt politicians?

Hold on! Positive change and advancement is also news. If only there were some of that.

Thaddeus longed for success with every fiber of his being.

This ever-changing society they lived in: Thaddeus wanted to be at the heart of it.

He could feel they were on the cusp of something big. Something life-changing. Something which would change the world forever.

And where am I? Reporting on all the stories no one else wants.

Never fear, old boy, there will be laughter again: I'm going to be laughed off the news bureau.

Thaddeus might only be twenty-five years of age, but he was not without a brain. Britain was at war with France for the first eleven years of his life. His own father was a person of influence in the war office, thereby fortunately not losing his life in the engagement. But Clifford Fulbright knew many who had lost their lives.

Not only am I a disappointment to myself, but I am a disappointment to by father. Granted, it was practically impossible not to be, so inclined to disapproval was his father.

Now we are doing somersaults and lighting candles commemorating the campaign.

Not to mention there are so many important milestones occurring in this age of industrial innovation, and what am I reporting?

Thaddeus kept up his reading of scientific journals; he couldn't fall behind or he was destined to cover the finishing schools, circuses, and health scares of his time.

Please, God, give me a real story.

Ah, the stories were there. He was living in amazing times.

But those stories were all being given to someone else.

Amidst all the sounds of typing, coughing, conversations, and general noise, Thaddeus felt a tap on his shoulder.

"The boss wants to see you." Penelope Watts, the boss' secretary, interrupted Thaddeus' self-indulgent pity.

"Right." Thaddeus rose, wondering what Egerton Smith, the owner and founder of *The Liverpool Mercury*, wanted. No doubt someone somewhere was walking a dog and Egerton thought Thaddeus was just the man to cover this extraordinary encounter. Possibly there was a falling leaf involved too.

In which case the story might go to someone else.

Mr. Egerton Smith was scanning the paper when Thaddeus walked into his office. He was a tall, well-built, formidable person, clean-shaven, with a high forehead, clear eyes, and a strong jaw, known to intimidate anyone who stood between him and the truth.

"Take a seat, Thaddeus."

"Yes, sir." Thaddeus waited for the pronouncement.

"Do you realize the *Liverpool Mercury* is the best paper in the city?"

"Of course. Everyone knows that. Even the competition."

"*Especially* the competition." The boss cleared his throat. "And the best paper in some other cities as well."

"No doubt due to it's international scope." As well as focusing on local news, the Mercury also reported on both national and international news, allowing the paper to circulate in Lancashire, Wales, Isle of Man, and London.

Thaddeus had to admit, his boss had not done too badly for a local boy. The young reporter looked squarely at Egerton waiting for the other shoe to drop.

"*The Liverpool Mercury* is a reformist paper. The *only* paper fighting for better housing and public health in Liverpool," Egerton added. "No other paper cares about the poor."

"Right. The other papers want to report on the high society and sensationalist events that will sell." This was one area where Thaddeus thought Mr. Smith didn't get it right. The Do-gooders never made as much money as the fear mongers.

The poor will always be with you. Besides, the poor aren't going to buy a paper. They can't read. The poor was not one of Thaddeus' particular interests. Unless he was the one who was poor.

Which is beginning to look like my future.

"Obviously we care about sales." Egerton frowned.

"Obviously."

"But we also want to report on the stories no one else will cover. Yes, sir, bringing the truth to light," Egerton added. "It's what the news is supposed to do. And do you know why, Fulbright?"

"To be the best paper in the United Kingdom?"

"Of course! And why do we want that?"

"To make the most money?" Thaddeus spoke from the heart.

Egerton Smith frowned. "If we do our jobs right, we'll make money. If your goal is to make money, Fulbright, you'll never be a great news-paper man. Focus on your actual job! That's the only way to be good at it." Egerton shook his head.

"And that would be?..."

"To bring the truth into the light! That's your job. The news exists that positive change may occur. Truth-based reporting. That's the power of the written word: To change the world for the better. That's the power of the media."

"Right." Thaddeus nodded, feigning admiration. *I wish you might change the type of articles you're giving to me.*

"Absolutely. *The Liverpool Mercury* is not being funded from pay-offs by the guilty wishing to keep the truth out of the paper," Smith added.

We might make more money if we were.

Not admirable but certainly profitable.

"*Serious* reporting." Thaddeus snorted, recalling the articles in his 'out' basket.

"What, Fulbright? Do you have a cold?"

"Sorry, sir." Thaddeus took a handkerchief out of his pocket. "Do go on. Fascinating."

"And in 1819 our man was at the scene in Manchester's St. Peter's Field, later writing a critical report of the behavior of soldiers at what became known as the Peterloo Massacre."

"Sometimes I think you know what's going to happen before God does, sir." For once Thaddeus leveled with his boss. No doubt about it, Egerton Smith had an instinct. Thaddeus' mood began to perk up.

"And what do you call countries without the media, Fulbright?"

"Dictatorships."

"Right!" Egerton smiled at him, a rare occurrence.

Something is up. Thaddeus didn't want to get his hopes up. *Why am I here?*

Egerton Smith pushed the paper towards Thaddeus, tapping on the paper as he did so. "Look at this."

"Sir, it's...it's only the advertisements..." Thaddeus muttered, his heart falling in his chest. *What now? Shall I be selling ladies' hats?*

"I know it's *only* the advertisements! Don't you think I don't know what is in my paper? READ IT! Read it out loud, Fulbright."

Thaddeus took a look at the advertisement which had formerly been under Egerton's finger in the middle of the paper and began reading,

"*THERE IS no class of Disorders to which cultivated Society is so subject as the NERVOUS, which invade alike the delicate female, and the robust and seemingly vigorous youth. Listlessness of mind, impaired strength and appetite, flatulence, head-ache, vertigo, and dimness of sight, more or less observable in them all. No remedy has hitherto been so generally beneficial in Nervous Disorders as the Cordial Balm of Gilead—*"

"No! No! NO!" Egerton yelled, tapping his finger on the article just to the right of the Lunatic Asylum notice.

· · ·

THADDEUS GAVE IT ANOTHER TRY, reading:

THE LIVERPOOL **and Manchester Railway** invites engineers and iron foundries to submit plans for locomotives to compete for the winning design. A trial will be held in October of 1829 in Rainhill. The winner will receive the contract to build steam locomotives for the newly completed Liverpool and Manchester Railway and receive a purse prize of five hundred pounds.

"WHAT DO you think this means, Fulbright?"

Thaddeus felt excitement take hold of him. It was a small advertisement and yet it spoke volumes. "I think it means something big is on the horizon. Very big. *Momentous.*"

"How do you mean?" Egerton Smith asked, showing the first signs of approval.

"The Liverpool and Manchester Railway is almost completed. The owners have not decided whether or not the locomotives will be the new steam locomotives or the rope-and-pulley variety. It looks like this race will determine the future of rail in Great Britain."

"And very likely the world," Egerton added.

Thaddeus whistled. "And who will be made rich from it."

Egerton Smith smiled. "Right. So you have been paying attention, Fulbright. It's going to be a huge event."

"I wouldn't think a scientific experiment would garner that much interest from the general public," Thaddeus considered.

"Not because of the outcome, but *because it's a race.* The masses don't care about the business decisions of the railways."

"Most attendees will have never seen a steam locomotive before," Thaddeus nodded, considering his boss' words. "And, instead of horses, there will be huge machines racing each other."

"Because these machines will go faster than any machine or animal has ever gone in the history of the world," Egerton Smith said. "Because, like never before, these locomotives will carry *people* in addition to goods. It's going to be a spectacular gathering unlike anything seen before. Which will excite and thrill the public."

"Naturally. These steam locomotives—these iron horses—are something glorious to behold. They are rather a cornucopia for the imagination," Thaddeus added.

"*Cornucopia...*" Egerton muttered. "*...*A goat's horn overflowing with fruit and flowers?"

"An abundant supply of good things, I should say," Thaddeus said.

"Ah...Just so." Egerton cleared his throat. "Mark my words, Fulbright, the developments following the Rainhill Trials are going to be even bigger than the race itself—which is saying something! *Our world will be unrecognizable in a short time.*"

Thaddeus nodded, his excitement growing. He couldn't disagree with anything his over-zealous boss was saying. "I daresay we can't imagine the world we will live in."

"We have to try!" Egerton exclaimed. "Give it a shot, Fulbright. How might steam locomotives change the world?"

"Hmmm..." Thaddeus knew this was a test, the outcome of which could change the course of his life. "Food and textiles will be transported from one part of England to another. The prices of textiles will decrease. People who have never been on holiday or left the place they were born will see other parts of England: we will be a more unified country. Work and education opportunities will be expanded."

Egerton appeared pleased. "So you're familiar with the locomotives, Thaddeus?"

"Naturally, they're the future. I have to keep up." *They're going to leave hot air balloons in their wake.*

"Have you seen any of the plans?"

"Not precisely, but I think I could put my hands on them when the time comes."

"And why is that?" Mr. Smith asked.

"I've talked to Ericsson and Braithwaite who have been working on horse-drawn fire engines with steam pumps. These fire engines are known for their ability to raise steam quickly."

"So...can you get a copy of those designs?"

Thaddeus shook his head. "Not a chance! Give away the blueprint to a fortune? Before the competition?" Thaddeus didn't want to laugh at his boss—at least to his face—and so he stifled a chuckle.

Egerton nodded. "They wouldn't want to give away their ideas for someone to steal. And after the race?"

"Hmm...Once the competition ends, and the contract secure, someone with the right contacts could possibly put his hands on the plans and publish them alongside news of the race."

"All technology is eventually shared." Egerton smiled broadly. "Could be a scoop! Do you think Ericsson and Braithwaite will be entering?"

"I'll ask. Wouldn't surprise me at all. The grand prize will make the winner rich. It's the perfect incentive for all these scientists looking for someone to fund their ideas. Not a lot of opportunities out there."

"Until now." Egerton nodded. "Seems like you're well informed, Fulbright."

"I try to be. It's my business."

"I like a young man who is ahead of the game."

"I'd put my money on anything Ericsson and Braithwaite build to be the winner," Thaddeus added. "Their designs are notably sophisticated."

Egerton studied Thaddeus. "So you're familiar with the steam engine."

"I've studied it. Fascinating, isn't it?"

Egerton slapped his knee. "I'm going to send you, my boy."

"Send me....?"

"To the Rainhill Trials for the race of the iron horses of course. You'll write the stories."

Thaddeus felt the dark clouds over his world open up as light and joy —meaning success, power, and prestige—descended upon him through the clouds. "Thank you, sir! I will do a good job for the *Liverpool Mercury!*"

And I'll write the most favorable articles I can about Braithwaite and Ericsson. If they win, they will be rich and famous men.

And I will be their special friend who helped them.

"You'd better, Fulbright! You have until October to read and interview everything and everyone affiliated with steam locomotives. Give me the stories to review personally. Interview all the prospective engineers you can find."

"Yes, sir!"

"Make sure you don't show any partiality. News reporting is objective."

"Of course, sir." *Unless it's one's friends who deserve to win. And a poor newspaper man who deserves a promotion.*

"Pay-offs alter the news and it is no longer truth, remember that."

I don't see how it's relevant. I don't have anything to pay anyone.

"Just one thing." Egerton rotated the ring on his finger, as he often did when he was deep in thought. "Do you think the steam locomotive will replace horses?"

"That's a radical thought, sir," Thaddeus said. "What do you think, sir?"

"You haven't answered my question."

"Does it matter, sir? I mean, if the steam locomotive changes the course of the world—the way we work, eat, and travel—it seems to me that is the relevant point. Whether or not there are still horses about, does it matter? There will still be cats in trees and dogs chasing cats as well."

"Everything matters to a newspaper man." Egerton frowned. "It's truth that matters....You have several months to answer my question, Fulbright. One way or another, you give me an answer. You can't be afraid to put forth the data—or even to speculate—if you're going to be a newspaper man."

"I thought speculation was a job for gypsies and their crystal balls," Thaddeus said.

"I've no objection to speculation if it is disciplined and logical," Egerton added. "In fact, it is the duty of every scientist and news-paperman."

"Yes, sir."

"You know, Fulbright, I took you on as a favor to your father. He was a great man in the war office."

"So I've been told many times. Thank you, sir."

"And I think we'll make a newspaper man out of you yet."

Thaddeus walked out of his boss' office floating on a cloud made of steam.

The only problem is steam can burn.

CHAPTER SIX

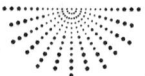

Above *Gorski's Butcher Shop*
12 Scotland Road
Liverpool, England

"Bㅤut Ma-ma, Mr. Davenport requires me to go to the Rainhill Trials," Sorcha explained. "It's just like I told you: he *asked* me to go!"

"Why in God's green earth would Mr. Davenport *require* you to go? Is he taking you himself? Is he proposing a tryst?" It was as if understanding dawned on Mrs. O'Shea. "Just as I thought. You must quit your job immediately, Sorcha. I would rather starve than sell off my own daughter!"

"Oh, Ma-ma, it's nothing like that at all." *Though Lawrence will be going.* "Mr. Davenport thinks I should go."

"And though I appreciate Mr. Davenport, he has no right telling me how to raise my daughter."

"It's nothing to do with that, Ma-ma. I keep trying to tell you. It's for work. He has a job for me to do."

"A *job*?" Mrs. O'Shea appeared aghast. "He wants you to *work* at the Rainhill races? Doing what?" she asked suspiciously.

"Mr. Davenport wants me to paint commemorative buttons of the Rainhill Trials."

Mrs. O'Shea nodded. "You are his best button maker."

Sorcha shrugged. "That's what he says."

"I'm sure Mr. Davenport knows."

"I only paint them, Ma-ma." *On porcelain, wood, enamel, pearl, and bone.* She pictured herself with her magnifying glass painting miniatures on buttons in great detail.

Who knew making buttons could be so lucrative? Or that she would be so good at it?

"Allowing him to sell those beautiful buttons to his wealthy customers," Mrs. O'Shea said.

Sorcha never thought she could make a living at art. *Everyone in her family was surprised as well.*

Sorcha always loved art but never thought it could put food on the table. Particularly being a girl, there were very few opportunities. There were children in the mines, doing dangerous work, working thirteen hours each day. Sorcha was so happy she could protect her younger siblings. Even her father couldn't get a decent job.

But Mr. Davenport didn't care if she was Irish or not. He cared about money in the till. Everybody wore buttons. There wasn't a garment or a pair of shoes not utilizing buttons as their means of fastening. Button-making was a big, money-making business. And beautiful, ornate buttons could fetch a pretty penny.

"And now you're keeping a roof over the entire family." Sorcha knew her mother loved their home and the stability it represented.

"You'd have to have a new dress, Sorcha, so people will think you are a fine lady and won't bother you," Mrs. O'Shea said, shaking her head. "Fabric is expensive, sewing is time-consuming, and the little time I have is devoted to my family."

"In the first place, I *am* a fine lady," Sorcha refuted.

"Yes, but mostly you have work clothes. It wouldn't do." Cecelia shook her head.

"In the second place, I'm quite a good seamstress myself."

"She is." Grandmother Oonagh agreed. "Don't know why we can't get any work out of her."

Sorcha was, in fact, a fine seamstress and adapted the fashions somewhat, lowering the waistline and broadening the sleeves.

For evening the look was still low cut and very much like the ball gowns ten years ago, but Sorcha never had any occasion to wear evening wear. Certainly not a ball gown.

I wish I could wear a ball gown just once. Sorcha sighed.

For a poor girl to wear a low-cut gown was to say she was cheap. If a wealthy woman wore the same gown, she would be elegant.

I wish I could go to a ball.

Or go anywhere, for that matter.

In truth, only wealthy Parisian women wore the newest styles, and, thereafter, wealthy Londoners. Country folk and the poor always took much longer to adapt the newer fashions, generally the hand-me-downs of their wealthy mistresses. Why, the fashions worn in Paris would likely not be seen in the English countryside for ten years.

As her mother was proof.

Sorcha glanced at her mother, who actually looked quite pretty sitting by the fireplace. She was a handsome woman, Sorcha thought, even though her mother had not kept up with the current fashions, wearing the Empire waist dresses popular when King George was the Prince Regent.

"If you think you'd like a new gown, Mother, I will help you make it," Sorcha offered.

"I don't like the new clothes. They aren't nearly as comfortable. Not to mention, they look ridiculous," Mrs. O'Shea said.

"Do you think so?" Sorcha asked. "Different maybe." Being a young person, in Sorcha's mind, looking fashionable *was* worth discomfort. True, the newer fashions had extreme proportions, as contrasted to ten years ago. The seam below the bodice kept moving lower, and the sleeves and the skirt kept getting bigger.

For both women and men, the silhouette was exaggerated and out of control.

But that's what makes fashion so fun.

"A working woman must be able to move in her clothes," Grandmother Oonagh added, looking up momentarily from her needlework. "We are not goods on display."

"Indeed we are," Sorcha replied. "Women always are."

"I'm not sure I like the new fashions either." Sorcha added. "But I have to keep up on fashion since that's my job. It pleases Mr. Davenport."

Mrs. O'Shea sighed. "If Mr. Davenport wants you to go to Rainhill, I suppose you'll have to, but you still have to have a chaperone."

"Mr. Davenport knows that." Sorcha cleared her throat. "He's sending his son Lawrence."

"His son? That won't do."

Sorcha didn't think so either, but she didn't want to say.

"How can a man be a fit chaperone for a girl unless it's a family member? It's the men a girl has to watch out for!" Mrs. O'Shea protested.

"Mr. Davenport's carriage driver will drive us. Lawrence and I will be in the carriage."

Mrs. O'Shea frowned. "Your immediate boss? I don't like it."

"I'm not that fond of Lawrence either. But what can he do? Even Lawrence wouldn't dare risk his father's reputation."

At least I hope not.

CHAPTER SEVEN

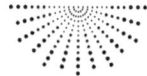

Davenport's Textile & Mercantile
Liverpool, England
August, 1829

"I don't know why you always favor Sorcha over everyone else, Father," Lawrence grumbled.

"Do you mean Miss O'Shea?" Henry Davenport raised his eyebrows.

"Yes, of course, Miss O'Shea." Lawrence cleared his throat nervously.

"Who should I favor if not Miss O'Shea?"

"Violet—Miss Villin—is a faster painter. Why don't you send her to the Rainhill Trials instead?" Lawrence considered that Violet seemed more likely to bestow her favors upon him than Sorcha did.

Sorcha might scorn me one too many times and lose her position. Lawrence smiled at the thought. *That would teach her.*

"Possibly faster, but certainly not as good of an artist. That often goes hand-in-hand." Mr. Davenport regarded his eldest son quizzically, as if this inverse relationship between speed and quality should be obvious.

Lawrence didn't appreciate the condescension. He felt his anger mounting, though he knew he must control his indignation in front of his father. "Miss Villin is very talented."

Very.

"Of course she is. But Miss O'Shea is *more* talented. She is an expert on all the technical aspects as well as the artistic touches. Her work is second to none. She will be able to reproduce a train with all its squares and triangles—which is no mean feat considering she is painting in miniature." Henry Davenport shook his head. "No, Miss O'Shea is the right one for the job."

"You know, Miss O'Shea doesn't show me the right respect. I am her immediate supervisor."

"Miss O'Shea disrespectful?" Mr. Davenport tapped his pen on his desk. "She is a confident and opinionated young lady to be sure—not always to my liking..."

"Most assuredly not!"

"—But I always assumed Miss O'Shea's hardships made her both strong-willed and driven. She has a strong work ethic. Which has put a great deal of money in our bank account. I'll thank you to remember that, Lawrence. As fast as you go through money, I would have thought you'd come to appreciate those whose labor puts the money in the bank."

"That may be so, Father, but would you like a woman bossing you about?"

"I would not. And neither would I tolerate my employee bossing me about, either. It sets a bad precedent."

"It most certainly does!"

"And yet, I've never observed Miss O'Shea to—"

"—You're never there when we're together, Father."

"Yes, I am. Quite frequently. That is to say, I'm in the artisan's room frequently talking to Miss O'Shea." Mr. Davenport wrinkled his brow, pausing to reflect. "But where you are Lawrence, I can't say..."

"I can't just hang about with the seamstresses, the painters, and the craftsmen. I have work to do."

"I suppose so..."

"And I tell you, Father, Miss O'Shea treats me in a contemptuous manner."

"That's strong language, Lawrence!" Henry Davenport lowered his head and considered his son. "Perhaps you were showing Miss O'Shea disrespect about a topic she knows more about than you do?"

"Sorcha—Miss O'Shea—takes an uppity attitude with me. As if *she* is better than *me*." Lawrence laughed.

"Naturally we can't have our employees placing themselves above us. Puts a spoke in the wheel." Henry shook his head. "Let me know if there are any other incidents."

"I certainly will." Lawrence smiled to himself.

Henry Davenport knew his oldest son was not perfect, but he thought Lawrence was merely sowing his wild oats, and Lawrence said nothing to disavow his father of that notion.

"He'll grow out of it as he has more responsibility", Lawrence had overhead many times.

The last thing I want is more responsibility.

"Now look here, Lawrence," Mr. Davenport added. "I know you'll be accompanying Miss O'Shea to the Rainhill Trials, but I don't want you to mix with any of the help—Miss Villin or Miss O'Shea. Blurring the lines is bad business."

"What do you mean by 'mix', Father?"

"I don't want you to marry any of these girls."

"I wouldn't dream of it." *Marry* them? Lawrence chuckled to himself.

"Most of them can't even read and write," Mr. Davenport said. "They —some of them—might be quite pretty, but they aren't suitable."

"True, they aren't very smart."

"I didn't say that. Some of them are very smart, but they haven't had the benefit of an education as we have." Mr. Davenport's jaw was firm. "The relevant point is they aren't of the same social station as we are."

Lawrence nodded in agreement. He may have pretended to hold many opinions which were not his own—such as a desire for hard work and responsibility—but he certainly believed in his own superiority. That he could agree too with completely sincerity.

Lawrence chuckled to himself. *I can't imagine taking Violet to the opera or the theatre. She likely wouldn't understand the story line and wouldn't know what was going on.* The adoration was nice enough, but she was good for one thing and one thing only.

"They bring nothing to the match—no connections, no wealth, no prestige, no social status. It would not be an advantageous match. I don't wish to be ridiculed by anyone over my son's choice of a bride. It's not good business." Mr. Davenport cleared his throat. "I don't want any red-headed grandchildren. People will think we're of Irish descent."

"Couldn't have that. Not very popular around here."

"No. I personally have no problem with the Irish. But as a prominent businessman, I have my position in society to think of."

"Of course, Father."

Henry Davenport leaned back in his chair. "But I do have a soft spot for Miss O'Shea. She's a very talented girl—and a hard worker. She's the best artist we've ever had. The wealthiest customers come to see us instead of our competitors. Most notably the *Compton House*."

"Compton House has more merchandise than we do, Father."

"*Compton House* might be bigger—with five full stories—but *Davenport's* has better quality merchandise. We don't need more, just better. Remember that, son."

Mr. Davenport stared pointedly at his son. "Don't you do anything to mess up our advantages over the competition, Lawrence."

"What could I do?"

"Don't let your drinking and gambling get out of hand. And no womanizing. A little fun I can understand, but your reputation is the most important thing you have. Never forget that, Lawrence."

"How could I?" *When the old man is gone, I'll do whatever I want. The business will be mine, and I'll have money to do whatever I want.*

"You weren't born with lands and a title, Lawrence. We have to work for a living."

You don't have to remind me of that.

"Only the very rich can afford to lose their reputations," added Mr. Davenport. He leaned back into his leather chair. "Still, work is not a bad thing. It builds character. Having everything handed to one is not good for anyone."

If it's good enough for the very rich, it's good enough for me.

"You know, Douglas is doing very well in the Household Goods Department. I'm thinking of promoting him to manager."

"Douglas? My younger brother?"

Mr. Davenport laughed. "Who else? What other Douglas is in the Household Goods Department?"

"That's a pretty easy department to run."

"Maybe. But Douglas has some innovative ideas."

I do too. And when I'm running things Douglas will be gone too.

CHAPTER EIGHT

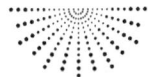

Davenport's Textile & Mercantile
Liverpool, England
September 1829

"Well, I don' see why you should get 'o go to Rainhill and I canna' go," Violet retorted to Sorcha. They both sat at their work stations painting their buttons, but they were still allowed to talk as long as they kept working, having more benefits than the other shop girls.

"I'm going because Mr. Davenport, who is my boss, ordered me to go." *I'm getting tired of repeating this. As if I have anything to say to anything.*

"You must 'ave done somethin' to trick him."

I'm beginning to wish I wasn't going. It isn't worth all the harassment.

"Like what, Violet?" Sorcha wrinkled her brow. "How am I going to trick or coerce Mr. Davenport?" *I doubt anyone could.*

"I don' know. But you did somethin'! It ain't fair!"

Sorcha rolled her eyes. "It is a working trip, Violet."

"And you get 'o go wiv' Lawrence."

"That is my punishment," Sorcha muttered under her breath. There was a great deal of noise in the factory, so it was easy to hide one's remarks.

"Wot? Wot did ya' say?" demanded Violet. She glanced suspiciously at Sorcha, who she suspected of trying to steal Lawrence's partiality.

Violet pouted. "I've seen 'ow Lawrence flirts wiv' ya', Sorcha O'Shea!"

"That is no fault of mine, Violet. Why don't you talk to Lawrence about it instead of to me?"

Violet laughed. "It ain't 'is fault, it's yours!" She added under her breath, "Tryin' to nick 'is fancy."

"And how is that?"

"By puttin' on yer posh airs an' all."

Sorcha rolled her eyes. "That might be how you attract men, but it isn't mine, Violet."

Violet laughed. "Wot other bleedin' way is there?"

"With your personality. With your conversation."

Violet looked at Sorcha as if she was crazy.

"It depends on the type of man you want to attract, Violet."

"I don' see that you have attracted *any*, Sorcha!"

You have a point. But if Lawrence is the best you can do...

Violet received many advantages, as everyone knew she was protected under Lawrence's umbrella. Violet had led Lawrence on for months, enjoying the special privileges at work, a little heady with the power, taking longer lunch breaks and throwing it in Sorcha's face, as well as talking badly about her to Bernice.

But Bernice, the floor supervisor, wasn't buying it. Bernice knew the quality of Sorcha's output, which was better than Violet's. And Bernice knew who the ultimate boss was: Henry Davenport. Still, it was a difficult path to walk.

"You're playing a dangerous game, Violet. You shouldn't be leading Lawrence down a path you don't intend to deliver on. Once you're there, you may not be able to turn back."

"Keep yer nose out o' me business, Sorcha!" Violet exclaimed.

"I'm sorry, I was just trying to help," Sorcha said. "Besides, you're the one who started by attacking me because the boss chose me. There is nothing I can do about that. I'm not going to lose my job because you're having a conniption fit."

Sorcha caught Bernice's eyes, begging for help. Bernice walked over. "Get back to work Violet and leave Sorcha alone to her own work."

Violet glared at her. "Oi, Leave me alone, or I'll tell Lawrence."

"Do your work, or I'll tell Henry," Bernice retorted.

Violet pouted and returned to her work.

CHAPTER NINE

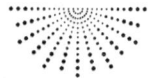

October 6, 1829
1ˢᵗ Day of the Rainhill Trials
Rainhill, England

"*There is no precedent to the spectacular race known as 'The Rainhill Trials'.*

The crowd is a mix of every walk of life—and, shockingly, everyone is welcome. High society nobs, parliamentarians, railroad officials, sporting men, constables, engineers, scientists, food merchants, shop girls, domestic staff, grandmothers in their shawls, coal-heavers, dustmen, Gandy Dancers, Navies, the soiled doves, pickpockets, grand ladies in their gargantuan hats and balloon sleeves, servants attending to their masters' horses and carriages, and, need I say it, even the news men are welcome.

The old and the young. All having an equally good time and happy enough to share the platform on this one occasion. Today and only at Rainhill everyone is equal on this stage.

Children are beside themselves with glee; the adults are as well, but some of the more self-conscious make an effort to hide their delight so as not to be thought improper and vulgar. Which is a waste of time since no one can see anything but the steam locomotives stealing the show.

Being cast out of the limelight by the iron horses and their race, all spectators are both frivolous and equal.

The rail is the great equalizer." – Thaddeus Fulbright, The Liverpool Mercury

"Isn't it the most thrilling experience of one's entire life?" Sorcha breathed in deeply, smelling the burning coal, the flowers, the cotton candy, the assorted foodstuffs, and the ale. Gentlemen in their frock coats and top hats, ladies in their crinoline hoop skirts, laborers in their Sunday best, and even jugglers and card sharps attempting to play a round—or arrange a card game at the local saloons after the day's races —while they waited for the race to begin.

I'm truly here. I can't believe it.

The Rainhill Trials—a race of the steam locomotives—was the most exciting event Sorcha had ever been to.

That anyone had ever been to. Except maybe the chariot races in Roman times or the Christians in the arena pitted against the ravenous lions.

It feels considerably more like a county fair than a technical trial. With all the hustle and bustle about, Sorcha was having difficulty maintaining her ladylike composure and hiding her excitement. Since arriving from Ireland, she had not been this far from Liverpool – 12 miles away! – and it had taken a full half-day's journey to get to Rainhill by carriage.

Sorcha wasn't alone in her exhilaration: over 10,000 people came from Liverpool and even further to watch the trials. The air vibrated with the energy of anticipation.

People knew something magnificent was on the horizon. All except Lawrence Davenport, her escort, that is.

"I'm sure there is something more thrilling." Lawrence gave her an inappropriate smile, letting his eyes move along her bodice.

Sorcha frowned and turned away, hoping she showed her distaste sufficiently. She began fanning herself with her fan.

This appeared to please Lawrence all the more. He took pleasure in knowing he had discomfited her.

What a sorry excuse for a human being—she could not call Lawrence a "man"—would wish to frighten a woman to express his dominance?

Sorcha willed herself to behave with more decorum than she felt.

"Do you think steam locomotives will replace horses, Mr. Davenport?" Sorcha wondered out loud as she watched the spectacle before them. She wasn't interested in Lawrence's opinion, but he was hovering about her and she wanted to impress upon him their professional relationship.

Hopefully that would keep him at arm's length.

Not that she couldn't take care of herself. Sorcha fingered the hat pin in her hat. Being a former police constable, Mr. O'Shea had taught his eldest daughter how to protect herself from predators. She hoped she never had to do so or she would no doubt lose her profitable job.

"Nah. Not a chance," Lawrence replied. He brushed up against her arm and she moved away.

She swatted his arm with her fan. "Please be a gentleman, Mr. Davenport. Your behavior does you no credit."

There was a flash of anger in his eyes.

Good. She had gotten her message across.

Sorcha smiled to herself as she watched her father on the tracks below. He might be a good policeman, but her Da was not the best chaperone. She was happy for him: Sean O'Shea was having a ball for the first time in a long time.

Sean O'Shea had to struggle to keep from falling into despair since they moved from Ireland. When her younger brother Danny died from the hunger and disease of living in Hockenhall Alley in Vauxhall, under such squalid conditions, that had been a terrible low point for her father. For all the O'Sheas, of course. But the Irish's pride was their family. The man, as the head, accepted responsibility for anything happening to the family.

But now Sean O'Shea was in his element. With the greatest of ease, Sean O'Shea directed pedestrians off the tracks as if he were a person of authority, assisted with the heavy work, stopped fights among the rowdy, and did a better job of policing the place than the actual Bobbies.

Mr. O'Shea's only error was thinking Lawrence was a respectable member of society.

Sean O'Shea wasn't the first person to be fooled on that count.

Lawrence rarely showed his true colors to anyone except females in the lower classes.

Granted, Sorcha might not look as if she belonged in the lower classes—she had sewing skills and had been educated at home, besides being an avid reader. She was, nonetheless, on the bottom rung in a class society.

"Why don't you think these locomotives shall take over the horses' work, Mr. Davenport?" Sorcha knew very well that the way to get along with men was to agree with everything they said, listen and rarely talk, and never voice a controversial opinion. Men liked to think they were smarter, their opinions raindrops from heaven. Many men didn't like a smart woman. Except for her father, who was proud of his daughters.

Ordinarily Sorcha didn't care if men approved of her or not. But Lawrence was the boss' son, so best not to irritate him—or to get too close.

It was clear Lawrence had taken a fancy to her. It wasn't to her advantage to offend him. She never led Lawrence to believe she had any exceptional interest, but he was persistent. Walking a straight and narrow line wasn't easy.

"The steam engines are unreliable, Miss O'Shea." He cleared this throat, shaking his head. "And dangerous. A fireman was killed and his engineer permanently maimed when an engine exploded not two years ago."

Sorcha covered her mouth with her gloved hand, her horror genuine. "How dreadful!"

"Steam will never be used for passengers—only cargo. It wouldn't be ethical to put humans in danger," Lawrence added.

You put humans in danger every day in your factory. Where does this sudden surge of conscience come from?

"Hmmm...I wonder. It appears there are a number of passengers riding in that locomotive—is it the *Rocket?*—you see that older gentleman carrying on and quite making everyone laugh. He appears to be the engineer."

"He's a buffoon!" Lawrence sneered. "Besides, along with the dangerous complications, the steam locomotives aren't that much faster than horses. How can it possibly be worth all the risks?"

"To the contrary...it looks like that locomotive carrying all those people is going quite fast!" she exclaimed.

"Those machines are impressive I grant you, Miss O'Shea. But it's all show."

"How many horses would it take to carry that many people, I wonder," Sorcha considered. "I would think at least twenty." *I'd like to ride that magnificent machine myself.*

Sorcha shivered as she beheld the steam locomotive entries on the tracks below, all so different and yet so marvelous. She had done her research in advance when Mr. Davenport supplied her with the newspaper articles, but to see them in person was breathtaking. They had vastly different appearances—and, she suspected, vastly different engineering. Just the proximity to the main components—the water, the coal fire, the throttle, the piston, the driver, and the engineer—varied so much, so surely the engineering was not equal.

Which arrangement was best, she didn't know. Sorcha knew she should take out her notepad and start sketching the locomotives, but she was too excited to do so. She couldn't possibly sit still and stare at a notepad!

There is time. Sorcha resolved to enjoy her first day. She didn't have the focus to do any work today!

"Are you cold, Miss O'Shea?" Lawrence put his arm around her shoulder.

Sorcha took the decorative umbrella she was carrying and dug it into Lawrence's foot.

I have just about had enough! Besides, pain spoke when words did not.

"Ouch!" He immediately began hopping and making a scene, yelping. "Damnit, Miss O'Shea, why did you do that?"

"Oh dear, did my hand go where it shouldn't have? That makes two of us then, Mr. Davenport."

"You hurt me, Sorcha!"

"I'm so sorry," she said with feigned sympathy. "Maybe you hurt me."

"By merely touching you?"

"Yes, where not appropriate or desired."

Lawrence frowned as anger crossed his expression. "I would take care to treat me with more respect, Miss O'Shea. I am your supervisor."

"I said I was sorry, Lawrence. And are you sorry for your improper advances?" She was fuming now.

"I-Improper?" Lawrence stuttered, turning beet red. Whether it was from embarrassment or anger, she didn't know. But it seemed to her the time had come to be direct. She had tried everything else to no avail.

"Yes, what else would you call it putting your arm around a young lady to whom you are not affianced?"

At that moment Sorcha caught her father's eye, who waved at her. *He had been scanning the crowd for her after all.* "Smile at my father, Mr. Davenport, so he knows he isn't needed."

Lawrence looked a bit ruffled, but he quickly waved and smiled at Mr. O'Shea. Lawrence understood the importance of appearances, if not of good behavior.

"Your father would never approve of your taking advances with his employees," Sorcha added. "I am not someone you are courting, as well you know."

Lawrence had made the threat to her that he could fire her, and she simply returned the threat. Lawrence wouldn't like her telling his father what had transpired. Of course, she would not wish to do so either. Better if she took care of it herself.

Hopefully, Lawrence would get the hint.

Sorcha glanced at *her* father who was trying to break up a fight on the tracks. She wasn't a child anymore and he couldn't always be around to protect her. Which was why she carried a umbrella and used it as her father had taught her. The hat pins in her hair would do a great deal more damage.

Sorcha didn't want to harm her employer, as ungentlemanly as he was. Maiming one's employer wasn't good for her continued employment.

And it wouldn't be good for Lawrence either.

Sorcha noticed a man in a working man's tweed suit glance her way and frown. He was tall and slim, handsome, and he had a pencil behind his ear. He carried a notepad.

"No, no, of course I am not courting you," Lawrence said defensively.

"Then why do you take liberties with me?" Sorcha frowned. "Are you saying you would take liberties with a woman you had no intention of properly courting?"

Lawrence looked away, for once silent.

Realization dawned, and Sorcha felt her fury rising.

Of course. Mr. Henry Davenport, Lawrence's father, would no doubt be violently opposed to any match between his son and an Irish immigrant.

How could I have been so stupid? There was no way on God's green earth Mr. Henry Davenport wanted Sorcha marrying into his family: he was a nice man, and she was eternally grateful to him, but Henry Davenport would consider the O'Sheas considerably beneath his family.

Lawrence's intentions were now clear to her, as well as the insult to her person.

"Because I....thought you were cold, that's all..." Lawrence acted apologetic, but there was the look in his eyes which said she had made an enemy.

"Lawrence Davenport, you are treating me as one of your low-bred women! How *dare* you!"

The memories of living in Vauxhall swept over her and she bit her tongue. More than anything in the world, Sorcha didn't want to let her family down.

But I cannot let someone compromise my virtue. Especially Lawrence: once a girl gave him an inch, he would take a mile. He would use his position of power to take advantage of her.

It has to be nipped in the bud now.

Sorcha was a valuable employee of Davenport's. That protected her from retaliation, didn't it? And anyway, she had never encouraged Lawrence's advances, so Mr. Davenport couldn't take it out on her, could he?

Lawrence had no real interest in her anyway. Would he see her destroyed when he wasn't even interested? Was his pride that great?

It was too bad Douglas wasn't her boss; he was an honorable man.

I wish Douglas were the eldest.

Lawrence was the type of boy who always had to be skating on the ice, who couldn't simply enjoy the many blessings he had been given, working hard out of gratitude.

Lawrence had to be risking everything all the time. He didn't know right from wrong—or, if he did, he would choose 'wrong' every time. 'Wrong' was more exciting and interesting to him. Upright behavior was to be avoided at all costs, which labeled him as a follower in his mind.

"Which locomotive do you think will win the race, Lawrence?" Sorcha posed, attempting to steer the conversation in another direction. She rarely addressed Lawrence as "Mr. Davenport". There was only one Mr. Davenport to her. Lawrence might be her supervisor, but for some time they addressed each other by their given names. Lawrence had breached formality first and she followed suit.

"The *Novelty*." Suddenly the man with the pencil behind his ear was standing on the other side of her. He tipped his hat to her as he studied Lawrence with suspicion. "Thaddeus Fulbright of the *Liverpool Mercury* if I might be of any assistance."

Lawrence butted forward. "Lawrence Davenport of *Davenport's Textile and Mercantile*."

"I've heard of you. Apparently the stories are true."

"What does that mean?" Lawrence demanded.

Thaddeus bestowed a look of condescension worthy of a duke upon Lawrence before turning towards Sorcha. "And you are, Miss, if I could make your acquaintance?"

"Why do you ask, sir?" He had appeared out of nowhere and she was not accustomed to giving her name to every stranger who asked. Besides, she was still a bit shaken up by Lawrence's effrontery.

Thaddeus glanced at her umbrella and tipped his hat to her. "Very well. I shall simply address you as 'the lady with the wicked umbrella.'"

Sorcha suppressed a giggle with the recollection. It would have been difficult to miss Lawrence hopping about if one were looking in her direction.

Thaddeus glared at Lawrence, adding, "It's a bit of a crush and there are all kinds of unsavory characters lurking about."

Sorcha threw the gentleman an appreciative glance for his understanding. She felt an instant comradry with him.

"Sorcha O'Shea," she replied. "True, there are, but I am managing."

She looked up at the handsome stranger with dark blonde hair and intelligent chestnut brown eyes. It was kind of Mr. Fulbright to check on her.

Fulbright. *I have seen that name before.*

"So I see." Thaddeus bowed. "Pleased to make your acquaintance, Miss O'Shea. And are you all alone here?" He glanced at Lawrence with an expression of scorn.

"Miss O'Shea is with me, naturally," Lawrence said.

"I mean, are you under anyone's protection?" Lawrence asked pointedly, having obviously observed her displeasure at Lawrence's grabbing her in public.

Sorcha liked this Thaddeus Fulbright. He had to know that Henry Davenport carried some weight in Liverpool, where he undoubtedly worked and lived, as well as observing that Lawrence was well-dressed in a tailored suit. And yet Mr. Fulbright was clearly unconcerned with Lawrence Davenport.

Whereas Lawrence dressed like an aristocratic dandy, Mr. Fulbright's attire was that of a professional man, consisting of a green and brown tweed morning coat, dark green pants, and a hurriedly tied cravat, surprisingly stylish. The young newspaper reporter knew how to pick his colors, which were flattering to his dark blonde hair.

But she didn't think he was a rich man. He looked to be young—around twenty-five years of age—and possibly was only beginning his career. He didn't have the leisurely or entitled air of a wealthy man but, instead, had the air of someone in a hurry to get somewhere and to do something.

I might do well to heed his example.

It seemed to Sorcha they had an immediate understanding and were, moreover, birds of a feather.

Mr. Fulbright wasn't accompanied by a man servant, nor did he carry a cane. Instead he had a pencil behind his ear. He wore a working man's John Bull top hat, a less exaggerated form of the top hat Lawrence wore.

"My father, Mr. O'Shea, is here." Sorcha replied, hoping her expression was telling. She pointed to her father who had his arms fully extended, attempting to keep pedestrians from going out onto the tracks.

"Is Mr. O'Shea one of the special constables employed here?" Thaddeus asked.

"A Bobby?" Lawrence laughed.

Sorcha smiled. "He wishes he were. He just attempts to create order wherever he goes." Sorcha glanced at Lawrence. "Mr. Davenport is my employer's son."

"I am your boss, Miss O'Shea," Lawrence corrected her in a tone of ownership.

Thaddeus raised his eyebrows and frowned at Lawrence once again. "Ah, yes."

Understanding clearly dawned. Thaddeus returned his eyes to Sorcha. "So you are employed by the Davenports, Miss O'Shea?"

"I am."

"And does Davenport's allow all of their employees days off to attend the races?" Thaddeus asked.

"It is a working trip for me. No doubt like yourself," Sorcha replied. Thaddeus looked perplexed, as if he couldn't perceive what job she was possibly doing while watching the races. Hopefully, Lawrence's unprofessional relationship wasn't an indicator.

Sorcha studied Thaddeus with interest. He was handsome in an approachable way, talkative, and with a bit of the knight in shining armor about him. She liked that. He had his feet firmly planted on the ground. He was focused, engaged and interested in his surroundings. He was a full four inches taller than Lawrence. Sorcha looked up into his chestnut brown eyes framed by dark blonde hair cut in a disheveled fashion flattering to his boyish features. "And you are a newspaper reporter, Mr. Fulbright?"

"I am. And what gave me away, Miss O'Shea?"

"You have a paper and a pencil. And you said you worked for the *Liverpool Mercury*. Honestly, I should have realized right away. I just remembered where I saw your name. You've been writing articles for *The Liverpool Mercury* on the steam locomotives."

"A far too liberal paper," Lawrence grumbled.

"*Progressive*, you mean. The future is never in the past," Thaddeus said.

"I guess that goes without saying," Lawrence said.

"Apparently you don't see the distinction," Thaddeus replied.

Lawrence moved closer to Thaddeus. "You know, Fulbright, you aren't needed here. I'm sure you have work to do somewhere."

"I do, soon enough." Thaddeus shrugged.

"No time like the present," Lawrence said with gritted teeth.

"Take care, Mr. Davenport," Sorcha said. "Mr. Fulbright is a newspaper reporter. I'm sure you don't want negative press of yourself, or, by association, of your business."

"If he says anything about me, I'll sue his paper for defamation of character!"

"It seems to me you already have that well in hand and don't need any assistance from me," Thaddeus advised.

Sorcha gasped but almost burst out laughing has she covered her mouth with her gloved hand.

Lawrence's eyes flew wide open.

"And anyway, the *Liverpool Mercury* never prints anything but the truth." Thaddeus added, appearing nonplussed.

"As an informed person, who do you think will be the winner of this exciting race, Mr. Fulbright?" Sorcha turned to Thaddeus. "I believe you said the *Novelty*?"

Thaddeus tipped his hat to her, apparently relieved to change the conversation. "Without a doubt."

"Why do you think the *Novelty* will be the winner, Mr. Fulbright?" Sorcha was genuinely interested in this well-mannered gentleman's opinion.

"My father agrees." Lawrence frowned, as if he didn't give a rat's ass what his father thought. She knew better though; Lawrence was constantly attempting to prove himself to Henry Davenport—as long as his efforts didn't involve work.

"Because *Novelty is* the best. Ericsson and Braithwaite are brilliant engineers," Thaddeus said. "The only real contenders are *Sans Pareil*—"

"Meaning 'without parallel' in French, or 'there is no equivalent',"" Lawrence interrupted, showing off his knowledge of French.

"—*Sans Pareil*, *Rocket*, *Perseverance*, and *Novelty* are the only real contenders," Thaddeus continued.

"What about *Cycloped*? Isn't your money on the horse, Mr. Davenport?"

"Yes," Lawrence said.

"Not a contender," Thaddeus chuckled. "*Cycloped* is just a horse on a treadmill powering the cart. It's not even a steam locomotive. It will be disqualified."

"It may be the only entry to make it all the way and fulfill the requirements," Lawrence objected.

"The *Cycloped* is no more able to win this competition than the *Manumotive*," Thaddeus shook his head.

"What is that?" Lawrence asked with a sneer, feigning boredom and superiority.

"The *Manumotive* was two powerful men pulling six passengers in a carriage. It was immediately disqualified from the competition," Thaddeus raised his eyebrows at Lawrence. "Neither man nor horse is a machine, but some entrants are having difficulty in comprehending the distinction."

"If there is a winner, the vehicle has to meet three criteria, one of which is go to over 10 miles per hour. It won't happen," Thaddeus said.

"Isn't that a ridiculously high requirement? I wouldn't think any of the entries could meet that," Sorcha exclaimed. "Ten miles an hour is unimaginably fast, isn't it?"

"No machine has ever gone faster than a horse on land in the history of the world." Lawrence sneered. "Why would it now?"

"A horse can't pull a boat though," Sorcha said, remembering her journey to Liverpool from Belfast.

"A steamship is useful, I agree." Lawrence straightened the flower in his buttonhole. "But in this case, it's all show."

"Here it comes! It's the *Rocket!*" Sorcha exclaimed excitedly before Lawrence could take exception.

"I'm impressed you know that, Miss O'Shea," Thaddeus said.

"As I told you, I've been reading your articles in the paper, Mr. Fulbright." *Very slowly and painstakingly. Certainly I saw the diagrams. I needed to study them for my assignment.*

"I owe my knowledge to you, Mr. Fulbright," she added with a smile.

He raised his eyebrows and then burst out laughing. Sorcha liked Thaddeus' easy-going manners. He was outgoing, but not one to put on airs.

"Why do you laugh, Mr. Fulbright?"

"Flattery and your feminine wiles won't work on me, Miss O'Shea."

"I'm counting on that, Mr. Fulbright. And an unswayable reporting of the facts."

"Why should you care about that, Miss O'Shea?"

She raised her eyebrows at him. "Why does anyone care about the truth?"

With the sight of the black and yellow locomotive moving down the track the crowd erupted into a spontaneous applause. Men's hats paid homage, handkerchiefs waved, there were shouts and gasps, all heads turning toward the *Rocket*. The wind created by the moving locomotive caused all the ribbons of ladies' hats to flow in the same direction.

"Ah, yes, the entry by the Stockton and Darlington Railway Chief Engineer George Stephenson," Thaddeus said somewhat bitterly.

"Oh? You don't like him, Mr. Fulbright?"

"Does it show?" Thaddeus asked. "He's an arrogant, loud old duffer."

"Many men are," Sorcha said coyly. "That doesn't mean he'll lose."

Thaddeus jerked his head around, smiling, his expression more appealing in an instant. "I see you have a preconceived notion of my gender, Miss O'Shea. Don't judge us all by the one. We aren't all the same."

"I never said so!" Sorcha retorted. "It is you who are overly critical, Mr. Fulbright. I suppose Mr. Stephenson is entitled to be proud. He must be quite intelligent to have risen to the title of Chief Engineer. He's the most respected engineer in all of England. Even I know that, and I have little to no knowledge of science."

Once again Thaddeus looked at her with admiration. "But I must correct you on one point, Miss O'Shea. Stephenson did not attend Eton or any of the finer schools. Have you heard him speak with his northern Yorkshire accent? He sounds like a country boy with no education. How can he compete with classically educated engineers like Ericsson and Braithwaite?"

Sorcha frowned. And just when she was starting to like Thaddeus Fulbright.

"I wouldn't be surprised if George Stephenson is smarter than all of them, no matter what he sounds like." Sorcha raised her chin. She couldn't stomach arrogance, pretention, and the assumption of superiority.

"No offense intended, Miss O'Shea." Thaddeus tipped his hat to her. "I must call it as I see it."

"I suppose, with my Irish accent you assume I am ill-informed, Mr. Fulbright."

"That hasn't been my impression at all, Miss O'Shea. I think your accent is delightful."

"Well, if you assume I was formerly educated, you would be wrong in that too, Mr. Fulbright."

60

Lawrence chuckled, until now observing the interchange from a few feet afar. "It seems you have out-stayed your welcome, Fulbright."

Thaddeus turned to Sorcha. "Call me 'Thaddeus'. Or 'Tad'. All my friends call me 'Tad'."

"I am delighted to learn that you have friends, Mr. Fulbright." Sorcha raised her eyebrows, returning her eyes to the track. *They either don't know you very well or are deaf.* "You share your criticisms so freely."

"In that, we are the same, Miss O'Shea," Thaddeus murmured under his breath.

Only in defense of those who are first attacked.

She smiled at him. "Where it is deserved, I suppose."

Lawrence slapped his thigh, chuckling. Sorcha was glad Lawrence had forgotten his anger. He was easily entertained at least.

"We'll see what this *Rocket* locomotive does. It's a clunky thing." Thaddeus consulted his pamphlet, ignoring her slight. "Weighs over four tons. The contest has a limit of four and a half tons."

Entering the tracks was a black and yellow locomotive, magnificent in its size and appearance. It started with a hissing sound and then moved to a "chug-a-chug" sound.

"Possibly it would have to be heavy in order to pull anything of note," Sorcha considered. "Isn't that a law of science?" The proof of Mr. Stephenson's brilliance was making a great deal of noise. With the magnificent distraction she couldn't help forgetting Mr. Fulbright's insults.

"Well I wouldn't ride it. Not for a King's ransom," Lawrence said.

Thaddeus murmured "You realize...the *Rocket* arrived damaged?"

"It doesn't appear to be damaged..." Sorcha observed. She had a habit of taking up for the underdog.

"When *Rocket* was uncrated at Millfield Yard, it was discovered that her back wheels were damaged by the transport."

"They are rolling now," Sorcha said, pursing her lips and tipping her chin in the direction of the *Rocket*. She would never agree to a man's assessment if her eyes told her something else.

"A pair of replacements arrived yesterday, but the journals were too large to fit the bearings. It was impossible to get the journals altered in time."

Sorcha turned towards Thaddeus. "So what did *Rocket's* engineers do?"

"At the last moment, they substituted a pair of cast iron wheels with square-ended axels taken from a tip wagon." Thaddeus smiled, obviously amused with the substitution.

"That shows a great deal of ingenuity," Sorcha said.

"So this is the third set of back wheels?" Lawrence asked, shaking his head as if the *Rocket* was doomed from the get-go.

"Exactly," Thaddeus said.

"Honestly, I've never seen anything so amazing in my life." Sorcha murmured, setting aside her annoyance with her pompous, arrogant companions in the excitement of the moment.

The iron horses aren't the only things filled with hot air.

"I suppose they work as well as anything can work on these massive monstrosities." Lawrence muttered. "They're an affront to nature."

"Don't include the *Novelty* in that group, it's a beautiful, elegant machine," said Thaddeus. "Which, by the by, is proving to be the crowd favorite."

"Because it is the most stylish?" Sorcha asked, enjoying talking to someone in the know. "I admit the *Novelty* is the sleekest and prettiest of the four." *Novelty* was a handsome, delicate machine in copper and blue, both lightweight and stunning. The *Rocket* was more industrial in appearance, bold and brash. "They are rather large, frightening machines overall."

"That's the nice way of putting it," Lawrence said.

"Still, I am inclined to believe *Rocket* has a chance of winning if built by the famous George Stephenson," Sorcha added.

Thaddeus shook his head. "*Rocket* must maintain an average speed of ten miles per hour. Short spurts of speed aren't going to meet the criteria. *Novelty* being lighter will naturally be able to go faster."

Sorcha suddenly hoped with all her heart *Rocket* would win and show this arrogant reporter.

"I've got to get in closer to the action. Duty calls." Thaddeus said. He bowed to Sorcha, as much as space would allow. "Very nice to make your acquaintance Miss O'Shea. I hope our paths might cross again." He glared at Lawrence, whose eyes were fixated on the track ahead. "Please let me know if I can be of any assist."

"I have every expectation of being able to take care of myself, but I thank you." Thaddeus Fulbright didn't seem like a flatterer—rather a no-nonsense sort of fellow—but certainly he possessed a certain chivalry if an obsession with class.

"I do like a young lady who can carry on a conversation." Thaddeus tipped his hat to her. He chuckled, whispering near her ear as Lawrence scanned the crowed, "As well as a young lady who knows how to wield an umbrella."

Sorcha covered her mouth with her gloved hand to stop herself from laughing. She looked sideways with smiling eyes at the reporter.

"Keep it near you, Miss O'Shea," he added.

"I thank you for your conversation as well, Mr. Fulbright. And I look forward to your reporting of this contest." Which was indeed true. This infuriating man could make one gurgle with delight one minute and fume with anger in the next.

"As do I." And Lawrence was gone, bounding onto the tracks.

"Oh, for goodness sake, where is my father?" Sorcha added, unable to find him in the crowd. "He's going to miss the race."

"I'll go look for him," Lawrence said disinterestedly. Sorcha suspected Lawrence was going to place a bet, rub up against women, and get an ale —and that she wouldn't see either of them for a while.

"Oh, don't, Lawrence, you'll miss the race. And you'll never be able to get back here at the front of the line."

He raised an eyebrow at her. "*Of course I will.* I'm Lawrence Davenport."

She shook her head as Lawrence moved through the crowd.

Lawrence might be someone in Liverpool, but here he is just one of thousands.

That's why I love it here! I was speaking to a *newspaper reporter* as if I were a high society lady!

Sorcha moved to stand next to an elderly lady seated on a bench. The lady moved over on the bench, offering a space to Sorcha, who thanked her and sat down. Being at the front of the line, the view was still good.

This is such a crush! Sorcha found that she liked the anonymity. Coming from a place where she was no one, here she was like everyone else. Establishing one's superiority was a lost cause.

Besides, all eyes are on the Iron Horses.

CHAPTER TEN

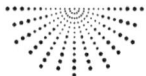

October 6, 1829
1ˢᵗ Day of the Rainhill Trials
The Opening Ceremonies

"*Huyton cars drawn by Mr. Stephenson's locomotive steam-carriage Rocket made a startling entrance, moving up the inclined plane with unexpected and considerable velocity, arriving on the course shortly after ten o'clock in the morning of October 6, 1829, the first day of the Rainhill Trials.*

The crowd gasped as the Rocket pulled into the starting point. Once arrived, all eyes upon them, who should depart the Huyton cars in front of the Grand Stand but the judges of the competition, each wearing a white riband in their button-holes. One understands their importance immediately.

What a beginning to the Rainhill races, catching everyone's attention in a grand gesture! No one can doubt that those who are fortunate enough to be here are about to witness a spectacular event.

The three gentlemen appointed by the Directors to act as judges of the race are: John Rastrick, Esq., civil engineer of Stourbridge; Nicholas Wood, Esq., mining engineer from Killingworth; and John Kennedy, Esq., of Manchester, a cotton spinner and proponent of the railway.

For a first event without precedent, the planners of the Rainhill Trials showed remarkable foresight in their handling of every detail, making every consideration of the attendees' comfort and pleasure.

For the accommodation of the ladies who might visit the course, a small coffee shop and a booth is erected on the south side of the railroad, equidistant from the extremities of the trial-ground. Here a band plays music, enlivening and entertaining the audience, adding to the grandeur and enjoyment of the occasion, and amusing the company during the day with pleasing and favorite airs, which must be acceptable to all attendees alike."

--Thaddeus Fulbright, The Liverpool Mercury

WHAT AN INTERESTING GIRL! Thaddeus thought to himself as he jumped back onto the tracks from the podium. *Pretty too, if that matters.*

Not to me it doesn't. Got nothing to do with me.

I thought she might have been in trouble from that rake, Davenport.

Recalling the interchange, Thaddeus frowned. Lawrence Davenport had a reputation about Liverpool. Word got about, particularly if one was in the newspaper business with one's ear to the ground.

Lawrence was wasting his fortune on gambling, wine, and women. Only Lawrence hadn't inherited his fortune *yet*. He was incurring lavish debts.

And, honestly, Henry Davenport wasn't *that* rich. He ran a successful business, sure. But one had to keep working to continue bringing in money. Margins in department stores were not without limits.

Granted, Lawrence would be considered rich—certainly by Thaddeus' standards—if he would stop giving his money away at the gaming tables.

Thaddeus never understood the point of that. How could it be pleasurable to turn over one's hard-earned money?

I suppose I answered my own question.

Thaddeus was raised with enough advantages, but his father was of the mind that his son had to make his own way in the world. Naturally Thaddeus didn't have money to squander; he didn't travel in those circles.

But he heard things.

The funny thing was, Henry Davenport was in his prime. He was no where near to the grave. It made no sense to be spending an inheritance long before one had any hope of realizing it.

Personally, Thaddeus thought that was a bad mindset anyway. One should never think of someone else's money as one's own. Until it was.

That mindset led to bad decisions.

Thaddeus sighed. *Yes, Sorcha O'Shea was very pretty.* Smart, too, which he liked. Some men were put off by smart girls, but it just kept life from being dull in his mind. There was only so long one could stare at a pretty face.

Thaddeus smiled to himself. No, that Sorcha O'Shea was not a shrinking violet.

It's just as well. It wasn't fortuitous to be a shy female in the vicinity of Lawrence Davenport.

One might even call Miss O'Shea a 'spitfire' given the right circumstances. She clearly was committed to protecting her virtue, apparently with success.

Thaddeus chuckled to himself. Miss Sorcha O'Shea appeared to be in control of the situation with her wicked umbrella.

And why is she here? What is she doing for the Davenports?

Miss O'Shea purportedly has a job: she works for the Davenports. She must be bringing in money of her own. It couldn't be much, though, as a factory girl.

What job is she doing? The whole thing had an illicit feel to it. But Miss O'Shea didn't show the slightest preference for Lawrence Davenport. Stabbing an umbrella in his foot wasn't exactly the language of love.

Thaddeus chuckled to himself. Miss Sorcha might work for the Davenports but she wasn't submissive to Lawrence Davenport.

Maybe it was Miss O'Shea's father who was working rather than her? Thaddeus had never seen an Irish Bobby before, but there was a first time for everything. Mr. O'Shea knew what he was doing: Thaddeus had seen Mr. O'Shea down on the tracks managing the rowdies.

Why do I keep worrying about things which are not my concern? I don't have time or money for a girl. I have more important things to attend to. This is my chance to make a name for myself in the newspaper business.

But if I did have time...

Thaddeus knew he was wrong about women more times than he was right. Definitely not his area of expertise. Most perplexing creatures on earth. Advanced science was easier.

Thaddeus shrugged. Solving the female puzzle required considerably more time than he had. Besides, understanding women was way down on the list of his priorities.

I would like to see Sorcha again to find out if I am right about her. Or not. Research. Practice.

I don't really care one way or the other.

Still, one needed to be a good judge of character in the newspaper business.

Insight could be helpful to one's career.

CHAPTER ELEVEN

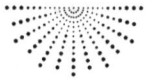

October 6, 1829
1ˢᵗ Day of the Rainhill Trials
The first steam locomotive race!

"*L*adies, gentlemen, and children in great numbers arrived from St. Helen's, Liverpool, Warrington, and Manchester, as well from the surrounding country, arriving on foot, by horseback, by cart, and in carriages of every description and comfort level.

All of Rainhill looks to be a race-course as on days of sport. None of the town's officials this reporter spoke to expected even half the number of attendees: on this first day of the race upwards of 10,000 people! There are not lodging houses or food services to accommodate them all. The spectators line both sides of the road for the distance of a full mile and a half! This reporter has never seen anything to match it.

The only evidence of class distinction is the placement of officials and dignitaries in the grand stand on the north side of the track, which holds approximately three hundred persons of high standing.

Another three hundred men employed on the line as special constables have orders to keep the crowds off the course. Despite all the reminders of the danger, *people persist in walking onto the tracks, putting themselves and others in peril. These Iron Horses weigh up to 4.5 tons going as fast as the unbelievable speed of 10 miles per hour! Never before in the history of mankind have we observed these speeds.*

"Enter the track at your own risk!"

– Thaddeus Fulbright, The Liverpool Mercury

THE *ROCKET* HURLED along at an unprecedented speed. In the history of time, human eyes had never beheld anything man-made going at these speeds.

Until now.

The Rainhill Trials is a first-in-the-world event.

Which meant, of course, that those driving these steam locomotives —and their passengers—were going faster than any human had ever travelled before.

Sorcha shook her head when she observed Thaddeus Fulbright standing close to the tracks. Though Thaddeus might admonish others to stay off the tracks, he was the first to break his own rules.

The crowd gasped as the locomotive continued to gain speed. Just when everyone was sure the Iron Horse could go no faster, red sparks flying everywhere, a new world record was set.

The crowd roared as the *Rocket* steam locomotive made a "chuff-ing" sound while throwing red sparks.

Sorcha knew from the program that the driver, the fireman, and the engineer were riding on the locomotive. The fireman kept the furnace going with fuel and refilled the water tank of the steam locomotive. The driver was responsible for the mechanical operations, including the handling of the brakes. The engineer oversaw the proceedings.

Usually. Sorcha was astonished to see the *Rocket's* engineer grinning from ear to ear, pontificating and putting on a show, waving to the ladies. George Stephenson appeared to be somewhere in his forties and in top condition, large and muscular.

The fair sex returned the gentleman's glances by waving their hand-kerchiefs, which only fueled his brazenness.

What a strange combination of occurrences. Sorcha was exceedingly amused at the unexpected sight of a middle-aged engineer—albeit handsome—flirting with the crowd on this momentous occasion. He was so full of energy, enthusiasm, and pure delight, completely uninhibited at what some might call a significant and serious event.

Somehow the title of "Chief Engineer" had not given Mr. Stephenson airs. His joy was almost childlike, not to mention his love of attention.

"He's quite a showman, isn't he?" A gentleman next to her remarked.

Sorcha turned abruptly to see a tall, handsome dark-haired man in elegant dress with a Lord Byron haircut watching the locomotive, smiling as if it were his own success instead of the engineer's.

He looks like a Duke! She thought to herself. *Talking to me, an Irish shop girl.*

Why is he talking to me?

My goodness, it certainly is my day for tall, handsome men. First, Thaddeus Fulbright—who was quite courteous to come to her assistance, if a bit of a snob when it came to education and class. And now this dandy, clearly of a different class from herself as well.

In truth, everyone was in a higher class than herself. But somehow she didn't feel her lower status so acutely in Rainhill.

"He does appear to love the limelight," Sorcha murmured, returning her eyes to the spectacle, in truth quite amused by the engineer's extravagant gestures.

"Without a doubt." The gentleman chuckled. "I would say to excess."

Despite not believing anyone better than herself, whatever society might say, Sorcha felt uncharacteristically shy before this impressive bystander. His fancy dress revealed a handsome figure and a gentleman of consequence. He had on a black super fine jacket with tails and four rows of gold buttons, exquisitely fitted to the waist. He wore an ivory silk waistcoat with a satin standing collar and an elegantly tied cravat, pants which conformed to his elegant figure, and a top hat, as if he were going to a fancy ball.

"No doubt he has earned the right to parade about." Sorcha giggled, genuinely enjoying herself despite feeling as if she didn't belong next to this stylish gentleman.

Sorcha wondered why her new acquaintance was so well-dressed— as if he were going to his own wedding, or receiving an honorary award at a university, or to another ceremony of great significance—for an occasion such as this, which some might consider nothing more than a day at the races. Maybe he was a dignitary, all of whom appeared to be similarly dressed.

Or maybe he really is a duke!

Even so, she couldn't help but think this gentleman's attire sedate in comparison to the spectacle Lawrence created with his outfit of striped silk trousers, a top hat, a red carnation in his lapel, and a long brown frock coat skirting from the wasped waist to his knees. The finishing touch of Lawrence's topcoat was puffed sleeves large enough to hold balloons.

The handsome gentleman next to her had *polish*. As opposed to pomposity.

She could tell the gentleman liked her observation. He added, "Yes indeed. The fanfare is well earned. The Chief Engineer can be very serious, and he can be cantankerous, but he has no reason to be today."

"Oh? And why not?" she asked shyly of her companion, feeling somewhat giddy in his presence. His proximity heightened her awareness. Though she might be quiet, Sorcha was not one to feel shy around anyone.

It's his moment," her companion replied simply.

Ironically, if the tall, dark gentleman had attempted to feign superiority over Sorcha, she would quickly gain her confidence, but, for the moment, his kindly, relaxed address made her feel a bit self-conscious.

I'll talk to him as long as he talks to me. Why not? He is behaving like a perfect gentleman.

Despite being so luxuriously dressed, there was no arrogance about him. The gentleman's easy manners did not strike her as condescending, intrusive or even flirtatious, but rather as sharing an enjoyable moment.

And his eyes! She was positively bedazzled by his sapphire blue eyes, glowing and warm, with so much intelligence.

Sorcha was not one to have her head turned by a gentleman, but she felt a flutter in her stomach and a tingling on her arms.

"He is showing off the *Rocket*," her companion added. "He knows what the machine can do and he fully expects it to win."

"Are you acquainted with the engineer, sir?" Sorcha asked, gaining confidence. She found that she liked men speaking to her as if she were a lady instead of a shop girl or a pub performer. Or an immigrant. Sorcha wasn't ashamed of who she was, but it was a nice change for other people not to be either.

"I should say so. He's my father, George Stephenson, the Chief Engineer of the Stockton and Darlington line," the young man said proudly.

Her eyes opened wide, even more impressed.

"Then you must be Mr. Stephenson as well?" she asked, her curiosity getting the better of her. This was a bit bold, even for her.

He bowed, tipping his hat to her. "I am Robert Stephenson. May I make your acquaintance, Miss? A proper introduction is somewhat difficult in these circumstances."

She smiled. It was a crazy circus with the shouting, clapping, and waving of hats and handkerchiefs. The excitement was palpable—it was absolutely electrifying.

This gentleman must be wondering why she was in such a raucous place alone and by herself. Sorcha suddenly felt embarrassed. Her lack of a chaperone revealed her station in life, obviously far beneath his own.

Sorcha paused and looked into his blue eyes, which now appeared hurt that she hadn't answered him. He tipped his hat and acted as if he were going to remove himself, realizing his inquiry was not welcome.

"Sorcha O'Shea," she replied quickly with a slight curtsey, anxious that he would not leave. Though he would no doubt take his leave of her shortly. "I agree, it is difficult to gain an introduction in such a crush as this. My father, Sean O'Shea, is somewhere about. He is not the most devoted chaperone, as you can see, but he tends to turn up if he is needed."

"I am delighted to make your acquaintance, Miss O'Shea, and I look forward to making his." He returned his hat to his head.

Robert smiled, relieved. He seemed to relax and reverse his retreat. He didn't appear to flinch in the slightest at her Irish name. But no doubt her red hair and green eyes had already informed him.

"I am delighted to make your acquaintance, Miss O'Shea, and I look forward to making his." He returned his hat to his head.

"You mentioned your father, George Stephenson. And what does the Stockton and Darlington transport?" Sorcha asked.

Oh my goodness, I'm chit-chatting with the son of England's most well-known engineer. Sorcha wasn't accustomed to hob-nobbing with famous people. Besides the fact that the son was quite handsome and charming, which didn't calm her nerves any.

You really must get out more, Sorcha O'Shea. How ridiculous to be so sheepish talking to a perfectly well-mannered young man.

I can't abide a missish girl, and look how I am behaving!

"Primarily coal. The line connects the coal mines at Shidon in Durham County to Darlington."

"Coal? I would hope the Liverpool and Manchester Railway, when completed, will transport cotton to Liverpool." She knew that to be Mr. Davenport's hope: all his costs would decrease.

And what is good for my employer is good for me.

The gentleman stopped watching the race for an instant to glance down at her with approval. "Precisely."

His expression turned to one of curiosity. "And is your father in the cotton industry, Miss O'Shea? Or, perhaps, he is an investor? You appear to have a particular interest."

"I do. I suppose you could say I am in the cotton industry—textiles—so the new line is of paramount importance to me." She added, "And to my family." At least that was truthful.

He smiled, his beautiful face framed by dark curls alight. "It is to many of us."

Sorcha felt a bit guilty for overstating her standing. As if her father were a cotton magnate or had money to invest. That was laughable!

I make buttons.

And now I am both missish and a liar!

I suppose I might say anything for that smile. Sometimes she wished, if they had to be poor, that her father was a parish priest. That was respectable poverty.

Sorcha immediately felt even more guilty. In truth, she didn't wish her father to be anyone other than who he was.

I am so fortunate to have such a father and I love him.

But it was so rare for a respectable gentleman without improper designs to be attending her. Perhaps she could be forgiven for not wanting this Apollo to be immediately repelled.

It will come soon enough.

"The *Rocket's* chief engineer appears very confident of his locomotive," she considered. "Some of the other engineers—well, *all* of the others—seem anxious about their locomotives, as if the contest came before they were ready. This is the first of the engineers to look as if he is enjoying himself." None of the other locomotives had raced, but they were all on display, their builders hovering about them.

Robert Stephenson turned to stare at her again, clearly surprised. "That's very astute of you, Miss O'Shea. The *Rocket* is the only locomotive which was actually tested before this race."

"Oh, and do you have confidence in this *Rocket* as well, sir?"

"I should think so. I built it."

CHAPTER TWELVE

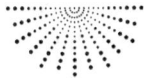

October 6, 1829
A new acquaintance

*R*obert Stephenson thought Miss O'Shea was the most beautiful girl he had ever beheld. She had strawberry blonde hair, aquamarine eyes, and wore a white lace dress from head to toe. She wore a wreath of pink flowers in her hair. He couldn't ascertain that she was wearing any jewelry. But her dress was exquisitely fashioned with expensive, one-of-a-kind, hand-painted buttons down the front of the dress as well as on the sleeves—unusual in their beauty—depicting various wildflowers. It was the only color she wore outside of her head-piece and her own natural coloring.

Sorcha O'Shea was like a fairy princess set down in this world of steam, black coal, tracks, scientists, businessmen, and industry, so out of place did she seem.

She said she was "in" the cotton industry. No doubt her father was a rich merchant and she took an interest in his business. It was unusual to encounter an Irish family which was prospering, but clearly this one was, as evidenced by this lovely girl's dress, appearance, and conversation.

Not that Robert cared if she was wealthy or not, though rich young ladies tended to be more demanding and less appreciative, having everything given to them. He preferred a bright girl from a working class family. His own father was born very poor. Robert was raised frugally but with everything he needed to succeed in life: George Stephenson saved every penny he had and gave his son an education, as well as food, a roof over his head, and love and encouragement. Something George's own parents were unable to do for him. But George Stephenson seemed to be born with confidence and determination.

And now....well, now....it was the happiest day of Robert's life. The entirety of their hard work and years of preparation came to fruition.

Today.

Of all days to meet this dazzling young lady. *Could it be that every good thing is happening to me today?*

Miss Sorcha O'Shea was bright and inquisitive. Robert liked a female who didn't only think about how she was to be amused and cossetted.

"You built the *Rocket?*" she asked, clearly impressed. "Not Mr. George Stephenson?"

"Yes, I designed and built it. We discussed any perplexing points of course. And certainly he taught me everything I know. Well, almost everything." He smiled.

"You can't be very old."

Robert laughed. That was a bit forward for this vision in white.

"Oh, I am sorry. I suppose that was rude." She looked down, but he noted that she didn't blush. She wasn't ashamed of her natural curiosity —and accurate assessment.

"Not at all. I am twenty-six."

"That must be very young."

"Young for what? I won't ask how old you are in return, Miss O'Shea."

"I doubt it's of any importance. I didn't build a locomotive." She smiled, her eyes sparkled, and the heavens parted. "You must be the youngest inventor-engineer to have entered a locomotive."

"I suppose I am," he said nonchalantly. "But naturally I had help. My father and I have a workshop together—technically an iron works company—and I am not hesitant to ask as many people for input as will help me. My father is a bit more…shall we say…*proud*…but I am not offended in the least if anyone will share their knowledge with me."

"You don't object to assistance, sir?"

"Not at all. I like to have all the facts before I embark on a venture."

"That is not always possible in this changing world."

"Indeed." He nodded, tipping his hat to her.

"You must have spent your entire life learning, Mr. Stephenson."

"I expect so." He nodded. "I beg pardon, Miss O'Shea, but the *Rocket* is preparing to start." Robert returned his eyes to the race. As much as he hated to take his eyes off Sorcha O'Shea, he had been working his entire life for the moment and it was unthinkable to miss any of it.

The whistle blew, the passengers departed from the *Rocket*, and the haul was attached.

The whistle was blown again and the *Rocket* began the first of its trials.

Rocket began chugging and spitting, steam blowing out of its blast pipe and smokebox, the wheels sparking the tracks. In no time, *Rocket* gained considerable speed.

"The speed is astonishing!" Sorcha exclaimed as the Rocket accelerated. "How fast do you think the *Rocket* is travelling?"

"The judges will tell us upon completion," Robert replied, a slow smile forming on his lips, even as he consulted his stopwatch. "But I have no doubt the *Rocket* will reach the required minimum of ten miles per hour."

"Even with the load?"

"Oh, yes. Definitely with the load."

"How will the *Rocket* manage?" Sorcha asked.

"For one thing, the *Rocket* has a separate firebox. Also, the *Rocket* uses a multi-tube boiler which passes the heated gas from the firebox through tubes within the boiler itself. The multi-tubes are a unique and radical design and a better heat conductor than a single tube since more surface is exposed to the heat." Robert stopped himself. "Forgive me. I hope I am not boring you, Miss O'Shea."

"Not at all. But aren't you concerned I may steal your design?" She glanced slyly at him.

Robert smiled. "I hope you will not. But it will not be long before the designs of all present today will be known." He shook his head.

"Then I shan't attempt to steal them!" she giggled.

"In general I find ladies are not interested." He gazed at the beauty before him. "And I find that I appreciate your interest."

"Well, I certainly wouldn't ask if I weren't interested," she replied quizzically.

Robert smiled to himself, his eyes directed to the tracks. Miss O'Shea was unique among women, interested in the details and not requiring his attention. She seemed pleased to merely share the experience.

She isn't too shy to make conversation. One of the many things Robert liked about Sorcha O'Shea. He disliked being in a woman's company doing all the talking while she stared adoringly at him, only wanting to say whatever she thought he might like to hear, as if she had no brain and no personality of her own. Quite tedious and boring.

"There are two tracks laid out, but it doesn't look like an actual race," Sorcha considered.

"Not in the purest sense of the word. The steam carriages will run one at a time." Robert replied. "This is the first of ten runs. The *Rocket* has to complete all ten runs, totaling thirty-five miles, while meeting the average minimum speed of ten miles per hour—and while hauling a considerable load. As do all the entrants."

"With two tracks, who knows what mischief may ensue." There was a sparkle in Miss O'Shea's eyes, adding to her allure.

Robert laughed. "Very true."

Miss O'Shea was clearly interested in the steam locomotives, but, on the other hand, Robert didn't know if she was at all interested in *him*.

I merely happen to be in the vicinity.

This was a new thought to Robert. Being young, handsome, and employed, Robert knew he had a bit of appeal in the marriage mart. But if a woman wanted a titled husband, or a rich husband, obviously he was out of the running. He was doing well enough with a home and a business—which required enormous investments! His funds were not limitless. He glanced at Sorcha in spite of the exciting race unfolding before them.

I hope she is not hanging out for a title.

Robert sighed. *But I do have the advantage of a famous father.*

They weren't in high society to be sure, given his father's northern brogue and lack of university credentials, but they might be soon. George Stephenson was already famous, but winning the Rainhill Trials would mean true notoriety.

I will be famous as well if we win. Robert smiled to himself.

"Actually, two locomotives could theoretically be tested at the same time," Robert added.

"Because there are two tracks," Sorcha said.

"Precisely. But, more importantly, the average speed cannot be less than ten miles per hour."

"It is a lightening speed!"

"It is. But it's an average." Robert smiled, looking at his stopwatch. "The *Rocket* is currently travelling over eighteen miles per hour."

"I am astonished, sir!" Sorcha waved her gloved. "This moment in time is truly magical."

"It's a world record! This is the fastest any human has ever observed *anything* moving," Robert said.

Sorcha lowered her hand. "As impressed as I am, I don't believe that is true. There is the speed of light. And the Peregrine Falcon."

Robert laughed, almost losing his hat. "I stand corrected."

Sorcha sighed. "But it *is* a momentous occasion."

"It certainly is." As he beheld her sparking eyes, he had to agree.

The run was completed and the average speed of twelve miles per hour with a top speed of twenty-four miles per hour for the *Rocket* hauling 13 tons was announced. There was wild screaming and cheering in the crowd. Astonishment and shock was channeled into shouting and waving. The noise was thunderous.

"It has been wonderful learning so much. But I'm sorry to detain you, Mr. Stephenson," Sorcha said. "You must wish to go and share congratulations with your father."

Robert laughed. "Everyone is surrounding Father. I couldn't even get close." He smiled at her. "I will join him shortly."

"But Mr. Stephenson! It is *your* locomotive! You must join him."

"Yes, I suppose I must," Robert agreed reluctantly. "But I hate to leave you here alone, Miss O'Shea. Your father is nowhere to be seen."

Sorcha pointed to her father managing the crowds on the track. "That is my father there. Believe me, he keeps an eye on me."

"I notice that gentleman keeps glancing your way. May I ask...is he an acquaintance?" The man in question was placing a bet, but he kept returning his eyes to Miss O'Shea. Naturally anyone would—she was quite beautiful, and not in the ordinary way—but Robert didn't like the other man's expression when he looked at her.

Robert felt his anger rising. He hoped that overdressed poppy posed no danger to Miss O'Shea. He was not very masculine in appearance, but his expression was too familiar.

"That is Lawrence Davenport of the Davenport Mercantile."

"Oh." His voice fell inadvertently. "So you know him?"

"Oh, yes. I rode in his carriage here with my father."

She is already spoken for. Of course she is. He was enjoying her company so much, he hadn't considered. *But, if Davenport is her intended, surely he would be here with his beautiful fiancé. How could he not be?* The idea gave Robert hope.

How can I ask her without being too forward?

"So the *Rocket* is in the lead. Who will race next?" Sorcha asked after an uncomfortable pause. It seemed to Robert there was something Sorcha didn't want him to know. And she clearly didn't wish to discuss Lawrence Davenport.

"The *Novelty.*"

"I understand from Mr. Fulbright the *Novelty* is a crowd favorite," Sorcha said.

"Mr. Fulbright? The reporter?" Robert asked, surprised. As he had been almost every moment of his time with Miss Sorcha O'Shea.

"A reporter for the *Liverpool Mercury.*"

"You know a great number of people here, Miss O'Shea." Robert chuckled.

"I wouldn't say so." Sorcha raised her eyebrows in bewilderment. "And yet—I find it strangely easier to meet new people here in Rainhill than at home in Liverpool."

"It is always easier to meet people on holiday," Robert agreed.

Sorcha laughed. "Oh, I'm not on holiday. Not actually. At any rate, I only know a very few people here." Her lips quivered. "But those few are simply among the most vocal."

"Not on...holiday?" Robert asked.

Sorcha shook her head, seeming to come to some resolve. "I'm actually here to work. As you are, sir."

Robert was immediately startled. *She might appear to be a heavenly vision, but maybe she is actually after my steam locomotive plans.*

CHAPTER THIRTEEN

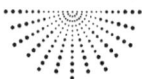

October 7, 1829
2nd Day of the Rainhill Trials

"*W*hat is the unique and distinct nature of this event that so many scientists, engineers, industrialists, businessmen, and manufacturers—more than ever before—have collected together on this one spot?*

In short, this convergence of the experts must reveal something of the scientific importance of this competition: The Rainhill Trials.

We cannot doubt it. But what of the cultural importance of the steam locomotive? What of the impact on our every day lives? What of the impact on the human race?

In the very near future we will all be living very different lives. An existence we cannot now even imagine."

– Thaddeus Fulbright, The Liverpool Mercury

TIMOTHY BURSTALL CONSIDERED HIS COURSE. Upon arriving at the Rainhill Trials, he was unpleasantly surprised by the progress of his rivals.

Rocket would be in the trials for a few days. *Novelty* would run on Saturday, followed by Hackworth's *Sans Pareil*.

And, finally, my machine, Perseverance, will run.

That gives me time to discover what my competition is up to and to make adjustments to my own entry.

True, *Perseverance* was damaged during transport when the freight cart pulled by horses overturned on the road to Rainhill.

The need for repairs put Burstall at the Forth Street Works with the full endorsement and sympathy of the judges.

No one notices me. I'm supposed to be here.

Timothy Burstall snooped around the Forth Street Works attempting to discover his competitors' designs.

He hoped to incorporate any designs he observed in his spying, altering his locomotive and improving her performance.

In effect, I have a full extra week over the other entrants to prepare my engine for the trials.

I'm entitled to it. I had a terrible piece of luck on the way here.

Hackworth could do much the same, but he claims to be a devout Christian and refuses to work on Sunday, meaning he will lose his last day to prepare before his machine performs.

Hackworth is an idiot.

Hackworth's *Sans Pareil* needed repairs after the transport too—*Sans Pareil* having a leaking boiler—but Hackworth *will not* fix it on Sunday.

Hackworth was also a friend of the Stephenson's. In fact, *Stephenson & Son* built the engine for *Sans Pareil*. Hackworth, in his turn, helped Braithwaite and Ericsson ready the *Novelty* for the race.

They were, all of them, friends it appeared. They don't seem to understand what a competition is.

Hackworth puts his future in the hands of the Lord.

Timothy Burstall put his future in his own hands.

CHAPTER FOURTEEN

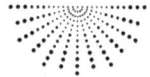

October 7, 1829
2nd Day of the Rainhill Trials

Sorcha and Thaddeus sat at Sorcha's now usual spot close to the band on the south side of the track, watching the *Rocket* undergo the next of its trials. The location was an excellent and comfortable vantage point.

Robert and George Stephenson rode the *Rocket*, Sean O'Shea helped manage the crowds, and Lawrence Davenport played cards with some surly characters he had discovered—or attracted, Sorcha didn't know which. *Birds of a feather.*

A regular social circle had evolved in this short time, one Sorcha would remember and cherish the rest of her life. Even those of questionable morality and of a loud and disruptive nature were part of the vibrant landscape now enshrined in her memory. Being an artist who was literally present to portray the event, all of the composition must be of interest to her.

Sorcha sighed. "Sometimes It is difficult to see over all the hats and umbrellas," Sorcha said.

"Not for me," Thaddeus said.

"Naturally, Tad. You are tall," Sorcha rolled her eyes.

"If it weren't for you ladies and your fashions, we would all have more room," Thaddeus considered.

"*We ladies!* We take up less room than you gents!" Sorcha retorted.

"Not with your clothes on," Thaddeus said.

Sorcha's eyes went wide open. "How dare you speak to me like that, Mr. Fulbright!"

"No impropriety intended, Miss O'Shea." Thaddeus tipped his hat to her, his blonde hair falling into his laughing eyes. "Unless you'd like there to be, then I would be happy to oblige you."

He gave her a sultry look and she gasped. But she found that she liked how she felt when he looked at her like that.

"Certainly not!" Sorcha objected feebly.

"All right then. Just stating the facts. I was only commenting on ladies' fashions. Ever since the Prince Regent became king in 1820, the styles have changed: wider skirts and huge puffed balloon sleeves which is *all* the rage in ladies wear. Those sleeves take up a lot of space and are a nuisance."

"Mr. Fulbright, I had no idea you were following ladies' fashions." Sorcha giggled, her anger dissipated. It was difficult to stay angry at Thaddeus; he always made her laugh.

"I'm not following them. They keep running into me and trying to suffocate me."

"Those balloon sleeves *are* a bit of a bother. Especially for a working woman," Sorcha agreed. "But, let's be honest, you're so tall there is no way a lady's sleeves would suffocate you, Mr. Fulbright."

"Unless she had her arms around my neck." He smiled at the thought.

Sorcha raised a disapproving eyebrow.

"The fitted bodices look nice though," Thaddeus said.

"Mr. Fulbright!" Sorcha swatted his arm with her fan. "Who do you think I am that you can take a vulgar tone with me?"

"What? You don't think they look nice? Forgive me, I had no idea." Thaddeus shook his head. "I don't know why you insult your own sex, Miss O'Shea."

Sorcha glared at him. "I ought to slap you, Thaddeus Fulbright! You need to acquire some manners for mixed company."

But in fact, Thaddeus was once again right: the empire waist gowns of the Regency era—when King George IV was the Prince Regent—were more comfortable and less constraining for a woman. And less bulky.

"Wouldn't that be boring, Miss O'Shea? Wouldn't you prefer a genuine conversation than one which is edited for ladies?"

"One can be genuine without being rude. Flirtatious innuendo is completely unnecessary to being genuine."

"Good to know." Thaddeus nodded then his eyes opened wide as an idea occurred to him. "Miss O'Shea. Did you think I was *flirting* with you?"

"Oh, that is rich Mr. Fulbright! First you affront me with intimate images and then you blame me for your ill behavior. There is no sincerity or genuine affection in you—you merely meant to unnerve me and watch me flounder like a fish—and I daresay you did. Quite ungentlemanly!"

"Insincere? No affection?" Thaddeus appeared astonished, a twinkle in his eyes. "Teasing is the sincerest form of flattery for me, I assure you, Miss O'Shea."

"Then I wish you might go an flatter someone else, Mr. Fulbright!"

"Do you?" He appeared perplexed, shaking his head. "But I cannot. Because my affection would not then be sincere. It is only for you, Miss O'Shea." He bowed deeply.

"Hmph!" Sorcha retorted, returning to her drawing.

"Do forgive me, Miss O'Shea, I meant no offence. There is nothing vulgar about ladies as far as I'm concerned. I was merely commenting on women's fashions. I find women quite beautiful—*one in particular*—but not their fashions."

"I am quite uninterested in your opinions on the subject, Mr. Fulbright."

"Oh, are you not, Miss O'Shea?" His good humor appeared to evaporate. "Whose opinions are you interested in then, if not mine? Engineers' opinions? Department store tycoons' opinions? The opinions of Royalty perhaps? It strikes me that you might be a bit snobbish, Miss O'Shea."

"Nothing of the sort."

His good humor returned almost immediately. "How is it you were allowed by your employer to come here? I must say I am grateful, but I am at a loss to figure it out."

"Have you devoted a great deal of time to solving this puzzle, Mr. Fulbright?"

"I must admit I have, and to no avail." Thaddeus wrinkled his brow. "What are you doing here, Miss O'Shea? I see you drawing in your notepad. Is it for Mr. Davenport? What do you do for him?"

"You are the nosiest person I ever met, Thaddeus Fulbright."

"Thank you." He brushed his hair out of his eyes, brushing her arm in the process.

Sorcha shivered for a moment. "It wasn't a compliment."

"Oh, it is to a newspaper man, I assure you. So what is your job for the Davenports?"

Sorcha sighed heavily, seeing that there would be no peace until she answered him. "I paint buttons." She pointed to the buttons on her dress.

"Oh, yes. Very pretty."

"I'm so pleased you like them," Sorcha said with a curled lip.

"Must be popular among the ladies," Thaddeus considered.

"They are."

"Still….one thing I don't understand is how you can dress so fine with a factory job," Thaddeus studied her.

"There appear to be many things you don't understand, Mr. Fulbright."

"Quite so," he chuckled, "but I'm attempting to unravel the mystery."

"And how do you fare?"

"I'm completely in the dark, Miss O'Shea. Many factory girls are starving to death. Factory employees, and especially women and children, are notoriously underpaid. How do you afford dresses which are, if I may say, particularly fine?"

"We have a roof over our heads and food on the table," she replied stiffly. "I am a good seamstress and I make my own clothes. We are not wealthy. We are only able to cover the essentials, I assure you."

"Hmmm…I know your father doesn't have excellent employment. What about your mother?"

"She's a chair bottomer, if it's any of your business, Mr. Fulbright."

Thaddeus shook his head. "Still doesn't explain it." He studied her. "What are your earnings, Miss O'Shea?"

Sorcha sighed heavily. "You're not around ladies very much are you?"

"No, actually not."

"Don't you have a mother?"

"Really, Miss O'Shae! Who do you think raised me?"

Sorcha raised her eyebrows. "You don't wish to know, I'm sure."

"Yes, I do have a mother, but she is rather suppressed, as is everyone who is in my father's company."

"You don't appear to be, Mr. Fulbright."

"Believe me, it required a great deal of work on my part not to be."

"What does your father do?" Sorcha asked.

"My father worked in the War Office and he was a pretty big name around there. Still is, I imagine. And he ran the household much the same as the War Office."

"Oh my! So…You finally have some freedom now that you're out and about."

"That is true. But I've had a great deal of freedom since I was thirteen years of age." Thaddeus paused. "Unless one considers being pummeled by older boys an absence of freedom."

"So you were mostly around the male of the species?"

"Absolutely."

"And now that you are encountering ladies, you have no idea how to treat them?"

"Actually, I don't think of you as a lady, Miss O'Shea."

Sorcha took her fan and swatted him with it. "Mr. Fulbright! How dare you!"

"I meant no offence."

"What did you mean?" Sorcha demanded.

"Certainly you are a beautiful specimen of the female species, no doubt about it, but you're more like my father than my mother. A very commanding personality. Maybe that's why I feel relaxed around you. You're very familiar to me."

Sorcha closed her eyes momentarily, attempting to control her temper. "I don't have a commanding personality! I am simply not inclined to let men take improper advances!"

"A great idea. But, all the same, if your button career doesn't work out, you might want to try the War Office."

She glared at him. "My button career, as you say, is doing very well, thank you."

"So, what do you say, Miss O'Shea? How much are you earning making buttons?"

She pursed her lips but realized Thaddeus wouldn't give her any peace until he solved the puzzle. And, the truth be told, she was a bit indignant over his obvious devaluation of her work. She motioned to Thaddeus to place his ear near her lips, which he happily obliged. She whispered in his ear.

"What!?!" Thaddeus exclaimed, jumping upright. "That's twice what I'm paid!"

"Maybe you should work harder, Mr. Fulbright. No doubt we are both paid by the piece."

"I am attempting to increase my production. Still…"

"It doesn't seem that way to me," Sorcha considered. "You waste a good deal of time from what I can tell."

Thaddeus looked at her with admiration. "You see? You have taken the words out of my father's mouth verbatim. Quite extraordinary!"

"It is fairly obvious to anyone with an ounce of perception," Sorcha exclaimed with exasperation. "As to my being paid double your salary, don't you think I'm worth it, Mr. Fulbright? I am the best button-painter in Liverpool. Maybe in London, given the chance. If you don't know my value, I assure you my employer knows how much income I produce for him."

"Most ladies make one-third what men do in the same profession."

"Oh, do you make buttons, Mr. Fulbright?"

Thaddeus shook his head, still appearing to be in shock. "At any rate, I'm gratified to know Mr. Davenport knows your worth."

"Are you, Mr. Fulbright?"

"Yes. I wish Mr. Egerton Smith knew mine as well. But he will soon." Thaddeus nodded reflectively, returning to his seat. "Like yourself, we have a king with expensive tastes. What do you think of that, Miss O'Shea? Do you know his coronation was possibly the most expensive in history?"

"I have no idea why you should compare my circumstances to the king's." Sorcha knew that while George IV was the Prince Regent, he ruled for his father, the mad king George III.

"Contemplating your great wealth put me in mind of the king. From there I merely wondered if the coronation was up to your opulent standards."

"My income may be more than yours, Thaddeus Fulbright, but it is still not much!" she retorted.

"Ouch! You are a viper, Miss O'Shea, did anyone ever tell you that?"

"Certainly not! Until I met you, Mr. Fulbright, I was mostly around pleasant people."

"Hmmm," considered Thaddeus, shaking his head. "It is quite futile to lie to me, Miss O'Shea. I've met your associates."

"Oh!" exclaimed Sorcha indignantly. "You are the conceited man Thaddeus Fulbright!"

"You can't have met many men then, Miss O'Shea." Thaddeus shrugged.

"Well then. Conceited, incorrigible, and infuriating!"

"Hmmm…You have stalled long enough, Miss O'Shea. And what is your opinion of King George's coronation?"

"Very well. I think it is a sin and a travesty when so many of his subjects are starving, poor, and without basic housing and sanitation." She turned her head towards the tracks. "Please, Mr. Fulbright, the sixth round is beginning. It is your job to pay attention."

He glanced at her and smiled. "Indeed it is, Miss O'Shea. And beautiful it is."

CHAPTER FIFTEEN

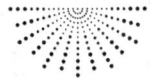

October 7, 1829
2nd Day of the Rainhill Trials

*P*ersonally, Thaddeus didn't care if young ladies put themselves out there or not. It was no never mind to him. Though he did like a genuine female, someone who didn't act like all the others...

Miss O'Shea is definitely not a carbon copy of another female...

Though she was charming, with intelligence, education, and even polish, he doubted if she had ever read "The Victorian Ladies Guide to Etiquette." Being modest, reserved, and traditional did not appear to be her area of interest.

Mine either.

To be sure, Miss O'Shea was more interested in bringing him down a notch than in proper etiquette.

As if I am conceited!

Ridiculous! It isn't my fault that I am intelligent and generally right.

He didn't have any argument with 'incorrigible' and 'infuriating' as he considered those to be qualities to aspire to.

And not that Sorcha O'Shea wasn't a lady: of course she was perfectly feminine.

Perfectly.

But she had a mind of her own and did not seem inclined to let anyone else do her thinking for her.

The kind of gal I like.

Thaddeus smiled. He seemed to be doing a lot of that since meeting Sorcha O'Shea.

Thaddeus knew he was relatively handsome—he had been known to turn a few heads—but he wasn't considered marriage material. Ladies soon lost interest. He couldn't afford a wife.

He was the budget option, and that's not where ladies started. Besides, he didn't have the type of manners that ladies liked.

Thaddeus frowned. Like Robert Stephenson's disingenuous, reserved manners which revealed nothing about him.

In a society which valued revealing nothing about oneself for fear of a misstep no wonder Sorcha O'Shea stood out.

Not that I want a wife. Too busy for that nonsense.

On the other hand, Egerton Smith was plenty wealthy. As the owner of the *Liverpool Mercury*, he brought in some real dough. If Thaddeus were to climb the ladder…

And it appeared Miss O'Shea might be able to support him! Thaddeus chuckled to himself. What was one more mouth to feed? He didn't eat that much anyway, and he wasn't particularly picky. A good stew, bread and butter, and an ale, and he was pleased as punch.

What am I thinking of a wife for? Ridiculous.

Sometimes he thought he annoyed Sorcha, and other times he thought she liked him.

Thaddeus hoped he hadn't misread the female species once again.

But why am I wasting time on something I can't possibly understand?

My brain must be addled.

Damn it! I've got to get my story to the Liverpool Mercury. Naturally, he was covering the Rainhill Trials races day-by-day.

I need to get my mind on my job. The trials were positively thrilling! He was surprised he was having any difficulty in doing so.

To be clear, he wasn't behind on his stories, he just seemed to let his mind wander a bit too much.

And always to the same subject.

Thaddeus glanced at the strawberry blonde beside him, her excitement charming and admirable. She was such a curious girl, so alive and inquisitive.

He sighed heavily.

The chugging of the wheels on the tracks, the hissing of the steam, and the whistle blowing reminded Thaddeus of his obligations.

"Excuse me, Miss O'Shea. Duty calls." Thaddeus tipped his hat and moved towards the tracks. Having a badge, he was allowed closer than the general public and allowed to interview the contestants in the race. "I suppose it is time to return to work."

Sorcha smiled at him and he almost let the thought of work slip out of his mind. He forced himself to look at the locomotives.

What exciting times we live in!

Thaddeus couldn't help but feel the thrill of this moment. That moment when everyone would look back and realize how significant it was.

Unknown at the time.

But I do know. We are all on the cusp of something great.

CHAPTER SIXTEEN

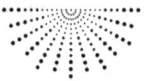

October 7, 1829
2nd Day of the Rainhill Trials

"*When George Stephenson surveyed the Liverpool & Manchester Railway, he made many errors of measurement, documented in the parliamentary proceedings of 1825. Mr. Vignoles had to be called in to perform another survey with the correct measurements. The chances for success by the Rocket must therefore be in question.*"

—written by a gentleman intimately acquainted with the circumstances of the case, Mechanic's Magazine

ROBERT STEPHENSON SNAPPED the newspaper shut, his anger rising.

"Whatever is wrong, Mr. Stephenson?" Sorcha asked. She sat in her usual section near the band where she could observe the proceedings closely while drawing in her notebook.

Robert was delighted to position himself next to Miss O'Shea while reading the morning newspaper, drinking his coffee purchased at the coffee stand, and awaiting the next step in the trials.

"I do apologize, Miss O'Shea." He was embarrassed at revealing his anger when a lady was present. "It's just that I get so tired of the insults hurled at my father. All jealous of his success."

"Most hatred stems from jealousy or fear." Sorcha nodded while sketching.

"At any rate..." he added "I built the *Rocket*. So I don't know why they are attacking Father."

The first phase of the trials was completed and Robert spent as much time with Sorcha as he could.

"I suppose because the *Rocket* was entered by the *Forth Street Works*, the company owned by both of you," Sorcha suggested.

"Yes. And Father is definitely the more famous of the both of us."

Sorcha looked up to stare into his eyes. "But that may not always be the case."

Robert felt her admiration and loved the feeling. "Perhaps not."

Sorcha glanced at the newspaper. "But, regardless, you are saying the article isn't true?"

Robert nodded. "It is true that Father made errors in the survey—he is more of a mechanic, engineer, and inventor than a surveyor. His mind needs the bigger problems to be solved. Mine is more suited to the minute details of data collection."

"You are a better surveyor than your father?" Sorcha asked.

"Possibly," Robert nodded modestly. "But there are many more good surveyors than there are of brilliant inventors!"

"Maybe some people are both." She looked at him intently.

"Moreover, it is not true—or right—for a person wholly unfamiliar with the mechanical workings of the *Rocket* to make predictions about the Rocket's performance based on my father's skills as a surveyor! When he didn't even build it!"

"Excellent point." Sorcha smiled wryly, returning her eyes to her work.

"Moreover, the 'gentleman' author is no doubt Mr. Vignoles himself, who is rooting for the *Novelty*!"

"My goodness, there is a great deal of back-stabbing. I feel as if I am on the stage of a Shakespearean tragedy," Sorcha exclaimed as her colored pencil paused in mid-air.

"I suppose when money and reputations are at stake, it is so. Ambition is surely the great motivator of the day."

"I think I was never in the midst of so many ambitious people. I hope none of them shall kill each other to be crowned king," Sorcha remarked. "And you are highly ambitious, are you not, Mr. Stephenson?"

"Yes." Robert nodded shyly, hating to reveal his greatest vice. He might be polite on the outside, but he was determined to win—or *die trying.* "For myself, I can say I have been working for this my entire life. But murder, no. Honestly, I have enough confidence in my own abilities to stand on that."

"But those who don't have the talent must resort to bad-mouthing." Sorcha glanced at him teasingly with a most becoming expression. "Try to understand, Mr. Stephenson."

"Oh, I think I do…" Robert considered, stealing a glance at Sorcha, so lovely as she worked.

"Hmmm….Mr. Vignoles seems very sure of himself," Sorcha remarked.

"He is an excellent surveyor, to be sure. He did not, however, assist in the building of the *Rocket*." Robert frowned. "And I venture to say my father's achievements far outweigh his own."

"It would appear that few can match George Stephenson's achievements."

Robert tipped his hat. "I do not mean to brag, but I must agree."

Seated on the bench together, it seemed to Robert people might overhear their conversation. "We are between races, Miss O'Shea. I wonder if we might take a stroll?"

* * *

IT MIGHT DO *you good to release some of your frustration,* Sorcha thought, though she appreciated Robert's familial loyalty. She had no doubt he would not be as upset if the article had insulted him instead of his father.

"I would like that very much, Mr. Stephenson. But do you think I would lose my place on my bench?"

"I expect I could reclaim it." Robert smiled, turning to a middle-aged woman. "Would you care for a seat? We will be taking a short stroll."

Sorcha packed up her colored pencils and her pad in her small satchel. She placed her shawl around her shoulders and opened her parasol, taking Robert's arm offered to her.

"Your father must be very intelligent," Sorcha remarked as they commenced their walk. "I had heard...*somewhere*..."—she didn't wish to reveal the source of her information—"that Mr. George Stephenson hadn't attended Eton or Cambridge, but surely he went...*somewhere*..."

Robert shook his head. "Father didn't learn to read and write until he was a teen-ager. He rose up through the ranks by showing everyone else up."

"He became an engineer while being...*illiterate?*"

"Yes, I suppose, if you put it that way. He did."

They commenced their movement, walking past the band as well as a small café with tables and chairs.

Sorcha gasped. "How is that possible?"

"Father kept solving problems the other engineers couldn't solve. Even the illustrious engineers brought from Eton and Oxford."

"Such as? Which problems did he solve?" Sorcha could scarcely believe what she was hearing.

It was difficult to walk, the crowds were so intense, but Robert Stephenson was tall, and recognizable, and people parted paths for him.

"Father's first big accomplishment was at the High Pit near Killingworth. Even the most experienced engineers couldn't figure out how to drain the water from the pit; the engine they brought in wasn't working. Ralph Dodds, the head viewer, was at his wit's end. He heard of my father's expertise with machinery and called on him at home. Father was only a brakesman at the time."

Ahead of them was the Skew Bridge, a sandstone construction, which took the main road over the railway. Across the tracks, on the north side of the track was the Grand Stand, where all the grand lords and ladies sat.

Robert should be there. Sorcha felt so honored and happy that he was with her.

Robert chuckled to himself. "When the engineers heard that Dodds had called on a mere brakesman to solve the problem which had confounded them, they were indignant and ill-disposed to assist George Stephenson."

"How could Mr. Stephenson solve the problem without assistance?"

"Father anticipated their arrogance and took his own men." Robert chuckled.

"So George Stephenson understood people as well as engineering," Sorcha considered.

"Indeed."

"How did Mr. Stephenson know the other engineers would not support him and attempt to cross him?" Sorcha asked. "I would have thought they would all work together to solve the problem."

Robert laughed. "If one is successful, there are always those who would like to see one fail."

Sorcha's brow furrowed. "I don't understand that. I always like to help others as well as receive their help if they are willing to give it."

"I am the same." Robert placed his hand on the small of her back briefly, as if he needed to touch her, looking at her with appreciative eyes.

"Did George Stephenson fix the engine?"

"He did."

"How did Mr. Stephenson drain the pit when no one else could?" Sorcha was astonished that this lowly brakesman outshone them all. Looking at Robert, she could see from his expression that he felt so much pride in his father.

Much as I feel for my own.

"Father knows his engines. In the early days he spent all his free time taking them apart and putting them back together."

"I suppose he is a mechanical genius. But whether it is a gift he was born with or developed through sheer determination, I don't know."

"A bit of both, I suppose," Robert said. "All I know is he didn't receive much help from anyone else in developing his gift and certainly had more than his share of disadvantages."

"And obstacles," Sorcha added.

There was every manner of person along their route wearing every manner of fashion. As they walked, they could see the *Rocket* on one of the tracks and the *Novelty* on another of the tracks.

"Why couldn't the Killingworth engine drain the pit?" Sorcha asked.

"It didn't take Father long to determine that the primary reason for the engine's difficulty was the insufficiency of the water spray utilized to condense the steam prior to the power stroke."

Sorcha giggled. "Naturally! How could the others have missed that?"

Robert appeared embarrassed. "Oh, I am sorry, Miss O'Shea, I must be boring you."

"Not at all, I assure you, Mr. Stephenson. So how did Mr. Stephenson fix the…insufficiency?"

"He enlarged the injection cock to almost twice its original diameter. He also raised the engine's reservoir of condensing water, thereby increasing its pressure."

"And George Stephenson's engine drained the colliery of the water?"

He stopped to look at her. His smile was so engaging. Sorcha couldn't believe such an accomplished man could be so humble and charming. *And that he is looking at me!*

There is nothing arrogant about him. Sorcha sighed. *I feel such a hopeless longing when he is about, as if he is a god instead of a man. I'm not sure I like being in a constant state of adoration. As if I will never be able to measure up to him and never feel myself to be his equal.*

Sorcha felt her cheeks color. *How embarrassing!* Some women were happy to adore their men, but it didn't feel comfortable to her. She wanted to relax and enjoy herself in a man's presence. She didn't want to constantly be comparing herself unfavorably to a man.

She supposed, for some ladies, it was enough to be adored by someone they greatly admired.

But that wasn't *living* for her. Delightful in the present, but difficult to sustain for long periods of time.

Still, she was enthralled for the time being.

"We should turn around and return to our seat. It won't be long until the next race." Robert took her elbow and Sorcha felt herself shiver.

"How long did it take your father's engine to drain the Killingworth pit?" She genuinely wanted to know.

Robert cleared his throat. "It took Father four days to make the repairs after six months of failures by the previous engineers. There was a small crowd of onlookers, some wishing him no success I am sure. And then he started up the engine."

"Why would they not wish him success? Because they had so many more advantages than George Stephenson and yet could not compete with him?" asked Sorcha.

"It is odd, isn't it?" Robert smiled, seeming to be at ease again.

"Some resent it when those who have worked hard for everything they have succeed. At any rate, Father got the engine started on Wednesday and by ten o'clock that night the water in the pit was lower than it had ever been. The engine kept working in spite of all the engine's nonstop laboring. By Friday afternoon the pit was dry enough to send down the pitmen."

"Mr. Dodds must have been so grateful. George Stephenson saved the Killingworth mine."

"Oh, I'm sure he did!" Robert's face lit up.

"Surely Mr. Stephenson was rewarded?"

"Dodds gave Father a bonus of ten pounds."

Sorcha gasped, disheartened by the finale. She colored in anger. George Stephenson made the company thousands of pounds, not to mention preventing great losses and inevitable bankruptcy. "Is that all? George Stephenson saved the company."

"Dodds probably had to recoup money after wasting so much on those who couldn't do the job." As they continued walking, many men were near the locomotives, performing various functions. The constables attempted to keep the crowds away from the locomotives. It was a regular circus!

"That ten pounds represented the first time my father was recognized as an engineer. It was the largest payment Father ever received on a job up to that point. He was very proud of that ten pounds."

"I expect so, but was he paid commensurate with his contribution?"

"It was the beginning of what you see here today, Miss O'Shea, so we can't complain. Dodds promoted father to the post of engineman at High Pit and increased his wages. Father had the last laugh on all the Eton boys. And now..." Robert Stephenson smiled proudly..."He is the Chief Engineer of the Darlington-Stockton Railway entering the first steam locomotive for use on a passenger rail."

Once again, Sorcha felt awed by the Stephensons, who responded to all of life's challenges with a positive and grateful attitude. The Stephensons didn't sit about being bitter and resentful: they were too busy working!

Sorcha had to admit that she sometimes resented the inequities of life. More for her parents and for Danny than for herself. Even so, it was hurtful when people looked down on her.

I am glad I am not one of the upper class, always trying to put on a show for everyone, like a fish in a fishbowl, not able to simply be myself. But I would like to be a bit higher up in society.

In Liverpool, I receive looks of disdain. Right now everyone is looking at me with admiration as I walk and talk with Robert Stephenson.

And I love it.

Sorcha sighed. *I'd best not let the it go to my head!*

There can be no question of Robert Stephenson being interested in me. I am merely in the right place at the right time. When I return home, he will move on from me faster than those steam locomotives can move.

Still, Sorcha was having a wonderful time, and she meant to continue to do so until the Rainhill Trials were over.

They passed a man selling pretzels, and the smell of the warm bread was inviting. "Would you like a pretzel, Miss O'Shea?"

"I certainly wouldn't object if you wish to share one, Mr. Stephenson."

He purchased a pretzel for her and, still walking, she held the buttery morsel in her handkerchief, offering him a bite. He bend down to take a bite.

It was delicious indeed, and welcome on this cool day.

"Hmm," Sorcha considered. "And how did the Rainhill Trials race come about? Something tells me your father was involved."

CHAPTER SEVENTEEN

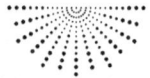

October 7, 1829
2nd Day of the Rainhill Trials

*R*obert laughed. "Very much so. I doubt if we would be here today if not for George Stephenson." He looked into shining turquoise eyes. *Remind me to thank him.*

"George Stephenson seems to have a hand in everything." Sorcha considered.

"The tracks were already laid. They were used with horse-drawn carriages built for the tracks."

"So all you have to do is add the steam locomotives?"

"If that's the decision of the directors, yes. The line has been deciding between a rope-haul system—essentially a pulley system—and a steam locomotive. The 'experts' say the rope-haul system is the best choice. My father went ballistic and wrote a letter to the board. The directors set up a race to decide the matter. And here we are."

"I expect you helped him with that letter," Sorcha said slyly.

Robert shrugged. It was true that writing was not George Stephenson's strong point. He still struggled a bit, having learned later in life. "I might have."

He was enjoying the extended wait although he should have been impatient. "Shall we have a cup of hot tea at the café, Miss O'Shea?"

"Oh, that would be lovely."

Sorcha O'Shea was the most agreeable girl of his acquaintance. Although Robert was used to ladies fawning over him, he felt her enjoyment was genuine.

Once situated at a table with a view of the tracks, Sorcha closed her eyes momentarily. "I feel I will always love the Fall henceforth."

"Oh?"

"The October weather is exquisitely comfortable—not to hot or too cold—the leaves are stunning colors." She positively glowed as she spoke.

And the company is both romantic and enchanting.

"Say, would you like a pot of chocolate instead of tea, Miss O'Shea?"

"I…I don't know…I've never had chocolate."

"You haven't? Why?" he asked, startled. How could anyone never have tried a hot cup of chocolate? It was more expensive, but surely… She was dressed so fine and indicated she was the daughter of someone in the textiles trade.

She blushed as if embarrassed. "Certainly I would like to try it if you like it, Mr. Stephenson."

Robert ordered the chocolate and the hot mugs and biscuits arrived quickly, the smell of cinnamon and cardamom wafting through the air.

Sorcha took her first sip and her face lit up as if she was experiencing pure delight. "Oh my goodness! That is delicious, Robert!"

She called me by my name.

He smiled, taking pleasure in her delight. "It is," he agreed. "Chocolate was once only available to the very rich."

"Many might still consider such a treat too dear." She looked away momentarily but suddenly began to laugh.

"What is it Miss O'Shea?"

"I fear I shall never be able to live without chocolate now," she giggled.

"You are not the first to say so," Robert murmured.

"The Rainhill Trials is a perfect blend of excitement and tranquility,"

Sorcha suddenly grew somber. "But...will there necessarily be a winner?"

"Oh, there will be a winner." Robert nodded.

"But you said it isn't like a race exactly, Robert. There is a difficult criteria to be met."

"Yes," Robert agreed. "But I have talked too much and too long about me, my family, and our locomotive. I'm ashamed to have been so vainglorious."

Sorcha motioned her head towards the tracks. "I suppose you have something to boast about."

Robert allowed himself the brief pleasure of studying her white lace, ruffled dress. He loved the way the ruffles fluttered in the wind when they were walking.

Sorcha O'Shea was definitely a leprechaun's fairy. "I must say, those delicate buttons on your dress are works of art. I hope you don't think I am being too forward but attention to detail is my profession."

"Thank you. They depict the wildflowers of Ireland."

"How exquisite. How did you acquire these buttons, Miss O'Shea?" Robert dipped a biscuit in his mug of chocolate, and Sorcha followed suit, smiling at him. He loved seeing her in this setting, so relaxed and enjoying herself.

"I painted them."

"You did? Your skill is exceptional, Miss O'Shea." He stared at the buttons, astonished. "You must have to use a magnifying glass to accomplish that level of detail."

"Oh, yes."

"It must require a great deal of focus."

She hesitated, as if she didn't wish to answer him. Then she seemed to come to some resolve. "Indeed it does. But it is my job."

"Your *job* is painting buttons?" Robert was confused. *Does she mean her contribution to the family is painting buttons? Her hobby? What does she mean by 'job'?*

"Exactly," she said, it seemed to him with a degree of both pride and embarrassment.

"Do you mean your contribution to your family, Miss O'Shea?"

"Certainly. But it is a job."

"Surely you don't mean a paid position?"

She sighed. "I do."

She's a working girl. An artisan. That explains it. Could that be the reason he felt so at ease with her? He now might be wealthy and able to aim higher in society, but his roots were in the laboring class—he had always been a working man—and he felt so much more relaxed with Sorcha than with young ladies who had been idle and self-indulgent all their lives. He and Sorcha came from the same background in a strong sense.

I like a working girl. Robert Stephenson didn't care what class Sorcha O'Shea was in. Robert's mother died when he was young. His father worked several jobs so that Robert might go to school. Robert knew he owed his father everything. Robert acquired the polish George never had, who was often ridiculed for his Yorkshire accent.

But does this mean then...is her father not wealthy? Is he not in textiles as she indicated? Sorcha struck him as a very articulate girl. Where was she educated?

Miss O'Shea had a great deal of polish for a working artisan.

"May I ask...where do you work Miss O'Shea? At your father's factory?"

Sorcha giggled and she seemed to lose some of her stiffness. She shook her head. "My father doesn't own a factory."

"But I thought you said...you were in textiles?"

"I am. Not my father." Sorcha took a sip of chocolate then looked up at him over her mug. "I work in a factory."

"Does anyone else in your factory have that level of skill?" Robert asked, doubtful.

So, she does not appear to be wealthy and she works in a factory. This explains her lack of airs and never having had chocolate before.

I could care less. But her address and her clothing does not indicate her station in life.

"In metallurgy, certainly, but, in all honesty, probably not in painting." Sorcha replied.

He liked an honest girl not afraid to toot her own horn.

"Do you ever paint regular-sized paintings?" Robert asked. "I expect it would be easy for you if you can paint in miniature."

Sorcha shrugged. "I actually am a fairly decent painter, but no one is going to buy a painting from a woman, much less an Irish woman."

"How would anyone know the gender or nationality of the painter?" Robert asked.

Sorcha raised her eyebrows. "Well, I don't have my own art gallery to hide behind."

I will give you one.

"Where are you originally from, Miss O'Shea?" Robert asked turning his mug round in his hand. He hoped he wasn't asking her too many questions, but he was fascinated by this puzzle unraveling.

"Belfast."

"So, technically, you're not an immigrant. We're all part of the United Kingdom."

"You are not like most British, Mr. Stephenson. The prejudice against the Irish is sometimes crippling." She smiled. "I'm not complaining. I feel very blessed here. I don't miss my homeland as much as my parents do: it is hardest on them. I have employment. Everyone wears buttons. *Everyone.* You see, you are wearing them."

"Of course I am. But they are not nearly so beautiful as yours."

"I can make one for you." She continued, seeming more relaxed, as if she had revealed a terrible secret and there was now nothing to hide. "Buttons can be made of steel, brass, silver, mother of pearl, ivory, wood, bone, glass, ceramics, enamel and even cloth. The patterns and detail can be stunning and intricate. I see yours are gold buttons made of brass."

"Is there a good living to be made in making buttons?" he asked.

"Surprisingly, there is for a skilled artist. I earn more income than everyone else in my family combined."

Robert stepped back, astonished. "You do?"

"Me, a factory girl, do you mean?" Her tone was polite, but he felt he might have hurt her, which was mortifying and the last thing he wished to do.

"Not at all! There's no shame in being a skilled artisan, but I didn't realize there was money in it either," Robert explained.

"We aren't wealthy by any means. But at least we aren't starving."

"I can see that." He glanced at her beautiful gown.

"Many children die from the conditions where the Irish live." Sorcha took out her handkerchief and wiped her eye. "*Where we used to live.*"

"Did you lose…?" His eyes flew wide open.

"One of my brothers. The conditions were so bad when we first moved to Liverpool."

"I'm so sorry, Miss O'Shea." He touched her hand though he knew it was improper. His heart went out to her.

"Thank you, Robert." She looked away. "I suppose one isn't supposed to discuss one's grief and misfortunes on a glorious day like today."

"The truth is rarely spoken in polite company." He nodded. "I find the superficiality difficult at times."

"Thankfully we aren't in polite company," she murmured.

Robert burst into laughter. "Speak for yourself, Miss O'Shea. I consider my company to be both polite and charming. And yet..." he glanced around "It's certainly a day at the races here."

"I don't think I've enjoyed myself more." She smiled.

"And where did you receive your education, if I may ask?" Robert asked.

"In Belfast. My father made a good living there but it was difficult work."

Suddenly a loud noise burst upon their conversation.

"What on earth?... That man hopping about there on the tracks and talking to everyone? My goodness, he is energetic! *Is it...could it be...Thaddeus Fulbright?*"

"It is. Quite enthusiastic. I'm afraid my father might punch him out if he doesn't stand back."

Sorcha smiled. "Mr. Fulbright is intent upon getting his story."

"Ah. Reporting must be an interesting job, I should think." Robert shook his head. "But it requires more brashness than I possess."

Sorcha raised her eyebrows. "Thaddeus Fulbright has no shortage of brashness, audacity and pretension, I assure you."

Having finished their chocolate, they returned to Sorcha's bench. The crowds had disbursed a bit since they were in between trials and Sorcha was able to recapture her seat.

"Sorcha Fae O'Shea, what have you been doing in my absence?" Mr. O'Shea arrived, eyeing Robert with suspicion. Lawrence Davenport was close behind.

"Oh, hello Da. Merely speaking to the *Rocket's* engineer!" She smiled mischievously. "Let me introduce you to Mr. Robert Stephenson. Mr.

Stephenson, my da, Sean O'Shea. And my employer Lawrence Davenport."

"G'wan!" Mr. O'Shea exclaimed, moving his head back in disbelief.

"It's true, Da." Sorcha studied her father, perplexed. "Surely you saw me speaking to Mr. Stephenson before?"

Mr. O'Shea looked embarrassed for his inattentiveness to his daughter. "Of course I did! But I didn't realize..."

Sorcha shook her head at her father.

Robert smiled to himself as he made the appropriate responses.

Sorcha *Fae*. She *is* a fairy.

CHAPTER EIGHTEEN

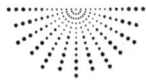

October 7, 1829
2nd Day of the Rainhill Trials

*N**ow the secret is out. Robert knows I am a factory girl.*

Because I was stupid enough to tell him! Why couldn't I keep it to myself a little longer? Nothing will come of this acquaintance anyway, but it would have been nice to pretend for a little while longer. This heavenly interval will be over soon enough.

I even bragged about what I earn! How vulgar! It was an extremely unladylike and uncouth thing to do.

In all fairness to myself, everyone keeps asking me how a factory girl can afford such a nice dress—and they expect me to be emaciated—so they rather back me into a corner. I certainly don't go about boasting of my salary! As if my income is anything to boast about anyway! It's just that we aren't destitute like we were. I suppose I am proud of my artistic ability: proof that 'pride goeth before a fall' as my Grandmother Oonagh always says.

If Robert Stephenson wins this race, he will be famous and no doubt wish to marry a girl of high society standing. Anything else would be detrimental to his career.

He won't even remember my name.

What ridiculous thoughts I am having. Robert Stephenson has no serious interest in me.

And why should I want him to? I just met him.

None of the men she interacted with today—Robert Stephenson, Thaddeus Fulbright, or Lawrence Davenport—would ever consider an alliance with an Irish girl from Belfast.

That is the relevant point.

Lawrence made quite clear what she was good for.

I was so insulted and humiliated. Sorcha had to admit to herself that conversation left her quite undone. For an instant she felt like the dirt beneath his feet.

It isn't like me to worry so much about what people think of me. Or to believe anyone could withhold any good thing from her: that was up to Providence.

God is greater than prejudice and social convention.

I must never buy into it. No matter how badly anyone treated her.

True, prejudice and greed killed Danny. *But as long as I breathe, I must resist the limitations of others.*

I must not let their limitations become mine.

But the interaction with Lawrence was akin to foreshadowing—even a prophecy.

This was the first time the reality of her marital prospects due to her nationality, class, position in the work force, and social standing became real to her. She supposed she had been stupid and naïve. It felt like having a glass of cold water thrown in her face.

She had never before thought of any man outside her class. Being thrown in with those previously unknown to her, and receiving such favorable treatment—by Mr. Fulbright and Mr. Stephenson, two out of three—was bittersweet.

It is an illusion.

Suddenly the sight before her brought Sorcha back to the present.

"Why are there so many cinders flying?" Sorcha asked. The Rocket was beginning the next of its leg, "chuff-ing" and throwing red sparks everywhere.

Robert, who was on the verge of departing, albeit reluctantly, replied, "The Rocket, and indeed all the other locomotives, do not have anything below the grate to catch the ash. So hot cinders can fall onto the track."

"It would seem to pose a fire hazard," Sorcha considered.

"It is not advisable to stand too near the tracks, for many reasons."

Staring at his locomotive in a trance-like state, Robert seemed to be reflecting upon the situation. "Possibly I should add a pan beneath the grate."

Just at that moment, a woman's dress began to smoke in the back. She was standing very near to the tracks, her huge hoop dress swinging back and forth and fueling the sparks. No one appeared to notice from the angle where they were standing.

No one about her appeared to be aware that she was about to catch on fire.

* * *

ROBERT WATCHED, horrified. He turned to look at Sorcha before realizing she had already rushed forward and leapt onto the tracks.

And I thought the Rocket was the fastest thing known to man.

Sorcha threw the woman onto the grassy part of the ground, telling her to roll. Rolling was made excessively difficult by the hoop skirt, but very important as the crinoline was extremely flammable. It was critical that the flames didn't reach the crinoline.

Sorcha seized the woman's shawl, beating the dress with all her might.

With Sorcha's quick response and the commotion she caused, *Rocket's* fireman jumped to the cart where the water barrel was housed. He doused the woman with a bucket of water from the big barrel of water in a cart pulled by *Rocket*, followed by another bucket carried by someone unknown to Robert.

But Sorcha's quick thinking saved the woman from bursting into flames. A woman who now looked like a drowned rat, drenched and appearing to take her fear and embarrassment out on Sorcha, Robert observed as he moved towards the scene of the near tragedy.

"I am completely soaked! And you might have broken every bone in my body, girl!"

"I only wished to keep you from burning up, Ma'am," Sorcha replied.

"Hundreds of women have died from their crinolines catching on fire, Ma'am," Robert added, having reached them by now and taking Sorcha's arm. "You should be grateful you aren't one of them. You have only to open a newspaper to read about it. And we saw the smoke coming from your garment!"

Apparently the lady did not read the newspapers, as she was not consoled in the least. As with most people, if it didn't happen to them, it wasn't real. And even if it did.

Robert turned to Sorcha. "Are you alright Miss O'Shea?" Her white dress was muddied, and her hair disheveled.

"Is *she* alright?" The drenched woman exclaimed. "*She* is not likely to die of a broken rib or a cold! She is the one doing the attacking!"

Distracted by the entrance of a Bobby, the unappreciative woman said of her rescuer, "Police Officer! I want you to take this woman into custody for attacking me!"

CHAPTER NINETEEN

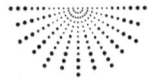

Rainhill Trials
The Challenger

"$\mathcal{M}$r. Robert Stephenson's Rocket attracted the most notice during the early part of the afternoon on the second day of the Rainhill Trials. Running without any weight being attached to it, the Rocket shocked everyone by travelling at the rate of twenty-four miles an hour! Shooting past the spectators with amazing velocity, the Rocket emitted very little smoke, but dropped red-hot cinders as it proceeded, the terrifying results of which will be revealed here shortly.

Cars containing stones were then attached to the Rocket; the combined weight of the Rocket with its cargo being upwards of 17 tons. This attachment of the load was in preparation for the essential part of the Rainhill trials: the condition of the locomotive being able to pull weight at a minimum speed.

The precise distance between the point of starting, near the weighing-shed, to the point of returning, was 1¾ miles. With a load of 17 tons, the Rocket travelled the space of 1¾ miles four times forward and four times backward, equal to 14 miles, in the space of 75 minutes. Including the stoppages, the average rate was 10½ miles per hour. The minimum speed was met!

Many of those present were astonished, not believing such a speed to be possible, particularly by such a cumbersome, heavy machine. It strikes one as counter-intuitive. One expects the tiny hummingbird to be fast, but an iron monstrosity?

The general consensus is that these iron carriages have somehow harnessed the power of the heavens.

In the fifth course the Rocket's rate of speed with a load of passengers equal to 13 tons was a full 15 miles an hour!

Our heads are spinning with what we witnessed here today.

In a challenge characterized by world debuts, excitement, thrills, and unexpected occurrences, there was yet another spectacular encounter at the second day of the Rainhill Trials. A phenomenal example of bravery was exhibited by a young lady from our very own Liverpool, a Miss Sorcha O'Shea, who leapt upon the tracks and extinguished a woman in flames, a Mrs. Rodney Ipswich, wife of a successful London merchant, who came very close to being one of the 250 crinoline deaths this year.

This is a family newspaper and, as such, one might not wish ladies' undergarments being discussed, but this is a life and death matter which must be brought to the public's awareness in all good conscience. A crinoline, made of horsehair and cotton or linen, is extremely flammable. Standing too close to the tracks, Mrs. Ipswich's gown was the recipient of the steam locomotive Rocket's flying cinders. Her dress began to smolder.

While everyone else stood about in shock at the horror unfolding before them, in a matter of seconds the quick-thinking Miss O'Shea threw Mrs. Ipswich to the ground, rolling her in the grass, thereafter thrashing the dress with Mrs. Ipswich's own shawl, previously an heirloom, narrowly averting a tragedy. Mrs. Ipswich was then doused in water by the Rocket's fireman and by a Mr. Thomas Skinner, a plumber by trade, who threw a bucket of water on Mrs. Ipswich, destroying her coiffure along with her pride.

For her part, the heroic Miss O'Shea wishes no recognition, but let it be known that she is an artisan painting commemorative buttons of this spectacular race for Davenport's Textiles and Mercantile in Liverpool. This newspaper man would not be surprised if owning one of those buttons painted by the young lady who exhibited such bravery at the soon-to-be famous Rainhill Trials will prove to be a collector's item.

Rather than being grateful for the heroic acts of those saving her life and preventing untold suffering, Mrs. Ipswich exhibited no small amount of animosity towards her saviors, complaining of bruising, humiliation, the destruction of her heirloom shawl, and catching her death of a cold. All unpleasant but not nearly as unpleasant as burning to death, in this reporter's informed estimation.

It is hoped that, upon reflection, Mrs. Ipswich will appreciate the brave service done for her as well as reconsider her fashion choices.

-- Thaddeus Fulbright, Liverpool Mercury

"Sorcha! You were like lightening!" Sean O'Shea and Robert caught up with her, but the deed was already done.

"I had to be, Da!"

Robert was in shock. "Miss O'Shea, are you alright? You put yourself in grave danger."

"I beg to differ. I am not wearing a crinoline."

"Miss O'Shea, let us retire to the Grand Stand where you can rest," Robert said. "I have some seats there. You must be exhausted."

Sorcha smiled. "That's very kind of you, sir, but what about my entourage?" She glanced at Mr. O'Shea who was somewhat dirty in his work clothes from being on the tracks. "I have regular visitors at my bench who might not be welcome among distinguished visitors. I don't wish to cut myself off from anyone I am supposed to be in touch with." She glanced at Lawrence Davenport. *Though certainly it would be nice to be cut off from some.* "Besides, the views are good from my bench. And I am comfortable doing my drawings."

"Yes, of course, whatever you wish, Miss O'Shea. It is a good vantage point from which to watch the next race."

Inadvertently, Robert glanced at the mud on the hem of her dress.

"It will probably have to wait until I return to my Aunt Hannah's home to clean," Sorcha explained.

"One of the consequences of heroism," Robert said with a smile.

The three returned to Sorcha's designated spot, where they found Lawrence claiming the coveted bench.

"Oh, wait, Da! The *Novelty* is up now! Let us speak later." Sorcha turned to Robert and asked, "You won't mind if we get excited over your opponent, Mr. Stephenson?"

"Your opponent?" demanded Lawrence. "Who is this gentleman? I saw you speaking to him earlier. You certainly have a lot of gentleman friends for someone here to do a job."

"Hush, Mr. Davenport, please mind your manners. If not to me, at least to the dignitaries. This is Mr. Stephenson, who built the *Rocket*."

"Let me shake your hand, young man!" Mr. O'Shea exclaimed with genuine excitement. "What an amazing sight that was! The *Rocket* seems to be the only locomotive here ready to race. We waited for them to put the finishing touches on The *Novelty*, and here it is."

It warmed Sorcha's heart to see her father happy. She hadn't seen him so enthused—almost bursting with joy—since they left Ireland.

In contrast, Lawrence frowned as he stared at Robert Stephenson. Sorcha observed that Lawrence was never happy to see anyone else succeed more than he did—a relatively low standard to meet—particularly another male.

Robert Stephenson did not appear to be much worried about the competition.

All of these three men exhibited different levels of excitement—running the gamut—at the same event.

I don't know how anyone can avoid being positively ecstatic. It is all so exhilarating!

Lawrence frowned. "You've been busy in my absence, Miss O'Shea. And not on your *work*."

"I will complete my work, Mr. Davenport." *Will you?* Sorcha shut her notebook and patted it. She wanted to give her full attention to the next race.

Robert Stephenson raised his eyebrows, but he was too much of a gentleman to comment.

But Sean O'Shea was not.

Sorcha saw the anger rising in her father's expression and she vehemently shook her head.

It was too late.

"Mind your own morals, Mr. Davenport, and I'll attend to my daughter's." Mr. O'Shea said. "From what I have seen, yours could use some scrutiny."

"Da!" Sorcha exclaimed, but her father's expression was unrelenting.

"How dare you!" Lawrence sputtered. "I don't have to answer to you, but the same is not true of Miss O'Shea! She answers *to me*."

Lawrence's proclamation had the opposite effect he might have wished.

"She does not," Mr. O'Shea said softly, but his expression revealed his fury. "However, *you* will answer to me, if you're not careful."

"You wouldn't dare!" Lawrence exclaimed, Mr. O'Shea's implication not lost on him.

"If you don't stop defaming my daughter's reputation, I certainly would." Sean's eyes narrowed.

And you have some nerve after your behavior at this event, Lawrence! I've not been gambling and hanging about with women of easy virtue! Sorcha fumed but she kept her mouth shut, as she wished her father would.

"It's none of your business," Lawrence retorted.

"You made it by business, sir, with your insults directed at my family."

"I'm not afraid of you, old man!" Lawrence backed up, indicating that he was more afraid than he said.

"But look!" Sorcha interjected. "It appears *Novelty* is finally ready to race!"

The interruption was a welcome one. Sean O'Shea cast a final glance at Lawrence, serving as a warning.

They all waited in anticipation of the *Novelty's* performance. The excitement was so thick it might have fueled the locomotives. The spectators were ready for the race to begin. The judges too were ready.

But, once again, the *Novelty* was not ready.

"Oh, there is that crazy reporter again, hopping about." Mr. O'Shea shook his head.

"I suspect he wants to observe from all the best angles," Sorcha considered.

"Or maybe he just likes to hop about," Sean O'Shea suggested.

"He had best get off the tracks or he may be run over," Lawrence said, muttering under his breath, "Not an altogether unwelcome outcome."

"Here come the constables, they will deal with him," Mr. O'Shea pronounced.

"If they can catch him," Robert said with a chuckle.

Sorcha giggled then covered her mouth with her gloved hands. As annoying as Thaddeus was, he was quite amusing.

A most welcome distraction.

"Mr. Fulbright definitely intends to get his story," Sorcha murmured.

While the group of newly formed acquaintances was standing on the podium absorbed in the trespasser on the tracks, suddenly Mr. O'Shea did a 180 degree turn and grabbed the man behind him by the neck.

"Lawd save me!" the bound man yelled. "What are you doing, you loon!"

"The question is what are you doin'?" Mr. O'Shea demanded, going through the man's coat and pockets with his free hand. Mr. O'Shea was a strong man, well able to handle both keeping the man pinned down and ciphering through his clothing.

"Ah-ha. And would this be your wallet, Mr. Davenport? I see there is an 'L' and a 'D' monogram."

"Bastard! Took my wallet!" Lawrence grabbed it from Mr. O'Shea's hand.

"Oh, and here's my coin purse," Mr. O'Shea said. "Not worth the effort, I assure you, son."

"No doubt Mr. Davenport will give you a reward for the retrieval of his wallet, Mr. O'Shea," Robert said.

Lawrence glared. "I'll do no such thing! No more than anyone should do!"

Robert raised his eyebrows. "And how much is in there? You would have been out all of it if not for Mr. O'Shea. Not to mention your beautiful leather wallet."

Mr. O'Shea kept his eyes glued on the culprit. "What is your name?"

"Jack."

"Jack *what?*"

"Nothing more. Just 'Jack'."

"Jack Jack is it? Now, you tell me your name, or I'll take you to the authorities right now."

"Y'are anyways aren't ya'?"

"It depends. You don't look or act like a practiced criminal. You're certainly not very good at it. What's your story?"

"I got 'is wallet from 'im!" Jack nodded his head towards Lawrence as if proof of his skill.

"Yeah, but he's a gobshite," Sean O'Shea said under his breath.

"What did you say?" Lawrence demanded.

"I was talkin' to Just Jack here," Sean replied. "I said 'you're a cheat'."

"I never did nothin' like this 'afore," Jack exclaimed. "But there ain't no work to be had round here. I'm terrible hungry."

"I can tell ya' right now, the food is terrible in prison," Sean said, adding, "What little there is of it."

"There will be jobs," Robert interjected. "The Liverpool Manchester line needs more men, and once the locomotives are built, there will be even more work. But we can't hire thieves."

"Oh, no sir, no. Wif' a real job, I don't need to. I never done nothin' like this afore. I just need work." The man was in his twenties and looked fairly strong, if skinny, though no match for Mr. O'Shea.

"I also need to know a last name," Robert said skeptically.

Jack swallowed hard. He seemed to be evaluating Robert. "Wif' all due respect, sir, why should I trust ye?"

"Because I have the power to help you, Jack," Robert replied. "What are your other options?"

Jack's eyes were hungry. "Bagshaw, sir. Jack Bagshaw."

Robert reached into his pocket and pulled out a card, scribbling on it. "Report to the Darlington Line, tell them I sent you. You'll start at the very bottom with the hard labor."

"Oh, thank you, sir! I'll work hard for youse. No one ever showed me a kindness 'afore."

"Don't disappoint me, Jack Bagshaw."

"Wait!" Sorcha exclaimed, pulling a sandwich out of her purse her Aunt Hannah made for her. "Take this."

"Thank you, Miss," Jack said.

Sorcha nodded. She was too excited to eat anyway.

"Now, you get out of here, Mr. Bagshaw, and don't come back," Mr. O'Shea said as he released the man. "And if I see you again, I'll report you to the authorities."

"You're going to let him go?" demanded Lawrence. "After he stole my wallet?"

"You have your wallet." Mr. O'Shea said, his expression suddenly solemn. "I don't think we'll see him again. He just needs to feed himself."

"I can't believe you rewarded a man for stealing!" Lawrence exclaimed. "He should be hanged."

"Men who have always had food don't know what it's like to not be able to feed one's family and to care for them," Mr. O'Shea muttered with sadness in his eyes.

"Why would you risk hiring a thief?" Lawrence asked of Robert.

"There's nothing to steal working outside on the railway. It's just him and the elements. It's hard labor and those who can't take it are sifted out pretty quickly."

Sorcha put her arm around her Dad, seeing he had taken a sudden downturn in spite of saving the day for everyone. "You're a wonderful father, Da. I couldn't ask for better."

"Danny might feel different."

"He's in heaven now Da. He knows we loved him and did our best. It's the world that let him down, not us."

Robert looked on with concern. "I lost my mother as a very young boy. No one deserved a wife more than my father, who takes care of his own parents. And certainly I deserved a mother. We can't understand the ways of heaven, Mr. O'Shea."

"I'm so sorry, Mr. Stephenson, for the loss of your mother." Sorcha sighed. "In spite of it all, I can't stop feeling God wants us to be happy."

"Nothing was stopping God from helping Danny—or Mr. Stephenson's mother." Mr. O'Shea dabbed his eyes with his handkerchief.

"My consolation is that Danny is with his heavenly Father now, Da. He's happy," Sorcha said quietly. "And he knows we love him."

Sean O'Shea's eyes returned to the tracks. "The authorities are allowing the *Novelty* to race without cargo." His remark appeared to be more of a question than a comment.

"The *Novelty* isn't ready to haul cargo, so they are giving her a break," explained Robert. "All of us only had seven months to build our locomotives and most did not have time for a trial run," explained Robert.

"Allowing the *Novelty* to run without cargo doesn't seem a fair comparison to the *Rocket*..." Sorcha murmured.

"No, but the *Novelty* will yet have to meet all the criteria to win," Robert explained.

"I see. *Novelty* will have to haul cargo at some point and then meet the minimum speed?" Sorcha asked.

"Indeed." Robert nodded.

"Then why even bother now?" snarled Lawrence.

"To get her warmed up. It's the trial run she didn't have the time to make before entering," Robert stated.

"Right. Just as the authorities allowed the *Rocket* to run without any cargo at the beginning," muttered Lawrence.

"That was to entertain the crowds," said Robert, laughing. "We already had our trial run. In the matter of the actual race, each locomotive will have to haul three times its weight in order to qualify—and that will be the official time."

"And each locomotive has to reach a minimum of 10 miles per hour hauling the cargo in order to win," Lawrence sneered, as if it were an impossibility.

Robert smiled. "Exactly."

Sorcha appreciated that Robert was always courteous—even to the ill-mannered!—something she found difficult to achieve.

"But you did a test before you came, Mr. Stephenson," Sorcha said. "You must have known if *Rocket* could meet all the minimum requirements."

"I did and I do." Robert nodded slyly with a gleam in his eyes.

They all waited anxiously, captivated by the *Novelty*, awaiting her departure. She was an enchanting sight: a beautiful, delicate machine in copper and blue, lighter than the green and yellow *Rocket*, which was less stylish and more industrial in appearance.

And then the *Novelty* took off. There was a cumulative gasp, amazed at the *Novelty's* performance.

The *Novelty* quickly reached an amazing velocity of 28 miles an hour!

The crowd was shocked. They had barely recovered from their amazement at seeing *Rocket* pass all heretofore speed records when *Novelty* went even faster. The engineer clung to the *Novelty* as it sped past them. The crowd cheered and the ladies waved their handkerchiefs.

The *Novelty* was the new crowd favorite.

CHAPTER TWENTY

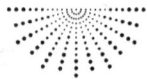

October 7, 1829
Rainhill, England

"*M*r. R. Stephenson's Rocket ran, without any cargo, at the rate of 24 miles in the hour, shooting past the spectators with amazing velocity.*

Today, right before our eyes, the Novelty surpassed the Rocket's speed, logging in at 28 miles in the hour!

Here in Rainhill, in the county of Merseyside, England, these two steam locomotives set world records for speed. Novelty and Rocket, seemed indeed, to fly, presenting one of the most sublime spectacles of human ingenuity and human daring the world ever beheld.

It actually made one giddy to witness these two marvels of engineering competing against each other—like two apex predators vying for the territory and the kingdom— filling thousands with lively fears for the safety of the individuals who were on these steam carriages.

Even those who supported the steam locomotive all along cannot believe what we are witnessing. Some thought we were watching a race, but in actuality we are watching the reality of our world change in the matter of one and a half minutes."

But as with any race, the question is 'who traveled faster'? The answer, my friends, is the Novelty! Not entirely unexpected for those of us who are behind the scenes. There are still certain formalities to complete, but after the impressive showing today one can easily predict the outcome of this race.

– THADDEUS FULBRIGHT, The Liverpool Mercury

"WELL THAT'S the shortest time to hold a world record in the history of mankind." Robert Stephenson laughed as his father, George Stephenson, joined them.

Sorcha was giddy with excitement. George Stephenson standing before her! The son was impressive, to say the least, but the father was a legend!

They bore a strong resemblance to each other, but whereas Robert had dark blue eyes and dark hair, George had pale blue-grey eyes and white hair. George was also taller and more muscular, being an extremely fit man.

From the picture of overall vigor George conveyed, Sorcha thought his hair must have gone white prematurely. True, George presented a less sophisticated manner than his formally educated son, an education which was no doubt earned by the hard work of George himself.

"Ah, but the trials ain't over yet." George winked playfully, not displaying the manner of one who had just lost a race. Sorcha stared at the father with interest.

In personality, George was more brash than his son. A person of high society who took issue with George's thick country accent—as opposed to the language of parliament—might even refer to him as 'vulgar'. That would have been unfair. But then, Sorcha knew what is was like to be judged for her accent by those who wished to feel superior.

Despite having been treated with hauteur and pretention, which might have deflated another, George had an arrogant, boastful manner. The elder Stephenson did not appear to suffer from low confidence.

In spite of their many surficial differences, there was a charming and heart-warming rapport between the father and son.

Sorcha liked Robert Stephenson's easy manners and humility—none of the bragging she was accustomed to in young men—when he certainly had reason to boast. She especially liked Robert's good nature: it appeared difficult to put him out of sorts, even when he might have cause for resentment. And it was no detriment in her mind that Robert was beautiful to the eye, reminiscent of the romantic poets.

Certainly no young lady can object to that.

"Can anyone doubt that the *Novelty* will win the Grand Prize?" posed Lawrence. "A full four miles per hour faster than the *Rocket*."

"Eejit," George muttered while bestowing a demeaning glance upon Lawrence. Robert showed no signs of being rattled.

Robert, unlike his father, was modest and reserved. But they were both highly ambitious and determined to win, of that Sorcha had no doubt.

"What did you call me?" Lawrence demanded.

George shook his head and looked away.

"You must be the famous Mr. George Stephenson?" Sorcha asked, curtseying, attempting to distract Lawrence. "It's such an honor to meet you, sir."

George bowed and lifted his hat to her. "And you are, lass?"

"Sorcha O'Shea. This is my father Mr. O'Shea. And this is Lawrence Davenport of the Davenport Mercantile."

Lawrence was agitated now. (Sorcha suspected he was still bruised and humiliated by his earlier encounter with her father.) "You didn't answer me, sir. I demand satisfaction." Lawrence slapped George's arm with his handkerchief.

George burst into laughter, as if a butterfly had just collided with his arm. "You're challenging me to a duel, boy?"

"I am." Lawrence was indignant.

"It's illegal in Britain, don't 'ya know?"

"That's of no concern to me."

"No respect for the law? Got a taste for Australia, do ya'? There are those of us who can't afford that luxurious journey. Got things to do here."

"Are you afraid old man?"

"Now don't get your bloomers in a bunch." George chuckled. "I ain't gonna shoot ya' son. But…if you like….we can have an honest fist fight. I'll warn ye though, I've won every fight I've ever fought."

"He's telling the truth," Robert murmured.

"You're an old man," Lawrence retorted.

"If that's what you think, then give it a go." George Stephenson cocked his head, winking at Lawrence in the manner one might speak to a 5-year-old. "Forty-five if I'm a day. And I can still out-work and out-fight any young man." George shrugged. "Just tryin' to save ya' some pain."

Lawrence surveyed the older man, who was much bigger and more muscular.

"I'm not going to wallow in the dirt," Lawrence sneered.

"Good on you, you hornswoggler!" George chuckled, slapping Lawrence on the back, thereby pushing him quite a distance. "It's fer the best. I've never lost. Probably all that hard work. You should try it."

"I'm not afraid of you, sir!" Lawrence stumbled to his feet.

"Not likely, you don't appear to have much sense. So let's call a truce?"

"You have insulted me, sir. I demand satisfaction!"

"I'm not sure I can accommodate ye there, I've got a gigglemug when it comes to the dandies. I just love 'em! They makes me laugh 'till I can't stop." To prove his point George continued laughing.

If there was one thing Lawrence didn't like above all else, it was being laughed at.

"I'll have you know, I'm an excellent shot, sir," Lawrence retorted.

"Using a gun is the coward's way out. Ye let the gun do all the work." George shook his head.

"You're the one who is a coward! You refuse to enter into a duel!"

"There's a lot of things I am, but a coward ain't one of 'em." George shook his head. "There, there young lad, I can see ye're of a delicate constitution. There's no cause for fightin' today. What do we have to be angry about? It's a glorious day, and we're all lucky to be here, ain't we?"

Lawrence stormed off.

Looking after him and shaking his head, George said, "Poor misguided fella'. He thinks the sun comes up just to hear him crow."

"And what is your opinion of the *Novelty*, Mr. Stephenson?" Sorcha asked, more and more mesmerized by the Chief Engineer of the Darlington-Stockton Railway.

"A very fine performance," George said politely, suddenly more serene.

"Are you concerned that the Rocket's top speed was 24 miles per hour and the Novelty's was 28?" Sorcha asked.

"*Novelty* is built for speed, to be sure. Even so, *Novelty* has never hauled its weight requirement, has it?" George asked.

"No." Robert shook his head. "But the judges are doing some calculations deciding how much the Novelty should have to haul."

"It won't be the same as the Rocket's weight requirement?" Sorcha asked, perplexed.

George shook his head. It was pretty obvious he didn't agree with the judges' decision. "No."

"And why not?" Mr. O'Shea asked.

"Because the *Novelty* is lighter," Robert replied. "It weighs less than the *Rocket*."

"So they are changing the requirements of the race for the *Novelty*?" Sorcha stated. "That doesn't seem logical or fair."

"Nope. Makes no sense to me." George laughed. "But then, I didn't have me intelligence demolished at one of them fancy schools."

"The *Novelty* did beat the *Rocket's* speed when neither was hooked up to its haul," Mr. O'Shea repeated.

"The *Novelty* has never shown that it can haul *anything*," George said. "It doesn't matter how fast it goes without a load. Carrying a load is the sole purpose of the locomotive. Nothing else."

"But the *Novelty* is a lovely machine," Robert said with a slight upturn of his mouth. "And the ride is smooth."

"When it comes time to haul something, which is going to be better, a locomotive what can haul more, or a lighter locomotive what can't be bothered as it might muss its coiffure?" George asked. "Are we going to say, 'But it's light, don't give it too much?' No business gives a damn how much the train weighs. They care how much it can haul!"

"But if two trains could haul the same load, a business would care if one train was faster than the other, wouldn't it?" Sorcha considered.

"That's a pretty big, 'if', Miss," George replied. "But yes."

"Do ye think *Novelty* can win?" Sean O'Shea asked, concerned.

"*Novelty* could win by the judges' rules." Robert frowned. "But I don't think it would be a good result for the Liverpool & Manchester line if she did."

"How do you mean?" Mr. O'Shea asked.

"The weight *Novelty* can pull is too light for a practical railway," George stated bluntly as was his custom. He had a way of getting to the heart of the matter.

"It is a very different thing to haul three times one's weight than to run a race without pulling anything," Robert added. "The Novelty is light and built for speed. The Rocket is heavier and built to haul goods. As my good father said, hauling goods is rather the point of the competition."

"That's right," George agreed. "It ain't a beauty contest of the most beautiful bird."

"Father! There are ladies present," Robert admonished.

"I've no doubt I noticed that before you did, son." George winked at Sorcha.

"This is Miss O'Shea's father. He may not take kindly to your crude conversation in front of his daughter," Robert added.

Sorcha could see Robert was in his element discussing trains with the other train-obsessed attendees: with the engineers and the muscle-bound men on the tracks (and those who were both). And yet he was concerned for her treatment.

Even her Da seemed completely at place here in this unique atmosphere, though it had something in common with the docks and the shipyards. But there was something both gritty and futurist about the tracks.

Sorcha smiled at her father, large and muscular. *Yes, this is the place for the manly men.*

"Beggin yer pardon, sir. You have a beautiful daughter and I've got nothin' but respect for her." George bowed before Mr. O'Shea.

"Sorcha ain't no shrinking violet. She can take care o' herself. I brought her up right." Mr. O'Shea smiled. "And, I must say, I am most impressed with the *Rocket's* performance today."

"Right she is, ain't she?" George smiled proudly. "You see, the *Novelty* was built to race. The *Rocket* was built to *win* this competition."

Sorcha studied George Stephenson. It was obvious he was going to be utterly disappointed if the *Rocket* lost. *Forth Street Works*, owned by father and son, was already accepting the prize in his mind.

"However it ends, this day was a first in history." Robert appeared reflective. "The fastest speed by a machine on land, I should say."

"Indeed. No one can take that from the *Rocket* – or the *Novelty*," Sorcha said.

"Oh, and look! Here is the *Cycloped.*" Lawrence exclaimed, returning to the group in better spirits, ale in hand.

"The *Cycloped* is just a horse in a cart moving the wheels—the wagon is powered by a horse walking on a drive belt," Robert said. "It isn't even a steam engine. Besides, why not have the horse pull the cart with the wheels on the track? That would make more sense."

"Folly, fudge, and flummadiddle! Nothing about the *Cycloped* makes sense," added George. "There is no way it is going to meet the 10 miles per hour requirement."

Sorcha found she enjoyed watching the races with the engineers. She was learning a great deal. And they were just as headstrong and opinionated as men at a bar! The band started up with "Buy a Broom" and she found herself wishing she could dance.

The *Cycloped* clocked in at 5 miles to the hour. A rather climactic end to the trial.

"Oh, no!" There was a huge crash and the horse fell through the floor of the Cycloped. "Oh the poor horse! I hope it isn't injured."

She started to run towards the horse when her father grabbed her arm. "Sorcha, the horse's party will attend."

"Oh, it is horrid!" Sorcha exclaimed. "How could they put that poor creature through this?"

Robert turned to Sorcha, obviously dismayed at her distress. "Would you care to take a ride on the *Rocket*, Miss O'Shea? You and your party of course. While the judges make up their minds about the weight the *Novelty* is to haul, we can entertain you on the other tracks with the *Rocket.*"

Sorcha's mouth almost dropped. "Of course I would!"

"Not a chance," Lawrence said. "And you shouldn't either, Miss O'Shea."

Sorcha's anger rose and she said what she had been thinking all day.

"It isn't any of your affair, Lawrence. You have no right to make personal decisions for me if I complete my work. *Which I will.*"

"No, but *I* do," said Mr. O'Shea. His mouth was firm, and then he broke into a smile. "Oh do go ahead, my dear, Mr. Robert will attend you."

"B-b-ut..."protested Lawrence.

Robert offered his arm and Sorcha took it, her father not far behind.

Sorcha was beside herself with excitement to be singled out, like a fine lady. Every time she felt she couldn't be treated with more kindness and regard, she was.

Somehow the tracks made everyone equal. At least today at Rainhill.

I feel transported to a different world.

A world where even a poor Irish girl is treated like royalty.

CHAPTER TWENTY-ONE

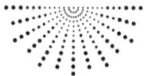

Riding the Rocket

"*B*ut is it wise to work the *Rocket* so hard?" Sorcha was concerned as they walked towards the locomotive, arm in arm. Many ladies who might have held their noses in the air at Sorcha prior to his trip glanced longingly at Sorcha, which was not lost on her. "Shouldn't you let the *Rocket* rest?"

Robert shook his head. "I thank you for your concern, Miss O'Shea, but *Rocket* is not a horse. She does not require rest in the same manner."

"Hmmm....And yet *Rocket* requires fuel and emits black smoke as waste. And replaces the horse—the only form of land transport we have ever known," Sorcha considered.

"I suppose the comparison is inevitable." Robert nodded. "But I assure you the *Rocket* is ready to perform."

Sorcha could not allay her fears. To many it appeared the *Novelty* was winning. "I only thought...forgive my intrusion...you might like to conserve your locomotive's energy until the contest is over?"

Robert Stephenson smiled knowingly. "The *Rocket*? She's in top form."

Sorcha was a bit embarrassed to have presumed she knew more than the inventor himself. She supposed it spoke to the easy discourse she had developed with Robert.

And I want the Stephensons to win. She liked Robert and George Stephenson so much.

"I grant you, Miss O'Shea…"Robert considered "…the Rocket has developed human-like qualities. She has a personality and is as alive as you or I in my mind." He smiled at Sorcha and she thought she might melt. "Not so beautiful as you, I grant you."

Robert was not prone to flattery which might be considered forward, but he was clearly excited and intensely alive, throwing caution to the wind.

Everyone feels it.

Sorcha waved her hand in dismissal of the flattery. "And much louder. I hope I am not spitting and coughing."

Robert laughed. "True. *Rocket's* manners are deplorable. She loves the attention."

"What a fine show you put on, sir." Sorcha sighed. "I was never so thrilled in my life as I am today."

He squeezed her hand. "Myself as well."

Sorcha turned to look at the other people waiting to ride *Rocket*. There was not much room on the platform and there were two men standing beside George Stephenson.

"Who are those men?" Sorcha asked.

"The driver and the fireman," Robert replied.

"And what do they do?"

"The driver is self-explanatory, I suppose," Robert replied. "The fireman shovels the fuel into the furnace as well as pumping water into the boiler. Both the driver and the fireman are highly skilled, and the fireman requires enormous strength and perseverance."

Sorcha's eye caught a tall, boyish man with ruffled hair. "It's you!" she said as he approached. "I wonder you are still alive!"

"And who might this interloper be?" George Stephenson asked, knowing full well this was not one of his invited guests.

Robert shook his head in concern. "This is Thaddeus Fulbright of the *Liverpool Mercury*, Father."

Thaddeus bowed, lifting his now crumpled hat, dusted with black soot. The pencil behind his ear fell forward but Thaddeus caught his essential tool mid-air.

George glanced at the pencil. "So you are a newspaper man, Mr. Fulbright?"

"I am, sir."

"Well, we've all got to do something," George grumbled, shaking his head.

"That's what my father says," Thaddeus replied good-naturedly. "He thinks being a reporter is a waste of an education."

"Aw, there I differ wif' him. It's the education that's a waste," George said. "At least you're getting your education in the real world by doing something."

All the would-be passengers stood about awaiting direction. There was clearly not much room on the platform of the Rocket where the driver, fireman, and engineer now stood. The locomotive had a wagon attached to it where no doubt they would all be herded like cattle. Even so, it was a great honor to be allowed to ride, of which everyone present was aware.

Just then a beautiful young lady, a brunette who looked to be about Sorcha's age of twenty years, caught her eye. "Oh, my goodness, I've seen your picture somewhere."

The young woman smiled and held out her hand.

"This is Miss Fanny Kemble," George Stephenson said.

"Miss Kemble is the rage of Covent Garden," Thaddeus explained in an uncharacteristically serious and no-nonsense manner, before winking at Sorcha, which made her blush.

"And appearing in Liverpool next, sir," Fanny added, smiling at Thaddeus.

"That's it!" Sorcha exclaimed. "I've seen your likeness on posters plastered all about Liverpool, Miss Kemble. I can rarely afford to go to the theatre, or naturally I would love to see you perform."

"Everyone can go to the theatre," Fanny said. "It's just a matter of where one sits."

"Or stands, as the case may be," George added.

It is true, Sorcha thought. The distinction was in where one sat: from the private opera boxes to the gallery to the pit which was standing room only with everyone smashed together like tinned fish.

"Indeed!" Thaddeus smiled broadly. "Theatre is the great equalizer where everyone can attend and ogle the other classes."

Fanny smiled at George for no known reason, but the gesture delighted him. Fanny had a way of charming everyone with a mere glance or a slight change in expression.

To Sorcha's surprise, Robert kept his eyes on her. And Thaddeus watched Robert for the most part.

"Yes, attendance can be difficult when one is usually working. Though…in all honesty…" Sorcha began shyly, "I did go to the theatre twice, standing in the pit, and it was a crush with standing room only, but I still thoroughly enjoyed it." Sorcha would definitely not go without her father, however, who could protect her from those who would take liberties in the confined spaces.

"And what show did you see, Miss?" Fanny asked, now interested in the other young lady present.

"'Hamlet' and 'She Stoops to Conquer.'" Sorcha had been particularly keen to see the latter as it was a comedy written by Irish playwright Oliver Goldsmith.

"Very good plays. You will be my guest then," Fanny smiled. "What is your name, Miss?"

"Sorcha O'Shea."

"Go to the Theatre Royal box office and there will be two tickets waiting for you, Miss O'Shea," Fanny said with a smile.

"The Theatre Royal in Williamson square?" Sorcha sighed. "Oh, that is so kind, Miss Kemble. I would love seeing you perform! That is a beautiful theatre. And I've never spoken to a real actress before."

So many things I have never done before the Rainhill Races.

Sorcha fully expected to go to the box office and find that Fanny Kimble had forgotten, but wild horses could not stop her from making the attempt.

"What will you be performing in Liverpool, Miss Kemble?" George asked enthusiastically.

"Romeo and Juliet," Fanny said.

"And what will ye be playing?" George asked.

Sorcha giggled, her laughing eyes looking sideways at George. "Juliet, of course!"

She felt guilty as soon as she said it, she didn't wish to make fun of a man who was already dear to her. But she need not have worried, George Stephenson did not appear even slight subdued.

"No one could be more beautiful in the role!" George exclaimed.

"Have you seen the play?" Fanny asked coyly.

"I have now!" George replied enthusiastically.

"Miss Kemble has no rival. She is also a wonderful actress. She has taken London by storm," Thaddeus said. "And soon, Liverpool."

Thaddeus' remarks were those of professionalism rather than flirtation as he smiled at Sorcha, making her wonder why he was looking at her.

Robert as well only appeared to have eyes for herself, Sorcha thought, which surprised her with this celebrated beauty here who continuously glanced Robert's way.

George Stephenson, on the other hand, was smitten by the young actress. He invited Fanny to ride on the footplate beside him.

So it looked like the rest of the party would be riding in the wagon.

Robert said in low tones to Sorcha, "It is a fact that Fanny saved her parents' theatre which was in enormous, unfathomable debt before she went onto the stage. Miss Kemble became the rage of London overnight with her talent and beauty, saving their business."

I like her even more. "She must be very devoted to her family. Quite admirable in a young lady."

Robert nodded, smiling at Sorcha. "It takes one to know one."

"What do you mean, Mr. Stephenson?"

"I take it you are a great help to your family, Miss O'Shea."

Sorcha nodded modestly. "No more than any daughter should do."

Everyone around them was chattering so as to make Robert's quiet tones unnecessary. "You are always working in your drawing tablet. Your father does not have a great deal of employment. Your employer showed you the great honor of sending his own son to be your particular escort" he cleared his throat "though I question how devoted Lawrence is to your safety. But that was obviously his father's intent. And your father appears to hold you in great esteem."

"Oh, Da would whether I had work or not."

"Yes, when a father is devoted to his children, the sentiment is often reciprocated."

Lawrence is the exception.

George assisted Fanny to the *Rocket* platform to sit beside him on the footplate. Just as everyone else began loading into the wagon, George Stephenson turned to one of his friends. "Stannard, put your boy up on the tub, he'll be out of harm's way."

"Father…I don't think it is the safest spot…" Robert protested.

"Now, son, this is the best place for the boy."

So the boy was lifted to the large tub, painted yellow and carrying the water, just behind the main platform where George and Fanny sat.

The other honored guests handpicked by George loaded into the wagon pulled by *Rocket*, including Robert accompanying Sorcha, and Thaddeus who slipped on amidst the commotion.

The locomotive started up and the passengers held on for dear life as they travelled ten miles per hour and higher. More than one sophisticated passenger screamed. Some seemed to fear for their lives as they sped on.

I am flying! Sorcha thought. Nothing could be more intoxicating!

Sorcha thought the day could hold no more excitement.

Never was I more wrong.

Robert placed his hand on hers, as if to brace her, as she held onto the rail. She felt a tingle travel through her body. He stopped short of putting his hand around her waist, probably not wanting her to think him forward, but he kept his eye on her. On occasion he braced her shoulder to keep her from swaying. To be there in that moment together completely present was heavenly.

"I beg pardon, Miss O'Shea, I don't want you to fall." Naturally she wouldn't as the passengers were tightly crammed into the space. Robert was smiling, and seemed to enjoy the ride as much as she did. Sorcha caught a glimpse of Thaddeus out of the corner of her eye who was frowning. How he could frown when they were having so much fun she had no idea.

Once the ride was over, Robert turned to her.

"And what did you think, Miss O'Shea?" Robert asked.

"It was thrilling beyond anything! There are not words to describe it!" she exclaimed. "We were soaring!"

Robert nodded, appearing pleased by her enthusiasm which some might call unladylike. "One cannot know the delight until it is experienced for oneself."

The ride completed, Stannard picked up his child. The boy's bottom was covered with fresh yellow paint.

"At least he stuck to the train!" George suggested. "The paint kept him from falling off."

Everyone burst into laughter. What a memorable close to the day.

Fanny added, "If the *Rocket* wins this competition, for the rest of his life that little boy can say he rode the Rocket, the template for all future train travel."

"And he has the pants to prove it!" Mr. Stannard chuckled. Though he didn't expect Mrs. Stannard to find the situation as amusing as he did.

"But *Rocket* won't win," Thaddeus murmured in Sorcha's ear as they stepped off the locomotive onto the tracks. "The winner will be the *Novelty*."

It seemed to Sorcha Thaddeus did not like the close regard Robert paid her. And that Thaddeus' enthusiasm for *Novelty* was somewhat forced, as if fueled by his dislike for Robert Stephenson.

How absurd! Sorcha knew how men were: they might not like a girl, but they objected to anyone else liking her.

It will all come to nothing. However, in the meantime, she had enjoyed a heavenly day.

I will never forget it as long as I live!

CHAPTER TWENTY-TWO

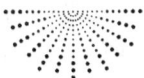

October 8, 1829
Day 3
The Rainhill Trials

TRIAL OF LOCOMOTIVE CARRIAGES

*N*ovelty, the London engine built by Messrs. Braithwaite and Ericsson, ran down to the grand stand with empty wagons. A large assemblage of Ladies and Gentlemen mounted, among whom were Dr. Traill and his family. With 45 passengers, the speed of Novelty while running the full course averaged 22 miles an hour! At one point Novelty carried the same passengers reaching the inconceivable velocity of 32 miles an hour!

And so it was that Novelty followed its first unprecedented showing with another show de force, this time carrying 45 passengers! This was not the official race to be sure, but the spectacle served to win more converts to the team rooting for Novelty.

We heard claims that Novelty could not haul weight. Now that claim is disproved in spectacular fashion!

The great engineering superiority Novelty possesses over the other locomotive steam-carriages entered in the Rainhill Trials became immediately evident today. The mechanical advantage consists in Novelty's having a pair of bellows constantly in action, the blast room which keeps the fire bright, and the steam up while the machine is running. This addition is unique in Novelty's design among all the contestants.

The Novelty's boiler is patented by Mssrs. Braithwaite and Ericsson, being altogether of an innovative construction. It is well known that the efficiency of an engine depends more on the boiler than on any other part. We are not privy to the engineering plans—naturally being closely guarded from competitors' eyes —but judging by the performance of the engine the mode of construction must involve some farsighted and valuable principles.

Although it is not known precisely how the speed was accomplished, all observed the results! We base these claims of superiority on verifiable data.

The Novelty possesses a valuable peculiarity that it carries within itself the water and fuel necessary for its operations, while Mr. Stephenson's Rocket requires a separate engine-tender linked to them, a tender which weighs about two tons. That weight should be included when calculating the weight of the Rocket, the result of which would put Rocket over-weight and disqualify it from these trials. Everyone should be subject to the same rules.

--Thaddeus Fulbright, Liverpool Mercury

SORCHA SNAPPED HER NEWSPAPER SHUT. *Disqualify the Rocket indeed!* She found her favorite bench near the band in the "ladies section", arriving early so she could claim the seat and do her drawing. Everyone of her acquaintance knew where she was because she was usually there.

What an underhanded ploy! She had thought Thaddeus Fulbright above such tactics.

Humans are a very strange species, Sorcha thought, closing the newspaper. With a distinct ability to manipulate the facts.

"You're looking awfully angry today, Miss Sorcha." Out of nowhere, the guilty party appeared.

"I am!" She pointed to the article in the paper. "Are you responsible for this biased reporting? It is practically slander."

"And just because you disagree with the content, you think you have the right to call the writer a slanderer?"

Thaddeus stood before her where she sat, his expression both indignant and dignified. He wore a dark green frock coat, beige slim trousers, and a dark brown cravat which was a jumbled mess; it might have been mistaken for a new, French design. He wore a watch on a gold chain and no other jewelry that she could see. He wore a John Bull topper, not as tall as the typical top hat.

Thaddeus was a tall, well-formed man on the slim side. His clothes were well-tailored.

Overall, he cut a fine figure, but she did not think he was very attentive to his toilette.

Just as he was not very attentive to the accuracy of his news reporting.

"You're supposed to report the news, not take sides," Sorcha retorted. "Instead of reporting, this is attempting to get an entry kicked out of the contest, thereby impacting the outcome."

"So you think *Rocket* should have its own set of rules which apply to no one else?" Thaddeus asked.

"The judges determined the rules—not I—and they determined the water barrel was not part of the equipment. If Novelty chooses to make it part of her equipment that is irrelevant."

"I must be true to my own perception," Thaddeus stated.

"I have not objection to that, as long as you are dealing in facts, and not emotion. It is not the *facts* you are devoted to, I assure you."

"Then what is it I am devoted to?" He moved closed to her face, his breath on her cheek, which was a bit unnerving.

"To your pocketbook and promotion, I would imagine."

"May I remind you that you take sides, Miss O'Shea? And are quite emotional?"

"Fortunately I'm not performing a service to the general public with the duty to report the news objectively."

Thaddeus shook his head while clicking his tongue. "You are quick to judge and insult, Miss O'Shea, I don't think you should point the finger at me."

"Hmph!" She then took her notebook and colored pencils out of her bag housing her umbrella, water, and lunch her Aunt Hannah sent along with her.

"Good day, Miss O'Shea." Thaddeus tipped his hat to her and departed. "I hope you may be in a better mood the next time we meet."

"As do I. Good day, Mr. Fulbright."

Sorcha thumbed through her notebook, which was beginning to fill up. She had drawings of all of the entrants: *Rocket, Novelty, Sans Pareil, Perseverance*, and *Cycloped*.

There had been ten entrants, but only five began the trials for one reason or another. And, of those five, only four were steam locomotives.

Rocket and *Sans Pareil* were the large locomotives, though *Rocket* had eight wheels and *Sans Pareil* only four. *Sans Pareil* was more squished together, with an exposed platform for the driver. A great deal had to happen in a small space, and everyone appeared to be crammed together.

Rocket was sturdy and inelegant, the engine carrying a big barrel of water in a cart it pulled. *Rocket* was brash, painted in bold colors of yellow, red, and green.

Perseverance was quirky, looking like a whisky bottle surrounded by four wheels. The *Novelty* was light, sleek and stylish with beautiful colors: blue and copper. All four were so different in appearance.

Now that *Rocket* had successfully completed its trials, Sorcha hoped to see even more of Robert Stephenson. He helped her a great deal with her drawings and was an excellent resource, knowing everything to do with steam locomotives.

He also knew how to make her heart stop in her chest.

Thaddeus was also quite helpful; information was Thaddeus' trade. Sorcha wished she hadn't snarled at him, even though he was biased. He was still kind to her.

Thaddeus also had laughing, chestnut brown eyes which continually lit up. Nothing was serious to him.

Whereas Robert had serious, sapphire blue eyes. He had a very pleasant manner, but Sorcha did not think he was generally gleeful: he was too busy with serious matters.

The two men could not be more different: Robert with his sideburns and a curly head of dark hair, always immaculately dressed, and Thaddeus with his dark blonde hair parted on the side and often in his eyes. He was always on the run.

Both men had become quick friends and decent chaperones in what could be a raucous crowd. In addition, they were a great deal of help to her in her project: Sorcha had no worries about being able to do an excellent job for Mr. Davenport. She sometimes simply observed during the day and drew in the evenings from memory—which wasn't difficult so vivid was every moment of her trip to Rainhill. Moreover, she had the luxury of working after nightfall as her Aunt Hannah and Uncle Nathan were relatively wealthy and did not begrudge the candles.

She sighed. Sometimes Sorcha let all the masculine flattery go to her head, but it was such a rare occurrence outside of the jeers on her walk to work that she vowed to enjoy it. It would no doubt be short-lived.

Sorcha reminded herself that neither of these gentlemen had any serious intentions. Men were well known to bestow their favors in directions where they had no thought of matrimony. As Lawrence was proof. But at least Thaddeus and Robert's intentions were not dishonorable, as Lawrence's had proven to be.

CHAPTER TWENTY-THREE

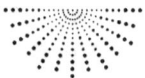

Carriage ride

On the close of the final day of *Rocket's* trials, it was time to return to Aunt Hannah's home for the evening.

Hannah Ahern, Sorcha's father's sister, was, in fact, delighted to put them up and to see her family again, though she had no interest in the going's on among the riff-raff and their fine machines.

Hannah made a good match, marrying an established businessman in the linen trade, who moved them to Rainhill upon retiring from the business when Belfast became more violent with the poverty and hunger. They had chosen a country lifestyle instead of Liverpool, London, or even Manchester.

Lawrence, Mr. O'Shea, Sorcha, and Robert Stephenson prepared to depart in Lawrence's carriage. Unlike his father, Robert enjoyed sociable drink and a touch of gaming. Robert invited Lawrence to play a game of cards with them at an elite game in town that evening—an offer Lawrence would never refuse, as Robert suspected, who wanted to learn more about Miss O'Shea's escort. So, the plan was to deliver Sorcha and

Mr. O'Shea to the Aherns and then head into town for the night's festivities.

"So. The Rocket has completed its trials, it appears." Mr. O'Shea considered.

"Yes. Today. The third day of the trials," Robert replied. The younger Mr. Stephenson was dressed exquisitely as usual, but more casually than he was on the ceremonial days—when he looked like he was going to a fancy dress ball. Today he was wearing A dark navy blue frock coat, light tan trousers, and a dark blue silk cravat, accentuating the color of his sapphire eyes. He wore a gold watch chain. His coat was fitted to his waist, accentuating his wide chest and fine figure.

"The *Rocket* met all its requirements and is a contender for the grand prize, is it not?" Sorcha asked.

"Very much so." Robert nodded. "Rocket has qualified. Now it's just a matter of if another locomotive can beat *Rocket's* numbers."

"When is *Novelty* racing?" Sorcha asked.

"Saturday," replied Robert.

Lawrence took out a cigar and began smoking it with smug satisfaction. Not having taken a great liking to Robert Stephenson despite wishing to join in his game, Lawrence said, " For *Novelty*, it is now only a matter of beating *Rocket's* numbers, which *Novelty* appears poised to do from its performance today."

"Possibly," Robert said noncommittally.

Sorcha raised her eyebrows at Lawrence. "Why do you think *Novelty* will win, Lawrence?"

"It's not just me! Certainly the majority of the attendees believe *Novelty* will beat *Rocket* after *Novelty's* preliminary bedazzling show of speed today."

On one point Sorcha could agree with Lawrence: undoubtedly *Novelty* was the crowd favorite. She overheard many conversations while sitting and drawing. Even the newspapers were drooling over *Novelty*, and it wasn't just Thaddeus doing so either. Maybe she had been too hard on him.

No I wasn't. Why should Mr. Fulbright lower his standards just because everyone else has?

"But are those forty-five passengers equivalent to the load Novelty will have to carry?" Sorcha asked.

Mr. O'Shea burst out laughing. Her Da was not one to adhere to the premise that *A woman is always to feign ignorance to be acceptable to the men.*

"I would estimate the forty-five passengers to be less," Robert replied in an unrevealing fashion, but he had a knowing twinkle in his eye as well. "But *Novelty* is a crowd pleaser and a show-stopper to be sure."

Sorcha glanced at Robert, interested by his discreet response.

I hope the gentlemen are not playing poker, because Robert is certain to beat Lawrence if they are.

It always seems as if Robert knows something the rest of us don't know. She glanced at Lawrence. *And it's always as if Lawrence doesn't realize what he doesn't know.*

Robert Stephenson handed Sorcha into Lawrence's carriage, followed by the men entering the carriage, and they began their journey.

"This house of your relatives is decidedly on the outskirts of town," Lawrence grumbled, anxious to get to the card game.

"Yes, they like living in the country," Sorcha said. "I'm sure everyone must if they can afford the land."

"What the deuce? Are you quite serious, Miss O'Shea?" Lawrence exclaimed. "Last place I'd like to be is out in the middle of nowhere."

"It is somewhere, of course." Sorcha rolled her eyes.

"Nowhere I'd like to be. With only sheep and chickens to keep one company."

"Isn't it funny how we were surrounded by people all day—*thousands!* —and now there is no one to be seen anywhere." Sorcha said.

Robert smiled at her, appearing to think it admirable how well Sorcha dismissed Lawrence's bad humor.

"Stop! Stop the carriage!" There was a loud voice outside the carriage.

Suddenly the carriage slowed. Obviously someone was in the road.

"What is going on?" Lawrence demanded.

"Stop or I'll shoot!" There was a man in the road with his gun pointed at the driver.

Suddenly a second man appeared at their window with a gun pointed at them. "Give me your watches and your wallets!"

"We don' ha' anything," Sorcha exclaimed in her most brogue-ish Irish accent. "We ear quite poor like you."

"He ain't." The outlaw pointed his gun at Lawrence in his top hat. "Or the other one across from 'im. They've got gold watches no doubt. Hand 'em over."

"Don't point that gun at me!" Lawrence squealed, perspiring with fear.

"I don't have much on me, but you can have my watch." Robert calmly handed his watch to the man. "Now move along. Don't hurt these good people."

"No! That ain't enough! Give me your wallets."

Mr. O'Shea had been quiet up to now, studying the robber with interest. "Look, that's just a few pounds. All the valuables are in the back in a chest."

"What? He can't have my things!" Lawrence regained a modicum of his courage when his wealth was at stake. "And you don't have the—"

Sorcha poked Lawrence in the side.

"Ouch!"

"Hand me the key," the thief demanded, guessing what Lawrence was about to say.

"I don't have it," Lawrence lied. "It's on the receiving end. We don't carry it with us."

Sorcha nodded approvingly. Lawrence might not be very brave, but he was a good liar.

"I'll have to come out to help you open the chest," Mr. O'Shea said. "I don't have a key. I do it by feel."

"Wait. Why would you help me?" the gunman demanded of Sean O'Shea. "Ain't he your friend? You're all riding high and mighty together."

"Me friend? I can't stand the sight o' him," Sean said with believable sincerity. "He treats me like a slave. Look at 'im decked out like a peacock. And look at what I'm wearin'." Sean pointed to his worn jacket, threadbare wool pants, and crumpled hat.

The gunman studied Lawrence. "Yeah. He looks silly."

"Silly? I'll have you know my waistcoat is silk!" Lawrence said indignantly.

"Shhh! Be quiet, Lawrence!" Sorcha admonished.

"I'll open the trunk if you let me go," Sean said. "And we have to split the riches. I want to get away from this high roller."

The outlaw in the front yelled, "Hurry up! What's takin' so long?"

"Shut up!" the second gunman yelled. Then he turned to Sean. "Yeah. OK. Get out," motioning with his gun.

"No Da! Don't go! You could get shot!" Sorcha exclaimed.

"Don't you try anything," the gunslinger said, "Or I'll kill you!"

"I don't have a gun, lad," Mr. O'Shea said. "Don't worry, dear, all they want is the valuables."

"Damn straight!" the thief said.

"Sorcha, give me your hairpin to open the chest." He winked at her.

Sorcha took one of the hair pins out of her coiffure and handed it to her father, knowing full well her father could stab the one with her hairpin. But that still left the other hoodlum with a gun.

Mr. O'Shea left the carriage with the bandit's gun on him.

Once Sean O'Shea was out of the carriage and the gun off them, Lawrence pulled the string for the driver to go on.

"No! Don't leave without my father!" Sorcha begged.

"It's our chance to get away! The gunman is going to shoot him anyway," Lawrence said.

"The driver won't go, Miss O'Shea. The other brigand has a gun on him," Robert murmured, squeezing her hand for a brief moment.

"He'd better go. Or he'll be without employment," Lawrence exclaimed.

"It is perplexing." Robert added in a whisper, "I'm surprised this one fell for such a strange story. Surely your father doesn't know how to open Mr. Davenport's trunk."

"Naturally he does not," Sorcha whispered. "Maybe they think Da is working for Lawrence. Look at their comparative dress."

"But it would make much more sense to take the watches and wallets and depart. A bird in the hand is worth two in the bush." Robert added under his breath. "I was prepared to give him my wallet, but he left before I could."

"Why did you poke me, Miss O'Shea?" Lawrence demanded.

"To make you be quiet, of course."

"Why should I be?"

"Because Da obviously has a plan," she whispered. "You won't help and you'll only get in the way."

Robert moved towards the carriage door. "I'm going to help. I'll try to disarm the one with a gun on your father."

"Wait!" Sorcha admonished. "You'll just get shot by the other one, Robert. I know my Da and he has a plan. You might interfere. Or worse, get shot."

Robert nodded, attempting to respect her wishes, but his expression was one of indecision. Sorcha motioned to him to move closer to the door, keeping an eye on things and ready to act.

"I don't know, Miss O'Shea," Robert confided. "There are four of us men and only two of them. We should not leave your father out there alone."

"Yes, but they both have guns," she said.

"I'm sure the driver has a gun too, behind the seat," Robert considered. "He just can't get to it."

Sorcha was sure Robert didn't wish to come to the culmination of his dreams and hard work only to die at the hand of outlaws, but he was acting admirably. Still, she felt he could do more harm than good by interfering with her father's plans. She knew that gleam in her Da's eyes.

Outside, Sean O'Shea made his way to the back. Bending down, he studied the lockbox on the back of the coach.

"Guess we'll just need to get started..." Sean put his hands on the lockbox and began fiddling with the hairpin in the lock while maintaining an erect stature. Suddenly Sean sounded alarmed. "Say. Do you hear that? Sounds like another coach coming down the road."

The highwayman was unable to overcome the panic this statement caused, turning his body as well as his gun towards the road behind them. Without thinking, he'd turned the gun away from his victim. O'Shea acted quickly, grabbing the thief's wrist in an iron grip. A slight twist of that wrist and the gun was in Sean O'Shea's hand.

The instant O'Shea disarmed the gunslinger, he placed him in front of his body to protect him from the second outlaw. The second fellow was of no greater intellect than his companion and began vacillating, aiming his weapon first at his cohort in front of O'Shea, then back at the driver, then back at O'Shea.

The driver took the opportunity to kick the second robber's gun out of his hand, jumping down from his platform and fighting the highwayman for his gun. The second villain was much smaller than the carriage driver, and it was no match.

Robert jumped out of the carriage despite Sorcha's admonitions.

"Get the rifle!" the driver yelled.

Robert jumped up to the driver's perch and reached behind the seat for the rifle, then jumping down with the rifle in hand.

Now that the two outlaws were covered, Lawrence pulled out a gun and joined Robert outside the carriage.

"What? You had a weapon all the time and sat in the carriage?" Robert demanded.

Clearly, Lawrence was waiting until the danger had past. He raised the gun to aim at the first bandit. Sean moved in between Lawrence and the outlaw.

"Stop, Lawrence! You could hit my Da!" Sorcha screamed. "Or Robert!"

"Wait! Don't shoot!" Sean O'Shea commanded. "Don't you see how small these men are? I think they are boys, not even full grown."

"That don't matter. He held me up. I'll shoot this 'un if he moves," the driver said.

"Right." Lawrence added. "Shootings too good for them."

"We're in no danger now. I doubt if there are even bullets in the guns." Sean O'Shea emptied the barrel of his assailant's gun: sure enough, no bullets.

Sean O'Shea easily took Lawrence's gun from him while the carriage driver grabbed his rifle from behind his seat, pointing it at the thieves.

"Take off your masks," Sean commanded. With two guns now on them, the second robber obeyed while Robert yanked off the first outlaw's mask.

Sure enough, they looked to be no more than fourteen years of age and possibly less, skinny and scrawny.

Mr. O'Shea motioned his head to the driver. "Check the gun."

The driver checked the gun for bullets, and there were none. "How did you know?"

"If they're so poor they have to steal, I don't know where they would find money for bullets." Robert kept his rifle ready to fire. "What are you two up to? Don't you know you could have gotten shot?"

"Who cares about that?" Lawrence yelled. "What about us?"

"What's so important that you could have lost your lives over?" Mr. O'Shea continued addressing the boys.

"We're so poor," the first boy said, his hair tasseled and his face grimy.

"Our mother is hungry and babies to feed. It drives us to misery. We thought if we could just pick up a few schillings, we might eat for a month. You know all these rich people here, and they won't miss it!"

"Why didn't you just take the watches and run then?" Robert asked.

"I got greedy. I saw a full larder for the winter in me head."

"And some real bullets so you could continue this line of work, I'll wager," Sean added.

The boy shrugged.

"Look. It's not a fair world. But, listen here boys, it's an even worse life in prison. If you're lucky. You could hang. And you wouldn't be any help to your mother then, would you?"

"No, sir."

"Don't entertain these ideas anymore," Mr. O'Shea added. "The laws in England are not lenient. Even to children."

"Yes, sir."

"What?" exclaimed Lawrence. "Take those outlaws to the sheriff! The pickpocket was bad enough—let's give him a job!—but this is ridiculous! Are we to let every criminal in England free?"

You're walking around, aren't you Lawrence? Sorcha thought.

The second boy motioned his head to the carriage with a grimace. "Why should I care about someone like that?"

"You don't have to care about him," Mr. O'Shea said. "Care about yourself and your family. You will be punished in the end no matter how undeserving someone else is."

"And what are your names?" Mr. O'Shea asked.

"I'm Kyle. And this is Quincy."

"Are you friends with Jack?" demanded Lawrence.

"Jack Bagshaw?" Kyle asked. "Yeah. We know 'im."

"I thought so." said Lawrence. "You all hang out in the same cesspool."

Kyle pulled forward with the obvious intent of laying a planter on Lawrence but Robert held him tightly.

"And your last name, Kyle?" Mr. O'Shea demanded.

"Smith."

"And your real last name? Don't mess with me, boys, or I'll take you in," Mr. O'Shea said authoritatively.

Kyle glanced at Lawrence.

"Don't worry about him," Sean said. "We'll deal with him later."

"No, you won't," Lawrence retorted.

Robert forcefully escorted Lawrence to the inside of the carriage. "Wait in here, sir. You'll be more comfortable."

"As if I have a choice."

"Upton," Kyle replied.

"Well, Mr. Kyle and Mr. Quincy Upton, I'm Mr. O'Shea. I'll know it if you're up to trouble again. Give Mr. Stephenson his watch back."

"Ah, they can have it," Robert said. "It's not worth much." It sure looked to Sorcha like it was worth a bit.

"Rewarding them for giving us all heart attacks now are we?" Lawrence yelled out the carriage window. "Take them to the sheriff!"

"Nah, they've learned their lesson," Sean O'Shea said in his normal booming voice. "Take the watch back, Mr. Stephenson. They've got to learn right from wrong."

Mr. O'Shea turned to his daughter. "Sorcha, get that basket of food your aunt packed for us and give it to them. She won't like it if we come back with anything."

"Yes, Da. She'd be very upset." Sorcha smiled to herself as she walked to the carriage. Da found a way to keep the boys from feeling like charity.

"And now you're going to reward those criminals?" Lawrence demanded.

"Yes, Lawrence, just as you are rewarded for bad behavior every day," Sorcha murmured.

"How dare you, Miss O'Shea! You will pay for that remark."

Fury overtook her being like a raging fire. "And if you ever put my father's life in danger again, I will move heaven and earth to make sure you pay, Lawrence." She fingered the remaining hairpin in her hat. "How dare *you!*"

Fear brings out the worst in us, Sorcha thought. But she meant what she said.

Lawrence squirmed a bit, ashamed of his own behavior. "I would have gone back for him."

"When? After he'd been shot?" Sorcha took a deep breath and patted his hand. "Calm down, Lawrence. We are all safe. And you haven't lost so much as a schilling." *Which I'm sure you will lose this evening.* "Isn't that enough?"

Seeing Lawrence's expression, clearly it wasn't.

Lawrence yelled as the boys walked away, "Say 'hello' to Jack for us!"

Back in the carriage, Lawrence muttered, "No doubt they'll all come back and kill us tomorrow."

As they started out again on their journey, the two young hooligans waving good-bye, Robert was curious. "How did you know, Mr. O'Shea, that those two did not pose a serious threat?" He cleared his throat. "Not that it wasn't impressive your disarming the one."

"I observed right away they were small and thin. It occurred to me they were boys. I honestly didn't think they had the money for bullets. Also, the way Kyle held the gun pointed at us, he didn't know how to hold the gun. When I gave them the cock-and-bull story about the chest in the back, and they fell for it, I knew we were dealing with young amateurs."

"That's my Da'." Sorcha smiled.

She glanced at Robert. As much as she liked Robert and had completely had her head turned by him—she felt as if she were being courted by a prince!—no man could compare to her Da.

"Yes, there was no reason to choose an out-of-the-way chest over readily available watches and wallets except for the dreams of youth. What child can resist a treasure chest?" Robert posed, smiling.

"And if you could break into the master's chest, why wouldn't you have already done it?" Sorcha added.

"No doubt when someone comes to kill us, you'll pat them all on the back and congratulate them," Lawrence grumbled. "But not before feeding them first."

Sorcha giggled in spite of herself, but added. "I'm still angry at you, Lawrence. You were ready to abandon my father."

"I would have fared just fine, Sorcha, as we now know, and then walked the rest of the way to the farmhouse," Sean said. "Actually, if they had been dangerous, I would rather the carriage left with you anyway. That would have been better than a blood bath."

"But surely not," Robert said. "There were three of us men—" he cleared his throat as he looked at Lawrence—"four, I mean, against the two of them. And…Mr. Davenport had a pistol."

"Well, I'm glad he didn't use it," Sean O'Shea exclaimed. "Someone might have gotten hurt."

CHAPTER TWENTY-FOUR

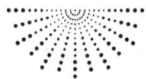

Novelty trials
Saturday, October 10, 1829

"I'm so excited to *finally* see the *Novelty* race!" It was Saturday morning and the *Novelty* was pulled onto the tracks.

"Aye!" Mr. O'Shea agreed. "It's been a wait. But then, the *Rocket* had to finish her trials. And well she did."

"Yes, but can *Novelty* beat the *Rocket?*" Sorcha asked anxiously. "Everyone seems to think so."

"Ah, well the opinions of *everyone* is usually not of much use." Mr. O'Shea smoothed his moustache. "But we'll soon see, won't we?"

Sorcha was both anticipating the outcome while wishing she could prolong the pleasure forever. "Da, I've never been so diverted in my entire life. I don't think I've ever been so happy. I wish it might never end."

Sean O'Shea nodded. "I know how you feel, me girl. I feel alive again. I haven't felt this good since we were in Ireland." There was a sudden sadness in his eyes. He was accustomed to being *useful*.

"Yes, doing what you were born to do," Sorcha said. "I don't know how the Trials would get by without you."

"Oh, nothin' of the sort," Sean waved his hand. "I'm just one o' many. But we all need occupation. I only felt like half a man 'afore we got here."

Sorcha sighed. "I never expected to be present at such a momentous event."

"Nor I," her father agreed, taking her hand. "None of it would be possible without you, my darling girl. You're such a blessing to me and your mother." He shook his head. "I hate that you have to work so hard."

"No harder than anyone else, Da." But, in truth, Sorcha was not a girl accustomed to being pleasure-bent. Nor was she accustomed to being entertained. She enjoyed her life, to be sure, especially when she was making music, or intent upon a painting, but her life was not one self-indulgence following another. It was largely work.

This is the first holiday I have ever had in my life.

I feel like a Queen.

George Stephenson waived at Sorcha and her father seated at her usual bench. There appeared to be an unspoken acknowledgement that the bench belonged to the particular friend of the Stephensons and it was often left vacated for Sorcha.

The engineers moved towards their new friends through the throngs of people, who generally made way for the Stephensons, being recognized by many, largely due to George Stephenson's antics.

"I feel like the guest of honor. Never did I imagine to be in such illustrious company," Sorcha whispered to her father in murmured tones.

"It is easier for a young, pretty girl than for an old, unemployed Irishman to make new friends." Mr. O'Shea winked at her.

"Oh, Da!" Sorcha shook her head. "They like us both."

"Maybe so. The Stephensons may be wealthy, and they may be famous some day, but they are, both of them, working men. They have earned their happiness in life and they appreciate everything they have worked for. I would rather see you with friends such as these than with those who have been given everything, however high-and-mighty they might act."

"Such as Lawrence?"

"Lawrence is a gobshite," Mr. O'Shea pronounced without pause.

"Da!" Sorcha looked about. "Take care you are not overheard."

"I shouldn't speak agin' me betters?"

"Oh, no, Lawrence is lazy, no good, and possibly down right evil." She generally shrugged off his advances but still smarted at his attempt to leave her Da with the outlaws.

"I dunna think so," Mr. O'Shea said. "He's a spoiled boy who was never been forced to grow up. Every opportunity his parents had to instruct him, they indulged him instead."

"You always give people the benefit of the doubt, Da."

"I dunna think he realizes his faults," Sean O'Shea added.

That is an understatement. Sorcha coughed discretely.

"Lawrence is not that old," Mr. O'Shea continued. "There is still hope for him."

Sorcha raised her eyebrows.

"Good morning, Miss O'Shea," Robert tipped his hat to her. "Mr. O'Shea."

"Good morning, young man," Mr. O'Shea said. "And Mr. Stephenson."

"You're lookin' in fine fettle this morning, Miss O'Shea!" George said.

Robert elbowed his father who wheeled around towards his son. "Well, she is! I never seen such a fine filly!"

"Thank you, sir." Sorcha smiled. In point of fact, she did feel herself to look particularly well. She wore an aquamarine taffeta dress with large, puffed sheer blue gauze sleeves, all adorned with gold trim and gold buttons. She wore an inexpensive gold cross necklace which had been her grandmother's. Her hair was braided and atop her head with corkscrew curls framing her face.

She had three dresses with her—the only three fancy dresses she owned, one of which given to her by her Aunt Hannah—but each day Aunt Hannah would have her dress from the previous day washed and pressed.

It was opulent extravagance! And she could stay up late and work on her drawings or read because Aunt Hannah and Uncle Nathan didn't begrudge the candles. In addition, her aunt and uncle had a cook who actually made breakfast for them every day as well as sandwiches to take to the event!

I am living in the lap of luxury! I wish it might never end.

"We can always count on you to save us a seat, Miss O'Shea," Robert smiled as he sat down beside Sorcha.

Sorcha smiled at Robert. "Did you beat Lawrence at the card game?"

"Unfortunately for him, I did."

"I'm not surprised," Sorcha said. *It seems to be a pattern.* "I hope he is not in an ill mood today."

Robert shrugged. "We don't play for high stakes, just for the enjoyment of the game. I don't think the loss put a hole in his pocket."

"I expect Lawrence tried to raise the stakes."

"He did, but we would have none of it." Robert shook his head. "We are just country folk, we're not high rollers like he is."

"Naturally, if you have to work for your money, you're not as keen to part with it," George said. "Though I wouldn't personally part with a farthing."

"You're not a gamester, then, are ye, George?" asked Sean O'Shea. They were long past formal address, except as suited them.

"Nope. Never developed a taste for it or for drink," George said. "Had no time to! I've got no time to waste. And no money neither!"

"Father is accustomed to utilizing every waking second of his day. He's extremely driven." Robert said. "Personally I don't mind a bit of relaxation at the end of the work day."

"The world ain't built by men sittin' about playin' cards," George observed.

"What is all this activity around the *Novelty*?" Sorcha asked, excited for the race to begin. In truth, *Novelty* was a gracefully fashionable machine with her copper and blue façade. "Are they going to add the carriages to her weight before the race?"

"Oh, yeah," George said. "They have to. The question has always been, 'how much weight'?"

"I've given it some thought, and I still don't comprehend the judges' thinking in not having the same load requirements for all the locomotives," Sorcha considered. "The point of the contest is to determine which locomotive can do the most work and haul the most weight at the highest speed. How can you find which is the best if you have the locomotives perform under a different set of rules?"

George chuckled. "You've put your finger on it, Miss. Giving one locomotive a lighter load defeats the purpose. But the judges are too high-minded for their own good. And for the good of the Manchester-Liverpool Railway."

"They do seem more like church deacons than businessmen," reflected Sorcha.

"There you are the right of it," George said. "They are Quakers, most of 'em."

"And yet for all their principles, they are rich," Robert added.

"Proof that good people can prosper, it seems," Sorcha considered. "Businessmen with principles. A rare breed."

Robert studied her, perplexed.

"Pardon me ignorance, but there isn't a Manchester-Liverpool Railway, is there?" Sean O'Shea asked.

George winked. "Not yet. But there will be if me and my son have anything to say about it."

"The track is almost completely laid," Robert smiled. "All it needs is a locomotive."

"So what have the judges decided?" Sorcha asked. "I can see they are attaching the load to the *Novelty*."

George turned to Mr. O'Shea. "Your daughter is quite a curious young thing. And smart."

"She is." Mr. O'Shea nodded proudly. "I've never seen anything Sorcha couldn't accomplish if she put her mind to it."

The older men winked and giggled about the ladies, Sorcha thought indignantly. They were middle-aged, being in their forties, but they acted like old men when it came to the women folk.

Robert, on the other hand, treated her with deference, as if she were a grown woman instead of a child.

Besides looking positively dreamy.

The younger Stephenson stepped in to interrupt the older men's snickering. "The judges made their decision to base the Novelty's burden on the pro-rated load the Rocket hauled by a weighted average according to their respective engine weights."

Sorcha raised her eyebrows. "What does that translate to?"

"The Rocket weighed in at 4 tons 3 cwt and hauled a load of 13 tons," Robert said. "The Novelty, much lighter, was assigned a load of six tons and 17 hundredweight to haul."

"Oh my goodness, so much less? About half?" Sorcha asked. "It doesn't seem fair in a competition to give such an advantage." As excited as she was about the beautiful *Novelty*, she hated to see her new friends lose.

"She'll make a Railroad Man yet," George said proudly, nodding his head towards Sorcha.

There was some grumbling over the judge's decision, but the Stephensons seemed relatively confident even so. Although George was vocal about his opinions, there being little filter between his brain and his mouth, Robert was not inclined to complain about that which he could not change. He approached unwelcome happenings with good humor and determination, Sorcha observed.

Sorcha hoped the Stephensons would not be disappointed in the outcome. She liked them so much.

The signal was given and *Novelty* reached the first post one minute and 20 seconds later. The crowd broke into shouts and applause.

Thaddeus Fulbright, now thrown off the tracks, joined them with his stop watch in hand. "That beats *Rocket's* best start by five seconds."

George Stephenson, also with stop watch in hand, nodded, frowning. It was over for *Rocket*: she had already run, and there was no beating her own time now.

"*Novelty* is moving much faster than *Rocket* did at the start of her trials," Thaddeus added.

"And *Novelty* also has half the load *Rocket* carried," George replied with a smirk.

Sorcha noticed Robert didn't say anything. He wasn't smiling either. But he was not a man who appeared defeated.

"And what is *Novelty's* official speed on this first leg?" Robert murmured to his father.

"16 miles per hour!" Thaddeus answered. "Almost up to *Rocket's* third best time over her entire 35-mile journey."

"It's a good showing so far," George agreed.

The Novelty's second run was not as spectacular, but still exceeded 13 mph, better than half of Rocket's first runs.

"Novelty is doing fantastic!" Thaddeus exclaimed.

"A most promising start," George agreed cautiously.

Sorcha nudged Thaddeus, glaring at him. "Don't crow."

The general feeling in the air was that *Novelty* was set to take the prize away from the Stephensons. Even so, Sorcha thought Thaddeus' gloating was in poor taste.

Thaddeus grinned from ear to ear. "I'll be writing all about it in the *Liverpool Mercury*."

"Take care you only include the *news*," Sorcha said.

"What do you mean, Miss O'Shea? What else would I be reporting?"

Sorcha pulled Thaddeus over a few feet for a private conversation, as much as could be had in the situation. They both kept their eyes on the tracks.

"The race isn't over yet," she said. "You had better not write in your paper any of the reactions of this private party, painting them in a poor light."

"Why not?" Thaddeus inquired. "I'm a newspaper man, Miss O'Shea."

"No one can say anything because you're here. Essentially, the party is no fun because you're present." Sorcha was surprised at her own rudeness, but she only stated the truth. Just as Thaddeus had done. *Sauce for the gander*, as it were.

"You wound me, Miss O'Shea." Thaddeus turned to smile at her, if only for an instant.

"Don't hurt my new friends," she stated pointedly.

"Oh, so they're your friends now?"

"Yes, just like your friends Braithwaite and Ericcson. I thought a newspaper man was supposed to be impartial?"

"And what about me? Aren't I your friend?"

"Hmmm. Ask me after I've read your account of this race."

"I tried to save you from that Casanova, Lawrence Davenport," Thaddeus objected. "Doesn't that buy me some credit?"

"I thank you for your intention."

"Miss O'Shea, you are so beautiful in your naivety."

She glared at him.

Novelty readied for her third leg, so Thaddeus and Sorcha returned to watch with the rest of the party. In all, the steam engines were required to make ten trips, equal to a total of thirty-five miles.

"Please, Mr. Fulbright, the third round is beginning. I must give the track my full attention."

But his eyes were already glued to the tracks.

* * *

"Oh, no!" Thaddeus looked horrified as *Novelty* began her third of ten legs. "Something is wrong."

"Do ya' really think so?" George posed, shaking his head. They watched water flying everywhere, shooting out all over the driver and the engineer.

"Oh my goodness, the water is gushing everywhere!" Sorcha stated the obvious, not accustomed to subtle humor from George Stephenson, who was generally anything but subtle. She glanced at George to see an expression of serious study in his pale blue eyes.

"It looks like our competition just blew up," George said.

"I wouldn't say that, precisely," Robert considered.

"Yep. She's definitely exploded." George pronounced.

"I hope that water isn't too hot," Robert was clearly concerned for his opponents' safety. He studied the recipients' reaction to the water and appeared relieved to conclude they were unharmed.

"What has happened?" Sorcha exclaimed.

"The pipe transporting water from the feed pump to the boiler has burst," Robert said, his eyes glued to the *Novelty*. "The bellows burst under the steam pressure. They're going to have to put a new seal on the boiler."

And in a flash, Thaddeus was gone.

George arrived at his conclusions, knowing well how a steam locomotive was put together. "The extent of the damage is likely only minor: the pipe can be repaired, but there are no facilities for doing the job on these grounds."

"The pipe will have to be sent to the village of Prescott," Robert added. "You know what this means, don't you Father?"

"Of course I do, son. It means it's showtime for the *Rocket* again!" George lit up.

"Someone has to keep the crowds entertained," Robert murmured to Sorcha. There was such a light in his eyes, a boyish delight in all the unexpected twists and turns of this wondrous event that she felt herself go giddy for an instance as she shared his mirth.

And in no time, the *Rocket* was again on the tracks mesmerizing the crowds, along with the antics of Chief Engineer/Showman George

Stephenson, a repeat of the last time the other locomotives were not prepared to perform.

Unencumbered with no load, the Rocket bedazzled the spectators, as George Stephenson no doubt intended.

With George and Robert on the *Rocket*, Sorcha turned to Thaddeus, who had by now returned. "I can't understand why you don't like George Stephenson. You must be the only person here who doesn't. He is the most delightful man."

"I assure you there are many who are not enamored of George Stephenson's blunt manner," Thaddeus said.

"And plain speaking. You don't like that George Stephenson always speaks the truth and never puts on airs," Sorcha added. "I would think you should like such a thing, your own manner being so direct."

But whatever Thaddeus' opinion, the crowd was clearly enthralled with the Stephensons.

"Do you think the crowd favorite is still the *Novelty?*" Sorcha asked.

"I do," Thaddeus said. "But their affection for the steady *Rocket* is growing." He shook his head, frowning and looking straight ahead at the *Rocket*. "If one is to choose between the alluring mistress and the faithful wife at home, sometimes the wife is less trouble and more comforting."

"Thaddeus Fulbright! You have the most vulgar manners. I assure you that George Stephenson cannot compete with your foul language!" Sorcha swatted him with her fan, which was becoming a usual occurrence. "The *Rocket* is as exciting as any...as any...Well! She is sufficiently exciting!"

"I apologize, Miss O'Shea. You are a lady and deserve better treatment. I don't know why I can't hold my tongue around you. I feel relaxed in your presence, I suppose."

"I wish you did not!"

"Do you?" His eyes held hers for a moment. "I do think *Novelty* is the best design, but I am also upset to see my friends so distressed. I feel it is undeserved. It has me distracted."

Sorcha felt her indignation melting. Thaddeus didn't wish to insult her and he did care about his friends.

EVERY DAY we are witness to new and more thrilling events than the day before.

The Rocket's engine unencumbered shot along the rails at an incredible rate of 32 miles an hour! So astonishing was the speed with which the engine darted past the spectators that this heavy iron machine somehow brought to mind the unlikely image of a swallow darting through the air.

It seems the iron horse is indeed a flying bird! The crowd's astonishment was complete, at least one observer exclaiming involuntarily, "the power of steam is unlimited!"

--Thaddeus Fulbright, The Liverpool Mercury

WHETHER THE CROWD preferred the *Novelty* or the *Rocket*, all now agreed that steam power was the ultimate power.

It does seem as if anything can be accomplished with steam, Sorcha thought with exhilaration.

CHAPTER TWENTY-FIVE

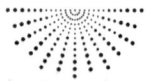

Rainhill Trials
Perseverance Runs
Monday, October 12, 1829

n answer to the naysayers who are doubting Novelty's strength and durability, it is necessary to address the circumstances of several petty accidents which have befallen Novelty, the London engine belonging to Messrs. Braithwaite and Ericsson.

As luck will have it, on the first day of Novelty's trial the valve of Novelty's bellows burst. Unfortunately the accident prevented Novelty from dazzling the attendees further until the injury could be effectively repaired.

But let us recall that the Novelty was built in four months! We are led to wonder at its success rather than to suffer any distrust arising in our minds because a few screws may have been loose or a wrong valve was turned by an inexperienced assistant, conceived by the ingenious inventors of this beautiful piece of machinery.

As the comparison is obvious to anyone, let it be noted that Mr. Stephenson has long contemplated bringing forward a locomotive engine for this railway, has been making locomotive engines for many years, is well accustomed to

*travel such engines along a railroad, and has had opportunities of exercising his
engine.*

*As for the remaining entrants, the engines of Mr. Burstall (Perseverance)
and Mr. Hackworth (Sans Pareil) remain to be tried.*

--Thaddeus Fulbright, Liverpool Mercury

SORCHA PUT DOWN HER NEWSPAPER. "Another exemplary example of
biased newspaper reporting. I am surprised your editor accepts this as
news."

"You forget, Miss O'Shea, my boss is reading the other newspapers as
well, who are mostly in agreement with my reports. I know you can't
believe it true of anyone, but he is more informed than yourself."

"It's of no consequence to me. Somehow I got the idea that you
wished to be an excellent newspaper reporter. Clearly I was mistaken."
Sorcha sighed. "Even so, I would think you would still wish to be the
best *man* you can be."

"Why should you care, Miss O'Shea?" He sat beside her.

"I'm sure I don't." Sorcha returned to her drawing. Disinterestedly
she asked, "And what of the other entrants?"

"Timothy Burstall has spent five days attempting to repair his locomotive," Thaddeus said. "It was damaged in transport."

"It seems they all were," Sorcha said, making little attempt to feign
interest.

"Yes, but if you dropped your baby, it would be little consolation to
you that other mothers had done the same," Thaddeus replied.

Sorcha raised her eyebrows. "You are saying I should have sympathy
for Mr. Burstall's plight?"

"Indeed I am," confirmed Thaddeus. "If you poured your heart and
soul into a creation—not to mention your money—and it was damaged
in transport, would you not be dismayed? Does that circumstance not
deserve our sympathy?"

"This sensitivity is a new side to you, Mr. Fulbright." Sorcha raised
her eyebrows. "I highly approve. I hope you may extend it to all of the
entries." She returned to her drawing.

"I wouldn't hold your breath, Miss O'Shea. My sympathy must be
earned," Thaddeus said loudly amidst all of the noise and bustle of the

day. The excitement for the trials had not died one bit over the week; in fact it was growing.

"Naturally, nothing can be given for free. Particularly goodwill." Sorcha shook her head, considering the unpredictable Mr. Fulbright.

"Except your criticism, which is generously offered, Miss O'Shea." He smiled sweetly at her.

She studied him for a moment. Thaddeus' dark blonde, disheveled hair fell into his eyes. He wore a brown frock coat, a brown John Bull topper, and well-tailored cream-colored pants which were slightly loose with small pleats at the hips, tapering to the ankles. He and was looking particularly handsome with his slim, muscular frame, as was the current fashion, besides being pleasing to the female eye she had to admit.

Despite his adherence to fashion, Sorcha was quite certain Mr. Fulbright would not be wearing a corset to obtain the effect. Thaddeus was much too down-to-earth, as well as being singularly disinterested in the opinions of others. She was frankly surprised he took any interest in hers, which he seemed to in general.

She was also surprised Thaddeus dressed so stylishly—though his cravat was hurriedly tied in a loose fashion and his hair was generally disheveled—as he was always in a rush, with a pencil behind his ear and a small bag on his shoulder. She had no idea how he kept his light pants from getting dirty the way he played around on the tracks amidst the steam locomotives. Maybe he had a second pair and hand-washed his clothes every night as she did at home.

"Excuse me, Mr. Fulbright?" Sorcha asked. Though she knew what he said. Even in their short acquaintance, she had grown so accustomed to Thaddeus that she could likely make out what he was saying even if no sound came out of his mouth.

Which was never.

"No need for excuses," Thaddeus replied distractedly, his eyes scanning the crowd as well as being focused on the *Perseverance* now being weighed.

"*Perseverance* looks like a beer bottle in the middle, doesn't it, with wheels on each side?"

It was Thaddeus' turn to raise his eyebrows, his head turning towards her. "How would you know what a beer bottle looks like, Miss O'Shea?"

"I am not living in a gilded cage, Mr. Fulbright. I am a working girl."

He kept staring at her, suspicion written across his face. "So they serve beer to the ladies working at your factory, do they?"

Sorcha sighed heavily. "Oh for goodness sake, I play in a band in the pub with my father. There, are you satisfied?"

Thaddeus burst out laughing. "*You*...You play in a pub, Miss O'Shea?"

"And what of it?"

"It's not a respectable activity for a young lady. Even I know that."

"And am I not a respectable young lady?"

"Yes...yes, of course...it would seem so."

"Then it must be a respectable activity since I play there and *I* am respectable."

"Which pub?" Thaddeus asked. He did appear surprised, but not shocked.

"*Ye Olde Hole in the Wall* at 4 Hackins Hey."

Thaddeus chuckled to himself, unable to cease his amusement.

"Thaddeus Fulbright! It is only music after all."

"I suppose *Hole in the Wall* is more like a boarding house serving food and drink."

"Well, naturally, my father wouldn't let me go there if he thought I was unsafe."

Thaddeus shook his head, muttering, "What will she do next..."

Sorcha scanned the crowd with her eyes, annoyed with Thaddeus, as she often was after five minutes in his company.

"Who are you looking for, Miss O'Shea?" Thaddeus was not so focused that he could not observe the beautiful Miss O'Shea.

"Oh, no one."

"Wondering where the Stephensons are?"

"I'm sure everyone is. They are rather the stars of this race, are they not?"

"And you feel quite special to have been singled out by the famous Stephensons?"

"Certainly not," Sorcha retorted. "I felt quite special before that."

The corner of Thaddeus' mouth rose in amusement. "And rightly so."

"Oh, it appears the weighing is completed," Sorcha observed.

"I happen to know the *Perseverance* weighs in at 2.9 tons," Thaddeus said.

"Oh, really? Rather light for this competition," Sorcha said, thumbing through her notebook. She had been keeping her notes.

"Yes, it is. But not as light as the *Novelty*."

"Oh, yes." Sorcha nodded. "The Novelty weighs 2 tons 3 cwt."

Thaddeus glanced at her notebook, then attempted to take it from her hands. "Let me see that, Sorcha. There's some good information in there."

Sorcha swatted his hand with her fan. "Get your hands off my things, Thaddeus Fulbright! I'm not sharing my findings with anyone."

"Not with *anyone*?"

"Most certainly not with you."

"Ouch! You hurt me, Sorcha! That's the hand I write with!"

"Well, this is the hand I protect myself with. That's what you get for grabbing at my possessions like a common thief. I have a job, too, I'll have you know, which is just as important as yours, Thaddeus Fulbright, and my notes are private."

"You might have just told me."

"I just did."

"Are you afraid the button spies will find your notes and beat you to the designs?" Thaddeus asked.

"Thaddeus Fulbright, would I make fun of your work or diminish its importance?"

"You do all the time, Miss O'Shea." Thaddeus sighed. "Well, at least, I know you are able to protect yourself. But seriously, Sorcha, I'm a newspaper man and I need all the information I can get my hands on."

"I'm sure you do, but there is nothing of interest to you in here. At any rate, it is mine, and I'm not sharing."

"I'll remember that the next time you want information, Miss O'Shea," Thaddeus replied with feigned indignation.

"I'm sure you are not privy to any information I require."

"Oh really? You might be surprised."

He shrugged. "Would you care for a lemonade?"

"I certainly would, thank you."

"Well, if I pay for it, I don't want you to give your attention to anyone else before I return."

Sorcha huffed. "If I do, I'll pay you back."

"Promise?" Thaddeus smiled sweetly.

Sorcha tapped her foot. "I'm not accustomed to lying."

"Very well. I'll be right back."

True to his word, Thaddeus returned quickly to Sorcha's bench with two lemonades.

The cold, sweet, tart drink was delicious! Sorcha was definitely feeling more friendly towards Thaddeus.

"What is your family background, Thaddeus? I have often wondered. You said one time, I believe, that your father thinks being a reporter is a waste of an education?"

"Very true." Thaddeus nodded.

"Why does he think that?"

Thaddeus laughed sarcastically. "How would I know? Perhaps he wanted me to go into the war office as he did."

"The war office?" Sorcha frowned. "I don't see why that is superior to reporting the news. A respectable position, to be sure."

"Do you think so, Miss O'Shea?"

"Naturally I don't think you are respectable, Mr. Fulbright."

"Naturally. That would require generosity and charity, which you would never bestow upon me."

"Hmmm…" Sorcha ignored him as she continued with her thoughts. "But newspaper reporting as a profession seems perfectly respectable."

"I shall inform my father of same."

"Where did you go to school, Thaddeus?"

"Eton. From the time I was thirteen years of age until I was eighteen."

"Away from home?" she asked.

"Right. Boarding School."

"And did you like it?" Sorcha asked.

Thaddeus laughed. "No one likes boarding school. Except the upper classman, perhaps. Beatings were every Friday."

"Oh my." Sorcha frowned. "I'm surprised your father didn't pull you out of the school."

Thaddeus' lips formed a thin smile. "He thought it would toughen me up."

"And did it?" Sorcha asked.

"Naturally it did. How would I be able to suffer your abuse otherwise, Miss O'Shea?"

At this point, Robert Stephenson turned up, tipping his hat to both.

"Miss O'Shea. Mr. Fulbright."

Thaddeus frowned. Why he wasn't happy to see Robert, Sorcha didn't know. "Well, I'm going to get a bit closer to the action. Good day."

"Good day, Thaddeus." Having exited, Sorcha turned to Robert. "Do you think *Perseverance* was able to make its repairs, Mr. Stephenson?"

Robert sighed heavily. "I do wish you would call me 'Robert' Miss O'Shea."

She laughed out loud. "And you refer to me as 'Miss O'Shea' in the same breath."

"I must show my respect to you," Robert said.

"And I you." *But I wonder what Robert would think of my playing music publicly.* She looked away. If it were a concert hall, that must be socially acceptable. But concert halls were primarily for classical music.

Maybe if I gave up playing in public venues I might be an acceptable wife to someone someday. Not to Thaddeus, of course, he is of no matter to me, and not to Robert because he would never have me. But to someone else…

The idea of ceasing to play felt so empty to her. Even for someone as great a prize as Robert Stephenson.

Who would I be then?

Sorcha didn't care what Thaddeus thought; he could go harass someone else if he didn't like it. Although he seemed more amused than anything.

Sorcha chastised herself for her annoyance. Honestly, Thaddeus was open to equal rights for women—he seemed to treat everyone the same —and she wasn't being fair to him: he didn't seem to put women on a pedestal, nor to treat her any differently than he did the men that she could tell. She wouldn't mind a bit more veneration and glorification, but, honestly, she didn't mind. It was difficult to get anything done if one didn't have one's feet on the ground.

Which accounted for her stiff demeanor with Robert, which she didn't like.

But she did like *him*. And she was afraid of being rejected by him.

"And the *Perseverance*?" Sorcha repeated, unable to hide her interest. "How does it fare?"

"I'm not certain. Word is at the Millfield Yard that Burstall was snooping about utilizing that time attempting to improve his steam locomotive rather than focusing exclusively on the intended repair of the *Perseverance's* air-compressing apparatus," Robert replied.

"Extra time which the judges were so kind as to allot to him," Sorcha said.

Robert nodded. "I trust you can keep that between you and I and you will not be repeating it to Mr. Fulbright?"

"Certainly not! Thaddeus Fulbright is incorrigible!" Though she was beginning to understand why. It seems he had been in a dog-eat-dog world from the time he was thirteen years of age. Thaddeus was remarkably good-natured, considering.

But I do not think he is an easy pushover.

"Just doing his job," Robert said. "All the same, I would not like to be quoted bad-mouthing any of my competition." Robert shrugged. "Anyway, no one can ever know for certain what Burstall's intentions were."

"And do you think Mr. Burstall was able to repair the air compressing apparatus?" Sorcha asked.

"I don't know." Robert shook his head. "But, at any rate, the *Novelty's* air compressing apparatus is superior, being a continuous flow, as opposed to being pulsed, as the *Perseverance* is constructed."

Sorcha giggled.

"What is it, Miss O'Shea?"

"Oh, excuse me! I can't help but notice that you seem to know the engineering design of not only your machine but of everyone else's."

Robert appeared subdued. "I suppose I do."

"And yet no one else understands your machine. How is it Burstall is trying to figure out what you already know."

Robert bestowed upon her a sly smile. "I couldn't say, Miss O'Shea. All we have to do is watch the performance and we understand how the other machines are built. That is to say, my father and I."

Sorcha smiled at Robert's reverting to speaking in technical terms as he was inclined to do. That's where his mind was and it couldn't be helped. Part of being brilliant, she supposed. His wife would have to become accustomed to scientific conversation.

His wife. Robert would never think of her as a wife. She was a poor Irish girl who painted buttons and played in a pub.

And he was a scientist.

Possibly a world famous scientist someday.

CHAPTER TWENTY-SIX

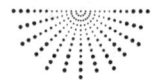

Private thoughts

*W*hy does Sorcha become positively ga-ga anytime Robert Stephenson is around? Thaddeus thought to himself as he stormed off.

Honestly, is Stephenson that much more than a pretty face? Sure, he built a locomotive, but he isn't going to win this competition.

Even so, Robert will still have a good job as the co-owner of the Forth Street Works. A decent living to provide for a wife.

Better than I have, to be sure.

I suppose there is no comparison between a businessman and a newspaper-man. And Stephenson is both a scientist and a businessman.

Why do I care? I don't want to marry anyone, least of all Sorcha O'Shea! *She has that fiery Irish temper. She's not happy unless she is picking a fight. She would never agree to 'obey' her husband.* Thaddeus snorted. *She would torture me to the end of my days.*

Still, I might like to find out. Thaddeus smiled to himself. *One could never be bored with Sorcha Fae around.*

Thaddeus immediately frowned again. *Sorcha is not interested in me in that way, she has made that abundantly clear. She is besotted with Robert Stephenson.*

Well, he can have her! Sorcha O'Shea was just a distraction and nothing more. Like all women.

A distraction from everything that mattered to him: fame and fortune.

A picture of Sorcha leapt into his mind and suddenly it all felt empty.

Thaddeus jumped onto the tracks.

I need to remember why I am here.

CHAPTER TWENTY-SEVEN

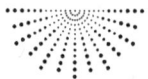

Perseverance
October 14, 1829

"*B*urstall upset his locomotive in bringing it from Liverpool to Rainhill and spent a week in pretending to remedy the injuries wherein he altered and amended some parts every day till he was last of all to start and a sorrowful start it was." – John Dixon, Resident Engineer Liverpool & Manchester Railway, as told to Thaddeus Fulbright, Liverpool Mercury*

SORCHA WATCHED *Perseverance* begin its trials with interest. "A week ago we would have been astonished at *Perseverance*. Now it seems rather ho-hum, doesn't it, Robert?"

"Oh, I wouldn't say so, Miss O'Shea," he replied. "The crowd appears to be quite diverted."

As am I. Sorcha glanced up at him. Robert was so handsome in his well-tailored suit and top hat with his sapphire blue eyes and dark, wavy hair curled about his face. Robert Stephenson had masculine features, but there was also a softness and a sweetness to him—a beauty, in the same vein as the romantic poets. She sighed.

Each day George Stephenson came to the trials in a serviceable tweed suit—probably his Sunday clothes—while Robert was dressed to the nines as if he were going to a fancy ball. Even if Robert manned the Rocket, his appearance conveyed the importance and the consequence of the moment.

Perseverance began her trials and was unable to reach above six miles per hour, chugging along with some effort. That would have been impressive if seen before *Rocket* or *Novelty*.

"Yes, after all the thrills and excitement, there is a bit of impatience with the struggling *Perseverance*," Sorcha said. "It's as if we're anxious to return to the real race and *Perseverance* is just in the way."

"There is no chance of Perseverance beating the *Rocket*," Robert agreed. "The only serious contenders left are *Sans Pareil* and *Novelty*."

Sorcha noticed Thaddeus down on the tracks with his friends John Ericsson and John Braithwaite, assisting however he might. *There is certainly an abundance of 'John's' and 'Timothy's' at this important contest. Timothy Burstall who built Perseverence and Timothy Hackworth who built Sans Pareil.*

Sorcha had to appreciate Thaddeus' complete and utter devotion to his friends. Thaddeus' faith never wavered.

"Are you nervous, Robert? Worried about the outcome I mean?"

"Hmmm....I don't really get nervous, Miss O'Shea; it serves no purpose. Only work produces results. And, after all, there is nothing I can do at this point, it is out of my hands."

She nodded.

"Still...much is riding on the grand prize. The future of my business...." He looked at her pointedly. "...my *future*."

"I expect you will have a future regardless of what happens, Robert."

The way he looked at her, her heart did a flip-flop in her chest.

"How is that, Miss O'Shea?" he asked softly.

"I expect you will be alright whatever happens, Robert . You're intelligent, you have a job, you have a future."

"There are other things in life besides one's career, Sorcha." He took her gloved hand and kissed it.

Could it be? Is he expressing a partiality for me?

"I'm not sure there is for you, Robert." Sorcha couldn't pretend she didn't know his character. She couldn't ignore what she had observed in this week.

She was so smitten and yet she couldn't imagine a life with Robert, even if he would stoop so low as to choose her. For a short time, she would be his main focus. But then she would be secondary. And it wouldn't be a close second. His brain was too great and his focus absolute. She wasn't sure this was the life she wanted.

On the odd chance it was the life he wanted.

He frowned. "What do you mean, Miss O'Shea?"

"Of course there are other things in life, but your work is central to your well-being."

"Yes, but I'm not like my father. I don't want to work every second of every day."

Is it true? Sorcha wondered.

She considered his words, smiling. "But you do want to win as much as he does?"

"Naturally. But mainly for the reason I don't wish to be stunted and stifled, unable to fulfill my calling. I would hate to be cut down at the knees before I discover what I can do." He sighed. "A creator wishes to create. Without the contract we will have much less to build. This is our chance to do something great."

"You were born to do it," she admitted. And she knew she was right.

"However," he took her hand. "I still have a heart. I still have dreams of a family."

Sorcha held her breath for an instant. Was he just making conversation? Or was this something he wanted her, in particular, to hear?

"And what do you wish for, Miss Sorcha O'Shea?"

"Honestly I am happy with my life right now. I couldn't have said the same a year ago. So I am so grateful."

"What do you enjoy about your life, Sorcha?" Robert asked softly.

"Playing music and painting. I would like a family of my own someday. I suppose everyone wants to find love." She sighed. "But first I would like to see my family settled and doing well—especially my father. I wish he could have a job more suited to him and my mother working less. Before I think about myself, I would like to see them better off. They depend upon me."

Why am I stalling? Why is it so difficult for me to express my regard for him?

"That is easily resolved for a person of means."

Right now you are in the business of winning this contest. As romantic as this moment was, it wasn't really about her. Robert's heart was visiting his other longings as a way to avoid facing his worst fear: *losing this contest.*

Romance was not paramount in his mind now, and she knew it.

He wants to win. And he wants to win with all his heart.

So that he can begin a new project. A major project.

She looked into his eyes. *I wish this was about me, but I don't believe it is.*

Sorcha had not thought much about falling in love; she was always so busy and there was not really anyone to turn her head in her circle. She had been infatuated with Enoch, but she barely spoke to him.

Sorcha didn't want to be part of Robert's fantasies. And she didn't think she was part of his reality.

Do I want to be?

At least not yet. It was too early to come to any conclusions.

Robert glanced at her book of designs. "And how have your designs progressed, Miss O'Shea?"

"Very well, I think. They will be quite difficult to reproduce in miniature, but not impossible. I like a challenge." She sighed. "Of course, I have to wait and see the outcome to know how to proceed with my design."

"May I see your book?"

"I doubt it will be of interest since you are so familiar with the subject," she replied hesitantly, but she placed her book in his outstretched hand.

"Miss O'Shea!" Robert exclaimed, perusing her drawings. "These are the drawings of a technical expert!"

"Even though the buttons are very small, I have to start with a precise drawing."

"All the more reason, I assume," he murmured. "Or the result would not be discernable."

"Yes." Sorcha nodded.

"These are so beautiful. I only saw you do sketches before."

"That's how they begin, of course." She giggled.

"I can't imagine how you will recreate them in miniature," he murmured.

"I have a magnifying glass. It is yet a challenge."

"I expect you would make an excellent surgeon." He turned the page. "Miss O'Shea...this portrait...It appears to be me...?"

"It is," she smiled. "If you are the winner, I must have a likeness."

"Oh?"

"In which case, the button will be very popular." She looked at him slyly. "Especially since you are very like Lord Byron in appearance." The intense blue of his eyes would be a dramatic touch, sure to grab one's attention.

Robert laughed. "I've heard that before."

His gaze was intense. Sorcha hoped he might say something like *'Whatever happens, I already feel I have won'* as he gazed into her eyes, but, instead, he said, "I certainly hope I may be the winner."

"I do too," Sorcha said with sincere feeling.

"Oh, and why is that?"

"The other candidates would not make as good a button."

Robert appeared startled then laughed. "That is a compliment I have never heard before. And why do you say so, Miss O'Shea?"

"Because...well...the other candidates are..." She blushed, placing her gloved hand in front of her mouth. *Old men*, she thought. "Not as young."

Sorcha cleared her throat. *And not as handsome either.*

"Ah...so you only do buttons of the young?" Robert asked pointedly.

"Certainly not! Mr. Stephenson! You are teasing me mercilessly!" Sorcha couldn't help giggling. "Do not make me say it!"

"I insist, Miss O'Shea!" He demanded.

"You know very well that you...you...*turn every head when you walk by!*"

"Yes, but which direction?" He asked with his poker face.

They both burst out laughing.

His eyes were smiling again and Sorcha was pleased to see Robert's spirit had risen.

* * *

SORCHA IS the most beautiful girl of my acquaintance. Her very presence was intoxicating. *I am definitely smitten.*

Robert felt conflicted. He had worked all his life for this moment, spending most of his waking hours towards the achievement of this goal.

A passenger railway. It was almost unthinkable.

I want to make those steam locomotives.

True, he wanted a family, and a charming wife—and who could be more charming that Sorcha O'Shea?

How much time he had to devote to courtship and marriage would be determined by the outcome of the Rainhill Trials. If he lost, he would be devastated—and able to pursue a wife. If he won, he would be elated and his time would be taken up. He would be lucky to have time to sleep and eat.

Many ladies would marry him at the drop of a pin, Robert knew that, but he didn't perceive that Sorcha was of that cut. She had her own interests.

Sorcha O'Shea will have to be wooed.

He liked her better than any other woman of his acquaintance, but he wasn't sure he had time for all that nonsense.

I have to get on with my life.

Many ladies understood that. Fanny Sanderson for one. And he liked Fanny very well. She was of sweet and constant temperament.

Sorcha was a tornado next to Fanny's calm waters.

Fanny sat in the Grand Stand and she no doubt had seen him walking with Miss O'Shea, but he and Fanny did not have an understanding. And Fanny would never cause a scene no matter the circumstances.

Fanny would make a perfect dignitary's wife.

But Sorcha...Sorcha was every man's dream: a fiery, lively maiden.

Could Sorcha tolerate his work schedule?

My life has been absorbed in engines for as long as I can remember. They were living on the brink of a social and industrial revolution, and Robert wanted to be part of it.

I am proud to be part of it.

Train travel would make jobs, education, and travel more accessible to the working person, making their lives better and the country stronger.

Robert had a beautiful picture in his mind's eye: A wife and children at home would make everything pleasant for him so that he would be free to devote his life to his work. Many women would like such an arrangement. He had no reason to doubt that Sorcha would. Surely she would wish to give up her factory job, to be married, to have a family, and a home.

And he wouldn't always be as busy as he is now.

Robert had never met any woman he liked so well as Sorcha. She was beautiful and intelligent. She would be a fine mother to his children and a fine wife for him.

Still, matrimony was for life and a very large commitment.

I wish we had longer to get to know each other.

Was he infatuated with Sorcha? Or was this the real thing?

Robert closed his eyes momentarily, envisioning the beautiful Sorcha O'Shae in his home, surrounded by their children, his maid setting the table for dinner.

His eyes opened wide as he realized there was a smattering of red-headed toddlers.

Robert laughed to himself, shaking his head.

I could care less that she is Irish, and not wealthy, and not in high society. I can give all that to her.

If I win this contest.

CHAPTER TWENTY-EIGHT

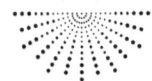

Sans Pareil Runs
Tuesday, October 13, 1829

"*B*urstall's locomotive Perseverance reached a top speed of 6 miles per hour during the first test runs without load, remaining well below the required minimum speed of 10 mph with load. Burstall then withdrew his machine from the competition and received an extraordinary expense bonus of £26.*

Consider that the average British worker is doing well to make £2 per week, or in the neighborhood of £8 per month.

To put this generous consolation prize afforded to Timothy Burstall in perspective, a skilled coach-maker, earning at the top of the working class income, can earn £5 per week. Below the coach-maker is everyone else. London omnibus drivers earn 34 shillings a week, less than £2, for a working day beginning at 7:45 am and sometimes ending past midnight. A poor laborer's wage is between £1 and £1.5 a week in London, covering only his rent and a meager table for his family. Some call these starvation wages.

And if a worker in the slop shops offers a shirt of poor quality to his employer, is he paid? No, he is docked for the wasted fabric.

This consolation prize for a failed effort could be an indicator of the wages to be earned on the railways." – Thaddeus Fulbright, Liverpool Mercury

"THIS IS a bit of an unkind article you wrote about Timothy Burstall. He did have expenses in building his locomotive," Sorcha said to Thaddeus.

"And yet you have no problem being unkind to newspaper reporters, Miss O'Shae. Why does everyone deserve your kindness except me? I have to ask myself."

"Still I like your pointing out the tribulations of the London poor," Sorcha added, ignoring his complaint.

"That wasn't my intent." Thaddeus shrugged.

"I have no doubt of that." Sorcha rolled her eyes. "What was your intent? To point out the generosity of the Quaker directors? I admit they are extremely fair-minded for businessmen."

"Yes. It is a wonder they make any money," Thaddeus frowned. "No, that wasn't my point either."

"To express your resentment at anyone who is given a break?" Sorcha continued with a sly smile. She had to admit that she and Thaddeus had lively conversations. About subjects of which she had some knowledge.

"You might have hit on it there, Miss O'Shea." Thaddeus shrugged. "But I believe my intent was to write a story which would improve my reputation and my salary."

"Indeed. I want to put food on my table." Thaddeus shook his head. "And yet I have observed you enthusiastically encouraging other men for being competitive and wishing advancement. I ask myself why you have singled me out for censure."

"It is your chosen field, I expect. Which is, by definition, meant to inform and enlighten the public. If you only wished to make money you should have gone into a different field."

"Perhaps my only skill is lying and deception."

"Such high ideals you have, Thaddeus Fulbright."

He stood and bowed to her. "Thank you, Miss O'Shea."

"I am inspired by your altruism and devotion to the betterment of mankind."

"Don't put me on a pedestal, Sorcha." Thaddeus advised, returning to his seat.

"Never fear."

"At least I don't have far to fall."

"I must admit, *Perseverance* was a bit of a disappointment," Sorcha considered. "Only six miles per hour without load. Although a week ago, I would have thought it extraordinary."

"I'm sure *Perseverance's* performance wasn't a disappointment to your special friend Robert Stephenson, whom you hold in much higher esteem than this lowly reporter."

"And whose fault is that?" Sorcha inquired.

"It is possibly *you*, Sorcha, who refuses to acknowledge the harsh realities of a working man's life."

"No one is better aware of that life than me!" Sorcha retorted. "But, as you point out in your article, even those who work must produce an item or service of quality."

"Ouch! That stings!" Thaddeus clicked his tongue. "You are a harsh taskmistress, Sorcha O'Shea. Is there no mercy in you?"

Sorcha glanced down at the newspaper in her hand. "To the deserving."

"You are my harshest editor, Miss O'Shea. And yet I do not answer to you." He raised one eyebrow at her. "If you tire of your present profession, you could always crack the whip at a slop shop, Miss O'Shae. This would channel your inclination to cruelty into productivity."

"Hmmm...Perhaps when my eyes and fingers fail me." She tapped her index finger on her cheek. "To answer your question, *Perseverance's* performance didn't appear to be unexpected to Mr. Stephenson."

"Ah, I see...Well, it's time for *Sans Pareil* to see what she can do. The anticipation builds." Thaddeus said as they watched the locomotive being moved onto the company's weighing machine by a large composite of muscular men, Mr. O'Shea included.

Thaddeus had often been in Sorcha's company since she stayed to the same spot on the podium. If someone wished to find her, it was not that difficult to do so, even in this massive crowd. Thankfully she could sketch and talk at the same time, so she had enjoyed a great deal more socializing than she did in her general workday. At the factory her main companion was Violet, who was more in the line of theatrics than conversation. Sorcha found her present companionship much more enjoyable.

Mr. O'Shea, though not having entirely relinquished his chaperone duties, appeared to be fine with either Mr. Fulbright or Mr. Stephenson in her company. If Lawrence presented himself, Sean O'Shea was not far behind, which let Sorcha know her Da was keeping an eye on her in spite of appearances.

"Your father has certainly been a great help at the Trials," Thaddeus considered, watching the muscular man on the tracks.

"He likes to work and to be useful." She raised her eyebrows.

"You don't think I am useful, Miss O'Shea?" Thaddeus asked, but he did not appear much offended.

"You are a gifted writer, Thaddeus, and you do have great curiosity and ambition. However…"

"Yes?"

"Although I do find this latest article refreshing, despite your less than admirable motives, I think you're sometimes biased for a newspaper man," Sorcha glanced at the newspaper again.

"Oh, just because I like *my* friends better than *your* friends?"

"I wouldn't think either would be appropriate for a newspaper man," Sorcha said.

"Oh, and why is that?"

"Objectivity. A newspaper man is supposed to be objective. It doesn't matter who your friends are as long as they don't influence your truthfulness. I mean, you can't start with what you want to believe and then fabricate the 'facts' to support your desired views."

"You are one to talk, Sorcha O'Shea." Now he was beginning to become annoyed at her unrelenting criticism.

"Yes, and how does my subjectivity impact anyone? When someone looks at my buttons will they be swayed one way or another?" Sorcha asked demurely.

Thaddeus laughed, releasing his anger. "It's difficult to say, Miss O'Shea. Those buttons are everywhere, watching everyone. I personally think they are part of a conspiracy and we are all being watched by surveillance committees."

Sorcha covered her mouth with her gloved hand momentarily. "Oh, my goodness, as in the Terror?"

"Yes. What else? The surveillance committees of the French Revolution are still with us."

Sorcha pictured her buttons with the eyes moving this way and that. *Most notably Robert's blue eyes.*

It suddenly occurred to her that she hadn't laughed so much in anyone else's presence. She mainly just stared adoringly at Enoch, unable to say much to him. And Robert, well, Robert was a god as far as Sorcha was concerned. And he certainly spoke in a foreign language only intelligible to scientists. Very few people on the planet earth understood engineering to the degree Robert Stephenson did. There might be five people in the world who did.

Although Thaddeus was no halfwit. His conversation was engaging and entertaining. Thaddeus liked to be in the thick of things, as did she. Thaddeus was a student in this thing called life. Like she was.

"You might be right, Mr. Fulbright."

"Every now and again I am."

"Hmmm..." Sorcha looked intently at Thaddeus. "What color are your eyes?"

"Brown. Why?"

"Just imagining..." *Would he make as good a button? Not really. Not as engaging. And yet...his smile is definitely engaging...*

"What? Why are you staring at me, Sorcha?"

"How would you feel about your eyes being green?"

"What bag of moonshine are you spouting now, Sorcha? It's difficult to keep up."

"I just don't know if you would make a good member of the Terror, Tad."

He stared at her as if she had lost her mind, his eyebrows furrowed. "That's good news. My Father won't have to have me killed."

"Maybe it's for the best. But remember, Thaddeus, your job is important. You are shaping opinions." She sobered. "And what do you think of the *Sans Pareil's* chances, Thaddeus?"

"*Sans Pareil* is a strong contender, to be sure, and may beat Rocket's racing numbers," Thaddeus said. "But I still believe when the *Novelty's* repairs are completed she will win."

"Possibly, "Sorcha mused. "I'm beginning to think no one has any idea what is going to happen. It's one surprise after another."

"I heard from a little bird that Mr. Hackworth was doing quite a bit of work on *Sans Pareil* at the last minute," Thaddeus added.

"Everyone was," Sorcha said. "Though I know Mr. Hackworth is friends with the Stephensons."

"Yes, the *Robert Stephenson and Company Ltd* built Mr. Hackworth's engine," Thaddeus considered.

"It seems odd, you know," Sorcha considered.

"It is. A conflict of interest to be sure for Robert Stephenson to build his competitor's engine."

"But *Forth Street Works* is the first company in the world created specifically to build steam locomotive engines. There must not be many options if one is looking for an engine."

"There are many ironworks shops, but not any others exclusively building steam engines," Thaddeus considered. "Perhaps Hackworth thought Stephenson would do the best job."

"Hmmm," Sorcha considered. "I wonder if Mr. Hackworth has been working on his locomotive since last week."

"Not on Sunday," Thaddeus shook his head. "Timothy Hackworth would no more work on the Lord's Day than he would cut his nose off. He might be confident and forceful, but, unlike some here, he is a man of principle."

"Who are you suggesting is without principles?" Sorcha asked.

Thaddeus shrugged. "It is a competition, after all, and the stakes are high."

Sorcha shook her head. "It seems to me that you make enemies too easily, Thaddeus."

"And it seems to me that you are a bit bossy, Miss O'Shea."

Sorcha giggled. "I suppose you are right, Thaddeus. I just want you to be the best man you can be."

"And you think I am falling short?"

"Perhaps. I see so much potential."

The weighing in complete, suddenly there was screaming and yelling on the tracks. For a religious man, Hackworth was making his fair share of the commotion.

"Oh my goodness, what now? I never was anywhere with so many surprises and unexpected events!"

Thaddeus tipped his hat to her, smiling as he departed. "For the benefit of the reading public, I must discover what is going on." Thaddeus leapt forward like a bee to honey.

Thaddeus positively loves conflict and contention, Sorcha thought, smiling to herself while shaking her head. *I wish there might never be any struggle, but the light comes on in Thaddeus' eyes when there is strife.*

It seems he is in the right profession after all.

Her father joined her soon thereafter.

"Why is there so much commotion down there on the tracks, Da?"

"The *Sans Pareil* is too heavy to compete," Mr. O'Shea replied.

"It weighs too much?" Sorcha asked.

"A full 600 pounds too much," Mr. O'Shea said. "The weight limit for a four-wheel locomotive is four and a half tons. Sans Pareil is 4 tons 15 cwt 56 lbs."

"Then why is Mr. Hackworth yelling?"

"He insists the weighing machine is wrong and that *Sans Pareil* is not overweight."

"You can't be serious," Sorcha said. "It's the same machine that weighed all the others."

"Mr. Hackworth is a very sincere and honorable man generally, so when he takes a stance people tend to believe his sincerity if nothing else," Mr. O'Shea laughed. "He can talk those judges into anything."

"We'll see if he can persuade the judges his locomotive weighs 600 pounds less than it does." Sorcha felt some sympathy for Mr. Hackworth. "It would be a shame to go to all that work and not be able to compete. And the *Sans Pareil* is so big surely it can haul a great deal."

Thaddeus then burst onto the scene again as he was wont to do. "The judges have decided to let *Sans Pareil* compete. If the *Sans Pareil* were to finish the trials – or even to win – then they will determine eligibility."

"These are the most accommodating judges I have ever seen in my life." Sorcha considered. "They bend the rules for everyone to give them an advantage over the *Rocket.*"

"Oh, I wouldn't say that," Thaddeus argued.

"I'm sure you wouldn't," Sorcha said.

"The judges are excessively fair and want to find the best steam loco-motive, however that may be accomplished," Thaddeus said.

Sorcha nodded her understanding. "So much is riding on the outcome of the trials."

The excitement built as *Sans Pareil* was wheeled onto the track.

CHAPTER TWENTY-NINE

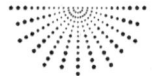

Rainhill Trials
Sans Pareil Trials
Tuesday, October 13, 1829

"*S*ans Pareil is an odd-looking locomotive, isn't it?" Sorcha considered.

By this time, Robert Stephenson appeared, joining the party as well. "I suppose they are all odd in their own way."

"No one could say these locomotives shared designs," Sorcha considered. "They all look so different."

"Yes, they are all notably different, both in engineering and aesthetic design," Robert agreed.

"They have some features in common," Thaddeus reflected. "Both Rocket and Sans Pareil are large locomotives, while Novelty and Perseverance are much lighter."

"Are the heavy locomotives similarly engineered?" Sorcha asked.

Robert shook his head. "Instead of *Rocket's* fire tube boiler, *Sans Pareil* has a double return flue."

"Are their advantages to each?" Mr. O'Shea asked.

"On *Sans Pareil*, the driver and the fireman ride on opposite ends of the engine," Robert said.

"Ah, yes," Thaddeus nodded his understanding. "That could create some problems."

"Quite so," Robert agreed. "There is nothing between the fireman and the blazing furnace and the sweltering chimney. When *Sans Pareil* lunges forward or backwards the fireman could be thrown into one or the other."

Sorcha gasped. "Oh, no! And what of the driver on the other side?"

"Even more dangerous, in my estimation," Robert said. "The driver is balanced on a narrow wooden platform six feet in the air with no safety rail."

"If he falls on the track, the iron wheels will slice him," Mr. O'Shea interpreted.

"A safety rail should be required," Sorcha objected.

Robert shook his head. "That would require laws. The government won't get that involved in private enterprise. At any rate, I wouldn't advise it."

"Who is the engineer?" Sorcha asked, concerned for his safety, while peering at the *Sans Pareil* being hooked up to its load.

"Why, if it isn't Timothy Hackworth himself," Robert said. "And his driver is William Gowan, a much trusted employee as I understand."

Sorcha did the sign of the cross and said a silent prayer for them.

"It sure looks like a heavy load," Mr. O'Shea remarked.

Robert nodded. "Full nineteen tons with the tender."

Sorcha wriggled her eyebrows. "*Rocket* only had to pull seventeen tons."

"*Only?*" Robert laughed. "And *Novelty* requirement is thirteen tons."

"This is the strangest competition I ever beheld," Sorcha murmured.

"The trick is to figure it out and to play the game." Robert shrugged.

Sorcha stared at Robert, surprised at his words. Robert Stephenson was such a genuine person, but she could see that he was also practical-minded and willing to do what it took in a competition. She didn't know how far he would go to achieve his ends, but she could see that he took note of the ways of the world.

I suppose one is not likely to win without drive.

"Obviously, one still has to build a quality product. Hopefully, the *best* product," Robert added. "But politics are a reality of life."

The race began, and once again, everyone was surprised, especially Robert Stephenson.

Mr. O'Shea whistled as he looked at his watch, not believing what he saw.

Sans Pareil's start was mercurial, passing the first post in one minute and nine seconds, even beating *Novelty's* astonishing debut, the previous record-holder.

"Heaven help us!" Sorcha exclaimed with the first lap completed. "How fast was *Sans Pareil?*"

Robert whistled to himself. "17 ½ miles per hour hauling 19 tons!"

"Isn't that faster than *Novelty?*" Sorcha asked.

"Yes. Faster than either of her legs." Robert frowned. "*Rocket* still has the fastest leg with cargo: 17 ½ miles per hour is *Rocket's* second-highest speed."

"But *Novelty*—and *Sans Pareil*—still have a chance to beat *Rocket's* highest speed," Thaddeus stated.

"Yes." Robert nodded, his eyes glued to the track.

The second leg was just under 12 mph, and the third leg at 15 mph. More importantly, though, *Sans Pareil* was still going strong.

If Sans Pareil tops 17 ½ miles per hour, she could beat Rocket and win the competition.

Robert is concerned. Sorcha could see it in his expression. Though he was not a man to curse or to throw tantrums: he was able to control his emotions in the interest of professional and gentlemanly behavior. He had a calm demeanor and was not one to reveal his innermost thoughts, which made getting to know him more difficult.

Whereas Thaddeus Fulbright was easy to get to know. Although she had not put much effort into getting to know Thaddeus. Sometimes she wanted him to be quiet.

The comparison between her new acquaintances couldn't help but come to mind.

Sorcha supposed intimacy took time with Robert. Hopefully it would come at some point. Certainly Robert was close to his father. It was encouraging to see a son respect and treat his father well.

She glanced at Robert who remained focused on the tracks. Possibly this was an apt description of his entire life.

Robert had not been as concerned with *Novelty*, but *Sans Pareil* was a robust and dynamic challenger.

"*Sans Pareil* is a work horse, but she is not an elegant performer," Thaddeus considered. The spectacle was loud and fire-y, like a spitting dragon.

"Do you mean to say 'even less elegant than *Rocket*', Mr. Fulbright?" Robert asked in spite of his intense following of *San Pareil's* progress.

"I'm inclined to think much less," Thaddeus replied. "*Sans Pareil* makes a great deal of noise and rolls about on the track with sparks and ashes flying everywhere."

"The facts align with your impressions, Mr. Fulbright," Robert agreed, "It looks as if half of *Sans Pareil's* fuel is being thrown out of the chimney unconsumed. Still…her performance is excellent." He shook his head, as if disbelieving. "I just don't know *why*."

"What do you mean, Robert?" Sorcha asked, her curiosity ignited. If this was a puzzle which was confounding the brilliant Mr. Stephenson, it had to be a complex dilemma.

"*Sans Pareil* uses *three times* the coke *Rocket* uses and almost twice the water. The engine is highly inefficient."

"Didn't you build the engine?" Sorcha asked.

"Well, yes, but according to the designs Hackworth gave us. We didn't deviate from his design. It would be unthinkable to do so."

3rd lap…4th lap…5th lap…12th lap…13th lap…14th lap…15th lap.

"Is *Sans Pareil* winning?" Sorcha asked.

"It's possible. If her performance is consistent," Robert said somberly.

Sorcha appreciated that this could be the saddest moment of Robert's life. And yet he didn't lash out in annoyance at her questions.

Since arriving at Rainhill she had come to understand there was going to be a railway empire—and whoever won this competition was going to be the king of that empire.

Royalty, as it were. Aristocrats by birth might be replaced by a new royalty: the kings of industry.

The winner was going to be very rich, very famous, and very powerful.

Sorcha smiled to herself. Studying Robert's expression, she didn't imagine he was thinking of this. He was only thinking that he wanted to be given the contract and to build locomotives. A master devoted to his art. If Robert was deprived of the means to create his art he would be utterly devastated.

Sorcha glanced at her buttons. Not for the first time, she thought she would like to paint on a larger scale.

"I don't understand it," Robert murmured. "*Rocket's* design is so much better and yet *Sans Pareil* is surpassing us."

Sans Pareil was on her 16th lap with only four more laps to go to complete her first 35-mile journey.

Spit! *Choke!* Suddenly a cloud of ash and steam erupted from *Sans Pareil's* chimney and she coasted to a stop.

"Did she mean to stop?" Sorcha asked.

"Something is wrong!" Thaddeus exclaimed.

"Indeed." Robert drew his eyebrows together as he studied *Sans Pareil* from their vantage point. Sorcha could see that Robert's concern and curiosity overroad his possible relief that *Rocket* was, once again, ahead.

CHAPTER THIRTY

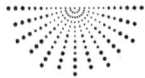

Accusations of Foul Play

"You sabotaged my machine!" Timothy Hackworth screamed at Robert Stephenson. "You built the engine that went into *Sans Pareil!*"

Thaddeus Fulbright watched with interest. "It is true, is it not, Mr. Stephenson, that *Robert Stephenson and Company Ltd.* built *Sans Pareil's* engine?"

"As well as *Rocket's,*" Robert said, turning towards the reporter with annoyance.

"It's a conflict of interest, is it not?" Thaddeus asked. "*Robert Stephenson and Company* built its competitor's engine which has now failed."

A private conversation became a very public one because Hackworth chose to make a scene. Robert kept his temper in check with great effort. "*Forth Street Works* is the first company in the world created specifically to build railway engines. Timothy Hackworth was always free to build his own engine."

"I wish I had!" Hackworth said.

"We did build the cylinders, but we built twenty of them," Robert turned to Timothy Hackworth. "And you selected, in your estimation, the best two cylinders. Do you really think we would build twenty bad cylinders?"

"Well, you certainly built one bad cylinder!"

"If that is true—and I don't say it is—I am exceedingly sorry. I would never sabotage a friend—or my business!" Robert replied.

"An excellent way to treat your friends!" Hackworth said indignantly.

"I could help you fix the engine," Robert offered.

"I won't let you near my engine!" Hackworth roared. "I notice that *Rocket's* cylinders are operative."

"The cracked cylinder may have to do with your engine's design and not with the cylinder I built," Robert considered in all seriousness. "The inefficient engine may have put too much strain on the cylinder."

"Why you....you'd better be thankful I'm a God fearing man or I would blast you from here to kingdom come!"

"I believe you already have, sir."

"It's too good for you, Stephenson!" Hackworth said. "I will be speaking to the judges about this, you can be sure of that!"

CHAPTER THIRTY-ONE

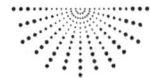

"*S*ans Pareil was in the lead. Timothy Hackworth's steam locomotive stunned everyone with its robust performance—reaching 17 ½ miles per hour while carrying 19 tons!—before coasting to a stop with a cracked cylinder, made, incidentally, by Robert Stephenson and Company Ltd, the builders of the Rocket, a competitor in the Rainhill Trials.*

Or not so incidentally. If anyone should be disqualified, does not sabotaging one's competition qualify?

Timothy Hackworth is convinced of wrong-doing and has loudly informed the judges—Mssrs. J.U. Rastrick, Nicholas Wood, and John Kennedy—of same. After consultation amongst themselves, the judges determined that Sans Pareil will run again on Friday the Sixteenth. So strong was her performance that, once the locomotive's repairs are made, the judges are convinced Sans Pareil will rank high in the list of competitors.

Even though Sans Pareil's weight was over the limit, there is talk among the judges it is still possible for Timothy Hackworth's Sans Pareil to be declared the winner of the Rainhill Trials!

Not since the excesses of the Prince Regent (affectionately called "Prinny") were brought to light, now our over-indulgent king, have we seen so much subterfuge, guarded secrets, conspiracy, extravagance, pageantry, corruption, fanfare, competition, and pomp and circumstance. As well as amusement, entertainment, and shock, for that is the labyrinth of our enigmatic king.

An apt description of what we have here at the Rainhill Trials. Add to all that accusations of sabotage!

It must be fate—possibly foretold in the stars—that the steam locomotive should enter the scene during the reign of King George IV.

The Royal Railways as it were."

– Thaddeus Fulbright, the Liverpool Mercury

SORCHA CLOSED THE NEWSPAPER, shaking her head. Thaddeus Fulbright was not one to temper his sensationalist tendencies.

If only he might utilize his ability to sway public opinion for good.

And not merely for personal gain.

Her eyes scanned the article again.

Still, there is nothing untrue in the article.

That must be an improvement.

He certainly might have ripped Robert Stephenson to shreds with accusations of misdeeds.

Sorcha knew Thaddeus was not afraid to do so.

She sighed heavily. *He isn't afraid of anything.*

He is my friend. And he was, indeed, gifted. *I wish to support him in whatever way I might.*

Unless he goes after other people unfairly.

Then he will know my wrath.

Sorcha didn't recall what Biblical verse that sentiment was from, but it certainly mirrored her feelings.

She knew it wouldn't make any difference—Thaddeus would be Thaddeus whatever she might say—though she could cause him a degree of discomfort.

And would enjoy doing so.

It is surprising he is still hanging about after all the arguments they had had. Most men would be on their way: they didn't like to be reprimanded by the 'inferior sex'.

Either Thaddeus had no regard for her opinions at all or they were actually fairly good friends that they could be honest with each other.

For some reason Sorcha hoped it was the latter.

CHAPTER THIRTY-TWO

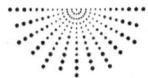

Grand Finale
October 14, 1829

"*T*hus shall mine anger be accomplished, and I will cause my fury to rest upon them, and I will be comforted: and they shall know that I the LORD have spoken it in my zeal, when I have accomplished my fury in them." – Ezekiel 5:13

"THERE ARE as many people here as there were on the first day of the trials," Sorcha exclaimed to Thaddeus.

"Possibly more. At least ten thousand people," Thaddeus surmised. "Maybe as many as fifteen thousand."

"The event just keeps growing and growing!" Sorcha exclaimed. She reflected on her own words. "Partly due to your sensationalist articles I expect."

"All true."

"That's debatable."

"The winner will be announced today," Thaddeus said.

The winner. The climax. The moment they had all been waiting for!

And it will soon be over. Sorcha felt saddened at the prospect at the same time she was beside herself with excitement to learn the winner of the Rainhill Trials.

Sorcha observed her father on the tracks helping to keep the crowds in check. Sean O'Shea had his work cut out for him today.

She was surprised Thaddeus wasn't down there too; if there was one thing she had learned about Thaddeus Fulbright, it was that he liked to be in the thick of things.

"The crowds are not surprising, I suppose. Everyone wants to know who the winner will be."

"Yes, *Novelty*," Thaddeus said.

"Do you still think so?" asked Sorcha, surprised at his dedication to his original premise.

"Yes. *Novelty* was last seen flying at the unprecedented speed of thirty miles per hour! Carrying forty-five euphoric passengers, no less."

"True…" Sorcha considered. "But *Novelty* only completed three runs."

"Yes, but she is fixed now," Thaddeus proclaimed confidently.

"And what about *Sans Pareil*?" Sorcha asked. "She did very well."

"Yes, *Sans Pareil* performed better than everyone expected, outrunning the *Rocket* in the first hour and in the turn-arounds."

"Has the *Sans Pareil* been fixed?" Sorcha asked. She knew Thaddeus was up on all the latest developments. While she worked on her drawings for her buttons in the evening, Thaddeus was always gathering information.

And her drawings were almost complete. But she needed to see who won the competition to settle the direction of the final paintings. Then, when she returned to Liverpool, the real work of transferring the drawings onto buttons began.

Sorcha wondered what Robert might be doing. *And where is he now?*

"Yes, the forcing pump was repaired and a new fusible plug put in place. However…" Thaddeus paused. "The judges are not going to allow *Sans Pareil* to run again after all."

"Why not?" Sorcha asked. It seemed everyone else had been given so many chances. "It doesn't seem right that *Novelty* should be given three extra chances—one still to come—and that the courtesy is not extended to Hackworth."

"*Sans Pareil* weighs too much. Simple. It didn't meet the entry requirements." Thaddeus shrugged. "The truth be told, my pals at *Popular Mechanics Magazine* are pretty angry too." He smiled at her. "They aren't as pretty as you when they're mad though."

Sorcha ignored the flirtation. "Why are they angry?"

"They think *Sans Pareil* is at least as good as *Rocket*. Possibly better."

"And do you?"

"Hmmm…in truth, no."

"Why not?" Sorcha was surprised Thaddeus favored *Rocket* in any category.

"*Sans Pareil* is not suited for large enterprise rail. High fuel consumption due to the flue-tube boiler instead of the multi-tubular boiler, which also limits the size the locomotive can attain."

"From what I've seen, Mr. Hackworth wouldn't take the judges' decision very well."

Thaddeus laughed. "You've got that right, Sorcha. The judges weighed *Sans Pareil* again, and Dixon said Hackworth 'must return to his preaching and own that he has been taught a lesson in humility.'"

"That remains to be seen," Sorcha said. "Though Robert said *Sans Pareil* shouldn't have performed as well as she did. But the fact remains that she did."

Thaddeus nodded. "True."

"And why don't your *Mechanics Magazine* friends perceive the flaws you do? Surely they must be mechanical experts."

"You would think so." He frowned. "Why don't you ask your engineer friend Robert Stephenson? I'm sure he will say the same. And I'm just as sure you will agree with him, as his opinion is clearly superior to mine."

Sorcha smiled at him. "Oh, Tad. Are you jealous?"

"Of course not! We're not a couple. Why should I care who you choose to mimic?" Thaddeus shrugged. "Anyway, I don't have time for courtship. I have my career to think about."

"That suits me as well." Honestly, the man was crazy. She would rather be courted by almost anyone than Thaddeus Fulbright. He was incorrigible and downright annoying. He had his moments when he was fun and interesting, to be sure, but one had to put up with everything in between.

"I thought it would." He frowned. "Though you appear to have time for both your job and suitors—as long as they aren't me."

"I suppose that is my business and not yours." She patted him on the arm. "But it has been fun, hasn't it, Tad? I hope we can stay friends."

"It's hard to say. It depends on my schedule. I might see you about, Miss O'Shea. Seeing as how we both live and work in Liverpool." He cleared his throat. "Maybe you'd like to go to the theatre and see Miss Fanny Price together?"

"Oh look! The *Rocket* is at it again." Now she knew where Robert was. She smiled, but in an instant her smile turned to anxiety.

Thaddeus whistled to himself, disbelieving. "Are they really going to try the Whiston incline?"

"And look, there are at least two dozen passengers." Sorcha said, unable to hide her concern.

"That's George Stephenson showing off again," Thaddeus grumbled. "I hope nobody may die from his escapades."

There was rapturous screaming as everyone grasped the rails of the carriage, the Rocket barreling to the bottom of the incline.

But George didn't stop there. He reversed the valve sequence then besieged the hilltop again, his passengers grinning from ear-to-ear, none the worse for wear.

"But this is more than a moment of fun and tomfoolery, Thaddeus added. "I have to say, in spite of Stephenson's theatrics, history just turned a corner."

"Whatever do you mean, Tad?"

"George Stephenson just won his debate with the owners of the Liverpool-Manchester line in this moment. And you and I were witness to it."

"His debate?"

"Over whether the stationery engine or the steam engine is a better fit for the future of the Liverpool-Manchester railway."

"I see," Sorcha considered. "He just proved that the steam locomotive can do the job better."

"Exactly."

"Even though he appears madcap and clownish, I don't believe George Stephenson ever has a moment of leisure," Sorcha added. "There is no wasted energy with that man. There is always a plan in everything he does."

"Or he has taken leave of his senses and decided to enter the state of madness on a full time basis instead of simply visiting on holidays."

"Thaddeus Fulbright, you are over-reacting as usual." Sorcha tapped her foot.

"What if George Stephenson hadn't made it?" Thaddeus frowned. "What would happen to all those people?"

"Oh, I think he had done all the calculations prior to the stunt."

"One can never be entirely certain where machines are involved."

"I suppose not." Sorcha sighed heavily.

He tipped his hat to her and smiled. "But who will win this competition is still up in the air."

She and Thaddeus were rooting for different teams, but there could be no question that all the talent here today was about to change the course of history.

CHAPTER THIRTY-THREE

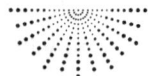

Grand Finale
October 14, 1829

"*Hackworth got many trials but never got half of his 70 miles done without stopping. Sans Pareil burns nearly double the quantity of coke that Rocket does and rumbles and roars and rolls about like an empty beer butt on a rough Pavement, moreover weighing above the contest limit of 4½ tons: the Sans Pareil consequently should have had six wheels. And as for being on springs I must confess I cannot find them out either going or standing, neither can I perceive any effect they have. Sans Pareil is very ugly and the boiler runs out very much: Hackworth had to feed her with more meal and malt sprouts than would fatten a pig.*

Hackworth must return to his preaching and own that he has been taught a lesson in humility."

– John Dixon, Resident Engineer Liverpool & Manchester Railway, as told to Thaddeus Fulbright, Liverpool Mercury

. . .

"Oh, look! The *Novelty* is about to begin." Sorcha exclaimed. She felt uncontrollable excitement.

Robert had since joined her, his eyes diverted to the track. This was the most tension she had felt during her time in Rainhill.

The race is between Novelty and Rocket now. Sans Pareil, Perseverence, and Cycloped have all been eliminated. Sorcha understood the stakes. She wrung her hands in anticipation.

This was a turning point for the Stephensons as well as for her. If looked upon in a certain way, up until now Sorcha and Robert were somewhat on equal footing. Robert was a working man, and she was a working girl. He was a professional man—an engineer—but Sorcha was a professional as well—an artist—though society might not reward her or acknowledge her in the same way as a man with equivalent skills was rewarded.

Also to her detriment, society looked down on the Irish, but that was social prejudice and had nothing to do with her skill level. She might be a factory girl, but she was not replaceable with anyone off the streets. Her skills were not low level, easily taught, repetitious functions.

One might think art to be less important than industry, but she was comparable in terms of her skill level and her work ethic.

But if Robert wins this race, we will no longer be on equal footing: there will be an ever growing chasm between us. His fame will soar to new heights, and he will go down in history. *I am a mere factory girl.*

I want Robert to win. Even if it means there is no hope for the two of us.

How could she not wish it? It was his dream and everything he wanted in the world. She cared about Robert—he was a good man who worked hard for everything he had—how could she not wish him happiness?

Robert took her gloved hand for an instant before releasing it. Social convention would not allow him too many liberties, not being her betrothed, but he couldn't help share this moment of excitement. It was a bit of a crush, and surely no one noticed.

The party all stood watching the tracks. Without speaking, Sorch crossed her fingers behind her back.

"So *Sans Pareil* was disqualified and *Perseverance* didn't come close to meeting the requirements," Thaddeus said, appearing out of nowhere, as he was wont to do. "Now is the moment of truth."

Robert nodded, not appearing delighted to see Thaddeus, but he was ever the gentleman.

Under her breath Sorcha said, "Mr. Fulbright, I'll thank you to show some consideration. Mr. Stephenson surely doesn't want his reaction recorded in this very personal moment, a moment which he has been working towards for his entire life."

"Naturally he doesn't. That's why I'm here." Thaddeus didn't budge. "It's my job, Miss O'Shea."

Sorcha glared at him. "Is it your job to be obnoxious?"

"I'm a newspaper man." He smiled. "I'm sworn to inform the public."

She raised her eyebrows at him.

"Don't distress yourself, Miss O'Shea," Robert intervened. "I am perfectly composed."

As you usually are. Sorcha smiled at him, her expression softening instantly. "As you wish, sir." She then turned to glare at Thaddeus.

"It's only my future unfolding before us," Robert murmured close to her ear.

"So you're here for the big race, are ya'?" George Stephenson joined them. He didn't appear to have a care in the world. Robert looked at him quizzically.

"Then it's back to work. No more goofin' off all the time." George added, looking at his son.

"Right. It's been one big holiday out here," Robert said.

"And where is your father, Miss O'Shea?" George asked.

"Didn't you see him?" she asked. "He's down on the tracks."

"Ah, yes. Crowd control. Only there ain't no controlling this crowd." George smiled, clearly enjoying all the activity.

In the bigger picture, the Rainhill Trials is the culmination of George Stephenson's life's work, as well as Robert Stephenson's, Sorcha thought. *But George has been waiting a good twenty years longer.*

"I'll be glad when it's over and we can go home," Lawrence said wearily. Everyone turned around in unison to momentarily gape at him before returning their eyes to the track.

* * *

1:25:40 pm

October 14, 1829

AND THE NOVELTY IS OFF!

"She's off to a slow start," Robert commented, looking at his watch. "The first leg was at eight miles per hour."

"The driver wants to be certain the boiler's joints will hold up under the new seals," George said. "After the explosion, they would have had to re-seal the boiler."

"It was a fire in the cinder, I believe, followed by the water feed pipe bursting," Robert considered.

"Right. The explosion." George nodded.

"At any rate, *Novelty* appears to be fully operational," Robert said.

George shrugged.

"Heavens! She's picked up speed," Sorcha exclaimed. "Looks like twice as fast."

"Exactly that. Sixteen miles per hour." Robert nodded.

The crowd roared in full anticipation of a spectacular showing followed by their favorite winning.

"Nothing will stop her now," Thaddeus exclaimed, waving his hat.

"Something might," George murmured. Robert was nervous, but George appeared non-plussed.

The third leg commenced as *Novelty* appeared to be preparing for victory.

"How fast is she?" Sorcha asked excitedly.

"About fifteen miles per hour," Robert said.

"Same as the Rocket," George said. "On average."

On the fifth leg Novelty headed westward, gliding towards the grandstand. As Novelty approached, ladies waved their handkerchiefs and men raised their hats.

The Novelty advanced toward them. In an instant there was an explosive gust of steam from the furnace.

Novelty glided to a halt.

It was 2pm. Novelty had been running for thirty-five minutes.

"Another explosion," George muttered.

Robert looked at Sorcha, then he picked her up and swung her around, kissing her cheek. She blushed, smiling into his eyes.

But it was a delightful feeling. And quite heady to be singled out by him.

I will remember this moment as long as I live.

"I apologize, Miss O'Shea, but I couldn't help myself."

"I'm so happy for you, Robert. You have won!"

It's over and I'll never seen him again.

Thaddeus pivoted towards George Stephenson, demanding "How did you know? How did you know *Novelty* would fail?"

"Why do you say I knew?" George asked with a sly expression and a wink to Sorcha.

"It was obvious by your remark that something might stop the *Novelty*." Thaddeus fumed. "Did you sabotage her?"

George laughed. "You're even crazier than I thought, son, and that's sayin' something!"

"Then how did you know if you weren't behind it?" Thaddeus demanded.

"When you've worked on engines as long as I have....I think I know my machinery." George raised his eyebrows. "And look, I don't need to sabotage anyone; I have the best machine. Why do I need to sabotage an inferior machine what's going to lose?"

"Just give it to me straight," Thaddeus begged.

"It's simple. The boiler had to be re-sealed. It requires days—if not weeks—to set properly," George said.

"So you're saying...if the boiler had had time for the seal to set...*Novelty* might have won?" Thaddeus demanded.

"It's possible," George nodded. "If wishes were nickels. And *Novelty* might have won had she been built better. *Sans Pareil* might have won if Hackworth had read the rules." George pointed to a bystander. "And that fellow might be the winner if he had worked for twenty years learning how to build engines then entered a locomotive."

"And *Rocket* would have won if she was ready when the contest started. Oh, wait, which was exactly what happened," Robert added.

"Right. I don't believe it was ever a joint in question. I had a good look at it," George said. "The Novelty's failure was not a joint but the collapse of a pipe conveying hot gases from the furnace to the boiler."

"So which is it, the joint or the pipe?" Thaddeus asked impatiently.

"Look here, Fulbright! Ask the builders of the *Novelty* themselves! Why are you asking us?" Robert retorted. "I'm tired of your haranguing my father because he has a better locomotive, condemning us then asking for our expert opinion in order to further your career. If you don't think we have any skill and are the inferior builders, why do you keep asking our opinion?"

Sorcha's eyes opened wide. She hadn't seen Robert angry before.

Thaddeus looked dumbstruck. *Good.*

"*Novelty* broke down three times over the course of the race," Robert continued. "She was given an extension to make repairs and the race went into the second week. Can the judges do any more than that? And there is no guarantee whatsoever that *Novelty's* engine wouldn't break down again, even if there was time for the seal to set."

"Or any guarantee that *Novelty* could haul anything of note," George added. "We worked hard, and *Rocket* won, and that's the bottom line. Put that in your paper."

Thaddeus bowed, then left without further adieu.

"What a buffle-headed gudgeon!" Robert exclaimed, shaking his head.

George stared after him. "That young reporter means well, he'll come 'round."

"Do you think so?" Sorcha asked, surprised that George Stephenson of all people was extending graciousness to Thaddeus.

George nodded. "Young fella' is just startin' out. Once he has 'o bit of experience and forgets some of his schoolin' he'll learn somethin'."

Sorcha couldn't help laughing. George had a way of lightening the moment. "I hope so."

Sorcha knitted her eyebrows, glancing after Thaddeus. She liked him in spite of her annoyance; he was a good man and a hard worker.

In all fairness, those were questions Thaddeus had to ask. So much rode on the outcome of the Rainhill Trials.

He got his answer.

CHAPTER THIRTY-FOUR

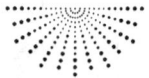

Rainhill Trials
Grand Prize

"*The Rocket is by far the best Engine I have ever seen for Blood and Bone united...The London Engine of Braithwaite & Ericsson called The 'Novelty' was a light one, no Chimney upright. She only weighed 3.7.3 and did not stand 10 ft high. A Water tank under the Carriage close to the Ground and Boiler Bellows were all covered with Copper like a new Tea Urn which tended to give her a very Parlour-like appearance. When Novelty started, she seemed to Dart away like a Greyhound for a bit, but in every trial she had some mishap: first an explosion of inflammable Gas which Burst her Bellows, then her feed pipe blew up, and finally some internal joint of this hidden flue...so that it was no go.*"

– John Dixon, Resident Engineer Liverpool & Manchester Railway, as told to Thaddeus Fulbright, Liverpool Mercury

. . .

"AND THE WINNER IS...THE *ROCKET!*" the judges declared. Robert and George Stephenson stood on the podium in front of the Grand Stand to receive the certificate, prize with contract to follow.

Sorcha and her party were honored to be included in the crowd so near to the podium; spectators were lined a mile down the tracks.

She saw a young woman glancing at Robert quite a lot. He spoke to her and she positively glowed.

I know the feeling.

Sorcha stood near the podium clapping. "What do you think Da? Is it not exciting? I'm so happy for the Stephensons."

"The losers didn't fare so badly either," Mr. O'Shea said. "*Sans Pareil* and *Perseverance* were given large consolation prizes of about 24 pounds each to help defray expenses."

"So much? Our entire family could live off that for a year!" Sorcha said.

Sean O'Shea laughed. "Yes, but could you build a steam locomotive with it, Sorcha Fae?" Sean O'Shea laughed. "And that's not all." He winked at her. "I've heard talk about the directors buying some of the other locomotives."

"Oh, really?" Sorcha asked. "Which ones?"

"The directors are in discussion about purchasing *Sans Pareil* as well as commissioning two locomotives from Braithwaite and Ericsson."

"Oh, my goodness!" Sorcha exclaimed. "I guess all the entries can win here."

"And yet—there are still hard feelings among many," Mr. O'Shea lowered his voice, though it wasn't necessary in the commotion. "Those rooting for both the *Novelty* and *Sans Pareil.*"

"The competition did take on the personality of a sports game," Sorcha agreed. "I never saw losers so angry!"

"Didn't seem to be much of a competition to me," Mr. O'Shea said. "*Rocket* was the only locomotive to complete the trials."

"Maybe if the others had had more time..." Sorcha said.

"Maybe. If wishes were horses then beggars would ride. And what about you, lass?"

"What about me?"

"Do you need more time?"

"More time for what?" Sorcha asked.

"More time to decide who you like best of your suitors: Mr. Stephenson or Mr. Fulbright."

"Don't be ridiculous, Da." She glanced at Robert on the podium—so handsome was he!—and sighed.

"Am I? You've been smelling of April and May since we arrived in Rainhill."

"They don't see me that way, neither of them."

Robert may think he does, but I am not where his heart lies. As for Thaddeus, *he is likewise too preoccupied with his career. And he would drive a woman mad anyway.*

"Don't they? And which do you like best?"

"There is no competition there," Sorcha smiled.

But I'll never see him again.

Sorcha was no idiot, she knew Robert liked her, but not *enough.* Maybe if there had been more time to get to know each other. They lived in two different cities—they were easily one-half day's travel apart on a good road.

And everyone knew there were no good roads in England.

Besides, even if they lived in the same town, Robert would likely not have time for her: he was extremely ambitious and very busy with his work. When he had to stand about with nothing else to do, he had no objection to talking to her.

But this is not real life.

Mr. O'Shea pressed. "And which gentleman is the clear winner?"

Sorcha shrugged secretively.

"Well, you know," Sean posed "I imagine Robert Stephenson is a bit of a knight in shining armor, but you may find that Thaddeus Fulbright has some of those qualities himself."

"Tad? Are you serious Da? He's only interested in one thing."

"And what is that?"

"Building a name for himself. And he doesn't care who he hurts to do it."

"You might be a bit harsh there, Sorcha. He is honest and forthright from what I can see."

"He is that."

"You can't fault him for having a different opinion from you, Sorcha."

"Oh can't I?"

"And, aside from that, Mr. Fulbright may yet develop stellar qualities if he is encouraged in the right direction. Seems to me he has never had anyone who was much invested in him. Not to mention that a knight in shining armor might be too busy fighting dragons to have time for the damsels."

There is more truth in that than you know.

"Thaddeus needs to grow up," Sorcha pronounced.

"Men have been known to do it." Sean chuckled to himself. "I see you've not thought much about poor Enoch."

"I find I like a man who has some conversation," Sorcha said. "With some indication there are thoughts in his head."

"Yes, one can only stare at the silent type for so long, no matter how beautiful to the eye."

Sorcha sighed, murmuring, "These past few days were the most exciting and romantic days of my life."

"Indeed me girl." Sean nodded. "Made possible by the railways."

CHAPTER THIRTY-FIVE

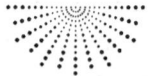

Rainhill Trials
October 15, 1829

"*C*ongratulations, Robert. I'm so happy for you." Sorcha said as he approached her after leaving the podium. *Your life will surely change so much now.*

I wish mine might, but I will return to working most of the time. Sorcha didn't mind working, or even working hard, but she had learned what it was to experience pleasure and leisure and to work in moderation, along with speaking with those who made her feel very alive in their presence, challenging her intellect and making her laugh.

She felt admired, even treasured.

Robert took her hand, seemingly unaware of everyone around them. "Please, Miss O'Shea, do join me in the café where we can have a private conversation."

There was enough of a din that they could talk without being over-heard in the café, even though people might stare at them.

Robert was famous now. He led her to a private table in the corner where he ordered some lemonade, being allowed some privacy.

"Miss O'Shea," he began nervously. "My next job will be attending to a new railway line in Leicestershire. But I wish…I hope I may call on you at some point in the future in Liverpool."

"Call on…*me?*" She swallowed hard. "Yes, I'm sure a visit would be wonderful." But she didn't expect it. *You'll be moving on with your life now….*

Her disbelief must have been written across her face because he continued, "Surely you can't think me indifferent to you, Miss O'Shea?"

"Why, no, I don't." And he had gone to a great deal of trouble to meet with her amidst his victory. But no doubt she would slip his mind in a week or two when they went back to their old lives.

Or she went back to her old life and he went on to his new life.

He took her gloved hand and she felt a tingle. "I feel we've only started to form an acquaintance, which now is cut short." He frowned.

"Yes, I wish there had been more time," she agreed.

"And yet…I feel…I do know you very well, Miss O'Shea, and I like all that I have seen," Robert added. "I feel there is something between us that could lead to…something more than *friends*…"

Sorcha felt her heart quicken at the thought.

Robert searched her eyes. "You look as if you don't feel the same, Miss O'Shea."

"I do…believe me, I do…" She saw him release his breath, a slight smile form on his lips.

"Then what is it, Miss O'Shea?"

I think you'll be very busy and my memory will fade.

But I would love to be proven wrong.

Or maybe I don't believe you because I don't think myself worthy.

Sorcha hoped that wasn't it. But she knew the ways of infatuation. "You will be travelling in far different circles, Robert, meeting high class ladies. I mean ladies of far higher social standing." Ladies who wouldn't even look her in the eye but would raise their chins and look elsewhere. She had seen a bit of that condescension here.

"You can't think that matters to me, Miss O'Shea. My father was raised very poor. We've earned everything we have."

"Yes, but…you will be thrown in with all the most famous people. You'll, no doubt, meet the mayors, possibly even the king and queen of England!"

He shrugged. "I suppose my life will change now. But mostly we'll still be working all the time. Our fame is dependent upon producing something. You know, my father and I, we are not so much focused on money and prestige, as we are on work. We like to work and we like to create things. We are no different from any other working people."

"Just smarter and more successful." She smiled at him.

Robert laughed, releasing her hand. "Miss O'Shea, I hope I am not premature. I just feel, when I am in your company, that I could enjoy being so...for an extended period of time...*forever.*"

"*If only...*Oh, Robert...But we're just getting to know each other. You can't possibly..."

Sorcha couldn't believe what she was hearing. *I wish it might be so.* When he was in the whirlwind of his new life, her 'company' might not be so enticing.

What is wrong with me? This is a dream come true. And I keep pushing him away. She couldn't help herself. Ever since they had met she felt he was so far above her, that he would judge her, that he couldn't possibly be interested in her, that he would be appalled if he saw her 'real' life. This had never felt attainable to her and she had never completely relaxed and been herself. Surely her intuition must tell her something?

He is welcome to prove me wrong!

She hoped he might come and visit her, and then they would see how things went.

If he came at all.

"And what do you think of me so far, Miss O'Shea?"

"Oh, my goodness, what is there not to like?" she giggled. *Obviously you are perfect in every way. Handsome, smart, and now rich.* "You have a character I like. Though maybe a bit too ambitious. In truth, I wonder if you will be working all the time."

Robert burst out laughing. "I do like to have a bit of fun, Miss O'Shea."

"I suppose I am a bit intimidated by you, Robert."

"You are so intelligent and beautiful, Miss O'Shea," he said softly. "I think there is something there."

"You may certainly call on me, Robert." *If you find the time.* "I would love to see you again."

Suddenly there was screaming over by the grandstand.

Robert jumped up. "Excuse me, Miss O'Shea, I must go see what is wrong. My father is still over there."

"Of course!" She stood and they both rushed outside the café to see what was happening.

CHAPTER THIRTY-SIX

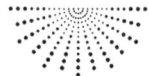

"You Won Because You Cheated"

"Stop! Oh no! He's got a pistol!" There was yelling and screaming over by the podium where George Stephenson was still standing. Sorcha clasped her gloved hand over her mouth in terror.

"You cheated, you bastard! You got rid of the competition!" the attacker yelled.

"And how did I do that?" George asked.

"You blew up the *Novelty*! But you had the *Sans Pareil* fixed even before the race!"

"I didn't do either. The *Rocket* won fair and square."

"No! No! Don't talk to him Dad!" Robert started to move forward and Sorcha grabbed his arm.

"Don't distract him, Robert, he may shoot you!" Sorcha said in a raised voice.

"I have to go and try to save my father!"

"I'm sure the shooter hates you just as much!" Sorcha was terrified for Robert's life.

"Look, Robert, look!" Sorcha admonished, clutching his sleeve. Sean O'Shea stood behind the shooter. She didn't know whether to be relieved or mortified.

By the time Robert gets there it will be over.

Please don't hurt my Da.

"My Da will take care of him," Sorcha said reassuringly, though she didn't feel reassured at all.

"Can you be certain, Sorcha? How can he possibly stop a madman?..."

She wasn't certain. She never knew if her Da would live or die. She only knew he had to try. He couldn't see injustice and not step in.

The shooter aimed at George, hesitating just enough for his victim to savor the fear of death.

From behind him, Sean O'Shea slammed the gunman's arm, driving it upward, and the shot went high and wild. There was screaming and running in every direction.

The assailant reached forward with his thumb and cocked the hammer back again while trying to hit O'Shea with his other fist in an attempt to dislodge the death grip on his arm.

"Dear God," exclaimed Robert, "the man has a double barrel gun. He's got another shot left!" At this realization, Robert hesitated no longer and rushed towards the scene, not thinking clearly at this point about what he could possibly do.

Sean O'Shea must have realized there was another bullet, though Sorcha doubted her father had ever seen one of the new-fangled weapons, a rich man's toy. Sean grabbed the madman's arm with both hands in a death grip and began throwing the assassin around through sheer strength. The gunman himself was no small man either, with long, scraggly hair and a wizened, scarred face.

This wasn't either's first brawl.

Instead of running for cover knowing that he was the intended victim, George Stephenson then kicked the assailant in the shins, causing him to bend his legs. The gunman, now outraged, pulled a small dagger from a sheath in his pocket with his free hand and began attempting to stab O'Shea.

Sean O'Shea grabbed his would-be murderer's wrist which was still holding the firearm. The gunman's knifing hand was free. George punched the gunman in the stomach followed by a swing to the man's side. O'Shea then kicked the man's legs out from under him.

"Do you surrender?" O'Shea demanded. "You must surrender for your own safety!"

The attacker fell onto the ground, crumpled, but managed to hold onto his gun. As he tried to raise the gun, George's boot went onto the attacker's hand while O'Shea retrieved the pistol with some difficulty, as the gunman's grip was intense.

"Surrender now!" O'Shea commanded. "You leave us no choice but to hurt you if you don't surrender."

The man looked up at Sean with hatred in his eyes. Obviously he could not endure the pain of failing at his supposed holy mission.

Just when the ordeal appeared to be over, the attacker threw his knife at George who dodged it. The deranged assailant then pulled out a smaller single-shot pocket gun, evidently his backup in case the fancy double-barrel pistol misfired. He aimed the Derringer at Sean O'Shea's heart.

Sorcha gasped.

Sean O'Shea fumbled for control of the pistol. The gun went off and shot the shooter, dropping the man flat to the ground.

"Oh, dear God," Sean muttered. "Damn fool. It didn't have to end this way."

Sorcha watched in horror. It might have been her father to die!

Sorcha ran forward now.

George Stephenson reached under the attacker's chin to check the man's pulse.

"He's dead," George pronounced.

"He would've killed me," Sean said. "And you, Mr. Stephenson."

"You don't have to tell me that, O'Shea. I was here, remember?" George patted him on the back. "Thanks for savin' me life. I owes ya' O'Shea." George chuckled. "I've never lost a fight, but this might've been the first."

"You probably would have fared better if I hadn't been here, George. Having someone else enter the fray just complicates the matter."

"In a fair fight that might be true." George raised his eyebrows. "This was anything but fair."

216

Sean looked at the Derringer still in the dead man's hand with the double-barrel pistol lying beside him. By this time Robert and Sorcha were by Sean's side.

"That's not a working man's pistol," George said pointing to the ornate crest on the side of the pistol. "Probably stole from his employer."

Sean leaned closer. "That pistol is made by James Wilkinson & Son." He closed his eyes and said a prayer for the departed, making the sign of the cross.

When Sean opened his eyes, Thaddeus Fulbright was admiring the pistol, several paid constables having joined them.

"Ah, Fulbright. Do you know anything about this?" Sean demanded.

Thaddeus looked up, astonished. "Certainly not! Are you accusing me of assisting in such a heinous act? I believe in slaying with words, not with weapons."

"I never thought you would kill. But maybe you knew about this in advance and didn't tell anyone," George said.

"Of course not!" Thaddeus retorted. "I have opinions, which I'm entitled to, but that doesn't make me a murderer or a conspirator! That's not in the realm of a gentleman."

"Nope. You got that right." George appeared satisfied. "I had to ask, just like you asked me some pretty insulting questions, wanting to hear the answer from me mouth. You're the only other person I know who took the races personally."

Thaddeus raised his eyebrows. "I'm not a murderer, sir. And plenty of people had issue with the outcome of the race, many from respected circles."

"And some not." Sean looked down at the dead man. "This is what comes from spreading lies and stirring everyone up."

Thaddeus rolled his eyes which he then returned to the pistol. "This is the crest of the 8th Earl of Katney. He resides near Liverpool."

"It will have to be investigated," The chief constable said, "But I expect we'll find the earl had nothing to do with this and the dead man was a former servant."

"Yeah." George shook his head. "The rich man is never guilty. That's something I've learned in me lifetime."

"I have to agree with the constable," Sean said. "The man was so full of rage, it was very personal for him. He wasn't working on anyone's orders." Sean glanced at Thaddeus.

"Oh, Da!" Sorcha threw her arms around her father. "I'm so glad you're safe!"

Sean nodded somberly, looking at the body before him. "You're not the only one me girl."

CHAPTER THIRTY-SEVEN

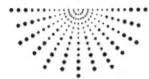

Rainhill Trials
October 15, 1829

"*We* may now consider the trial of Steam Engines at an end, though some say prematurely. With a great deal of discontent among both experts and spectators alike, the dye is cast and the outcome is irrevocably attached to the future.

Whether prematurely or not, we may consider the trial of Steam Engines at an end.

Among those competing for the grand prize, Mr. Burstall's engine Persever-ence was not sufficiently powerful to compete with the other three. Mr. Hack-worth's engine Sans Pareil was disqualified for being overweight. In consequence of the number of petty accidents which occurred to the London Engine, the Novelty, Mssrs. Brathwaite and Ericsson took their engine to pieces after the Saturday's performance, unadvisedly it may now be considered, and the re-glueing of the joints did not have time to set.

The course is thus left clear for Mr. Stephenson. We congratulate him, with much sincerity, on his receiving the grand prize of 500 pounds and a lucrative contract to outfit the Liverpool Manchester line in passenger steam locomotives. Quite the contest win indeed!

But it cannot be denied, in the interest of accurate reporting, that the grand prize of public opinion was won by Mssrs. Braithwaite and Ericsson: for their decided improvement in the arrangement, the safety, the simplicity, and the smoothness and steadiness of a locomotive engine. However imperfect the Novelty's contest performance may have been, nine-tenths of the engineers and scientific men now in Liverpool predict that the principle and arrangement of this London engine will be followed in the construction of all future locomotives. The beautiful mechanism of the connecting movement of the wheels, the absolute absence of all smoke, noise, and vibration, and the elegance of the machinery—in short, the tout ensemble—proclaim the perfection of the steam locomotive.

If there had been sufficient time, who knows what the Rainhill Trials outcome might have been? It is much to be regretted that the Novelty was not built in time to have the same opportunity of exercising which Mr. Stephenson's Rocket had and that there is nowhere in London or its vicinity any railway where experiments could have been performed. It will evidently require several weeks to perfect the working of the Novelty and the proper fitting of her joints.

All fairness aside in the selection of the winner of this one contest, the Rainhill Trials, the question of steam locomotives in general is now answered to the satisfaction of all. That is, the argument between the fixed engines vs. steam locomotives is now unequivocally resolved.

***The steam engine has won the contest and has soundly won!** Which steam engine should have won is a matter of some disagreement but not the engine itself."*

– Thaddeus Fulbright, Liverpool Mercury

"Much sincerity indeed!" Sorcha exclaimed as she flapped the newspaper in Thaddeus' face. "You congratulated Mr. Stephenson while inferring that he didn't deserve to win!"

"It's a newspaper man's perogative." Thaddeus shrugged. "I reported the facts."

"I notice that you perform all manner of atrocities under the umbrella of being a newspaperman," Sorcha retorted. "The *Rocket* won fair and square. The *Novelty* couldn't haul the goods. And then it blew up for a finale!"

"But when the *Novelty* raced…it was a beautiful sight." Thaddeus sighed, recalling the happy memory now etched in his brain. "The thrill, the excitement. Many engineers thought *Novelty's* sleek design was perfection."

"Because of the way the *Novelty* made you feel is why you wrote this. It has nothing to do with logic and what actually happened."

"Oh, and are you without feelings, Sorcha O'Shea? And can it be how you feel about Robert Stephenson which colors your favorite?"

"True. The *Rocket* would be my favorite whether it won or lost. But the fact remains that the *Rocket* did win! A fact you seemed to overlook!"

"I believe I say that in the article."

"No. You say that, had it been a fair competition, *Novelty* would have won."

"In my opinion—and in the opinion of many experts—that is true."

She shook her head. There was so much misinformation out there that the public would believe anything. "This is not objective reporting, Thaddeus Fulbright, it is wishful thinking and imaginary fiction."

"Then why do so many experts agree with me?"

"Who knows why people are blinded by beauty, elegance, and their own desires? People often start out with what they want to believe then set out to prove it."

"I'm required to present the experts' arguments, as opposed to yours, Miss O'Shea," Thaddeus retorted.

"As opposed to the facts, Mr. Fulbright! The experts also thought the stationery engine was a better choice than the steam engine." She sighed. "I just want you to be the best newspaperman—and the best man—you can be, Tad, and this is not it."

"And if you, Sorcha O'Shea, were the best woman you could be, maybe you would hold your tongue now and again!" He was indignant. "It is insulting to malign my integrity, Sorcha O'Shea. If you were a man, I would call you out."

"If you were a man, you wouldn't have written it! It's nothing more than a passel of lies to justify your insupportable position."

Sorcha had not often seen Thaddeus angry, but she could see the indignation in his eyes.

"Miss O'Shea, I have tolerated a great deal of plain speaking from you with equanimity, but this is too far to attack my objectivity. Don't you know it is not becoming or lady-like to boss men about and to correct them?"

"Perhaps so, but when men are wrong, someone should tell them so."

CHAPTER THIRTY-EIGHT

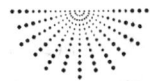

Rainhill Trials

*T*he Rainhill Trials is now concluded and all participants and observers are returning to their comparatively uneventful lives.

For how could anything compare to the past ten days filled with glimpses into the future beyond our wildest imaginings?

Except for, of course, the winner of the trials, Robert Stephenson *&* Co., which will now be astonishingly busy harnessing the power of steam to build the locomotives for the Liverpool-Manchester Railway: the first railway in the history of the world to carry passengers!

The thrill of this event, for those of us who were there, may never leave us. We all await with excitement the opening day of the Liverpool-Manchester Railway, which may not be too far in the very near future, as told to this reporter by George Stephenson himself. The same George Stephenson who may reasonably be thought to have pioneered the railway, which will no doubt prove to be one of the most important technological inventions of the 19th century, powering us into the future.

George Stephenson, now being called the "King of the Railways" was aptly named after the reigning kings of the United Kingdom. Which King George is *his namesake, we don't know, but it must be noted that there is a bit of the "Mad King George" in him. That is not merely this reporter's opinion: observing George Stephenson driving Rocket with reckless abandon, the exclamations "Crazy!" "Maniac!" "Unhinged!" "Mad!" and "Lunatic!" were often heard among the awestruck crowd.*

Let us just say, if we may, there is a fine line between genius and insanity, and George Stephenson walks that line. Or possibly his character is merely an effervescence and lust for life, shocking in its rarity. One thing is certain: George Stephenson can put on a show!

Robert Stephenson may have designed and built the winning locomotive **Rocket**, *but, without George Stephenson there could be no Robert Stephenson & Co. It was George Stephenson who insisted on the use of steam engines over stationery engines, and who cofounded the first company in the world to build steam locomotives (Robert Stephenson & Co, e.g. "Forth Street Works"), along with his son Robert Stephenson, Michael Longridge of Bedlington Ironworks, and Edward Pease, a woolen manufacturer from Darlington with a decided interest in the transport of goods.*

These four partners stand to become very rich indeed with the contest win— or, shall we say, the turn in the tracks?—inspired by the Rainhill Trials.

It might be said there were no losers in the Rainhill Trials: there were only entrants who failed to win. The directors bestowed prizes upon all of the steam locomotives entered, some quite substantial. **Sans Pareil**, *which was disqualified for being too heavy, was awarded an astonishing 24 pounds. Not only that, but the directors purchased* **Sans Pareil** *for 550 pounds to be used on the Bolton & Leigh Railway.*

In spite of that unheard of consolation prize, San Pareil's builder Timothy Hackworth complained about that massive sum, as he complained about every-thing during the Trials, saying the astonishing amount didn't cover his expenses. Never was a loser rewarded so much while complaining so unre-lentingly.

Perseverance *came in fourth among the steam locomotives, only reaching a speed of 6 miles per hour. Even so, builder Timothy Burstall had the audacity to propose building a locomotive for the Liverpool-Manchester Railway, which was naturally denied by the Directors. Burstall was awarded 25 pounds to help defray his Rainhill Trials expenses, again, an astonishing sum to someone whose entry was of no use to the Liverpool-Manchester Railway. Essentially, a gift.*

The Directors of the Liverpool and Manchester Railway are generous indeed, consisting of merchants and businessmen from Liverpool and Manchester: Henry Booth, Charles Lawrence, Lister Ellis, Robert Gladstone, John Moss, and Joseph Sandars.

*Then, there is, of course, the crowd favorite the **Novelty**. Against George Stephenson's recommendation—which seems a bit uncharitable, given Stephenson's win—the directors placed an order with Braithwaite and Ericsson for two locomotives, to be named William IV and Adelaide, the next in line for the throne. Which may not be long in the future considering King George's declining health.*

Only time will tell who built the best locomotive, but certainly no one can say not everyone was given a chance. It can no longer be thought true in evidence of the actual events which have transpired since the winner was declared.

– Thaddeus Fulbright, Liverpool Mercury

"I SUPPOSE THAT IS A BIT BETTER," Sorcha said as she read Thaddeus' notes to be published.

"A bit better?" Thaddeus complained. "It was pure torture and went against every feeling."

"You still got your snub in." Sorcha raised her eyebrows.

"What's the point of being a newspaper man if I can't do that, I ask you?"

"I suppose you must be true to yourself, striving to corrupt the facts and demean those who don't deserve it with your witticisms and inferences," Sorcha acquiesced.

"Very good of you to allow me that, Miss O'Shea," Thaddeus grumbled. "I hope you are quite pleased with yourself in your latest emasculation of men."

"I live for nothing else, I assure you," Sorcha replied.

"That is a truth most evident." Thaddeus cleared his throat. "I notice you don't exert your efforts upon every man."

Sorcha raised her nose in the air. "Some are too masculine for even my powers."

"Ouch!"

Lawrence, Sorcha, Mr. O'Shea, and Thaddeus prepared hastily for their return trip to Liverpool. Lawrence liked to be on friendly terms with the newspapers, his only area of good sense, Sorcha thought, so he asked Thaddeus to join them in the Davenport's carriage.

Thaddeus was delighted to increase his comfort level, not having to fight for a tiny spot on the mail coach, squished in between the smoking older gentleman and his plump wife, as he had been on the road to Rainhill.

All of the party had a different perception of their departure. Lawrence was delighted to return to Liverpool, considering Rainhill to be much too boring as well as lawless. Thaddeus was pleased: he had his story. Mr. O'Shea was sad to leave his duties but relieved to be abdicated by the local constable: it was determined the killing of the assailant was an accident of self-defense as well as a service to those present.

A happy accident, Sorcha thought. *Or, perhaps it wasn't an accident; Da did not make mistakes in his aim.*

Da had no choice in the matter but to turn the assailant's gun on himself for the safety of all concerned. But those would remain her private thoughts. Some things were better left unsaid.

Not generally a philosophy she lived by, but she was not about to endanger anyone, least of all her Da.

Sorcha herself was the only one of the party sad to leave Rainhill. She completed her assignment, to be sure, but she was disappointed to leave Robert just when they were becoming acquainted.

I'll never see him again. Not to mention he was beginning his new life while she returned to her old life.

Naturally Robert thanked Mr. O'Shea profusely for his bravery in saving his father's life, and naturally he held both the O'Sheas in high esteem, but she and Robert never had an opportunity to speak privately again.

Sorcha sighed. That was a 'holiday romance' cut short, she supposed. Now she knew what the experience meant: both a 'holiday' and a 'romance', neither of which she had previously experienced. To be sure, Sorcha read all of Jane Austen's and Maria Edgeworth's novels, much to her mother's chagrin, who imagined her daughter would develop romantic ideas. But reading about something was far different than experiencing it!

Until now Sorcha had felt no serious pangs of the heart. Was it because Robert was so perfect, or was it because there was something there? At any rate, 'it must be improper that a young lady should dream of a gentleman before the gentleman is known to have dreamt of her'. Sorcha read that in Northanger Abbey, and the line burdened her now.

'Beware how you give your heart'. Jane Austen was right.

Now it is back to work. Her hand went over her notebook, which told the story of her grand adventure.

Never to be forgotten as long as I live.

CHAPTER THIRTY-NINE

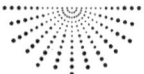

The Factories
Davenport's Textile & Mercantile

"Whatever is wrong, Violet?" Sorcha asked. She returned to her work station at *Davenport's Mercantile* to find Violet, who had a desk beside her, crying.

Sorcha brought her drawings back from the Rainhill Trials and was working on sample buttons to show Mr. Davenport.

"I canna' say." Violet continued weeping into her handkerchief.

Sorcha stood up and took her co-worker's hand. "Violet, can I help with something?"

"No." Violet shook her head while sobbing. "No one can."

Violet was generally volcanic, but that was theatrics. Sorcha had never seen Violet so upset: she was genuinely distressed.

Not many people even glanced at them because everyone had tight deadlines and were carefully watched by the shop steward. At any rate, they had seen workers upset before.

Factory work was hard, especially for children. Children 9-16 years were limited to 12 hours/day of work and nine hours on Saturday. So a

69 hour work week for a nine-year-old! Owners were required to provide a lunch break at least.

Adults were still worked like animals, particularly immigrants, but Sorcha and Violet had higher status because of their skills—artisans who were not easily replaced had status with Mr. Davenport—Violet even more so because of her association with Lawrence.

Sorcha and Violet were not on assembly lines—they worked independently—which greatly improved their working conditions. Though they still worked exceedingly hard and were high producers, especially Sorcha.

The noise was so loud that it made talking difficult, something Sorcha usually appreciated sitting next to Violet, but she was worried about Violet in her present state. When it was time for their lunch break Sorcha left with Violet, heading behind the building to sit with her.

"Violet, why don't you trust me?"

"I can't trust no one, Sorcha."

"Why not?"

"There's nothin' you can do, Sorcha. An' if people find out I'll be cast aht!"

"Cast out? What could you possibly do that would…?" Once outside, Sorcha pressed her. "What is wrong, Violet?"

"It canna' get any worse!" Violet burst into tears.

Fear gripped Sorcha's heart. "Are you with child, Violet?"

Violet shook her head up and down, sobbing.

"Oh. I see." Sorcha swallowed hard. *This is not good.* Violet wasn't married, so she would be ostracized, lose her job, and not have any way to feed and house herself and her baby. "Thank goodness you have a family. Still, it would be much better if the father of the baby marries you."

"Na, you don't see, Sorcha! Me family chucked me out of the 'ouse. I ain't got nowhere to live."

"Oh, my goodness. How could they? Their own daughter?"

"They said I was a slut and I could move into the poorhouse." Violet gasped.

"The workhouse? Oh, no! That is so unkind!" Sorcha bit her lip. "Who is the father? Can he be made to marry you?"

Violet shook her head, refusing to answer.

"Is it Lawrence?" Sorcha asked.

Violet burst into tears. Sorcha put her arms around her. "And what did Lawrence say when you told him?"

"'E said it weren't 'is baby. I told him there weren't no one else, but he didn't believe me."

"Oh, he believed you all right, Violet!" Sorcha said angrily.

"Do you think so?" Violet looked up hopefully as if this had never occurred to her.

"Of course he does! He just refuses to do the honorable thing." *He always does.*

"But he said…"

"He knows he's the only one." *You've been smitten. Everyone has seen it.*

"He is! I swear on me life! But he don't want to marry me, Sorcha. He said he never will. I thought…I thought he loved me. He said so."

Lawrence says a lot of things. Almost none of it true. Sorcha couldn't believe Violet would fall for Lawrence's lies, but maybe she really was that naïve.

Sorcha shook her head. *Oh, Violet, how did you let it go this far?*

"It's difficult to believe those we love would lie to us and betray us. I'm sure it hurts," Sorcha said consolingly. She knew she shouldn't condemn Violet right now when Violet had been abandoned by everyone she loved, offering her nothing but criticism.

"I've gotta' 'ave a job, Sorcha! Lawrence kept makin' demands, and I quite fancy 'im. What was I to do?"

Seriously, Violet, did you think that was the only option open to you?

But Sorcha had been at the receiving end of Violet's haughty display of superiority for months as well as the pawn in Violet's games, so she knew Violet had entered into this relationship with her own motives, not always admirable.

Still, Lawrence was a heel and was behaving abominably. Maybe Violet always imagined Lawrence would marry her.

It seemed Violet truly loved Lawrence. Clearly her heart was breaking. "Do you want to marry Lawrence, Violet? Even after he has treated you so badly?"

"Lawd, yes!" Violet sighed. "I don't blame him for not wantin' to marry me. I'm a nobody and he's…he's…a proper gent."

Sorcha felt her stomach twist into knots. "You're every bit as good as

Lawrence, Violet. And no gentleman would treat a lady this way. A gentleman wouldn't have demanded you go to his bed without marrying you first."

Violet shook her head with her obvious desire to take up for Lawrence, tears beginning to well up again.

Sorcha could see there was no point in bad-mouthing Lawrence, because Violet would have none of it. Sorcha would have thought the bubble had burst, but Violet remained strong in her devotion.

"Do you love Lawrence?" Sorcha asked, disbelieving, although she saw the truth in Violet's eyes.

"O' course I do. Who wouldn't?" Tears began rolling down her cheeks. "But wot difference does it make?"

"And which hurts worse, Lawrence's rejection or your family's?"

"Lawrence's, o' course."

Sorcha was aghast. She could see that Violet was enamored of Lawrence, for some reason. He must appear suave and debonair to her. As well as powerful, accomplished, and attractive to the eye.

"Personally, I would rather be in the workhouse than married to anyone who treated me that way," Sorcha said. She hoped to fuel some anger in Violet, but it didn't appear to work.

"Oh, no! You can't know what yer bleedin' sayin', Sorcha. I can't think of anything worse. They may even separate me from me baby!"

"Oh, that's horrible! I forgot about that. Separating a baby from its mother is a very cruel practice," Sorcha considered. "One would have to have no heart at all to do such a thing." *And consider the poor to be no better than vermin.*

Being poor was a great sin in the eyes of society, so the poor must be punished. Government thought these cruel acts would deter the poor from being poor.

As if anyone wanted to be poor.

"I'd do anythin' to protect me baby," Violet said. "Even something sinful."

"My father always tells me to do the right thing, no matter how bleak it appears. Don't despair and let your troubles lead you down an ungodly path. Go on the right path and it will work out." As evidenced by Violet thinking she had to give in to Lawrence. The worst that could have happened if she had resisted is she would have lost her job. Now she had a much worse problem: she would soon be unemployable with an extra mouth to feed.

"This ain't the time for your sermonizin' and actin' all superior," Violet said bitterly. "*It won't work out.* I won't be able to get another job. I'll be in the poorhouse for the rest of my life." Violet sobbed.

"That won't happen, Violet. You don't have to quit work yet. And you can come and live with me. You can sleep in the same room with me and my sisters."

"I can?" Violet looked up from her sobbing, not believing the kindness shown to her by someone whom she had not always treated kindly.

"Yes. We will do what your family should have done."

"And when Mr. Davenport gives me the ol' heave-ho?" Violet gasped.

"You can paint buttons at my house. I'll take them in as if I painted them and I'll give you whatever money I make from them."

Sorcha knew very well Violet's buttons wouldn't be recognized as her work, but Davenport would still buy the buttons. Violet was his number two painter. They were paid by the piece. He couldn't keep a pregnant, unmarried employee for everyone to see but he wouldn't throw away money either.

"You're not without skills, Violet. You may be able to rent your own place with the proceeds, but you can stay at my home as long as you need to."

Would Violet continue with her backstabbing? Maybe. But what could Violet do to her now? The poor girl was at the end of her rope.

"Violet, if you come to my house, you must be courteous to all my family, and you must never steal anything or put any of my siblings in harm's way. Or even my family would throw you out. Then it really would be the workhouse."

"Oh, I wouldn't! I wouldn't, Sorcha!" Violet put her arms around Sorcha, still crying. "Oh, Sorcha, I can never thank you enough. You 'ave saved me life and me baby's life."

"I want to help you as much as I can, Violet. Now you must stop crying and go back to work. We must have the appearance of working normally, or Bernice will get mad. She can't be giving exceptions right and left or she gets in trouble. Bernice won't put her own job at risk, I assure you. And, as hard as it is to face, Lawrence may no longer come to your defense."

"Do you think not? I hadna' thought of that. Because…because…"

"Because he doesn't want the baby and you are a reminder of his misdeeds."

"I won't kill me baby, I won't!"

"There is no need to Violet. It wouldn't win Lawrence back anyway."

"You don't think so? Why not?"

"He told you himself he doesn't want to marry you. You must realize now he never did."

"Oh. It was just so he could…." Violet sobbed.

Sorcha took her hand. "Don't cry, Violet. He can't take your baby from you. We have to go back to work. We'll figure it all out in time."

"Yeah. Yeah, we gotta' do that." Violet dried her eyes. "I must go back to work."

"And Violet…" Sorcha added. "If Lawrence tried to get further…*favors*…from you, don't let him unless he marries you first!"

"Oh? Do you think I can make 'im?" Violet looked hopeful.

"I don't know, but you certainly won't if you give him everything he wants at no cost to himself. Have some respect for yourself, Violet, and make him respect you, too!"

"Alright, I will, Sorcha. I will for you."

"No, Violet. Do it *for you*. You deserve better than this ill treatment."

Violet shook her head. "I don't deserve nothin'."

"In the eyes of God you are as important as anyone, Violet! Never let anyone treat you as inferior!"

CHAPTER FORTY

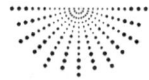

Mr. Davenport's office
Davenport's Textile & Mercantile

"These drawings are very good, Miss O'Shea."

"Thank you, Mr. Davenport. Next I will transfer them onto the buttons."

"There is something else I must talk to you about." Henry Davenport leaned back in his chair.

Sorcha knitted her eyebrows. There was disapproval emanating from her employer, even after presenting her excellent sketches. It didn't make sense. "Yes, Mr. Davenport?"

"Lawrence tells me your conduct was less than becoming at the Rainhill Trials."

Sorcha's eyes flew open wide, disbelieving her ears. "Lawrence said *my* conduct was unbecoming? In what way?"

"Among other things, he said you didn't treat him with the respect he deserves."

"I most certainly did. I treated Lawrence Davenport with exactly the respect he deserves. Probably much more." His words struck a nerve after dealing with a distraught Violet carrying Lawrence's child all morning.

"He says you took an unladylike attitude with him and talked down to him. Frankly, having observed your feisty temperament on occasion, it strikes me as believable."

Sorcha was not a shrinking violet, but she had always had a good working relationship with Mr. Davenport, so she was surprised by these words.

"In the first place, it isn't true. I did my job, did I not?" She pointed to the drawings.

"Lawrence also said you flirted with other men there, not reflecting well upon the reputation of the *Davenport Mercantile*."

Sorcha gasped and her hand flew to cover her mouth. "He...said... what?" Sorcha felt the blood rise to her head as her fury rose. "That is absolutely untrue, Mr. Davenport. I behaved with perfect decorum at all times."

"Do you deny that you were speaking to other gentlemen?"

"Of course not. Speaking. There were many ladies and gentlemen present who often initiated conversations with me. But I assure you my behavior was always above reproach," Sorcha retorted. "There was a bench where I sat to do my work and I sometimes spoke to people who spoke to me. I didn't realize being unfriendly was a condition of my job. I was always in public."

"Lawrence said that another gentleman even took your hand."

Sorcha knitted her eyebrows together. *What could he be speaking of? Perhaps when the Rocket won? Oh, yes, Robert took my hand for an instant.*

Sorcha closed her eyes momentarily. She couldn't let this stand. "That was a dear friend of mine—and, incidentally, the winner of the contest. He took my hand and I congratulated him."

"So you don't deny it?"

"Why should I? I did nothing improper. And how do you suppose Lawrence behaved towards *me*, Mr. Davenport?"

"I suppose he treated you with respect as befits his station." Mr. Davenport cleared his throat. "And yours."

"Then you haven't been paying attention, sir." Sorcha felt she had to call Henry Davenport on his misconceptions, or he would believe what

Lawrence said about her. "I am shocked that you didn't question these accusations, sir."

"That's what I am doing, Miss O'Shea."

"This strikes me as more of a conviction than an inquiry." Sorcha knew she had to take a chance on clearing her good name. A lie just kept escalating and growing bigger. "If you are actually interested in my side of the story, Mr. Davenport, then let me inform you that while I was working, Lawrence was flirting, drinking, and gambling."

"I don't like your tone, Sorcha. This is just what Lawrence said."

"I don't like having my reputation maligned, sir, when I have done nothing to deserve it. Mr. Davenport, I went to Rainhill as you requested. I did my job while I was there. I was courteous to Lawrence unless he was discourteous to me. The truth is, Mr. Davenport, that Lawrence is always flirting with me and treating me like I am a strumpet. And I'm not the only one. He treats every pretty girl in his department in exactly the same way." *Which I'm sure you know but have chosen not to see.*

"Your attitude is very unbecoming, Miss O'Shea. I'm beginning to think Lawrence had the right of it."

"Because I am taking up for myself against these false accusations? And did Lawrence tell you that one of the shop girls is now with child and he is the father?" She didn't want to reveal the name and get Violet dismissed. Moreover, if Mr. Davenport took the story to Lawrence without a name, and Lawrence revealed the name, that would be an admission of Lawrence's guilt.

Mr. Davenport gasped. "Miss O'Shea, that is a dreadful accusation!"

"No, Mr. Davenport. It was a dreadful act. And now Lawrence is making accusations against me as a way to continue his vices and to get revenge on me for repulsing his advances. You need to do something about Lawrence, Mr. Davenport. He is constantly making improper advances to the women in his employ, lording his power over them. He has no respect for the girls, and no respect *for you* to compromise your business in this way. When are you going to make him grow up and behave like a man? And he has no intention of doing the right thing by the girl with whom he has fathered a child and marrying her."

Mr. Davenport's face was turning red in anger over the supposed actions of his son, but he turned his anger onto Sorcha. "How dare you speak like this to me, Miss O'Shea!"

"I didn't commit these acts, Mr. Davenport. Lawrence did. So why are you angry with me for telling you the truth? You attacked my good character when I walked into this room after I did a job for you, or I would never have told you. You think it acceptable to attack my character while the one pointing the finger is the one with the questionable character."

"How dare you, Sorcha! How dare you speak of my family in this way."

"Not of your family, Mr. Davenport, *Lawrence*. Douglas is beyond reproach. He is a man of character and discipline. He has a work ethic and he respects his employees. He should be running the store, not Lawrence."

"You are stepping outside your station, Miss O'Shea," Henry Davenport said angrily. "You have no right to direct me."

"Maybe I do, since I have suffered at Lawrence's hands. I most certainly wouldn't have said anything if your son hadn't spread lies about me while mistreating every woman in his employ. And I have to clean up the mess when the mother of his child comes crying to me. Is that my mess to clean up? Or yours? I'm only telling you because *only you* have the ability to make Lawrence do the right thing." *An ability you haven't exercised up to this point.*

Mr. Davenport grabbed her drawings, opening his desk drawer and placing the drawings in his desk. He took out a few pound notes and handed them to her. "Miss O'Shea, leave the premises immediately. Your employment here is terminated." He shook his head. "I can see it was a mistake to hire an Irish girl."

Sorcha was shocked. Mr. Davenport had always been nice to her and she never thought he could treat her this way. But she was determined that Mr. Davenport not see how he had hurt her. "You can insult me, Mr. Davenport, however undeserved, but do not insult my homeland. It is quite possible that my father saved your son's life at Rainhill. And I know that my father saved George Stephenson's. My Irish father has character, bravery, and he knows right from wrong. Which is more than I can say for you, at the moment, I am sorry to say it, sir. I thought I knew you better than this, and I thought you were a gentleman."

Mr. Davenport opened his mouth then closed it, his eyes concerned. She wondered if he was not completely insensitive, though he gave a good impression of being so.

Sorcha stood, moving her eyes towards his drawer, biting her lip. She knew Violet couldn't paint buttons with her drawings. She doubted Mr. Davenport would find anyone else who could. But she didn't want to insult Violet to Mr. Davenport.

Sorcha got to the door, turning to look at him before she exited. "I have tolerated much and I have worked hard for you. If you wish to punish me for your son's behavior, it is only going to hurt your business, Mr. Davenport."

Sorcha closed the door behind her. She leaned against the door momentarily as her eyes filled with tears.

CHAPTER FORTY-ONE

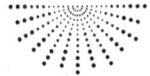

Reflections

*A*fter Sorcha left the room, Henry Davenport leaned back in his chair, thinking back to a conversation he had with Sorcha O'Shea some months ago.

This conversation made him wonder if there was truth in what Lawrence said.

Sorcha was, indeed, a young lady of strong opinions which she was not shy to express.

Opinions which sometimes make no sense.

In truth, Henry enjoyed his conversations with Sorcha and didn't mind her extreme, radical views. They were a source of amusement to him, keeping him from falling into boredom. Ever since his wife Eleanor had passed away, Henry had been very lonely. Eleanor had been a lively and uncommon woman, surprisingly well read, and he missed their far from predictable conversations. Sometimes his wife's unpopular opinions made him angry, but he still missed them.

But it was a fact that Miss O'Shea didn't seem to know which side her bread was buttered on. Henry didn't want any employees who brought unwelcome attention to his business.

"Lawrence saw you at an abolitionist gathering protesting slavery, Miss O'Shea. You realize, of course, that we rely on the cotton industry in the United States, which owes it's success to slavery?"

"Be that as it may, I will never support the enslavement of another human being," Sorcha replied softly.

"I am glad you can afford your high ideals, Miss O'Shea. Fortunately for you and your family I cannot."

"With all due respect, you might feel differently if you were the one to be enslaved, sir. You might think there is another path."

There was a large anti-slavery group in Liverpool, the center of the trade, where more than 4,000 slave ships had sailed out of the ports. There was so much opposition now in Liverpool, but the Davenports—and even the MP—supported the slave trade.

"So you don't deny, Miss O'Shea, that you have been to the abolitionist meetings?" he asked.

"Certainly not. My free time is my own. Or does your belief in slavery extend to me?"

"N-n-no! I didn't mean that, Miss O'Shea! I merely meant I can't have rabble-rousers in my employ!"

"Being an Irish immigrant I understand being a second-class citizen." She raised her chin, adding softly. "It cannot be right to treat humans as property."

"It's a bit hypocritical to be employed by the textile industry but to take such a stance, Miss O'Shea. I don't see how you'll do well in business."

"I want to work hard and I want to be a good employee, but business is not my primary concern, Mr. Davenport."

"And what is your primary concern?"

"I want to be a person of integrity, to love and be loved, and create beautiful art."

"That is admirable, Miss O'Shea. But, really, your outrage is misguided. There have been no slave ships in Liverpool since 1807."

"Yes, Mr. Davenport, but, as you well know, slavery is still legal in the British colonies. It is reprehensible. Until slavery is outlawed in both Britain and her colonies, I will continue to protest."

Mr. Davenport scoffed, shaking his head at the foolishness of youth.

CHAPTER FORTY-TWO

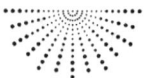

The streets of Liverpool

*W*hat will I tell my parents? How will we live? Will we have to move back to Hockenhall Alley? Sorcha gasped. *Oh, please God, anything but that.* Sorcha ran out into the street crying.

Thump! Sorcha ran into someone who was walking at a forceful pace along the street. The impact of their movements caused her some pain. "Ouch!"

"Sorcha?" The gentleman asked her. He took her by he elbow. "Are you alright? Are you hurt?"

She shook her head noncommittally. "Hello, Tad."

In an instant he saw that she was crying. "Sorcha, whatever is wrong?"

Thaddeus had obviously been in a hurry to get somewhere.

"Don't worry yourself, Thaddeus. And you appear to be busy."

"No. Not at all. It can wait." He was now completely focused on her. "Why don't we go to the *Neptune Coffee House* on High Street and we'll share a pot of tea?"

Sorcha nodded without talking. Telling Thaddeus her troubles was not going to solve anything, but she wouldn't mind a cup of hot tea.

And it would be a welcome delay to telling her parents she had both lost her job and gained a boarder. Another mouth to feed.

Disastrous work for one day.

"Oh, no! I just thought," Sorcha said, stopping in her tracks. "Violet doesn't know my address."

"Violet?"

"She works in Davenport's… she's in trouble…"

"Violet…I remember Lawrence mentioning a Violet…" Thaddeus was talking to himself now as he was wont to do.

"I don't want to go back!" Sorcha sobbed. "But I have to tell Violet…"

"Wait! No! This Violet needs your address?" Thaddeus didn't understand, but he comprehended that Sorcha's address needed to be communicated to Violet. He raised his eyebrows. His expression said that he also didn't know why Sorcha couldn't tell her, but Sorcha must have her reasons.

"I'll tell her. What is your address, Sorcha?"

"12 Scotland Road."

Thaddeus took out his notepad and wrote it down. "Does Violet have a last name?"

"They'll know who she is inside."

"Stay here, Sorcha. Do you promise me you'll stay here and wait for me?"

Sorcha nodded.

Thaddeus tore the paper from his notebook, ran into the building, and in no time was back by Sorcha's side. "I gave the note to the secretary who assured me he would give it to Violet."

How is my family going to pay for an additional person now that I have lost my job? Sorcha felt her grief well up inside her. Of all things she hated to be a burden on her family. She had taken such pleasure in improving her family's lot and now she had messed everything up by not swallowing her spleen and keeping her mouth shut.

Maybe Violet will contribute something for food. She still has employment. Sorcha gulped.

Who knows? Mr. Davenport might have sacked me either way. He seemed determined to believe bad things about her. *Easier than believing bad things about his son*, Sorcha supposed.

Thaddeus dotted her eyes with his handkerchief then put his arm in hers, leading her forward. He didn't dare put his arm around her out in public, but he appeared to know that she needed support.

They made their way on the winding road, passing horses and carts, as well as a few private carriages of the wealthy, to the Neptune Coffee House.

Although High Street was parallel to Scotland Road where she lived, Sorcha had rarely been on High Street. Scotland Road housed many immigrants, being close to both the docks and to the outskirts of the city center. Of course, Sorcha walked to and from work every day—there were no other options for a poor girl—so they had to live somewhere reasonably close by to their employment.

To work. Sorcha sobbed again. *What will I do without a job?*

Naturally I'll have to get another job. But it would likely be under considerably worse conditions, with longer hours and less pay. The factory acts of 1825 and 1829 stopped the employment of children under nine, except in silk mills where children under nine could still be employed. With the enactment of the factory acts, children ages 9-13 could not work more than eight hours without a lunch break—but they could be worked 12 hours per day! This "restriction" of a mere 69 hours per week for a 9-year-old, which factory workers complained about as being too much government interference, did not apply to women and men, who could be worked even more. One would think factory owners would get better work out of employees they were not working to death.

She supposed she should be thankful for the job she had had at *Davenport's*, which delayed being forced to join the work force most women were subject to. And she still had some savings under the floorboard.

Thaddeus led her to a table where they were seated. Sorcha patted his hand, embarrassed to ask. "Do you think…might we…?"

"What is it Sorcha?"

She suppressed a sob. "Do you think we might order chocolate? Of course, if it's too expensive…I've only had it once before…I shouldn't ask when you've been so kind…"

Thaddeus laughed. "Of course we might have chocolate, dear Sorcha."

Thaddeus ordered the pot of chocolate and some biscuits. Sorcha couldn't help looking about the coffee shop as a guilty pleasure: the wood paneling and books created a warm atmosphere, along with the scent of the coffee, tea, cream, and pastries.

She had never been in a coffee shop except at the Rainhill Trials, which was much more hectic and had none of this relaxing atmosphere.

Sorcha smiled as she remembered the café. The last time she had been there was with Robert. It had not been that long ago, but it seemed like a lifetime ago.

I miss Robert. Those were happy days. The happiest.

She remembered looking into his sapphire blue eyes and wishing they didn't have to be separated, feeling giddy just looking at him.

Then she looked at Thaddeus, with whom she felt relaxed, and she was actually glad she didn't have to bear this pain alone. She had felt as if she would burst with grief only a few minutes ago.

Thaddeus studied her with concern, his blonde hair falling into his chocolate brown eyes. Somehow she felt comforted just being in his presence. Funny that someone who had annoyed her on so many occasions was such a comfort to her now. *I suppose because I know him so well and there is nothing I have to prove to him.*

Should I be here alone with a man? She looked around and saw several couples, but not too many. There were many ladies, all well-dressed, with obvious female companions, who weren't as well-dressed. The ladies present tended to be in twos or threes.

Sorcha shrugged. It was a public gathering, and poor women didn't have the luxury of chaperones as the wealthy did. Even though she knew Mr. Davenport's accusations of impropriety weren't true, she supposed Mr. Davenport's words still stung and she was feeling defensive and self-conscious.

The chocolate arrived and the warmth felt so good both in her hands holding the mug as well as drinking the sweet, hot liquid. Biscuits were also served, which Sorcha happily took. Somehow the combination, as well as being with Thaddeus, lifted her mood so much.

She wished this moment might never end.

I wish I might never have to go home and explain my mistakes.

* * *

"WHATEVER IS WRONG, SORCHA?" Thaddeus asked. He was pretty sure it had something to with work since she should be at work now.

Sorcha didn't answer.

"Is it Lawrence?"

Sorcha bit her lip. "In a manner of speaking."

"What happened Sorcha?"

She still couldn't answer.

"Is it Mr. Davenport?"

"Yes." She nodded. "He dismissed me."

"He what?" Thaddeus couldn't believe his ears. "How could he shoot himself in the foot like that?"

Sorcha shook her head. "He was very angry. Lawrence told his father I was disrespectful to him and that I behaved improperly at the Rainhill Trials."

"WHAT?!?" Thaddeus appeared shocked. Then he started to chuckle. Almost everything made Thaddeus laugh, even terrible occurrences. As usual, the ridiculousness of the situation occurred to him.

Annoyance replaced Sorcha's grief. "It isn't funny, Thaddeus Fulbright! This is tragic where my family and I are concerned!"

"I didn't know there was a way to behave improperly at the Rainhill Trials. Between the pickpockets and the fighting, the bar was set pretty low." Thaddeus shook his head, his gaze intent upon her as he attempted to compose himself, generally failing. "How were you improper, Miss O'Shea?"

"Without decorum. Shamelessly. Apparently I threw my cap at every man who came around."

"Only one to my knowledge."

"I certainly did not! At least I wasn't improper."

"Most assuredly not." He appeared to be deep in thought.

"Maybe this was a mistake. I shouldn't have told you." She started to rise.

He grabbed her arm and pulled her down forcefully. He appeared suddenly serious. "This is ridiculous, Sorcha. You're the least flirtatious woman of my acquaintance." Thaddeus felt his face flushing with anger. "The bastard!"

246

"Please! We're in a public place," Sorcha whispered.

"Well he is one. We all know you tolerated more at Lawrence's hand than you should."

"I told Mr. Davenport that Lawrence is disrespectful to the women in *his* employ, and, worse than that, he is a womanizer. Which, of course he is."

"Sorcha." Thaddeus felt a sudden alarm, touching her hand gently. "You weren't as blunt with Mr. Davenport as you are with me, were you?" Sorcha should take up for herself obviously, but Sorcha was not inclined to mince words and she had no diplomacy. A man might be able to get away with it, but never a woman.

"I told him the truth if that's what you mean."

Thaddeus sighed heavily. "Whatever possessed you to insult Davenport's son? Why didn't you just say the accusations weren't true?"

"Well, I did!" Sorcha bit her lip. "I don't know how to tell only half the truth. I had to defend myself. Of course, Lawrence only wants to deflect scrutiny off himself onto me. Accusing me of what he is doing. Which is usually what the guilty do."

Sorcha wrinkled her brow. "Or maybe he was mad because I rejected his advances and he wanted revenge, I don't know."

Thaddeus felt a sudden alarm. "Sorcha, you're saying Lawrence made advances…?"

"Of course, he always does." Sorcha shook her head. "Oh, you mean… no. No more than usual."

"Did he…*touch* you?"

"He tried, but my umbrella made fast work of that." Sorcha smiled for the first time.

"Ah yes, I recall." Thaddeus smiled, adding somberly, "And were there other times?"

"Usually it is just flirtation, which is bad enough, but he seemed to feel he could take more liberties away from the work place."

"Bloody scoundrel!" Thaddeus muttered.

Thaddeus suddenly recalled the message he took to Violet. "Why does Violet need your address? Is she coming for a visit?"

"A long visit."

"Is she coming to live with you?"

Sorcha nodded.

"Why? Doesn't she have her own family?"

"She has a family."

In an instant understanding dawned. "Is Violet with child?" Thaddeus asked.

Sorcha's eyes flew open wide. "I shouldn't say. I promised I wouldn't."

"Is Lawrence the father?"

"How did you know? I didn't say." Sorcha giggled in spite of herself. "You're a better newspaper man than I thought, Thaddeus Fulbright."

"Simple deduction." Thaddeus grew serious. He had an idea, but it might get him in trouble with his boss. Egerton Smith was a friend of Henry Davenport's.

"It isn't my place to…"

"Don't worry, Sorcha."

"What are you going to do, Tad?"

"I'm going to have a little talk with Davenport."

"Oh, no! Please don't! You shouldn't."

"Why not? He can't hurt you anymore now, Sorcha."

"I expect he can!"

"I guarantee there is nothing he can do to you now." Thaddeus muttered under his breath, "Or he'd better not try."

Sorcha shook her head. "I don't like the idea."

"Are you afraid he'll go after you?"

"Well…*yes*. He's a powerful man in Liverpool. He could blacklist me from any job. I have to have work. Surely you must see that." She dabbed her eyes with her handkerchief.

"What happened to your drawings of the Rainhill Trials, Sorcha?" Thaddeus asked softly.

"Mr. Davenport has them."

"Who is going to make those buttons? Violet?"

Sorcha laughed. "No one else at Davenport's Mercantile can."

"How to get those drawings…" Thaddeus said to himself.

"Oh, that's not a problem. I have copies."

"You do?"

"Of course. I have the sketches and then I made copies for Mr. Davenport."

"Why?" Thaddeus asked.

"Because he wanted the sketches but I also need drawings to make the buttons."

"Could you make those buttons at home?"

"Of course."

"Why don't you set up your own shop then, Sorcha?"

"My own shop? Doing what?"

"Making buttons of course. You told me yourself no one in the city can match your work. You could display some of your paintings as well."

"A button shop. What a strange idea." Sorcha murmured. "But who would buy them?"

"The same people who buy them now. The wealthy elite."

"Oh, I don't think they would buy from an Irish girl."

"If they want the buttons they will! No one has trouble letting the poor do their work. Especially if it is a product they can't get anywhere else." Thaddeus reflected. "You could rent some space next to an established Haberdasher."

"Rent? That means I have to have money." Sorcha thought of her savings under the floorboard, but it made her extremely uneasy to think of spending it. The idea of investing in a business was completely foreign to her: that was for rich people.

"Yes, but to make money. You're only receiving a fraction of what Davenport is selling your buttons for. You would keep more of the profit."

"I don't have the money to pay rent." Sorcha shook her head. "Well, not much. And we'll need it now that I don't have a job." She gasped at the sound of her words.

"You don't have a job at this moment in time. It is possible a Haberdasher would want you in the space. It elevates their consequence. You would have to make some buttons to take around and show to merchants, of course."

"I could do that in a few days."

"Well, then, there is another option for you, Sorcha."

"Hmmm. I could at least try it to see what happens before I look for other factory work."

"Right. If no one is interested, at least you tried, and you've only lost a few days." Thaddeus smiled. He put her hand on hers. "But I expect something will come of it."

Sorcha shook her head. "Mr. Davenport wouldn't like it."

"I'm sure he wouldn't. But did you like getting fired?"

"Certainly not."

"And would you still be working for him, making those buttons, if he hadn't dismissed you?"

"Of course."

"Did he pay your for the drawings?"

"Yes."

"So you're even. You gave him some drawings for the payment and your debt is paid. Mr. Davenport indicated that the debt was paid."

"Yes, but I'm sure he has no intention of my making buttons from those drawings."

"There aren't any laws saying you can't reproduce those images, I guarantee it. He doesn't own the images and it's not his business what you do now. He has dismissed you from his life," Thaddeus said. "It will all work out, Sorcha. You'll see. You have a great deal of talent and you'll come around."

He patted her hand again and she felt strangely warm towards him. She didn't know Thaddeus Fulbright had this much kindness in him.

"It turns out you are my friend, Tad." Sorcha smiled at him. She did feel much better. The future still terrified her, but she now felt a way would present itself.

He has changed.

Or maybe she just never knew him.

"I am. And to think you criticized me for being loyal to my friends before." He cocked an eyebrow at her.

"I guess I did. Thank you, Tad. I feel some hope where I thought there was none."

"There's always hope." He took another sip of the warm chocolate, looking up at her over the rim of his teacup with a sinister expression. "And people aren't as all-powerful as you think. If you know where their weaknesses are."

Sorcha giggled. "That's the cut-throat Thaddeus Fulbright I know."

He raised his eyebrows in a foreboding manner. "Sometimes cut-throat is what is called for, Miss O'Shea."

CHAPTER FORTY-THREE

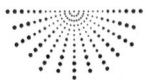

Mr. Davenport's Office
Davenport's Textile & Mercantile

"Thank you for seeing me, Mr. Davenport." Thaddeus said as he entered Henry Davenport's office.

Henry Davenport smiled from behind his desk. He was pleased with the effectiveness of his advertising in *The Liverpool Mercury*. "Have you seen Norton with the advertisements for this week? We have some exquisite offerings to rival London's fashions."

"Yes, I've picked up the advertisements. Now that the Liverpool Mercury railway line is not so far off, the woolens and cottons should be coming even more quickly from Manchester." Thaddeus said. "You might receive them before London does."

"That's what I've been told," Henry said. "The new line is the passenger line, but the *Forth Street Works* will be building newer and better cargo locomotives now that the steam engine has taken hold."

"That's what everyone expects. I had quite a few conversations with the engineers while I was in Rainhill." Thaddeus said. "As a matter of fact, I met two of your employees at the Rainhill Trials. I was in close contact with them for almost two weeks."

Davenport cleared his throat. "Yes, my son Lawrence was there."

"I remember him well." Thaddeus raised his eyebrows. "And your button designer was there as well, a Miss O'Shea?"

"We're going to have a new line of buttons commemorating the Rainhill trials." Henry Davenport opened his desk drawer and pulled out Sorcha's drawings, showing them to Thaddeus.

"Beautiful!" Thaddeus said. "I would love to place an ad about these buttons in the paper."

"In due time." Henry cleared his throat again. "They aren't ready yet."

"Aren't you worried that, since you dismissed Miss O'Shea, no one else will be up to the task?" Thaddeus shook his head. "She'll still make them, I'm sure, but she won't give them to you since you have broken your ties with her. I wonder who she'll sell them to?"

Henry jaw dropped and his face turned red. "She'd better not! Or I'll have the law after her."

"Oh? And what law would she be breaking in creating something only she can create?"

"She developed those drawings on my dime!"

"You don't own the images of the *Rocket*, or the *Novelty*, or the *Sans Pareil* for that matter, Sir. 15,000 people saw the objects of those drawings. There is no English law to protect the reproduction of images." Thaddeus smiled warmly. "Miss O'Shea gave you the drawings for payment so the transaction is complete. It's not her fault no one else can transfer the images to buttons."

"All the paper needs to know is that I will have exclusive rights to those buttons!" He shuffled the papers on his desk.

"I wouldn't count on that, sir. Now that you have dismissed Miss O'Shea, she is free to do what she will with the images in her head. I expect you have destroyed her loyalty, which was all you had to begin with. You don't own an artist. Particularly if you aren't paying her."

"It's nothing to do with you, Fulbright!" Henry Davenport narrowed his eyes.

"It is if you torment Miss O'Shea, continuing what your son started. It has a lot to do with me, sir. It's the *Liverpool Mercury's* business to report on injustice in society, the poor and the mistreated and

abused, those who are taken advantage of by greedy persons and institutions."

"There's been no injustice! I have treated Sorcha very well, giving her
an excellent salary. She is an ungrateful Bridget."

"Until you dismissed her for complaining that your son was
assaulting her along with other women in your employ. In exchange for
her mistreatment, Miss O'Shea has done an excellent job for you and
made you a lot of money." Thaddeus took his pencil from behind his ear
and began making notes.

"What are you writing?" Henry demanded.

"Merely noting your racial slur against Miss O'Shea."

"Everyone knows what the Irish are! No business owner should have
to be disrespected by his employees! She was downright rude to me.
Unladylike. I wouldn't take that from a man much less a woman!"

"You wouldn't have to, sir. Your son wouldn't be taking advantage of
his male employees the way he takes advantage of your female employees. I understand he's impregnated one of them."

"He has done no such thing!" Henry slammed his fist on his desk as if
to add weight to his rebuttal.

"We'll see in 9 months, I suppose."

"That's none of your business, Fulbright! And why is it your
concern?"

"The news is always my concern."

"You won't publish this in your paper! Egerton won't allow it."

"Maybe he will and maybe he won't. But I'm giving you a chance to
make it right before we both find out, sir." Lawrence shrugged. "This
could be a big opportunity for me to report a breaking news story. What
do you think of these titles: 'Heir to the Davenport Mercantile violating
his innocent female employees', or 'Department store owner's son
impregnating female workers'?

"You wouldn't dare!" Henry Davenport blasted, jumping out of his
chair, his face red.

"Of course I would! It's news. But I'm willing to curb my own ambition and go against my reporter's instinct if you do the right thing, Mr.
Davenport."

Henry Davenport pointed his finger at Thaddeus in a threatening
manner. "That's blackmail!"

"Not at all, sir. It's reporting. The story is true." Thaddeus shook his head. "Look. I was at the Rainhill Trials. I saw your son in action: flirting with the ladies, drinking and playing games of chance in the evening. I saw him with my own eyes. I am an eye-witness to Miss O'Shea's story: Lawrence was constantly imposing himself upon Miss O'Shea. That's how I met her, observing your son taking liberties, attempting to put his hands on her person. It was disgraceful. Miss O'Shea could have called the police right then and there."

"How dare you! I'll see you lose your job, Fulbright!"

"What is this? Fire everyone day?" Thaddeus laughed. "Egerton Smith might dismiss me—which I doubt, I never met a man with such a heart for justice—but if he does, another paper will pick up my story about how *Davenport's* treats their female employees. I won't be out a job. In fact, this story could be the boost my career needs. This is a story so big I don't need the *Liverpool Mercury.*"

Why am I putting my job on the line for Sorcha O'Shea? For all his bluster, Thaddeus was taking a big risk. He had just gotten a raise in salary and a promotion. He was going somewhere with the *Liverpool Mercury.* He would have to start on the bottom rung with another paper.

And yet, this was why many became newspaper reporters: to tell the truth. To reveal what people didn't want revealed. To make a positive change.

Thaddeus smiled to himself. Egerton Smith had gotten to him.

Let's hope he doesn't boot me out the door.

He became a newspaper man because he was aggressive, fearless, and nosy, he had a gift for language, he didn't want to be shot on the battlefield, and he didn't want to sit behind a desk. He liked to be physically active, but he didn't favor backbreaking work. It seemed the best option.

There was something else, too. When Sorcha was before him crying, Thaddeus felt as if his heart was breaking too.

Henry Davenport did that to her. Thaddeus frowned looking at the man before him.

Thaddeus had always experienced Sorcha O'Shea as brave, confident —and even *commanding!* She had been reduced to a puddle at the hands of injustice.

Henry Davenport broke her. It got Thaddeus to thinking about the effects of male exploitation of women. (Or the debasement of anyone for that matter.)

Thaddeus thought of Violet, who had been assaulted by her employer; her crime being she was young, pretty, and naïve.

Thaddeus considered how a person's treatment could shape their personalities—and sometimes break them.

It broke his heart to see that fiery Irish lass reduced to a person who felt helpless, afraid, and without confidence.

It isn't right. If there is anything I can do to change it...

"What do you want, Fulbright?" Davenport demanded.

Thaddeus grew somber. "Rehire Sorcha. Don't punish her for what your son has done. No one else is going to be able to paint those buttons anyway." Thaddeus stood from his chair, adding softly, "And, most importantly, don't interfere with Sorcha O'Shea's attempts to make a living for herself. Do not sabotage her efforts."

Henry Davenport glared at the young reporter, not indicating that he had any intention of complying.

"She merely wants to use her gifts to feed herself and her family. And, honestly, sir," Thaddeus continued. "if Lawrence marries that girl and the baby is born in wedlock there is no story."

"You want my son to marry that slut?"

"Oh, so you do think Lawrence did it?" Thaddeus chuckled in the contemptuous, mocking manner he had, tipping his hat to Henry Davenport. "But you blame the factory girl, the one who owed her job and her salary to your son? Lawrence definitely had the bargaining chip it seems to me."

Thaddeus shook his head smiling, as if he enjoyed the joke, taunting Henry Davenport.

"He's not a blackmailer like you, Fulbright!"

"Much worse I'd say." Thaddeus moved towards the door, waving his arm in a mock salute. "I'm just trying to help you out in advising you how to erase all my stories. That's helping you, not me." Thaddeus shrugged, a certain sadness in his one. "Anyway, I'm not the one who is interested: it's the people of Liverpool who are fascinated by the misdeeds of the rich and powerful. If no one did anything wrong there would be no story and no one would care." Thaddeus whistled to himself. "Frankly, Mr. Davenport, your eldest son is a goldmine for me; I know him well. He's not a man, he's a leech upon society. He preys upon women."

"Get out of here, Fulbright!"

"Yes, sir. You're right. No reason to give away my best lines. I'll save it for my article." Thaddeus tipped his hat. "Have a good day, sir!"

CHAPTER FORTY-FOUR

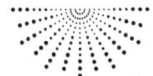

Newspaper offices of *The Liverpool Mercury*

haddeus didn't think he'd ever seen Egerton Smith so angry. "You went after Davenport? One of my oldest friends and biggest advertisers?"

"I didn't go after anyone. I directed Davenport to stop his son from assaulting his female employees. Otherwise, I would report on his son's actions in order to protect the female working classes." Thaddeus shrugged. "Davenport has a choice. Any other newspaper wouldn't give him the opportunity to make it right."

"Is it really that dire, Fulbright? It sounds like a sensationalist exaggeration."

"Lawrence Davenport is preying upon his female employees, that's the simple truth. How many? I don't know. How many is too many? You tell me, Egerton. And the father is further punishing these ladies by dismissing them when they tell the truth about it. The father is punishing his son's victims."

"Hmmm…" Egerton straightened his dark cravat, tied loosely around a white shirt with high points up to his ears. He was a broad-chested, manly, formidable person who turned heads wherever he went. "What about this Miss Sorcha? What does she claim Lawrence did to her?"

"I saw it myself with my own eyes, Mr. Smith. That's how I met Sorcha O'Shea. Lawrence was getting too close and grabbing her. She was attempting to push him away, so I ran forward to assist her. After such observations, and after being in Lawrence's company for a week, I have no doubt that Violet's story is accurate." Thaddeus shook his head. "In fact, I'd be surprised if there aren't more."

"But you can't prove it."

Thaddeus shrugged. "In nine months—more like eight—there will be evidence. And I *can* prove that Miss O'Shea got fired."

"Do you have a personal interest in this girl?"

"She's a friend. But that's not why I believe her story. Really, Egerton. Don't you keep your ears to the ground? Stories of Lawrence's conquests and gambling debts are everywhere."

"But do you have to ruin the father's business?"

"I'm not ruining anything. Henry Davenport has that well in hand. He is allowing his business to be damaged by turning a blind eye and choosing to turn his head the other way. I told him to do the right thing by his female employees or I'll print the story."

"That's blackmail."

"Funny, that's what Davenport said."

Thaddeus stood. "Look, Egerton, if you don't care about this story, I'll take it to another paper. Then Henry Davenport can't hold you accountable. I owe you that much. If I have to go to London, someone will want it." Thaddeus shook his head. "But if you don't care because it's only women involved—and therefore no one of importance—then maybe you need to search your own conscience as well. Who do we care about? Rich business owners? Do they really need our help? And why is it only the poor who have to have morals?"

Egerton nodded, motioning with his hands for Thaddeus to sit down. "I'll make a newspaper man of you yet, Fulbright."

"So what course do I take now?"

"Don't go back to see Davenport. I'll go see him. Then I'll let you know what story you're going to write."

"You're not going to squash my story?" Thaddeus asked suspiciously.

"No. But I am going to give you a raise."

CHAPTER FORTY-FIVE

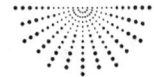

12 Scotland Road
Vauxhall, Liverpool

"*T*he girl is ungodly." Grandmother Oonagh muttered while mending her laundry.

"If Jesus can forgive her, I suppose I can too," Cecelia murmured while paring carrots for the stew. There were two Dutch ovens cooking in the fireplace: one for bread and one for stew. "She's been a help around here, she does her share."

"I should hope so, she eats like a horse," Grandmother Oonagh retorted.

"She's got a wee one cooking in the oven," Cecelia said, moving to pare the potatoes. She glanced at the Dutch oven in the fireplace which was cooking the soda bread. "God has given us all enough. We need to share."

Grandmother Oonagh shook her head. "She's a child having a child."

Cecelia nodded as she pared potatoes, grateful for the food. The meat from the butcher was sizzling in the fireplace, filling the room with delectable smells. "I agree, she's not as grown up as our Sorcha. But few girls are."

"She'll only return to her old ways, given the chance."

"Possibly so." Cecelia sighed. "But what would you have me do, Grandmother Oonagh? Kick her out on the street as her own family has done? It's no wonder she don't know right from wrong."

"Hmph!" Grandmother Oonagh sputtered. "Well, she might learn a thing or two by example."

"She does seem grateful," Cecelia considered.

"When she's not crying like a baby," Grandmother Oonagh added.

"That's the way of a woman with child," Cecelia said. "She's worried for the future of the child. She's thinking about someone else besides herself for the first time in her life."

"I never cried with none of me babies!" Grandmother Oonagh said proudly.

"I'm sure you didn't." *You never show the slightest sensitivity at anything.*

"Too much work to be done for that foolishness." Grandmother Oonagh picked up another garment.

* * *

"Hello!" Sorcha yelled from the front door, as she entered the kitchen. "Oh, it smells wonderful in here!"

"Check the bread, will you Sorcha?" Cecelia asked.

"What's this, Ma-ma?" Sorcha stopped at the kitchen table where she saw a children's book in her mother's place. She murmured aloud, "The Life and Death of Cock Robin."

Cecelia looked up from her chopping. "Oh. Molly is teaching me to read."

Sorcha smiled. "That's wonderful, Ma-ma."

"Humph!" muttered Grandmother Oonagh.

"Don't make too much of it!" Cecelia waved her knife in the air. "I just want to check out the recipe books from the lending library so's I can cook better for my family. I get tired of me own children having to read everything to me!"

"Naturally, Ma-ma! It's all for the family." Sorcha added under her breath, *"You should never do anything for yourself. That would be a sin."*

"Where have you been Sorcha?" Cecelia asked.

"Oh, just looking for a job."

"Did you have any luck?" Cecelia asked.

"Well…. I met a Madame Arquette who is a very elegant lady. And a seamstress. She may be interested in some of the girls' lace. Molly's is particularly good."

"Finest I've ever seen," Grandmother Oonagh considered. "And Felicity's would be too if she would but focus on her work."

"Felicity is only ten, Grandmother."

"When I was ten, I was not so lazy."

"Felicity does a fine job on the washing and pressing." Cecelia came to her daughter's defense. "I think she prefers that over the detail lace work."

"Hmph!" Grandmother Oonagh muttered, her eyes focused on her sewing.

Sorcha lifted the lid on the Dutch oven, smelling it's contents before lowering the lid. "Mrs. Arquette owns a dressmaker's shop on High Street."

"*High Street*," Cecelia emphasized. "Aren't we moving up in the world?"

"Not as yet." Sorcha shook her head. "We were just talking about possibilities. Madame Arquette was unsure of me, but she certainly liked my buttons."

"That's a start. I'm sure something will turn up," Cecelia said. "But I'd really hate to see you become a factory girl working the machines. Seventy hours a week is exhausting, even for a young person."

Sorcha bit her lip before turning to hug her mother. "I'm so sorry to put you through this."

"Because you can't keep your mouth shut, girl!" Grandmother Oonagh proclaimed.

Sorcha moved to hug her grandmother, who kept on with her handiwork. "And who do I get that from, Grandmamma?"

"Your mother's side of the family," Grandmother Oonagh muttered.

Cecelia whirled around, still holding her paring knife. "That's not true, and well you know it, Grandmother!"

Grandmother Oonagh shrugged.

"At any rate, Sorcha will get employment." Cecelia returned to her work. "It's just a matter of where."

Sorcha began to set the table.

"Oh," Cecelia added. "There's a letter came in the post for you, Sorcha."

Sorcha ran to the table in front of their couch and picked up the letter, gasping.

In the return address section was a design representing the *Forth Street Works*.

Robert Stephenson.

CHAPTER FORTY-SIX

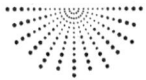

Mr. Davenport's Office
Davenport's Textile & Mercantile

"What are you suggesting I do, Egerton? Make Lawrence marry the girl? She's just a factory girl. She's not in any way a suitable bride for a Davenport."

"Do you know who she is?" Egerton asked.

"I have my suspicions." Davenport frowned.

Egerton cleared his throat. "Make your son accept his responsibilities, Henry. The only other option is to set the girl up somewhere in the country to have your grandchild. Is that what you really want to do, to reject your own flesh and blood?"

"I never thought you would turn against me, like this, Egerton," Henry Davenport said.

"It's my job to report the truth, Henry. I have professional and personal standards. I can't turn a blind eye to what my friends do and report on everyone else. That's hypocrisy and transparent to my readers."

"Why is it any of your business?" Henry demanded.

"If it weren't for the girl, it wouldn't be," Egerton replied. "She has been sorely used by your son. There is no other way to put it."

"What are you going to do?" Henry demanded.

"I'm going to run the story on shop girls, factory girls, and seamstresses either way—it's news and that's my job. But I won't name names if you give Miss O'Shea her job back. In that case I would then run a more anonymous piece on working girls in the city without naming names, with many of the same facts."

"Blackmail again."

Egerton Smith shook his head. "I'm giving you a chance to save face I wouldn't give to anyone else, Henry, because you are my friend."

"Why do you care about these girls?" Henry demanded.

"Because they were done an injustice. Because someone in a position of power is allowed free reign."

"Are you talking about my son?" Egerton stood.

"I've known you a long time, Davenport. You're a good man. But you aren't doing that boy any favors, and you certainly aren't doing yourself any," Henry added, "A businessman has a reputation to maintain."

"You don't have to tell me that!"

"Someone needs to rein in Lawrence. He's living like a titled lord." Egerton lowered his voice. "Look, Henry, because you're my friend I'm willing to do you a favor. I'm willing to run the story anonymously. But I'm not going to help Lawrence continue preying on the women of this city unless you give me your word you're going to do something about it."

Henry tapped his pencil on his desk. "You've said quite enough, Egerton."

"And what is your answer?"

"I'll let you know."

Egerton stood to leave. "Don't take too long." He tipped his hat. "And don't let me hear that you have cast the mother of Lawrence's child out into the streets or I'll be all over that."

In that moment Henry knew that kind, sensitive Egerton Smith, who cared about the people of this city, also had a backbone.

CHAPTER FORTY-SEVEN

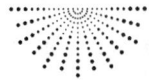

Forth Street Works
Newcastle upon Tyne

"*H*ow are the locomotives progressing son?" George Stephenson asked.

Robert wiped his brow. "While *Rocket's* brilliant performance at the Rainhill Trials removed all the directors' doubts, their purchase of *Rocket* and order of four more engines in her image—all to be delivered within three months—is perhaps overly ambitious."

George chuckled. "Do you think so, Son? I say 'the more the merrier'!"

"I'm sure you do, Father."

"Word is it, we'll need even more locomotives for the opening of the Manchester-Liverpool line."

Robert closed his eyes momentarily. "How many more?"

"I'm thinking a total of eight trains."

"*Eight trains,*" Robert repeated. "Including *Rocket?*"

"Yep. So you'll only have to make three more trains after you've completed this order."

"*Only.*" Robert sat down for a minute.

"No time to sit, son!" George admonished him. "Get to work."

In fact, George had never looked happier. The busier he was, the happier he was.

"When is the Liverpool Manchester Railway opening, Father?" Robert asked.

"We're planning for September 1830."

Robert raised his eyebrows. "*Ten months.*"

"Plenty of time," George pronounced.

"What about Novelty? I heard the Directors were still interested," Robert asked.

"Once *Novelty* was supposedly repaired, it was tried out again, but continued to break down. Though they build a beautiful work of art, Braithwaite and Ericsson cannot build an engine which can maintain a sufficient supply of steam." George shook his head. "In spite of this, the directors placed an order for two more locomotives, *William IV* and *Queen Adelaide*. Which will naturally perform no better than *Novelty*. And they won't be at the Liverpool Manchester opening."

"Surprises me. Braithwaite and Ericcson have had success with the steam fire engines in London," Robert considered.

"Yep. Not as much to haul."

"And what about *Sans Pareil*?"

"That's going to the *Bolton & Leigh Railway*," George said. "Nope. You've got seven trains to make."

"You know, father, I'd like to do something else in life besides make trains."

George laughed. "Maybe you should have thought of that before."

"It's not that I don't like making trains—I love it!—and I'm happy we won—"

"You were born to do it, son."

"Yes, but it's not all I want to do," Robert objected.

"What else do you want to do?" George asked.

"I'd like to get married…you know, to have a family…" Robert said.

"Well do that too then." George shrugged.

"It's a little difficult to court a young lady when I'm working every waking hour!" Robert protested.

"Ladies don't care about men working too much," George pronounced. "They like the secure life you can provide."

"Maybe so. But I have to find time to propose!"

"How much time do you need?" George asked, perplexed.

"At least two days travel time."

Suddenly George wheeled around, an idea capturing hold of him. "Tell me, son, do you have an Irish lass in mind?"

"I do."

"Isn't this a bit sudden? You've only known her two weeks." George asked. "Wouldn't you like to get to know her a bit better first before you become a tenant for life?"

"I certainly would!" Robert replied, frustrated. "But when am I going to do that? We're a day apart and I've never been busier. Better to get her here and we can get to know each other better after we're married. I don't want to lose her."

"That's not the way it's usually done, son."

"I'm well aware of that!" Robert retorted.

"Do you really think she's the right one for you?"

"Why not? She's pretty, she's smart, she'd be a good mother to my children."

"Yes. But she might want a bit more of your time than you can offer."

"I thought you said ladies don't care about that." Robert eyed his father suspiciously.

"That one might," George considered. "I thought you were thinking of someone else. Someone you've spent a bit more time with."

"Maybe I would like to work a bit less and offer Sorcha that affection," Robert replied.

"Not for the next year, you can't. It might be good to find a gal who doesn't care how much of your time is taken up."

Robert sighed. "I think it a better idea to find a gal who is the best match for me."

"I agree, son."

"But do you love Miss O'Shea?"

"Of course I do! She's a lovely girl. I like everything about her."

"Hmmm...What about Fanny Sanderson?" George pulled up a chair and sat down. "What about her? She's a lovely girl, too. And she's right here in town and love-struck. No doubt she wouldn't mind your long working hours."

"What do you have against Miss O'Shea?" Robert sat opposite his father and pulled out his pipe. He'd been working long hours and was ready for a break.

"Nothing a'tall! Brains and beauty, to be sure. But I don't see Miss O'Shea leaving her family in Liverpool. Even for a prize like you. Oh, I saw it, she had her head in the clouds over you, but I don't think she knows what she would be getting into. Not every girl wants to give everything up for a man who is rarely home." George leaned forward, smiling. "But some are."

"It's the wife's place to leave her home for her husband," Robert stated.

"True…" George considered, "But Miss O'Shea feels a great responsibility to 'er family."

"I'll take care of them." Robert shook his head. His heart was filled with longing for the happy moments he spent together with Sorcha. Her image kept running through his mind. "I can't get Miss O'Shea out of my mind."

"Infatuation. And you're so overworked your mind naturally moves to fairy tales."

Sorcha Fae. She is a fairy indeed.

"You're wrong, Father. I know I would be happy with Sorcha."

"Oh, I don't doubt it, son. But I'm not sure she would be happy *with you*." George leaned back in his chair.

"There's only one way to find out," Robert murmured.

"Give it a whirl! What have you got to lose?"

CHAPTER FORTY-EIGHT

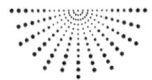

The Slop-Sellers and Their Victims
Suicide of a Poor Needlewoman

by Thaddeus Fulbright, The Liverpool Mercury

*N*either humanity nor shame moves the slop-sellers, who "grind the face of the poor, and afflict the soul of the needy."

The needlewoman's handler fares sumptuously every day off the labor of the needlewomen, who starve. The vitality of the poor needlewoman is siphoned off like a slow death by poisoning, replaceable by the next young woman. Utilizing their life force, the handler enters into the 'respectable class' while the needlewoman remains one of the undeserving poor.

A fine young woman, Eliza Kendall, industrious and virtuous, was driven to suicide, unable to support life upon the wages of shirt-making. Miss Kendall worked at home doing needle-work "slop work". The shop paid 1¼ shilling to 3 shillings, or a maximum of 1/3 pound, for each shirt, requiring four hours hard work per shirt.

On this wage Miss Kendall breakfasted, but did not look to have dinner. She often went for 24 hours without food while working 15 hours per day, using the money she might have used for food to light candles instead.

Unable to sustain this miserable existence, Miss Eliza Kendall, only 19 years of age, threw herself into a secluded spot of the River Mersey.

Is the murder of our young British women through nothing less than slavery "respectable"? Talented, hard-working, and industrious. Ask yourself how a skilled young woman of only nineteen could have lost all hope?

Miss Kendall worked for a Mr. Norman, who employs up to 200 girls, reminiscent of men who manage women for illicit purposes. The manifest tendency of this system is the destruction of life.

Thousands of females in this vast metropolis are daily subjected to the same toils: long hours and hard work for less than a sustenance wage. All Miss Kendall asked for in return for her hard work was to be housed, fed, and clothed under the meagerist of conditions.

Is it better for young ladies to leave the home and to travel to the factory? you may ask. But there are other villains to prey upon the virtue of pretty, young workers in the factory. This reporter knows of another case in a local Liverpool Department store where a young woman succumbed to the advances of her employer only to be made with child, abandoned by both the father of her child and by her own family.

Will this girl—little older than a child herself—be cast out onto the street while her child's wealthy family treats her with indifference?

The purpose of truth-based reporting is to illicit positive change, as my employer, publisher of the Liverpool Mercury, informed me: "That's the power of the written word: To change the world for the better."

We will put my editor's supposition to the test.

This reporter will give a full reporting with names and places if the father of this child does not do right by a young factory girl who naively believed his promises of love and marriage, hoping to escape a life of constant toil and an early death.

For, as seems to be the case, the "respectable class" cares more about their reputations and their image than they care about their own children—and the employees who make them rich.

May we strive for a more Christian existence where good triumphs evil.

Time will tell.

. . .

SORCHA PUT down her newspaper and smiled. *Thaddeus Fulbright, you may bring about a better world after all.*

CHAPTER FORTY-NINE

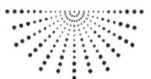

Mr. Davenport's Office
Davenport's Textile & Mercantile

"Thank you for coming to see me, Miss O'Shea," Henry Davenport said.

Sorcha didn't reply, merely nodding. She didn't know if Mr. Davenport had asked her here to insult her further. She had shown him the courtesy of following his bidding, and that was as far as she could go until she knew the reason for the summons.

"I'd like you to come back to work for me, Miss O'Shea," Henry Davenport said.

"And why have you changed your mind about me? Or did you?" Sorcha asked as politely as she could muster. She appreciated the gesture, but Mr. Davenport wanted to gloss over the insult he had given her—not to mention the economic threat to her family's existence—and pretend it hadn't happened.

Perhaps he feels backed into a corner by Thaddeus' article and has no change of heart at all. In which case, she wouldn't wish to be in Davenport's employ: she would surely be punished.

Mr. Davenport squirmed in his seat. "I don't believe now that you were the one at fault, Miss O'Shea."

Sorcha was surprised by his answer. "And who was at fault?"

Mr. Davenport threw his pen on the desk. "Damn it, Sorcha! I said I was sorry. Don't make me say something I don't wish repeated!"

Sorcha placed her index finger on her cheek. She knew this was difficult for him.

And she also knew he wouldn't lie. Lawrence would, but not Henry.

"I thank you, Mr. Davenport. But I need to know if I can trust you again: Did you change your mind about me?"

"I did."

"And why is that?"

"Well…I've spoken with the girl, and she appeared quite sincere to me. Not particularly bright, but sincere."

"And did I not appear sincere, sir?" Sorcha bit her lip. She didn't wish to be ungrateful; it took a great deal for a man of Mr. Davenport's stature to admit he was wrong to a mere woman.

"You did, Miss O'Shea." He sighed heavily. "But you must realize that it is extremely difficult to confront the idea that one's children may be less than honorable."

"Yes, sir, I'm sure it must." *Having one's reputation insulted is most unpleasant, I completely understand.* She leaned forward in her chair, speaking earnestly. "But Douglas is completely above reproach."

"So maybe I did something right," Henry muttered. He cleared his throat. "And what do you say, Sorcha? Will you come back to work for *Davenport's?*"

"I very much appreciate the gesture, sir, but not at this time." Part of her did wish to return to *Davenport's Mercantile,* but even more she wanted to try her hand at something new. She felt empowered since— quite literally—running into Thaddeus.

"*What?*" Mr. Davenport exclaimed. "Why won't you come back? How will you get by?"

"I have another opportunity I'm pursuing."

"What is that? Whatever it is, I'll increase your salary."

"Thank you, Mr. Davenport, and I may take you up at some point, but right now I am excited at the possibility of expanding my skills and horizons. You don't know what it's like, Mr. Davenport, to be a slave to someone else."

"You were not my slave, Sorcha! And I do know what it is like to work for someone else."

"So you have answered your own question, sir." Sorcha's lips formed a slight smile. "I was very well paid for a woman and I thank you. I enjoyed my work here and I felt pride in it. But I learned that you, as my employer, could drop the shoe at any time—through no fault of my own —and I was out on the street with nothing. You'll understand if I don't wish to go through that again."

"It won't happen again, Sorcha. I said I was sorry and I meant it."

"I believe you do, Mr. Davenport, which is to your credit. But I've already committed to another endeavor."

"And what is that, Sorcha?" he demanded.

"You know, I'm not entirely without talent. There are other textile manufacturers."

"Are you going to one of my competitors, Sorcha?" Mr. Davenport boomed.

"Actually no. But I am free to do so if I choose." She was beginning to get a little annoyed that Henry Davenport was so angry. He clearly felt entitled to her creative work as well as to an explanation. "Just because I worked for you *does not mean that you own me*. And just because I am a factory girl and an artist doesn't mean I am any less important or ambitious than you are, Mr. Davenport. I am free to chart my own life and to pursue my dreams, just as you are."

He laughed. "But Sorcha…you…you're a…*woman*."

"I'm aware of that, sir."

"It is men who run the world. That is not women's place to be competing in the marketplace."

Sorcha stood. "I am not obligated to share my dreams with you or to answer your questions. I came out of courtesy because I thought we were once friends. But I get the impression you view me as your possession. Surely you cannot intend this?"

"You worked for Davenport's, Sorcha! You owe me so much."

"I do. And you owe me too."

"How can you do this to me, Sorcha?"

"I haven't done anything to you, Mr. Davenport. I'm only pursuing my own happiness. And none of this would have happened if you hadn't terminated my employment. I very likely would have been loyal to Davenport's for the rest of my life. It might be a good lesson for you on how to treat people whose work you value."

Even now, she liked Mr. Davenport: he had the capacity to grow and to change, in spite of his prejudices. She didn't want to upset him, and she didn't want to criticize him too much, or it might shut down the small steps of improvement he was willing to take.

Sorcha understood Henry Davenport had to maintain control, but it was a good lesson in life not to treat someone with disrespect just because they are poor and not powerful.

As for me, I am going to open my own button shop. Madame Arquette, a modiste, wished to increase the prestige of her dressmaker's shop and had offered Sorcha a small space to the side of her waiting room. Sorcha's one-of-a-kind buttons were an asset to Madame Arquette and of great interest to her clientele.

Every dress and every pair of boots are made with buttons! she reminded herself.

Sorcha didn't require a great deal of space, and the setting would be a great improvement over the dark, small corners of *Davenport's*, not to mention the endless noise of the employees and the machines. It was no wonder factory employees became hard of hearing.

Even more importantly, as her own business owner, if her business did well Sorcha could hire who she wished, potentially creating employment for her mother and her sisters. When Violet started to show and Mr. Davenport inevitably let her go, Sorcha could hire her. Violet couldn't be seen to be unmarried and pregnant or tongues would wag— Madame Arquette would never allow the reputation of her shop to be damaged—but Sorcha could put up a screen for Violet to work behind until her time came. Or Sorcha could simply transport Violet's buttons from home.

Madame Arquette understood the plight of the poor woman as well as being pragmatic. As long as Violet did not draw attention to herself or scare customers away, and the goods were produced, Madame Arquette had no objection.

"If you cross me, Miss O'Shea, you'll be sorry!" Mr. Davenport boomed.

"Cross you how, Mr. Davenport? By taking money out of your pocket and putting it into mine? This is what you men do every day. It's called *business*."

"Well, y-yes, by conniving with my competitors! Watch your step, Sorcha!"

"I won't be doing anything illegal, Mr. Davenport, so there is no need to threaten me." Sorcha began moving towards the door. It occurred to her that she had been utterly distressed during their last conversation and, this time, she pitied Henry's ignorance and was much less afraid of him.

"But I paid for you to get those drawings! You never would have been able to go to the Rainhill Trials without me!"

"I gave you the drawings you paid for."

"But I have no one who can create them!"

"That was your decision and not mine to dismiss me. Let me remind you that you set this ball into motion, Mr. Davenport."

"Don't you dare make those buttons when they are supposed to be exclusive to *Davenport's*! Or you'll be sorry, Miss O'Shea!"

He seems to think that his humiliating apology commands my absolute obedience.

Sorcha was slightly afraid of Mr. Davenport's threats. But her courage, curiosity, and desires were stronger.

And she knew that the degree of his anger was an indicator of her talent. He wouldn't be angry, after all, if he didn't want what she had.

I should never let an angry person seeking control over me make me believe I am less than I am.

Sorcha had taken care to seek out a shop owner who was of a practical mind, a like mind, and a kind heart, as Sorcha couldn't abide snobbery and cruelty. Hopefully Madame Arquette would appreciate which side her bread was buttered on as Mr. Davenport had been unable to do.

Sorcha knew she had Thaddeus to thank for this idea, as she would never have ventured out or thought it possible without his encouragement and insight. He had grounded her outlook when she needed it. It had never occurred to her that she could be in charge of her own life.

Women aren't supposed to be able to do that. A man was always in charge.

Sorcha smiled thinking of Thaddeus. Who would have ever guessed that an arrogant, pontificating, self-righteous man would be the pathway to her independence?

It turns out there is more to Thaddeus than meets the eye. He had more depth and kindness than she had originally thought.

She had always liked Thaddeus as a friend—he was fun and interesting to talk to and they had a rapport from their first moment of meeting—but now she wondered if there was something more.

She felt a warmth when she thought of him.

Sorcha couldn't help but recall that Robert had wished to take care of her. Thaddeus believed she could take care of herself.

Staring at the displeased man before her, reminding her of an ungovernable five-year-old, Sorcha smiled.

In spite of his ill treatment of her, Sorcha was indebted to Mr. Davenport. He was better to her than most men had been. He recognized and appreciated her talent. He had paid her well. They had had a good working relationship until Lawrence got involved.

And Henry Davenport was no longer a threat to her.

True, Mr. Davenport was a product of his time, but wasn't everyone? It was ridiculous to expect people to be perfect, independent of their culture and upbringing. She wasn't going to let Henry Davenport abuse her, but she didn't want to burn any bridges either.

Sorcha handed him her calling card. "Mr. Davenport, if you wish to buy buttons from me, this is my address. The rate is twice what you paid me here."

"Twice! What are you thinking Sorcha?"

"It's a fair price. But I'll give you all the Rainhill Trials buttons at half off." *Since you paid to send me to Rainhill.*

"Give me? I own those buttons!"

"No you don't, not anymore. I left your employ at your command, remember?"

"But, Sorcha...I asked you back!"

"That's my offer, sir. But after the Rainhill Trial buttons, there is no discount for you."

"Then my buttons won't be exclusive," Henry Davenport objected.

"As a favor to you, because of the history we enjoyed, I won't sell the Rainhill Trials buttons to anyone else."

"I should think not! It's only right." Henry Davenport pouted.

She reached the door and put her hand on the doorknob. She turned to smile at her former boss, adding "If you pay my price."

She closed the door behind her.

CHAPTER FIFTY

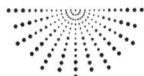

Ye Olde Hole in the Wall at 4 Hackins Hey
Liverpool

haddeus slipped in and sat in the back in the shadows, attempting not to be seen.

Sorcha was playing the mandolin and Sean O'Shea the fiddle. There was a beautiful boy, an Irish tenor, singing. Sorcha joined in at times and she had a lovely voice as well.

They performed "The Rose of Tralee" and Thaddeus was mesmerized watching Sorcha. She was completely unself-conscious, as if only the music existed.

Thaddeus was swept away by the tale of a doomed love affair between Tralee merchant William Mulchinock and the beautiful kitchen maid Mary O'Connor who worked in William's family's great house.

As the tenor sang to Sorcha, Thaddeus could easily see her as the beautiful Rose of Tralee, as if the tenor were the heir to the manor and Sorcha was Miss O'Connor.

Much like my doomed love affair, I suppose.

Still Thaddeus could not be unhappy listening to Sorcha. Pensive and wistful maybe—possibly *bittersweet* was the best descriptor—but not sad: he liked to be in her company, even if she didn't know he was there.

THE PALE MOON was rising above the green mountain,
    The sun was declining beneath the blue sea;
    When I strayed with my love to the pure crystal fountain,
    That stands in the beautiful Vale of Tralee.

SHE WAS LOVELY and fair as the rose of the summer,
    Yet 'twas not her beauty alone that won me;
    Oh no, 'twas the truth in her eyes ever dawning,
    That made me love Mary, the Rose of Tralee.

THE COOL SHADES of evening their mantle were spreading,
    And Mary all smiling was listening to me;
    The moon through the valley her pale rays was shedding,
    When I won the heart of the Rose of Tralee.

IN THE FAR fields of India, 'mid war's dreadful thunders,
    Her voice was a solace and comfort to me,
    But the chill hand of death has now rent us asunder,
    I'm lonely tonight for the Rose of Tralee.

SHE WAS LOVELY and fair as the rose of the summer,
    Yet 'twas not her beauty alone that won me;
    Oh no, 'twas the truth in her eyes ever dawning,
    That made me love Mary, The Rose of Tralee

THADDEUS THOUGHT SORCHA SPOTTED HIM, so he ducked more into the shadows.

I want to enjoy this moment watching her, without her awareness. If she saw him, he would have to look away to avoid being too forward.

And I don't want to take my eyes off her.

He knew he could never have her. *But at least give me this.*

True, she does have a viper's tongue at times, he thought. But he couldn't help himself. *She is everything. I love her.*

She was as pretty a girl as he'd ever seen.

But that isn't why I love her. She had a depth to her. As if there were very few subjects she hadn't thought about. She was smart, insightful, talented, and perceptive.

And Sorcha was kind and devoted to those she cared about—even those she didn't even like. Take Violet Villin, for instance.

Sorcha had a heart for justice: a heart which had put him to a lot of trouble.

But there is not much hope to win her affection in return. Thaddeus had no idea what that would take. *If I knew, I would attempt it.*

I might be able to afford a wife now. Thaddeus was making more money now—largely thanks to Sorcha and her constantly pushing him to be a better newspaperman—even a better *person* with a broader knowledge of the world.

I never particularly wanted to be enlightened. Or sensitive and caring. He had just wanted to be successful and wealthy.

Knowledgeable and informed of course, but Thaddeus hadn't wanted these tugs on his heart. It wasn't always popular. And above all, he wanted to be popular and in the mainstream of things.

Thaddeus knew very well there were people who would vilify being kind—he supposed he was guilty at times—for caring about the perspective of others, and attempting to put oneself into the shoes of those less fortunate. They called one naïve, soft, too sweet.

Those without a heart couldn't understand kindness and criticized one for it.

Cruelty is a survival instinct. Without a heart it was easier to step all over others, easier to take what one wanted, and easier to get ahead.

The same people who would vilify Violet Christlike, Sorcha said.

And now she was trying to get him to go to the Abolitionists' meetings.

It wasn't enough that he had championed the voices of working women and children. The poor.

Honestly, he never wanted to be a reformer or a progressive—he was a lifelong Tory after all! *Now what am I? A Whig?*

God forbid.

Do you know what Whigs stand for? Thaddeus asked himself. A bunch of damn populists, that's what they were.

Working for the everyday man.

Thaddeus smiled as he watched Sorcha. *Why do I torture myself when I can't have her?*

I can't help myself.

Well, it doesn't matter anyway. She won't have me.

Sorcha was like Mary O'Connor who had fallen in love with the lord of the manor. She was destined for a grand life.

Thaddeus sighed.

She really is the Rose of Tralee.

CHAPTER FIFTY-ONE

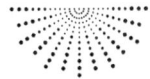

Davenport's Textile & Mercantile

"What are you trying to do, Lawrence? Destroy my business? It's time for you to act like an adult."

Henry Davenport frowned. "You set this entire thing going telling me Sorcha disrespected you and behaved without decorum at the Rainhill Trials. Now I realize it was actually the reverse. You lied to me, Lawrence! And Sorcha says she won't come back! I've lost my best button maker, and I put that at your door."

"I didn't lie! Sorcha is constantly taking an attitude with me!"

"Only in response to your advances." Henry Davenport frowned.

"I have to take a firm hand with my employees or they'll walk all over me," Lawrence retorted.

"Firm, but fair. There is a difference in managing the staff and using them for your own ends."

Lawrence shrugged. "There is no managing Sorcha. She is incorrigible, as you now know. And you're yelling at me instead of at her!"

"Why did you do it, Lawrence?" Henry demanded, ignoring his son's sniveling. "Because your pride was hurt? Because you wanted revenge? If you destroy the business, you won't have any of the wealth you now enjoy. Do you never think of the business?"

* * *

"I THINK of it all the time." *I wish it was mine.*

Lawrence had never seen his father so angry.

Well I am angry too. How dare he treat me like a child.

Mr. Davenport tapped his hands on the desk. "Did you get this girl Violet with child?"

"Who knows? It could have been anyone."

"But it might have been you?"

"Might have been."

"I can't believe you treated one of *my employees* like a strumpet!"

Lawrence shrugged. "Just a bit of fun."

"You have to marry the girl now," Henry Davenport commanded. "I'll not have any grandchild of mine be a base born child!"

"*Marry her!* Are you crazy, Father? She's a factory girl! I doubt she even knows how to read and write."

"You should have thought of that before you took her to your bed, Lawrence. Now she is pregnant with your babe. You'll have to educate the child and the mother together." Henry sighed. "Miss Villin may yet acquire some town bronze. She's very motivated."

"It could be anyone's baby. She's a slut. That should be obvious."

"I've spoken to the girl. As uneducated and simple-minded as she is, she doesn't have eyes for anyone but you, God help her. And I don't think she's lying. I believe that is my grandchild. For once in your life, Lawrence Davenport, you are going to accept responsibility for your actions!"

"And what if I say 'no'?"

"I'll take you out of my will and fire you from your job."

"You wouldn't dare! I'm your first-born son!"

"Believe me, I'm aware of that. I'd like you to be aware of it and start acting like it, Lawrence, paying honor to that position instead of disgracing my name."

Lawrence bit his lip. He was accustomed to being doted upon and regarded with pride. This was the most humiliating experience of his life.

"The arrangements have been made. I have already applied to the Bishop for a common license to avoid the reading of the banns for all to hear and to comment upon." Henry Davenport continued. "You will be married in a private ceremony in Holy Trinity Church in two weeks time with myself and your brother Douglas as witnesses. I am saving your mother the distress. After which time Miss Villin—I mean, 'Mrs. Davenport'—will move into our home where you will have the east wing of the house."

"Does Violet know about all this?" Lawrence didn't argue as he couldn't be without income or a job. As much as he didn't wish to marry Violet, even more did he not wish to be without money, home, or employment.

What else am I going to do?

"Yes," Henry Davenport answered.

"And she wants to go forward with it?"

"I never saw a person so happy." Henry Davenport frowned. "She appears to think her life with you will be a heavenly existence. Please don't disappoint her. *Or me.*"

No worries, Father. When you are dead you won't have anything to be disappointed about. And I will be running this store.

CHAPTER FIFTY-TWO

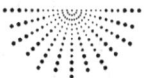

Ye Olde Hole in the Wall at 4 Hackins Hey
Liverpool

haddeus slipped in and sat in the back in the shadows, attempting not to be seen, which he was usually able to accomplish when Sorcha was performing.

Generally Sorcha was playing the mandolin, but this time she sang. Thaddeus thought he had never heard a voice so beautiful.

I'M A SIMPLE IRISH GIRL, and I'm looking for a place
  I've felt the grip of poverty, but I'm sure that's no disgrace
  'Twill be long before I eat again, tho' I work hard and I try
  For I'm told at every door 'No Irish need apply'.
  Alas! For my poor country, which I never will deny.

NOW I WONDER what's the reason that the fortune-favored few,
  Should throw on us that dirty slur, and treat us as they do.

They all know Paddy's heart is warm, and willing is his hand,
They rule us yet we may not earn a living in their land
Oh to their sister country how can they bread deny
By sending forth this cruel line, 'No Irish need apply'.

WE DID NOT ACT *the same when they anchor'd on our shore,*
For Irish hospitality opens every door
Pat would give his last potato, yes, to the weary stranger still,
And whisky, which he prizes so, never would deny
Then whyfore do they always say 'No Irish need apply'?

NOW WHAT THEY *have against us, sure the world knows Paddy's brave*
For he's helped to fight their battles, both on land and on the wave,
At the storming of Sebastopol, and beneath an Indian sky
Did you mind Lieutenant Massy when he raised the battle cry?
Pat raised his hand, their General said, 'All Irish might apply'.

THE GAME IS UP. *She's spotted me.* Sorcha moved towards Thaddeus' table.

Damnit! I meant to slip out before she saw me. Thaddeus didn't really want to talk to Sorcha tonight. *It was just a reminder of what he couldn't have.* He wanted to watch her from afar.

As I am destined to do for the rest of my life.

"Tad! Why didn't you tell me you were coming?"

"It was a last minute thought," he said, motioning to the waiter. "A couple of mugs of ale, please."

Sorcha shook her head. "Not for me."

"Would you like a rum punch or a ratafia? That's what the other ladies are having," The waiter said. Speaking close to her ear he added, "The ratafia is pretty watered down."

Sorcha nodded.

"You didn't want ale, Sorcha?" Thaddeus asked when the waiter departed.

"My mum says it isn't ladylike." Sorcha shrugged.

"Scandalous!" Thaddeus exclaimed.

Sorcha giggled. "I do have a small beer at home, but my mum says a lady doesn't drink beer or ale in public."

"Let me get this straight, Sorcha." Thaddeus was distressed and flabbergasted. "There is someone who you listen to?"

Sorcha smiled. "On occasion."

"Never any occasion where I have been present." Thaddeus shook his head. "Forgive my stupefaction, Miss O'Shae. I have suffered quite a shock." Thaddeus looked about the room. "There seem to be a number of ladies here. Some having an ale."

"I mean, would you wish to be seen with an intoxicated woman, Tad? I would no doubt be considered a low bred woman with ulterior motives."

"Do you have ulterior motives, Sorcha?" he asked hopefully. "Other than sharing a drink?"

Sorcha pursed her lips in disapproval.

"Anyway, it's no never mind to me what people think. I'll write them up in the paper if they bother you, Sorcha." *I've done it before.*

Sorcha laughed. She always looked angelic when she laughed. Her eyes and her entire face lit up.

"Did you like the music, Tad?"

"Very much."

Sorcha sighed. "My mother says no man will marry a woman who plays in a pub. That I have resigned myself to spinsterhood."

If only. Then I might look pretty good to her.

"Is something wrong, Tad? You aren't even smiling."

"In the first place, there is a different set of rules which apply to the upper class than to working class girls." Thaddeus shrugged. "In the second place, Sorcha, if someone loves you, he won't care."

"My mother doesn't seem to think so." Sorcha shrugged. "Though I don't like it when men think their wives and children are an extension of him, as if they are property! And not separate people."

"Under British law, a wife *is* a man's property," Thaddeus stated. "She and everything she owns becomes his property upon the marriage."

"I don't think that is right." Sorcha frowned. "I'm talking about God's law, not man's law."

Thaddeus took a swig of his ale. "Woman did come from Adam's rib, after all."

"She improved upon it." She grew somber. "But it seems to me the only course for a woman is to remain single—in that way she can keep all her property. And her autonomy."

Thaddeus wrinkled his brow, perplexed. "Do you have that much property, Sorcha?"

"Well, no, but I might someday. Still, I wouldn't like to think my husband would own everything I have! And myself as well!"

"I suppose you should only marry someone you trust to respect your wishes, Sorcha." His expression was soft as he looked at her. "And who treasures and adores you."

"I don't think it is a good idea to hand over that much power."

"You seem to be thinking a lot about marriage, Sorcha." Thaddeus felt a fear grip him.

Sorcha's eyes grew wide open. "Not at all."

"Then where do all these reflections come from?"

"I'm just pondering the need men seem to have to control their wives and children. I see it everywhere. It's difficult to find a man who doesn't wish to control everything around him."

"Are you looking for someone, Sorcha?"

"Not really. But I have received a great deal of criticism for this that or the other over the course of my life. It wears on me sometimes."

"Such as?"

"Oh, for having an opinion, for opening my mouth, for expressing myself, for being different from someone else, for playing music in public, for not being quiet, shy, and demure for example."

"Oh, my God, Sorcha. It's not as if you're shooting people in the street. You're just playing music."

"That's a radical viewpoint you have, Thaddeus Fulbright."

Thaddeus sighed sadly. "Yes. I expect it is. It seems to be a pattern lately."

He fixed an accusing stare upon her, shaking his head.

"What is it, Tad? Why are you looking at me that way?"

"I hate to tell you, Sorcha, but you are a radical reformist."

"Oh? How exciting! Now there is a word to describe me. Do you think it's a bad thing?" Sorcha asked.

"Only if they put you in jail for it." He paused. "I suppose, if you're really concerned about losing your rights—and your non-existent property—you could have a partner outside of marriage."

Her eyes opened wide and she slapped his hand. "Thaddeus Fulbright, what kind of a girl do you think I am? My mother would drop dead at such a notion!"

"And your Grandmother Oonagh," he added.

"Oh, no," Sorcha shook her head. "She would take a shot gun and force the young man into compliance!" Sorcha giggled. "Grandmother Oonagh would make quick work of the whole affair."

"She's a woman who knows her own mind, that's for certain," Thaddeus agreed. "And she makes sure everyone else knows it too."

"When I first met you, Thaddeus—I'll be frank—"

"You always are, Sorcha."

She ignored that. "At the time I thought you were narrow-minded and prejudiced, not particularly open to new views."

"Those were the good old days. I can barely remember." Thaddeus frowned. "I do recall it was certainly less exhausting. It's very tiring always having to step into everyone else's shoes. If I'd wanted to do that I would have become an actor."

"But now...it's as if..." Sorcha paused, ignoring his retort as she was wont to do.

"It's what?" Thaddeus asked.

"Tad, are we friends?" Sorcha asked.

Thaddeus was a bit taken aback by this, as he always was in Sorcha's company. He took her hand in his. "I hope so Sorcha."

"I do too, Tad. I hope we are always friends."

We will always be friends. Thaddeus sighed heavily, saddened by her words. But he rallied to the moment. "I hope you can count on me, Sorcha."

"I do, Tad," she said softly.

"Wouldn't you like to dance, Sorcha?"

"I would, Tad." She got up from her chair. "But it's almost time for me to play again."

"You can spare a dance."

The music began. "Oh, it's the Gallopade," Thaddeus said.

"What is that?" Sorcha asked.

"Do you know the waltz?" Thaddeus asked.

"I suppose so."

He put his arm around her waist and they began to dance around the room in an elegant manner with two other couples.

"Oh my goodness, Tad! It's very fast. And you're such a fine dancer!"

"I have to keep up. I still go to London, you know."

"Oh, why is that?" Sorcha asked.

"My family lives in London, of course."

"I didn't realize you were such a man about town, Thaddeus Fulbright!"

"Oh yes you did, Sorcha O'Shea! You know very well that I have *connections*."

She laughed, thoroughly enjoying herself, and she began to get breathless.

"Yes, the Gallopade is much like the waltz only a little bit hoppier with shorter steps. And faster," Thaddeus said.

Sorcha could hardly keep herself from laughing. She was obviously enjoying herself immensely as he swung her about the room.

Looking into her smiling face, Thaddeus felt his heart well up inside him.

I will love you forever, Sorcha Fae.

CHAPTER FIFTY-THREE

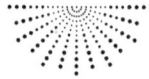

Saturday night
Slaughterhouse
Liverpool

"It's not fair!" Lawrence muttered as he nursed his ale at the *Slaughterhouse* Pub, a drinking establishment so called because it was located next to a slaughterhouse on Drury Lane. "I'm going to be strapped to some stupid girl without a brain."

"Why do you call her stupid?" his companion said.

"She believed what I told her!"

His companion snickered. "Yeah. Stupid dame."

"Right." Lawrence paused. "She's pretty enough though."

The other man shrugged. "Plenty of pretty dames. You don't 'ave to marry 'em."

"That's what I think, Panda." Lawrence looked at his companion, so nicknamed due to black circles around his eyes and pale blonde hair. "What right does my father have to tell me who to marry?"

Panda shrugged. "Maybe cuz' he's footin' the bill?"

"Right." Lawrence nodded. "Wish I could find another way to make money."

"You can't do nothin', Lawry, except chase women and gamble money away." Panda lowered his voice. "The only way you'll be free is to rid youself of the one 'oldin' the reins."

"My own father?" Lawrence felt a wave of shock run through his body. Even for all his fantasies of his inheritance, and his general dislike of his family, the idea was distasteful to him. He couldn't do anything like that with his own hands. Not even now when he was livid. "I don't know, Panda. I'm madder than a hornet, that's for sure, but the very idea…"

Sure, I'm so mad I wish he was gone.

"You don't 'ave to do it yerself." Panda shrugged. "But think of it. If he was gone, you don't have to marry the girl, you can keeps chasin' skirts —And you can inherits the business, see?"

"That would solve my problems, but…" Lawrence said uneasily.

"You want me to dos it or not?" Panda asked. "I can't hang out here all day."

"Mind if I join you?" An older man walked up to their table with an ale.

Lawrence looked up. "Mr. O'Shea?" Lawrence shook his head. "We're havin' a private conversation."

* * *

"THAT'S what I'm afraid of. "Sean O'Shea pulled up a chair and set his ale on the table but he remained standing. He motioned to Panda to get lost.

"Look. I'm not leavin'." Panda said. "We're discussion' business."

"You can discuss it later or I'll throw you out of the pub now," Sean O'Shea said.

"You don't work here's," Panda objected. "You can't throw me out."

"Care to find out?" Sean asked.

Sean worked as a bouncer at *Ye Olde Hole in the Wall*, about one-quarter mile away, but Sorcha saw Lawrence walk by with Panda and told her father. Sean had an instinct for trouble.

Panda rose from his chair, having apparently heard of Sean's fighting skills. "I'll sees you later, Lawry. Let me know."

"Yeah," Lawrence said.

"I just want to have a brief word with you," Sean said.

"Why not? My day can't get any worse."

"Why are you hanging out with low lifes like that, Lawrence?" Mr. O'Shea asked, not beating around the bush. "Panda is lower than a snake's belly in a wagon rut."

"It's none of your business who I hang out with, old man," Lawrence replied.

"I overheard what you were talking about," Sean O'Shea said.

Lawrence's eyes flew open wide. "I didn't mean it. Just shooting the breeze. Anyway, Panda's the one who said it not me."

"You looked like you were considering his proposal."

"Not a chance." Lawrence shook his head. "I can't believe you can't tell when someone is joking, old man!"

Sean raised his eyebrows.

"Are you going to tell anyone?"

"That depends. But I'll make sure if it happens, someone will know."

"*Bloody Hell!* I can't get a break!"

Why is it people who have the most complain the most?

"Seems to me that you have a lot more breaks than most and you ruin them all yourself."

"Go to hell, old man!"

"You might be goin' there yourself if you carry this out." Sean took a sip of his ale. "You'll have the devil to pay. Look, I know you're angry, son, but you don't want to go this far. You'll never forgive yourself for it. Your life will be much worse, not better. Why don't you cool down first?"

"You should have just turned me in to begin with. Now I might go after you."

"I don't think you're that evil. I think you're just a spoiled child who needs to learn to accept responsibility and become a man. This marriage might be the best thing for you."

"Damnit! I wish the old man would retire. I just want to run the department store."

"And run it into the ground? You don't have the maturity or the skills to run it yet. Give yourself a chance to learn. No one expects you to be born learning how to do things."

"My father does," Lawrence grumbled.

"You need to start appreciating your life, son, and using whatever you have at your fingertips to make it better," Sean said. "I wish I had your opportunities. I can't even get a job doing what I already know how to do because I'm Irish."

"So what are you going to do about it?" asked Lawrence.

"Do the best I can at whatever job I'm given."

"Sounds pointless. You're not going anywhere."

"Maybe. But if I kill someone out of anger, I'm only going to jail."

"Yeah. But you don't understand. I'm supposed to be doing a lot better. I'm supposed to inherit Davenport's."

"And are you supposed to be frittering away all the profits? You don't appear to have an interest in business. Is there anything you like to do besides being a wastrel?"

"Not really."

Sean looked up to see a man in a dark overcoat and a hat low on his face glancing over at them from the bar. The man in shadow seemed to be watching them intermittently.

"Well that's a shame." Sean cleared his throat. "At any rate, don't go after any of your family members. That's all you really have. You'll regret it. And stop hanging out with Panda and his sort."

"Why should I?"

"You realize, of course, that, if you went through with this, Panda would hold it over you for the rest of your life, extorting more and more money?"

Lawrence swallowed hard. "Nah. Not once I've paid him."

Sean laughed at Lawrence's naiveté. "Panda is anxious to do it. Not for whatever you plan to pay him, but for what he can make off you for the rest of your life. He sees it as a goldmine."

"Ah, nah. That would break the code. Not a very gentlemanly thing to do."

Sean raised his eyebrows. "Neither is what you are considering."

"I guess not. But I didn't really mean it." A tear moved down Lawrence's cheek.

"Make sure Panda knows that. He might carry it out before you can change your mind."

CHAPTER FIFTY-FOUR

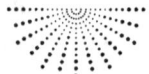

Ye Olde Hole in the Wall at 4 Hackins Hey
Liverpool

Sorcha returned to the stage after their dance. This time she and Enoch were singing in Irish. Thaddeus knew a little Irish—one had to, living in Liverpool—and recognized the song as "The Rising of the Moon", a song about the Irish Rebellion of 1798, only thirty-one years ago. It might have meant trouble to sing the song in English in England, so it was sung in Irish.

Thaddeus sighed heavily. His awareness of injustice was a heavy burden. *Worse for those who endure injustice than for me, though.*

Funny how he used to always pity himself and believe he was the most put upon person, and now he realized it was somebody else.

Now that he loved Sorcha, he couldn't help but think about persecution based on race and wonder how prejudice had affected her family.

If it had to do with Sorcha, he had to care about it.

Of course Thaddeus was aware of the oppression which led to the Irish revolt against British rule—and the subsequent crushing of the Irish. Captured and wounded Irish rebels were not treated as prisoners but were executed, usually by hanging. Somewhere between ten thousand and fifty thousand men, women, and children died in the Irish Rebellion.

AND COME TELL *me Sean O'Farrell, tell me why you hurry so*
  'Hush, mbuachaill, hush and listen,' and his cheeks were all aglow
  I bear orders from the captain, get you ready quick and soon
  For the pikes must be together at the rising of the moon

AND COME TELL *me Sean O'Farrell, where the gathering is to be*
  At the old spot by the river; quite well known to you and me
  One more word for signal token; whistle out the marching tune
  With your pike upon your shoulder at the rising of the moon

OUT FROM MANY *a mud wall cabin; eyes were watching through the night*
  Many a manly heart was beating for the blessed warning light
  Murmurs rang along the valleys to the banshee's lonely croon
  And a thousand pikes were flashing by the rising of the moon

ALL ALONG THAT *singing river that black mass of men was seen*
  High above their shining weapons flew their own beloved green
  Death to every foe and traitor! Whistle out the marching tune
  And hurrah, me boys, for freedom, 'tis the rising of the moon

AS HE LISTENED to the haunting tune, Thaddeus drifted away into a sleep-like state, thinking of a certain Irish maiden who had removed any desire for an ordinary life.

CHAPTER FIFTY-FIVE

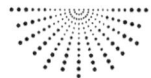

Saturday night
Slaughterhouse
Liverpool

The man in the overcoat moved towards Sean O'Shea and Lawrence.

It was obviously a heated argument; Lawrence was visibly discomposed, in a tormented state.

"Yes, yes! I'll talk with Panda!" Lawrence exclaimed. "It was insanity, and he was the one who suggested it anyway."

"May I sit down?" the stranger asked.

"What's your business, stranger?" Sean O'Shea asked. "We're having a private conversation."

"I beg your pardon. I'll wait. I have business with you alone, Mr. O'Shea." The man tipped the brim of his hat up.

Suddenly Sean recognized him. "Robert Stephenson!" Sean exclaimed, suddenly smiling. "How good it is to see you! Sit down. Why are you here?"

"I'm here to see you, Mr. O'Shea." Robert pulled up a chair. "A passersby said they had seen you."

"Bloody hell! Every person I never wanted to see again has shown up tonight," Lawrence said, rising from his chair. "We're done here anyway."

"Heed what I said," Sean advised, returning his eyes to Lawrence. "I'll make sure someone in a position of authority knows what we discussed today. They would be ready to pounce if anything happens."

"Don't worry, O'Shea. I just had a moment of madness. You might think I'm worthless, but I've not sunk that low."

"I didn't think so, Lawrence. Take care you don't."

Lawrence walked away, both of the seated men trailing him with their eyes.

"Anything I can help with?" Robert asked.

"Nah," Sean said. "I think he'll come round. He's facing responsibility for the first time in his life and it's a bit of an adjustment. He's a bit of a baby, but he's not a demon."

At least I hope not.

It actually made sense to disclose the story to Robert. Someone else must know in the event he'd overestimated Lawrence.

It would worry his wife too much. *Can I trust Thaddeus with the information?* He had to figure out someone to tell.

Sean turned to Robert. "And what brings you here, son?"

"Personal and business, I suppose. Naturally I want to pay my respects to Miss O'Shea."

"She'll be happy to see you."

"And are you *all* well?" Robert asked nervously.

"We are. Sorcha has had a bit of upset at her job, but it will work out."

"Oh? And what happened?" Robert asked with concern.

"I'll let her tell you about that. You can call on us tomorrow."

"Very good. And as for business, I'm here about a job."

"For your work then?"

Robert laughed. "No, as it happens, it's a job for you, Mr. O'Shea. I hope you'll do us the honor of accepting it."

"For me? What do you mean?" Sean couldn't believe what he was hearing.

"Well, as you know, my father and I have the contract to build the locomotives for the Liverpool-Manchester line."

"Of course. As a result of the Rainhill Trials."

"Quite right." Robert nodded. "Well, my father and I have been in discussion with the directors of the line. As it happens they don't have enough railway constables for the line. We told them we knew someone who would be excellent for the position."

Sean felt the sun rise in his world but he didn't dare believe it—it was too good to be true. He was almost at a loss for words, a rarity for him. "Are you saying?...a railway constable?...a policeman for the railways?"

Robert nodded, his expression serious. "Yes. All the railway lines have their own private police force. We saw you in action on numerous occasions with your knowledge of human nature, your natural leadership, and your fighting skills, and we know you to be an excellent choice."

"Me? The directors would hire me? An Irishman?" Robert was bursting for joy.

"They don't care what nationality you are, as long as you can do the job. We have no doubt that within a short time you would gain the trust of your fellow constables and work your way into a leadership position."

Sean rubbed his eyes, as if it might bring him back into reality. His heart began to pound. He couldn't remember when he had been so happy. He had come to believe he would never find good work again.

"So I would be working all along the line? That's a lot of distance."

"It won't be much distance for the locomotives." Robert smiled. "You'll be picked up every morning in Liverpool and dropped off at the same."

"Thank you, sir. I can't tell you how happy this makes me."

Robert held out his hand and Sean shook on it. "You'll make the directors happy too, we have no doubt."

CHAPTER FIFTY-SIX

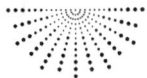

Sunday after church
The family at home

"Robert! It's so good to see you," Sorcha said. She was delighted to see him. Though it felt like seeing an old friend instead of a lover. She had been through so much in the past few weeks, it was no wonder her emotions were muted.

In all fairness, her heart sped up upon seeing him—as she was sure any woman would experience in Robert Stephenson's presence, she wasn't blind, nor was she immune to the intensity of his gaze. But her feelings were of a superficial nature, she knew, as she might feel for any famous, handsome man lavishing his attentions upon her.

She wondered what Robert thought of their humble dwelling as he stood before them in full regalia.

She felt some embarrassment as Robert entered her very plain and simple, bare home. How different her home must be from Robert's home in terms of appearance and size. Thank goodness they weren't still living in the slums.

Their dwelling was small and there was hardly any furniture with little to no decorations except what the children made and the ladies of the household sewed.

What am I thinking? My home was good enough before I met Robert. It felt like a palace in fact.

Their home was serviceable, and the family was so grateful to have it. There was a fireplace and warmth, both literally and emotionally.

I am an honest, hardworking person with good character, so I have no reason to feel ashamed of anything.

"I'm so happy to see you, Sorcha." He kissed her hand and his eyes were intent upon her.

"This is my mother, Mrs. O'Shea. My Grandmother Oonagh. My brothers Colin and Jamie and my sisters Molly and Felicity. My father, you know." Sorcha made the introductions.

"This is Robert Stephenson who is making the steam trains for the Liverpool-Manchester railway being built." Sorcha turned towards her family.

"The iron horses?" Jamie asked excitedly.

"Yes." Robert nodded. This admission only served to ignite Jamie even more.

"Can we ride them?" Jamie was turning red in the face now.

"I expect you will," Robert said.

Sorcha was concerned her brother might faint from the excitement. "Calm yourself, Jamie, all in due time. It won't be today or tomorrow."

Jamie's face fell, while Colin punched him in the side, shaking his head. Molly and Felicity stared at the wonder which was Robert Stephenson while Grandmother Oonagh pursed her lips.

"Why don't you sit down, Mr. Stephenson?" Sean O'Shea said, leading their guest to the couch, where Sorcha sat beside Robert and Jamie sat across from him, enamored of his cane and top hat now on the end table beside him. Indeed, Robert's elegance seemed out of place in the small, sparsely decorated apartment.

Sean shook his head at Jamie. "Leave the seats for your mother and grandmother—and for me," Sean said. "You children can sit next to the fireplace."

"But Da'! Mama is in the kitchen makin' tea." Jamie clearly wanted to sit as close to Robert as he could manage.

"Yes, but when she has finished she will sit on the chair next to the fire, as is her custom."

In point of fact the kitchen was only a few feet away in the same room. Mrs. O'Shea brought the tea and biscuits into the living area where she served the guests and the adults. Grandmother Oonagh stared at Robert as much as Jamie did.

It is no wonder! It is as if the Prime Minister entered our humble abode! Sorcha suppressed a giggle.

"And how long has it been since we've seen each other?" Sean asked.

"I'd say about a month, sir," Robert said.

"What a grand time Sorcha and I had at Rainhill!" Sean added.

Grandmother Oonagh frowned. "Idleness is the devil's work."

Sean chuckled. "Weren't none of us idle, I can tell you that, Maimeó! Least of all Mr. Stephenson here." Sean turned to Robert. "And I expect you've been busy since we last met?"

Sorcha could feel his arm touching hers, the couch being a bit small, and her awareness of him was acute. *He's really here! I thought I'd never see him again.*

In truth, Sorcha was happy to see Robert. But she was so intent upon managing all the changes in her own life that she was not feeling the intense longing she had experienced before in his presence. Naturally she still thought the world of him and knew him to be an exceptional and honorable person.

"Very. We've been working long hours to get another four locomotives ready," Robert said. "We only have three months to do so."

"And will they be like the *Rocket?*" Jamie asked. "The one what won?"

"Similar. The new locomotives will actually be even bigger and carry heavier loads."

"And when will the Liverpool Manchester railway open?" Sorcha asked.

"We have some months to go yet. We only did just win the contest." Robert turned to smile at her and Sorcha felt the warmth of happiness at a dear friend's success. "The directors are thinking September of next year. So about ten months from now."

"It must be very exciting," Mrs. O'Shea said.

"It is, Ma'am. But there is barely a moment to catch our breath, we are so busy. I suppose we never pause to think what we are feeling."

"And will the iron horses actually carry *people?*" Colin asked.

"Yes, son. The first railway for passengers," Robert said.

"*Rocket* already carried people," Sean added. "Sorcha and I rode *Rocket* at the Rainhill Trials."

"Yes," Sorcha nodded. "We were among the lucky few."

The children made the appropriate sounds of wonder, gasping and murmuring. Grandmother Oonagh made the sign of the cross.

"Do ye think anyone will actually ride the new iron horses when it's not just a silly race?" Grandmother Oonagh asked. "Is anyone that stupid?"

"I hope so!" Robert laughed.

"Grandmother! Please don't be rude to Sorcha's friend," Mrs. O'Shea exclaimed. "Mr. Stephenson is a very important man and his visit is an honor." Clearly Cecelia did not wish to scare away any of Sorcha's potential suitors.

"I'm accustomed to non-believers," Robert said, smiling. "Yes, Ma'am, we anticipate a large crowd."

"To watch the idiots get on it, yes, but to actually ride it?" Grandmother Oonagh persisted, undaunted by her daughter-in-law's reprimand.

Having set his top hat on the coffee table, he ran his hand through his dark curls. "Yes, Ma'am. There is a great deal of interest in the steam locomotives."

"Hmmph!" Grandmother Oonagh muttered. "There's a lot of interest in sin too."

Sorcha thought Robert controlled his laughter with difficulty, he was such a polite man.

Grandmother Oonagh stared at Robert as if he must be the chief offender in his fancy dress. Nor did she think much of his intelligent. "Those locomotives will never replace horses."

"They go a lot faster than horses!" Jamie admonished.

"Indeed they do." Robert nodded approval at Jamie. "And they carry a great deal more as well."

"Hmph!" Grandmother Oonagh let her opinion be known.

Sorcha giggled to herself, thinking how Thaddeus had a bit of fun with Grandmother Oonagh, pushing back until she was almost ready to give up the fight. At first this treatment made her very angry, but now she was starting to respect Thaddeus. Maybe even like him.

"And what brings you to Liverpool, Mr. Stephenson?" Mrs. O'Shea asked.

"Oh, you can call me 'Robert' Ma'am. I'm here on business." Robert glanced at Sorcha, adding, "For the most part."

"He's actually offered me a job, Cecelia," Sean said. "A good job."

"A job?" Cecelia exclaimed. "Whatever do you mean? I don't abide with splitting up the family."

"Oh, no," Robert said. "Mr. O'Shea will board the train every morning and return every evening. He'll be a railway constable."

"A constable?" Cecelia O'Shea smiled. "How can that be?"

"All the railway lines have their own private police force. The directors observed Mr. O'Shea in action at the Rainhill Trials. He saved my father's life as well as the lives of others. He was, frankly, remarkable. All the directors support his hire." Robert cleared his throat. "Well, all but Mr. Craggy, but he's impossible to please, and he doesn't support the steam locomotive either."

"Oh, thank you, sir!" Mrs. O'Shea was breathless. "That is most welcome news. I hate the danger, but Sean was born to do it."

"I agree, Ma'am." Robert turned to Sorcha. "I'd ask you to take a stroll with me in the park, Miss O'Shea, but I don't believe there are any public gardens in Liverpool as there are in London."

"There are public gardens in London?" Sorcha asked.

"Yes," Robert nodded. "Hyde Park."

"Is it nice?" Sorcha asked.

"Oh, it's beautiful. You know, even in the excitement of the city, the human animal needs fresh air and green things."

"Ah, yes," Grandmother Oonagh smiled for the first time. "As in Ireland."

"And where do you live, Mr. Stephenson?" Mrs. O'Shea asked.

"In Newcastle upon Tyne," Robert said. "The Forth Street Works, my company, is in Newcastle."

"That's quite a distance from Liverpool, isn't it?" Mrs. O'Shea asked.

"Yes, but it won't be once the steam locomotives are installed." Robert took a sip of his tea.

"We have no public gardens in Liverpool but there are some nice grounds at St. Anthony's Church on Scotland Road if you and Sorcha would like to take a walk and catch up on your doings?" Mr. O'Shea suggested.

Cecelia raised her eyebrows.

Sorcha blushed, though she knew her Da was trying to give them an opportunity to have private conversation and Robert was too polite to press it.

Being quite familiar with Robert, Sean clearly approved. It was a bit awkward since Robert was going to be Mr. O'Shea's boss.

Having obtained her hat, day coat, gloves, and umbrella, Robert donned his top hat and cane and they embarked on a stroll. It was a lovely day with crisp, salty air and sunshine—though it wouldn't be long until winter arrived.

Robert took her arm in his. He seemed concerned as he looked about. "It doesn't seem like the best neighborhood for a walk."

"Yes, but during the daytime, it's no problem. I walk this way by myself often," Sorcha said.

Robert frowned, as if he would like to spare her the difficulty. He glanced at his watch, noting "It is three o'clock in the afternoon."

"Thank you for giving my father a job, Robert," Sorcha said as they walked.

"Mr. O'Shea earned it, believe me," Robert said. "He impressed everyone at the Rainhill Trials."

"Nothing could ever mean more to me than seeing my father happy."

They reached the church and found a bench to sit on. Robert turned and faced her and took her hands. "Sorcha, I know I'm just starting out, but I think I have a strong future."

"There can be no doubt of that, Robert."

"You're the sweetest, smartest, most talented girl I've ever met. I want us to be together. It is my greatest wish that you should marry me and become my wife, Sorcha."

Sorcha felt her heart flip in her chest. *It is like a fairy tale dream come true.*

But something doesn't feel right. "I thank you for the honor, Robert, and my feelings are very strong for you, but I can't help but feel we're not the same. As much as I like you—maybe even love you. Who wouldn't?—I don't think we would suit."

"What do you mean, Sorcha? How could we not suit?"

She raised her eyes to meet his. "I think I am too wild for you, Robert."

"Oh, Sorcha," he kissed her hand. "You're perfect. You're beautiful and intelligent. What more could I want?" He sighed. "How can you not think we would do well together?"

"You're so wonderful, Robert, and I daresay I adore you, but you seem like someone I could never measure up to. I don't want to be jealous and envious of my husband; I would lose my sense of who I am."

"It doesn't seem insurmountable if there is love," Robert suggested.

"Perhaps you are right. But I wonder what I would do with myself all day?"

"What do you mean, Sorcha?"

"I am accustomed to work...And to being around a great deal of people—my family and co-workers."

"Your job would be to manage me, the household, and, I hope, children."

"I'm sure it is a dream come true for the right woman. It's a bit too confined for me. I can't sew and paint all day for my own gratification. I want to do something that touches the world also. As you do."

"You don't think it would be enough to be together, Sorcha?"

"In my dreams, I do. But I'm not sure it would be enough in real life. Right now I perform music and make buttons—it doesn't seem very respectable for the wife of Robert Stephenson, does it?"

Robert laughed. "You wouldn't need to work for money, Sorcha. Of course, you could still paint and create art for pleasure."

Am I insane? To give up a life with more leisure when I am so over-worked? What am I thinking? And I like Robert so well. Worship him, in fact!

But I don't want a life of being alone while my husband pursues his dreams.
Hardly seeing my husband.

"But not for anyone to see. For leisure. Painting all alone in my room." Sorcha considered. "I would love not to have to worry about money, but I want to create something to leave behind. My work matters to me as yours does to you, you must understand. I wasn't made to be in the house attending to domestic matters all day."

Robert sighed. "I had hoped...I thought...there might be children."

"I love children, too," Sorcha said.

"And what about playing at the pub?" Sorcha asked.

Robert appeared startled. "You play at a pub? Is it that important to you, Sorcha?"

"I love playing music."

Robert colored at the image which came to mind. "I would never ask you to give up playing music, Sorcha. But playing in a pub might not fit with your social standing as my wife. There will be official ceremonies and affairs of state. I will be traveling around England meeting dignitaries and people who are pillars in their respective communities. I'm not asking you not to be yourself. I always feel you are perfect just as you are. " He knitted his eyebrows. "I'm sure you could find another outlet for your music. Surely there is another way for you to play music."

Sorcha smiled knowingly. "I expect so. But...I can't see us together somehow. I think the world of you and I daresay I love you," Sorcha said. "But like a friend. It doesn't feel real. It never has. It's like some fantastic fairytale. Where everything I like to do I can't do anymore. I would be taken care of like a pet pug."

Sadness permeated his being. "Oh, Sorcha, it isn't like that at all. I love you and I want you to be my wife. I think we would be happy together. We always have been when we're together."

Sorcha's heart was breaking as she looked at him.

Am I letting my Prince Charming go?

"So do I, Robert." She smiled. "I know you will find the perfect woman for you. I do wish it could be me. But somehow I have never been able to picture it. You know I think in pictures." She added, "And I wish we had had more time to get to know each other before the demands of your job forced you to get your ducks in a row." *Or your wife all lined up.*

"If only we lived closer together, maybe..." He squeezed her hand with great longing in his eyes.

Suddenly a terror gripped her heart. "You wouldn't...you wouldn't end my father's employment, would you, Robert?"

Robert looked at her aghast. "Do you think so little of me, Sorcha?"

In an instant she felt a terrible pang in her heart. "Oh, no, of course not, it's just that he has been through so much, and I would hate to think that I..."

Robert released her hands and forced a smile. "I couldn't let him go if I wanted to. My father and the directors are keen to have him."

Sorcha smiled up at him, and they continued their walk.

"Is there someone else, Miss O'Shea?"

Sorcha nodded. "I think so."

"What…is special about him? What does he have that I don't?"

"I can be myself with him," Sorcha said simply.

Robert stopped in his tracks and turned to her. "You can't be yourself with me?"

Sorcha shrugged. "The first layer, yes. But I think I would have to give up some of myself to play the part."

Robert raised his eyebrows. He faced forward and they walked on.

He's going to make some woman very happy. She knew Robert would be fine.

I only hope there is someone for me.

CHAPTER FIFTY-SEVEN

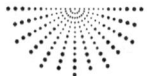

Belle Femme
Liverpool

"If you please, I'm here to see Miss O'Shea." Thaddeus walked into Madame Arquette's shop *Belle Femme* only to greet an expression of discomfort from the proprietor joined with an icy stare from an overbearing matron along. The shy daughter was more favorable in her assessment but allowed no voice in the matter.

Madame Arquette was serving tea to her clients while she displayed fabrics and designs. Madame Arquette knew, as did all successful mantua makers, that providing the appearance of exclusivity and luxury while prolonging the shopping experience was necessary to her success.

Thaddeus tipped his hat to the ladies. The older two frowned, but the young woman smiled. Thaddeus was, after all, tall and handsome with his dark blonde hair. He dressed fashionably, if not extravagantly.

"Isabelle! Pay attention!" The condescending Mama swatted her daughter's arm with a fan.

Sorcha looked up from her desk which faced the store window. She had a collection of beautiful buttons displayed in Madame Arquette's part of the shop.

Sorcha smiled and stood up, walking over to Thaddeus with an outstretched hand. She whispered, "Why are you here?"

"I'm glad to see you too, Miss O'Shea," he replied. "I came to see you, naturally."

"We can't talk here, it would disturb Madame Arquette's clients. Shall we go for a pot of tea at *Neptune's?*" she asked in hushed tones.

"Excellent idea." Thaddeus agreed with a nod.

Sorcha quickly put on her hat, gloves, and coat, grabbing her umbrella. "I'll be gone for a short time, Ma'am," she said to Madame Arquette with a curtsey. Isabelle looked at Sorcha with envy.

As Sorcha was leaving she heard the matron say to Madame Arquette, "Surely your button designer doesn't leave the store with a man and no chaperone?"

"He's from the newspaper. It's a professional relationship," Madame Arquette replied with raised eyebrows. "And they'll be in a public place to discuss business."

"Business indeed! Business is a man's realm. For goodness' sake, young ladies today!" the matron huffed, her stiff coiffure bouncing up and down as she shook her head.

Who does she think Madame Arquette is if not a business owner?

Sorcha sighed heavily. *I may have to bring one of my sisters in as a chaperone. Or just have Thaddeus tap on the window.*

Outside Thaddeus asked, "How is your new position progressing, Sorcha?"

"Oh, it's wonderful. I love it." Sorcha smiled sideways at him. "I can leave on occasion and go for a coffee and biscuit if I wish."

"What about that woman who was objecting to my escort?"

"Madame Arquette doesn't care as long as she has exquisite buttons on display which no one else has."

"She'll care if you offend her clients."

"I will have to make adjustments to avoid the appearance of impropriety." Sorcha shrugged. "I suppose doing my job isn't enough. It's shocking that women aren't allowed their own lives outside of work." Sorcha shook her head. "Why are spinster women treated so badly? As if they are only half-women? As if all they do is chase after men?"

"Shocking!" Thaddeus exclaimed. "But it would be even worse if unmarried women didn't chase after men. In which case all they would do is knit and dote on their cats."

"Far worse!" Sorcha giggled. Thaddeus could always put her in a good mood. "Everyone knows an animal lover is a threat to society."

"Yes, and a woman must get married, otherwise she will commit the worst sin of all," Thaddeus added.

"And what is that?"

"Not have babies of course."

"Repent!" A street preacher was yelling as they walked. *"Make an immediate decision for your salvation!"*

Sorcha nodded. "Yes, it is far better to be a widow than a spinster."

A whip cracked on hesitant horses as a carriage driver moved his carriage through the crowds.

"But you needn't worry as long as you create beautiful, unique buttons, Sorcha." Thaddeus grew serious. "I suppose you are learning the power in being in possession of a unique product in demand. No doubt you just show up to work when you wish and leave when you feel like it."

Sorcha raised her eyebrow at him. "Honestly, I could do the work at home and just supply Madame Arquette with the buttons, but being present allows me to paint something specific to the client."

"I expect your clients love that."

"Oh, they do. I have even painted children, grandchildren, and fiancés on the buttons. As well as pets and favorite flowers." Sorcha added softly, "For ladies with money, there is no limit to the things they can imagine want."

As they walked along the carriage wheels hitting the pebblestone road created a slight hissing sound.

"Forgive me, but buttons are not a very bold way to announce ones loved ones," Thaddeus considered.

"That is the point, Mr. Fulbright. It's a sort of game to hide one's heart's desires on oneself in miniature." She shook her head. "As a newspaper man you must learn to perceive the theme."

"Oh, I see. Much like the language of the fan," Thaddeus considered.

Sorcha nodded. "Clients love that they can have something so personalized. And the buttons become a family heirloom."

"I suppose one could have one's enemies painted on the buttons, too," Thaddeus said. "Something like a voodoo doll on one's chest."

Sorcha glanced sideways at him, suppressing her laughter. "Why must you either not grasp my point or take the train of logic one step too far?"

He shrugged. "I don't know. Too many university classes in philosophy I suppose."

"You are blaming your insolence on education?"

"Why not?"

Sorcha paused for reflection. "Back to the subject at hand, actually buttons are somewhat hidden, like a delicious mystery. Only visible upon close inspection. One might even hide one's true love from one's parents."

"Is that what you have done, Sorcha?"

She stopped in her tracks, almost colliding with a child running. "What do you mean, Thaddeus?"

He shook his head. "Never mind."

Once arrived at the *Neptune Coffee House* they were fortunate to find a seat next to the window. "So, what will it be, Miss O'Shea? Tea, coffee, or chocolate?"

She glanced sideways at him.

"I perceive the mischief in your eyes, Miss O'Shea! Chocolate it is!"

"Do you mind, Tad?"

"I would never deny you anything within my power to provide, my dear."

The rich, steaming chocolate and biscuits were served. Sorcha took a sip of her chocolate and sighed blissfully. "I never thought I would have such a delightful existence."

Thaddeus had concern in his eyes. "And are your earnings sufficient, Sorcha?"

"Even better than they were," she said.

"What are you doing with the extra money?" Thaddeus asked.

"I'm saving for a place of my own."

"Maybe I should marry you." Thaddeus considered. "Then you could take care of me."

Sorcha laughed, as she was wont to do in Thaddeus' presence. "Actually I am thinking of investing in the railways."

"That does seem more likely to produce a return," Thaddeus considered. "You're going to be an investor, Sorcha?"

She shrugged, taking a sip of chocolate. "I'm thinking of it as a savings account."

Thaddeus nodded. "Actually, though I'm not a gambling man, I believe the railways are a sound investment."

Suddenly she sobered. "Is your job going well, Tad?"

"Never better," Thaddeus said. "After the interest in my story on the shop girls of the city, Egerton has me covering every plight of the working class. The more misery, the better. And there is plenty of it here." He sobered. "You know, Liverpool is growing so fast. The crowding is leading to disease. Especially in dank basements."

"I'm sure I know that." Sorcha saddened.

Thaddeus had a sudden idea. "You know what this town needs, Sorcha?"

Sorcha shook her head.

"A public garden!"

"Oh, you mean like Hyde Park?"

He looked at her, surprised. "How do you know about Hyde Park, Sorcha?"

"I'm not illiterate, Thaddeus Fulbright." Sorcha shrugged. "I've heard talk."

"What do you know about Hyde Park?" Thaddeus repeated.

"I understand it is where the *ton* go to exhibit themselves."

Thaddeus laughed. "Yes, Hyde Park is a place to see and be seen—even kings and queens join the promenade—with carriages and horse riders prancing about, as well as the dandies, macaronis, and foreign dignitaries, but it is a public park. A place for parades, clandestine meetings, and even duels. Everyone is welcome."

"I gather Hyde Park is rather large?"

"350 Acres."

"Oh, my goodness. In the middle of the city?" Sorcha asked.

"Yes, in Westminster. The park was established by Henry VIII in 1536 when he took the land from Westminster Abbey that he might use it as a hunting ground. Hyde Park was opened to the public in 1637."

"How do you know so much about it, Tad?"

"Information is my business." He glanced up from his teacup. "And my family lives in London. Near Hyde Park as a matter of fact."

"Why don't you live in London then?" Sorcha asked. "Surely London needs reporters."

"If you knew my father you'd know why. I like to create some distance between us."

He could see the wheels turning now. "I'm sure you could help bring this public garden about, Tad. You know everyone in town."

"I suppose I do."

"Where there is an idea it begets reality," Sorcha considered. "But is a public garden your interest, Tad?"

"Why not? I've no objection." He smiled, and his blonde hair fell into his chocolate brown eyes.

* * *

IF YOU WANT A GARDEN, *it shall be done, my love.* Thaddeus cleared his throat, looking away. "More green spaces would deter the spread of disease."

Sorcha paused for a moment, staring at him quietly.

"Why are you looking at me that way, Sorcha?" *I hope I didn't reveal too much of my thoughts.*

"The sunlight came through the window, highlighting your hair, and you look very handsome."

"Thank you, Miss O'Shea. Do you need some hartshorn? Are you feeling faint?"

"Why?" she asked.

"You're complimenting me, of course. Are you well?"

Sorcha rolled her eyes, as if to regain her composure. "If your articles could save lives, wouldn't that be wonderful?"

"It would." Thaddeus nodded. "And green spaces would improve people's moods—and improve courtship."

Sorcha wrinkled her eyebrows. "What do you mean, Tad?"

"We wouldn't have to meet in the tea shop all the time. There would be alternatives out in nature and the fresh air."

She looked at him shyly. "Are you courting me Thaddeus Fulbright?"

"I would if I thought I had any hope….Although you've already done enough damage, Sorcha. Maybe I should leave it at that."

"What damage are you referring to, Thaddeus Fulbright?"

"I didn't think I was interested in any of these human interest stories until I met you, Sorcha. All of the sudden I care about other people. Care about someone other than myself."

"That's good isn't it?"

"I hate it." Thaddeus shook his head.

"Why?"

"Because I'm miserable all the time." He took a bite of biscuit. "Why else?"

"Why should you be miserable?"

"Think Sorcha. Now you are the one being obtuse. Because I am made aware of the misery of others. That makes me sad."

And because caring about you and what happens to you set up a longing in my heart that cannot be fulfilled. He sighed. *I think about you all the time, my love.*

Thaddeus sat up straight, as if to increase the formality between them. "Sorcha, did you hear of Robert Stephenson's marriage to Fanny Sanderson?" He watched her reaction intently.

"I did. I'm sure I wish them happy."

He straightened his cravat with his free hand. "You don't wish it were you instead of Fanny?"

Her eyes opened wide. "Thaddeus Fulbright, you are the nosiest person I ever met!"

"Well? Do you?"

She sighed heavily. "I don't. I don't think we would have suited."

"Wouldn't have suited? Robert Stephenson is a good man. And going to be very rich."

"Indeed. However…as much as I like him—which is a great deal—he is a bit too stuffy for me." She smiled.

"I suppose you can't say that about me," Thaddeus considered.

"Oh, no!" Sorcha giggled. "And…I think I would rather be *cherished* than simply needed. Much in the same way a housekeeper is required."

Thaddeus took her hand and leaned towards her, saying softly, "I cherish you. I want us to be together. I want to marry you. I love you, Sorcha Fae."

Sorcha gasped, taken by surprise. She glanced out the window. "Passersby can see us Tad!" She pulled her hand away.

"What do you say, Sorcha? I've just proposed marriage to you. Do me the honor of a reply."

"Thaddeus Fulbright, I...I...I love you too." She took her fan out of her purse and opened it behind her head so as not to be seen by those walking by the shop. "But this is not the place..."

"You do?" he exclaimed, studying her intently. "Like married kind of love? Or friend love?"

Oh, please dear God, let me love Sorcha forever.

"Both. We go together well. I'd like us to be together."

Thaddeus couldn't believe what he was hearing. *This is the best day of my life.* "I would too, Sorcha! More than anything in the world. But..."

"But what?" Sorcha asked.

His mood fell momentarily. *I have to tell her the truth.* "I never thought I would be good enough for you, Sorcha."

"Oh, I'm sure you are." She smiled mischievously. "Or you will be soon."

He leaned over the table, his face close to hers. "I've a mind to kiss you, Sorcha O'Shea."

"Don't you dare, Thaddeus Fulbright! You can't do that in here!"

"You've made me so happy. I never thought you reciprocated my affection."

"And why not? I am an open book to read."

"You're so mean to me, it's difficult to tell." Thaddeus returned to his seat. "Look, Sorcha, some people never find anyone to love them—or to spend their lives with. I've been alone for so long, since I was thirteen, really. I never want to take it for granted."

"This is an odd place to make a declaration." She looked around the coffee shop, placing her gloved hand on her mouth.

"Where should I have done it?" Thaddeus shrugged. "Liverpool hasn't built the park yet."

"What about the Theatre Royal in Williamson Square?" Sorcha suggested. "Fanny Kemble is performing there tonight. My two tickets should be there."

"Oh, that's a much better idea," Thaddeus agreed. "I wish I'd thought of it. That's a grand theatre and very opulent."

"I've heard it's quite elegant."

"I feel like I need to give you an engagement gift—earrings or a necklace or a friendship ring. I know my father would insist upon it."

"Oh, I don't think that is necessary."

"But would you kiss me in the middle of the entrance hall of the Theatre Royal, Sorcha?"

"I don't know if that's quite proper. It might ruin my reputation!"

"I want to kiss you now, Sorcha."

"Not here!" she said, blushing. "All right, perhaps the Theatre Royal. Or….if we're in a carriage on the way?"

"That's a good idea. Definitely a carriage. And we should have a nice dinner planned for the occasion. Just one more thing," Tad said.

"What is it?" Sorcha asked.

"Are you going to say 'yes'?" Thaddeus asked, his eyes hopeful. He took her gloved hand and kissed it. "Will you spend the rest of your life with me?"

"Do you need to know now?" Sorcha asked.

"Naturally I do. I don't want to be out the expense of buying you a gift if you're going to say 'no.'"

Sorcha covered her mouth, suppressing her laughter. Regaining her composure, she said, "That's not very gentlemanly, Thaddeus Fulbright."

Thaddeus shrugged. "Maybe not. But it is opportune. And I do like a wife who knows how to manage money—as well as make it."

Sorcha sobered. "Do you think we will do well together, Tad?"

"It's going to be exhausting, Sorcha, with your constantly pointing out the ills of the world—and my shortcomings. And wanting me to do something about it. And…*I'll be so happy to be with you.*"

She tapped her fingers on her chin. "It could be a fun time, as I think about it."

He took her hand against her protestations. "The best. I think we'll have an interesting and unpredictable life with a great deal of laughter. It's fascinating times we live in, Sorcha."

Sorcha had to agree. "Yes, Tad. It certainly is." She smiled at him. "I have another question."

"Yes?"

"Where shall we live?"

"Where do you want to live, dearest?"

"Oh, I was thinking of London, perhaps. I've never been, you know."

"I am partial to Liverpool. It's something of a cesspool. The over-crowding, the crime, the disease. I would have thought it exactly your cup of tea, Miss O'Shea."

"It all lends itself to the intrigue," Sorcha agreed.

"Yes, Liverpool is perfect. Many opportunities for a newspaper man."

Sorcha considered. "Though I'm sure you could find the underbelly of wherever you went, Thaddeus."

"True. With that in mind, we could always go to London for our honeymoon."

"That or Paris," Sorcha considered. "But I'll plan the honeymoon. I don't want to go to gambling dens or cocaine dens on my honeymoon." Sorcha knew very well they couldn't afford a honeymoon, and that any money they had would go towards a home of their own, but she appeared to enjoy playing along.

"Sounds a bit dull. But as you wish, my love. We can always get back to the fun when we return. As long as I'm with you, it will be as wonderful as all those places."

Sorcha and Thaddeus did kiss. On the steps of the Theatre Royal under the moonlight with all the people coming and going.

He pulled her close to him.

"Thaddeus! I didn't realize you are so strong! I can't move."

"Good." He leaned down to kiss her. His lips touched hers, so soft, and he was relieved to find them eager to meet his.

All the world stood still as he kissed her, a moment he would remember forever.

"Sorcha, you're the only girl for me," he whispered at the end of their long engagement kiss.

"Oh, my goodness, Tad, I feel like I am floating on air."

"Take my arm, my love. Our carriage awaits."

They stepped inside and he allowed her to feel a great deal more.

CHAPTER FIFTY-EIGHT

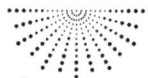

"*The Irish hate our order, our civilization, our enterprising industry, our pure religion. This wild, reckless, indolent, uncertain and superstitious race have no sympathy with the English character. Their ideal of human felicity is an alternation of clannish broils and coarse idolatry. Their history describes an unbroken circle of bigotry and blood." – Benjamin Disraeli, Prime Minister*

"YOU CAN'T BE SERIOUS, Thaddeus. You wish to marry an Irish girl?" Clifford Fulbright was formidable sitting behind a large mahogany desk in his study.

"Quite serious. Why wouldn't I be?" Thaddeus asked. "I love her."

"Haven't you heard of the 'Irish Problem' Thaddeus? The Irish are a terrible influence upon society. A bunch of rabble-rousers and trouble makers who don't appreciate their benefactors."

"Hmmm…you don't say, Father? Interesting." Thaddeus nodded appreciatively. "There's always the possibility they wish to rule themselves."

"Irish Home Rule? Don't be absurd!" Clifford huffed indignantly. "Why haven't the Irish conquered and colonized the earth if they are so deserving of self-determination?"

"I don't believe Ireland wishes to colonize anyone. They only wish to rule themselves."

"Don't be dense, Thaddeus!" his father commanded.

"I'm not intending to be. I don't see that there is any connection."

"England has the right to rule because She *does* rule. It is not chance but racial superiority which has made Britain the ruler of all the world."

"Ah, so now we come to your point. Racial superiority." Thaddeus wrinkled his brow. "Are the Irish of a different race? We're both white, are we not?"

"And furthermore," Clifford Fulbright continued, "If the Irish were entitled to independence, they would be independent. They are brainless commoners."

"I see you've given this a great deal of thought, Father. But possibly you've missed a point or two. So if a thief comes into your house and steals your possessions, you will congratulate him and not press charges? And offer him your wife as well?"

"Of course not!" Clifford Fulbright boomed. "What nonsense are you spouting?"

"After all, the fact that the thief took your things is proof that he deserves them." Thaddeus nodded reflectively as if seriously considering the argument. "We can take whatever we want because we are superior to you?"

"That's not what I said Thaddeus!"

"It certainly was, expounding the superiority of the aggressor. Only consider, Father: an aggressor is not superior: he's a bully who has no respect for the rights and claims of others. To take what is not yours is mere thievery. Perhaps it is we who are the criminals."

Clifford frowned. "What have they taught you in school, Thaddeus? It is the War Office which has paid for your schooling, Thaddeus."

"I'm very aware of that, Father."

"The Irish are backward and lazy. Violent and alcoholic," Clifford said, taking a sip of his whiskey.

"The O'Sheas are a lovely family. I count myself fortunate to be welcomed into their family." Thaddeus raised his eyebrows. "I hope you can extend the same courtesy, Father. I wouldn't wish to think an Irish family has better manners than you do."

Clifford tapped his fingers on his desk. "Are they wealthy?"

"Not at all."

"So they are poor?"

Thaddeus shrugged. "It's not a crime."

"Yes, I've seen your articles on the poor." Clifford frowned. "Is the girl Catholic?"

"Yes, Miss Sorcha O'Shea and her family are Catholic."

"Then it won't be legal to marry her. You can't be married in her church."

"I am well aware of Hardwick's Marriage Act of 1753," Thaddeus said.

"A marriage must be performed within the Anglican Church to be legal," Clifford Fulbright reiterated.

"I have already applied for a special license," Thaddeus said. "We will have our marriage legalized in an Anglican church then we will be married in her Catholic church."

"An unofficial ceremony." Clifford shook his head.

"British law is not the only reality," Thaddeus said.

Clifford stood up and banged his fist on his desk. "I forbid this marriage, Thaddeus!"

Thaddeus remained calm. "You may do as you wish, Father. But I'm going to marry Sorcha. She is the most wonderful thing to ever happen to me. I've never been more sure of anything in my life."

"You defy me, Thaddeus?" Mr. Fulbright appeared shocked.

Thaddeus stood, tipping his hat to his father. "If you don't wish to see any of your grandchildren, let me know now so I can take your name off the guest list, Father. I must warn you, though, Mother would be none too happy about it."

Thaddeus reached the door of the study. He turned around to behold his father's stupefaction.

"Oh, and by the by, Father, I've changed parties. I'm now a Whig."

Clifford Fulbright's jaw dropped. He looked as if his son had just informed him he had assisted the infamous serial murderer William Burke in killing countless unsuspecting citizens in order to sell the victims' bodies to medical schools for research.

Thaddeus knew well that this was the greatest insult of all. An Irish daughter-in-law Clifford Fulbright might be able to stomach, but a Whig for a son?

Never.

CHAPTER FIFTY-NINE

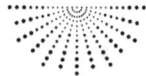

The Wedding
May 15, 1830
Liverpool

he long-awaited nuptials of this reporter Thaddeus Fulbright and his beautiful bride Sorcha Fae O'Shea (at least long-awaited by the groom; the bride has only just consented to marry that fortunate fellow) took place on May 15, 1830, at the bride's church, St. Anthony's, a beautiful and majestic gothic cathedral in the city of Liverpool.

Red carpet led to the altar surrounded by five exquisitely beautiful stained glass windows. The enormous organ was on the second story in the organ loft. On either side of the organ recess were two 17th century painted panels depicting Nativity and Epiphany scenes.

Miss O'Shea positively took the groom's breath away when he first saw her.

The stunning bride's wedding dress was a simple white silk satin with a raised waist, puffed sleeves to her elbows, and a décolletage accented with lace below her lovely shoulders. The dress was decorated with orange blossoms. With her strawberry blonde hair and aquamarine eyes, the bride was in no need of ornamentation at all. Even so, Miss O'Shea was breathtaking with a flower wreath of orange blossoms in her hair, as well as a veil. She carried white callas lilies and English bluebells.

Speaking of ornamentation, Miss O'Shea's wedding dress had ivory buttons hand-painted by the bride herself and depicting herself, her husband-to-be, yours truly, and certain significant Irish symbols such as the rainbow, the shamrock, the Celtic Cross of St. Patrick, the Claddagh as a token of friendship and love, and the Celtic Knot, indicating no beginning or end.

This reporter can say beyond a doubt that Miss O'Shea was the most beautiful bride to ever walk down an aisle. Dear reader, if you doubt this reporter's objectivity, let it be known that he was not the only one to say so, though certainly he is the greatest authority on the subject.

Even our beloved Queen Adelaide in her marriage to King William in 1818, with no expenses spared, who wore a satin dress superbly trimmed with Brussels point lace and silver tassels, as well as a wreath of diamonds in her hair, did not present a more stunning image than Miss O'Shea walking down the aisle with her father, Mr. Sean O'Shea, soon to be a constable on the Liverpool – Manchester railway.

Surely those present on the occasion of the wedding ceremony of Sorcha O'Shea and Thaddeus Fulbright represented a broad range of Liverpool society, including friends and family, many of the Irish community, as well as pillars of the community such as Mr. Everton Smith, owner of the Liverpool Mercury, and Mr. and Mrs. Lawrence Davenport of the Davenport Mercantile. Also present were the groom's illustrious parents, Clifford Fulbright, lately of the war office, and his wife Mrs. Lucinda Fulbright, who provided a honeymoon to London for the newly married couple, a city which the bride had long expressed a desire to see, with a particular interest in Hyde Park.

Everton Smith, the groom's employer, generously provided oysters and a roasted pig for the wedding reception, which was otherwise catered by friends and family with Irish Soda bread, baked cabbage, stewed tomatoes, potato pancakes, deviled eggs, and baked beans. Ale was provided by Ye Olde Hole in the Wall. The luscious 5-tiered wedding cake of vanilla buttercream was made by the bride's mother Mrs. Cecelia O'Shae and paternal Grandmother Oonagh.

Music was provided by the father of the bride and his band. At the reception the unconventional bride even sang "The One I love" to her new husband, much to the gratification of all present. There was not a dry eye in the grand hall, least of all the groom's.

The groom made a gift to his bride of a simple gold ring depicting the

Trinity Knot, which he promised to have inlaid with emeralds when he might afford to do so. The bride subsequently expressed indifference to worldly riches, despite their being of use to those of us living in the world.

Following a short honeymoon in London taking in the sights, Mr. Thaddeus Fulbright and his bride will be establishing their home in a small flat on Fleet Street.

No one could be happier than this reporter, who counts himself to be the luckiest of men. To be sure, no one would have thought when he left Liverpool to cover the race of the steam locomotives at the Rainhill Trials that he would return with a heart already given to one Sorcha Fae O'Shea, then a button-maker at Davenport's Department & Mercantile still holding exclusive rights to the depictions of the Rainhill Trials races (and now with her private line of elegant designs at Madame Arquette's Belle Femme).

To be sure, this humble reporter owes his happiness to this illustrious steam locomotive competition, followed by many readers, which introduced him to the beautiful and intelligent woman who consented to be his bride.

May all be as happy as this reporter now finds himself, with a future as bright as it is unpredictable and exciting.

-Thaddeus Fulbright, The Liverpool Mercury

RIDING in a carriage to London with her new husband—as there was not yet a train to that cosmopolitan city—Mrs. Sorcha Fulbright smiled as she folded the newspaper which would go into her keepsake chest.

She was well aware that most people in her social class could not afford a wedding. A small party before the priest after the reading of the banns would have been the sum of it.

Though not extravagant, Sorcha thought there could be no wedding this side of heaven more lovely than hers.

And a honeymoon! She never imagined she could have one! Granted, she would be staying with her in-laws, but as long as Thaddeus was there she was happy. And she would see London!

Her father-in-law was a bit icy at first, but he was coming around, as evidenced by the invitation.

Sorcha closed her eyes momentarily, remembering walking down the long aisle with her father.

I have never been so happy in my life.

Thaddeus took her hand. "We will spend our honeymoon in Mivart's Hotel in Mayfair and then move into my parents' residence after three nights."

"Oh dear, can we afford it?"

Thaddeus smiled. "Indeed we can. Mr. Mivart is a friend of my father's."

"I don't wish to take advantage," Sorcha whispered.

"I certainly do," he murmured in her ear. He leaned over and kissed her deeply, expressing his own intent so convincingly.

"Thaddeus Fulbright, you can't be behaving this way all the way to London!"

He took her in his arms and held her to his chest, kissing her thoroughly. "I fully intend to, Mrs. Fulbright! And for a great deal of time beyond that!"

She looked at her husband, his eyes so full of hope and promise.

Sorcha sighed. "I suppose we must to something to pass the time."

He laughed and kissed her again.

"I am sure this is the best honeymoon anyone ever had," she murmured.

The End
And the Beautiful Beginning

MAGICAL AMULET

If you enjoyed this book, ***please consider writing a review or rating the book***. Reviews and ratings are the magical amulet of authors today: without reviews, our books have no visibility on Amazon – and readers do not find them. You would be surprised at the jump in visibility **one review** creates. If you like a book, the surest way to insure an author can continue writing for a living is to write a review. Yes, ONE review makes a difference!

Another way to help an author out is to follow him/her on Bookbub. Authors have had their careers made on Bookbub, which is really the only platform for self-pubs:
https://www.bookbub.com/settings/authors#authors-search

Thank you for reading this novel. If you enjoyed it, this alone means the world to an author. We love to hear from our readers. Personal notes are always appreciated. I am not the most techie person, so, if you don't hear back, it means I didn't see your note. I am still in the 19th century, after all. I can be reached at suzetteholl@gmail.com or
http://suzettehollingsworth.com/contact/.

Sign up for my newsletter for new releases, sales, giveaways, and insider info.

http://eepurl.com/bsJHXL

Like me on facebook "Suzette Hollingsworth",

https://www.facebook.com/HistoricalMysteryRomance/

ALSO BY SUZETTE HOLLINGSWORTH

"Daughters of the Empire" historical romance:
THE DESTINY CODE: the Soldier and the Mystic
(A closet Victorian psychic and a British soldier)
THE SERENADE: the Prince and the Siren
(A Royal romance)
THE RESISTANCE: The Contessa and the Shadow Knight
(a World War II spy novel)

"The Great Detective in Love" romantic historical mystery:
Sherlock Holmes and the Case of the Sword Princess
Sherlock Holmes and the Dance of the Tiger
Sherlock Holmes and the Chocolate Menace
Sherlock Holmes and the Vampire Invasion

"Romancing the Rails" traditional historical romance
"Race to Rainhill": A Dawn of the Railways Romance

Next:

A London spinster daringly embarks upon a railway journey and finds romance

(Title forthcoming)

ABOUT THE AUTHOR

Suzette writes on the cusp of historical romance and historical fiction interwoven with high adventure.

Suzette's writing style combines wit with elegance and can be described as "A Jane Austen and Robert Downey Jr. meet on the African Queen type of Historical Romance". She writes an entertaining, humorous read with an authentic historical setting. All of her series utilize actual historical figures extensively researched. Suzette's goal for the reader is an historical immersion experience.

You can contact Suzette http://suzettehollingsworth.com/contact/. If you enjoyed this book, please post a rating or write a review, which enables the author to continue writing for a living.

Suzette Hollingsworth grew up in Wyoming and Texas, went to school in Tennessee (Sewanee), lived in Europe two summers, and now resides in beautiful Washington State with her cartoonist/author husband Clint, Go-Go Destructo, George Clone-y, Captain Jack, and StingRay. She loves to be in that creative place which writing, music, and dance offers. She enjoys travel and snorkeling; she has a dream to visit Switzerland and to swim with the whales in French Polynesia.

I have a wonderful memory of riding the train with my mother and sister (from Rock Springs, Wyoming to Los Angeles). I loved eating in the dining room with the sound of the wheels going round and round and a red rose on the table. My mother let me have tomato juice with breakfast! I still love tomato juice with pepper (and other additions). At that time (the 1960s) it was not expensive to have a private compartment or we couldn't have done it: the trains just lined the aisles with beds and curtain closures. Anyone could have come along and snatched children out of the beds! It just amazes me. And yet we were all more than fine. It was a fantastic journey and memory.

Suzette's goal in writing historical fiction is that you, the reader, will engage in a magical journey and time travel through her books. She is very excited about her next series of Railway romances, highlighting the golden age of rail.

Full Steam Ahead!

AUTHOR'S NOTES

I hope this novel has made the very exciting and romantic period which constitutes the beginning of the railways come alive for you, communicating something of the era and the ambiance while telling a love story.

From what we have been taught, it sounds unbelievable that a woman in 1830 could make enough to support a family outside of an illegal or lurid profession. But I actually have a friend, Michele Martin Kelly, whose Italian great-grandmother brought her entire family to America (New York) from Italy, supporting them all by making buttons! I was astonished to learn this: that button-making could be that lucrative and that *a woman* could support her family before women could even vote!

To be sure, there weren't zippers or Velcro, and everything utilized buttons for fastening: clothing, dresses, pants, jackets, even hats, bags, and undergarments.

We sometimes think a premise couldn't be true because we are indoctrinated with what *the majority* did: the majority of women could not make anything but dirt poor wages outside of prostitution or inheritance (so far as we are told). It is true that social, legal, political, and economic conditions were terrible for women prior to the 20th century. But there are always exceptions to the norms, and our minds have to entertain the possibilities to arrive at the reality.

An excellent book and resource is "**The Rainhill Trials: The Birth of Commercial Rail**" by Christopher McGowan, which delves deep into George Stephenson's character and antics as well as into the politics of the time. I was shocked to learn that some things never change in terms of human behavior. For example, the Rocket was the clear winner of the Trials (no other locomotive even completed the trials!) and yet there was, in truth, a large segment of fans who were claiming the competition was unfair and that one of the other locomotives should have won. Go figure. There is a lot of fascinating behind-the-scenes information in McGowan's book.

Robert Stephenson:

Robert Stephenson was a real person, the builder of the *Rocket*, and the son of George Stephenson "the father of the modern railway".

Robert's mother did, in fact, die when he was three years of age. **The only variation from the truth is Robert's love interest.** In 1829, three months before the Rainhill Trials, Robert married **Frances Sanderson**; the couple had no children, and he did not remarry after her death in 1842.

"My dear Fanny died this morning at five o'clock. God grant that I might close my life as she has done, in true faith and in charity with all men. Her last moments were perfect calmness."- Robert Stephenson's diary entry on 4 October 1842.

Every descriptor of George Stephenson is true according to historical records. **George Stephenson** began work without a grade school education and was illiterate until he returned to school to learn to read and write. I believe George was promoted to engineer while illiterate. He was a mechanical genius and a determined and disciplined person.

Robert had a long and illustrious career as well. Robert's death was deeply mourned throughout the country, His funeral cortège was given permission by the Queen to pass through Hyde Park, an honor previously reserved for royalty.

A staunch conservative, Robert Stephenson was elected unopposed as a Member of Parliament for Whitby in 1847, serving in that capacity until his death in 1859 of nephritis (inflammation of the kidneys).

Robert Stephenson was a lifelong friend with Brunel, probably the two most famous engineers of the age. Reports are they partied together:

drink and cards. Brunel was more temperamental and not as well liked on a personal level as Robert. Robert Stephenson had a likeable, kind, polite personality and he was well-liked. He was also able to induce people who might otherwise be his competitor to help him with his projects, Brunel being an excellent example. i.e., Robert could win people over. In his turn, he helped and assisted others.

Although George gave Robert more advantages than he himself had, Robert still had to make his own way. It is clear that George Stephenson taught his son a strong work ethic from an early age.

Sorcha O'Shea is a fictional character and Robert Stephenson was a real person (historical figure).

"Born on 16th October 1803 in Northumberland, **Robert Stephenson's** early life displayed few clues that he would become one of the greatest engineers of the 19th century. While his father George had been born to poor and illiterate parents (George was himself illiterate until the age of 18), Robert's start in life was only marginally better. His father was a brakesman at the local colliery, and by the time he was three, his mother Agnes had died of tuberculosis. The infant Robert was subsequently left with a housekeeper while George departed for Scotland to look for work, eventually returning to the colliery at Killingworth, where he became an expert in steam machinery: the first step in an illustrious career that would make him the 'Father of Railways'. Despite having little formal education, George was determined that his son would benefit from one, and at the age of 11, Robert was sent to the Percy Street Academy in Newcastle, where he borrowed books that he would study with his father. In 1813, Robert was apprenticed to a local colliery manager, during which time he constructed a mining compass that he would later use to survey the High Level Bridge in Newcastle upon Tyne."

https://www.theengineer.co.uk/content/in-depth/late-great-engineers-robert-stephenson/

George Stephenson remarried **Elizabeth Hindmarsh**, who died 1845. He then married **Ellen Gregory**, who he was married to until his death in 1848. George was a very hard worker and a saver, he didn't drink or gamble, and he took care of his parents until their deaths. "Stephenson financially supported the wives and families of several who had died in his employment, due to accident or misadventure, some within his family, and some not."

https://en.wikipedia.org/wiki/George_Stephenson

The fight scene at the Rainhill Trials is fictional. There were no doubt fights and brawls over the eight days, but this specific fight didn't happen to my knowledge. There was a great deal of animosity towards the winner, even from reputable sources such as the *Popular Mechanics Magazine*, even though the Rocket was the only locomotive to complete the trials.

Railway personnel:

Locomotive. A typical steam locomotive had an engine and a tender for carrying fuel and water for the boiler. Two crew members worked in the engine's cab: **the engineer ran the locomotive, and the fireman managed the boiler and helped watch for signals**. Both jobs were highly skilled.

https://americanhistory.si.edu/america-on-the-move/lives-railroad

The Iron Horses:

It's very interesting that many of the descriptions of the trains were in terms of horses. Presumably because horses were the mode of transportation everyone was used to, trains fell into that same category (transportation), so the mind tended to draw comparisons. We still talk about machines in terms of "horsepower".

Rainhill Trials Prizes:

Rocket: 500 pounds and contract to build the locomotives for the Liverpool-Manchester Railway*

Sans Pareil: 24 or 26 pounds (equivalent to 2400 pounds today). Plus, after all the fuss Hackworth stirred up, the directors purchased Sans Pareil for 550 pounds (which Hackworth also complained about, saying it didn't cover his expenses) which was used on the Bolton & Leigh Railway for 15 years.

Perseverance: Burstall proposed building a locomotive for the company, which was denied, but Burstall was awarded 25 pounds to help defray his Rainhill Trials expenses.

Novelty: Directors placed an order with Braithwaite and Ericsson for 2 similar but larger locomotives (William IV and Queen Adelaide), against George Stephenson's recommendation, neither of which worked very well, rejected by the Liverpool and Manchester Railway– (McGowan, p.224)

Value of 1829 British pounds today | UK Inflation Calculator

in2013dollars.com

https://www.in2013dollars.com > inflation > 1829

£100 in 1829 is equivalent in purchasing power to about **£14,046.13 today**, an increase of £13,946.13 over 194 years. (multiplier is 140)

The Steam Locomotive Entries into "The Rainhill Trials":

By Unknown author - Illustrated London News. Image taken from http://www.edgehillstation.co.uk/resources/rainhill-trials-in-the-illustrated-london-news/, Public Domain, https://commons.wikimedia.org/w/index.php?curid=30617765

In the foreground is *Rocket* and in the background are *Sans Pareil* (right) and *Novelty*.

Stephenson's Rocket picture:

Public Domain, https://commons.wikimedia.org/w/index.php?curid=216014

Hacksworth's Sans Pareil drawing:

By The Mechanics Magazine, Public Domain, https://commons. wikimedia.org/w/index.php?curid=215835

Burstall's Perseverance drawing:

Public Domain, https://commons.wikimedia.org/w/index.php? curid=216004

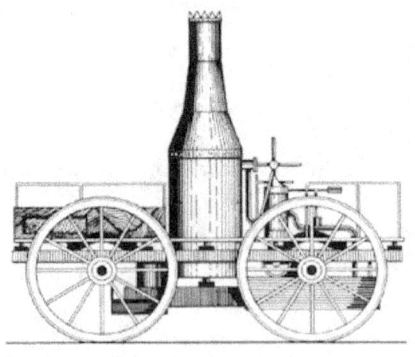

Ericsson and Braithwaite's Novelty:

Public Domain, https://commons.wikimedia.org/w/index.php?curid=216302

Brandreth's Cycloped:

By Elijah Galloway - 'History and Progress of the Steam Engine', by Elijah Galloway (1831)., Public Domain, https://commons.wikimedia.org/w/index.php?curid=73136158

A succinct summary of the Rainhill Trials (Wikipedia):

The length of the L&MR that ran past Rainhill village was straight and level for over 1 mile (1.6 km), and was chosen as the site for the trials. The locomotives were to run at Kenrick's Cross, on the mile east from the Manchester side of Rainhill Bridge. Two or three locomotives ran each day, and several tests for each locomotive were performed over the course of six days. Between 10,000 and 15,000 people turned up to watch the trials and bands provided musical entertainment on both days.

Cycloped was the first to drop out of the competition. It used a horse walking on a drive belt for power and was withdrawn after an accident caused the horse to burst through the floor of the engine.

The next locomotive to retire was ***Perseverance***, which was damaged in transit to the competition. Burstall spent the first five days of the trials repairing his locomotive, and though it ran on the sixth day, it failed to reach the required 10 miles per hour (16 km/h) speed and was withdrawn from the trial. It was granted a £25 consolation prize (equal to £2,340 today).

Sans Pareil nearly completed the trials, though at first there was some doubt as to whether it would be allowed to compete as it was 300 pounds (140 kg) overweight. However, it did eventually complete eight trips before cracking a cylinder. Despite the failure it was purchased by the L&MR, where it ran for two years before being leased to the Bolton and Leigh Railway.

The last locomotive to drop out was ***Novelty***. In contrast to *Cycloped*, it used advanced technology for 1829 and was lighter and considerably faster than the other locomotives in the competition. It was the crowd favorite and reached a then-astonishing 28 miles per hour (45 km/h) on the first day of competition. It later suffered damage to a boiler pipe which could not be fixed properly on site. Nevertheless, it ran the next day and reached 15 miles per hour (24 km/h) before the repaired pipe failed and damaged the engine severely enough that it had to be withdrawn.

The ***Rocket*** was the only locomotive that completed the trials. It averaged 12 miles per hour (19 km/h) and achieved a top speed of 30 miles per hour (48 km/h)) hauling 13 tons, and was declared the winner of the £500 prize (equal to £46,810 today). The Stephensons were given the contract to produce locomotives for the L&MR.

The **sealant** at the time was cement-like, and the Novelty's boiler would have required more time for the seal to set. (Christopher McGowan, The Rainhill Trials). But then, generally in a contest, the entrant is as is: judges don't give one two, three, four opportunities to make repairs! It seems these judges truly wanted to get the best locomotive and were giving the entrants every opportunity to provide their best effort.

Fanny Kemble, a famous actress of the day who truly did save her parents' theatre, described her first ride on a locomotive as follows:

"We were introduced to the little engine which was to drag us along the rails. She (for they make these curious little fire-horses all mares) consisted of a boiler, a stove, a small platform, a bench, and behind the bench a barrel containing enough water to prevent her being thirsty for fifteen miles, — the whole machine not bigger than a common fire-engine. She goes upon two wheels, which are her feet, and are moved by bright steel legs called pistons; these are propelled by steam, and in proportion as more steam is applied to the upper extremities (the hip-joints, I suppose) of these pistons, the faster they move the wheels; and when it is desirable to diminish the speed, the steam, which unless suffered to escape would burst the boiler, evaporates through a safety-valve into the air. The reins, bit, and bridle of this wonderful beast is a small steel handle, which applies or withdraws the steam from its legs or pistons, so that a child might manage it. The coals, which are its oats, were under the bench, and there was a small glass tube affixed to the boiler, with water in it, which indicates by its fullness or emptiness when the creature wants water, which is immediately conveyed to it from its reservoirs. There is a chimney to the stove, but as they burn coke there is none of the dreadful black smoke which accompanies the progress of a steam vessel. This snorting little animal, which I felt rather inclined to pat, was then harnessed to our carriage, and, Mr. Stephenson having taken me on the bench of the engine with him, we started at about ten miles an hour. The steam-horse being ill adapted for going up and down hill, the road was kept at a certain level, and appeared sometimes to sink below the surface of the earth, and sometimes to rise above it. Almost at starting it was cut through the solid rock, which formed a wall on either side of it, about sixty feet high."

Newspaper Articles:

Almost all of the newspaper articles purportedly written by Thaddeus Fulbright were taken from actual newspaper articles written in 1829 and 1830 by someone else (Thaddeus is a fictional character), as found on **"British Newspaper Archives"**, with some changes to the wording for modern clarity.

For accuracy's sake, I thought it important to go to actual historical records which described the events first-hand, not because I want to take credit for the writing of others. Most of the articles were not signed by the author, just the newspaper name, or I would certainly give credit.

The newspaper sources are the **Morning Post, Bury and Norwish Post, Lancaster Gazette, Manchester Courier, Chester Courant**, and **English Chronicle and Whitehall Evening Post**.

"Suicide of a Poor Needlewoman" was an actual article written at the time describing the plight of the poor and, in particular, of seamstresses doing piece work. It's all true. From **Henry Mayhew's "Labour and the Poor, 1849-50"**.

It's not a matter of plagiarism because these works are in the public domain, adding greatly to the historical accuracy of an historical fiction work such as this, but a writer should not take credit for another writer's works.

Arguments over the 'Fairness' of the Rainhill Trials and Who actually should have won:

I never expected to come across rage and disinformation around the winner when I began my research! I initially believed I was simply researching the particulars of a race.

It is an historical fact that, in spite of the *Rocket* being the only steam locomotive to complete the trials, there were many people who thought *Novelty* or *Sans Pareil* should have won the Rainhill Trials (even scientists and reporters, including *Popular Mechanics* magazine). I.e., in spite of the facts, there were those who started with their feelings and then came up with the "facts" to support their feelings.

Sound familiar? I have taken these biased and enraged reports almost verbatim from the newspaper reports of the day (see British Newspaper Archives).

Regardless of the outcome, both of the losing contenders were given many opportunities to prove their worth and to succeed. The directors purchased the *Sans Pareil* from Hackworth for 550 pounds once the cracked cylinders had been replaced. *Sans Pareil* was used on the Bolton

& Leigh Railway where it remained in regular service for the next fifteen years. (McGowan, p. 229)

As for Braithwaite and Ericsson, "Once *Novelty* had been repaired it was tried out again at Rainhill, but it was not a success and continued to break down." (McGowan, p. 224). Even so the directors placed an order for two locomotives with Braithwaite and Ericsson (named *William IV* and *Queen Adelaide*), which were "so painfully slow that on two occasions one of Stephenson's locomotives had to assist with a push." (McGowan). Braithwaite and Ericsson were, by accounts, likeable and gentlemanly, and apparently had success in other endeavors, especially in steam fire engines.

I found this recurring theme during the Rainhill Trials fascinating in its relevance today:

1. the power of the media to subvert the news. (I love and revere the media, there is no democracy without the media: an overriding characteristic of dictatorships is to have no free press. I am pointing out the power of language to persuade and alter the perception of reality)

2. the twisting of the facts by those who want to believe something other than what is actually happening before their own eyes.

When I was in college, I took a political science course in which our assignment was to read the same event described by both a liberal and a conservative newspaper. In the liberal paper, certain people were described as "freedom fighters". In the conservative paper, the same people were described as "terrorists". Which is true? The point is that some concepts presented as facts are actually opinions. Simply be aware of that when formulating your own conclusions.

The inability to identify conspiracy theories is particularly pronounced in America, possibly because we want to "protect" our children from thinking, as well as from uncomfortable truths. Children in Europe are taught in school how to identify these theories based on 1. Who is behind the theory? 2. What is their agenda? 3. What is the emotion the source wishes to illicit? 4. What does the source want you to believe and why? And, naturally, 5. Follow the money.

https://www.theguardian.com/education/article/2024/aug/10/uk-children-to-be-taught-how-to-spot-extremist-content-and-misinformation-online

I admire Germany as a nation and a culture because Germans are able to learn from their mistakes. They adamantly teach about the holo-caust in schools because they don't want any repeat of the same mistakes. **It is against the law to *deny* the *Holocaust* or to propagate Nazi and anti-Semitic hate speech.**

Feli from Germany describes the German school system she attended:

https://www.youtube.com/watch?v=DMNJk1LNV0w

Contrast this to Florida, where it is illegal NOT to deny history: i.e., it is a REQUIREMENT to deny history. It is illegal to talk about racial inequality, Black history, and the wrongs done to African-Americans. How can an American deny slavery and segregation? And that slavery's legacy might have an impact? The "Stop WOKE Act", enacted in 2022, prohibits K-12 public schools from teaching a list of concepts, including that someone is inherently privileged or oppressed based solely on their race, sex or national origin. As of this writing, certain elements of the "Stop Woke Act" were just reversed by the 11th District (a conservative district) as applies to the workplace, but it is my understanding that education issues are still being fought in the courts. And the state of Florida may yet appeal to the Supreme Court.

https://www.youtube.com/watch?v=ODnAYsfcynM&t=1s

This is not meant to influence the reader to be either liberal or conservative, but to be open-minded and a seeker of truth. (And to recognize when someone is attempting to influence you to further their ends! Identify their motivation.*) Why would we wish our own children to be ignorant, uneducated, afraid of the truth, and insensitive to the lives of others? Germany wishes their children to grow up strong and aware of the suffering caused by their forefathers so it never occurs again.

*My motivation is that I believe in compassion, kindness, and equal-ity. I want to learn what it is like to be in someone else's skin, either of this time period or another.

Learning about other cultures and admitting one isn't omniscient is anathema to American culture. This pride and arrogance is harmful to actual growth and improvement as a person and as a culture. (Which is contradictory because a tenet of Christianity is humility and admitting one's sins before God) **One can have self-confidence and self-love and still be open to knowledge and wisdom.**

One of the most fascinating, intriguing, and thought-provoking movies I ever saw was "Where to Invade Next", a documentary/comedy (it's very funny), in which actual heads of state of various countries are interviewed in order that we might learn from what they are doing right.

I love the concept: why don't we look at what other countries are doing successfully and see if we might learn from them? There are much poorer countries with much better health care systems, much lower crime rates, much more harmony between the races, higher education standards, considerably less gun violence, and happier people. Why don't we at least ask what they are doing differently? You might not agree with what other countries are doing, you might not want it in your country which is your right (I certainly didn't agree with everything), but it is self-defeating to close oneself off to knowledge. Get the information first and then make a decision.

Conspiracy theories, misinformation and the twisting of the facts is a subject very near and dear to my heart and I make no apologies for that because, first, caring about the truth is relevant to the historical facts of this novel and, second, false narratives are destructive of freedom, democracy and human relationships—even deadly. How can we as a people make good decisions unless we're able to weed out the propaganda, identify the snake oil salesman, and face the truth? *In a democracy, everyone should have a voice.*

Irish revolution:

After the English revolution brought Cromwell and his parliamentary forces to power, **Cromwell sent armies to crush resistance in Ireland with extreme brutality**. In whole areas, the Irish population was exterminated or forced to flee. Scottish or English protestant colonies were then established.

In March 1649, Westminster appointed Oliver Cromwell to lead an invasion of Ireland in order to crush all resistance to the new English Commonwealth and to avenge the alleged massacres of Protestant settlers in 1641-2. Irish land was also a valuable commodity, almost 70% of which was still held by Catholic landowners.

https://downsurvey.tchpc.tcd.ie/history.html

How did English policies harm the Irish?

Irish culture, law and language were replaced; and many Irish lords lost their lands and hereditary authority. **Land-owning Irishmen (nobility) who worked for themselves suddenly became English tenants.**

Suppressing the religious and linguistic practices of the Irish Catholics were a few of Britain's many strategies that contributed to the weakening of Ireland as a whole (Franks). Under the Penal Laws of 1695, the Catholics could not hold commission in the army, enter a profession, or own a horse worth more than five pounds.

As the English gradually expanded their reach over the island by the 16th century, **religious persecution of Catholic Irish grew** – in particular after the accession of Elizabeth I, a Protestant, to the throne in 1558.

With the partition of Ireland, the relationship between Ireland and Britain changed dramatically. While the Republic of Ireland distanced itself from Britain, the Protestant majority in Northern Ireland clung fiercely to its British identity, and Catholics there suffered discrimination in employment and housing.

How many Irish died under English rule?

The combination of warfare, famine and plague caused a huge mortality among the Irish population. William Petty estimated (in the 1655–56 Down Survey) that the death toll of the wars in Ireland since 1641 was **over 618,000 people**, or about 40% of the country's pre-war population.

https://www.irishcentral.com/roots/history/irish-maids-new-york-racist-slur

Irish women working as domestic servants faced anti-Catholic and racist prejudice, with middle-class homeowners often calling them "Bridget" or "Biddy".

Where did most Irish immigrants settle in England?

Manchester was one of the big three destination cities for Irish immigration to England. In sheer numbers, London was the largest but the Irish % was proportionally small. **Liverpool was undoubtedly the most Irish city.**

Where did most Irish immigrants settle in the 1800s?

Irish men and women first settled in the United States during the 1700s. These were predominantly Scots-Irish and they largely settled into a rural way of life in **Virginia, Pennsylvania and the Carolinas**.

Distance to the Rainhill Trials:

Rainhill is 12.6 miles from Liverpool. The Liverpool to Manchester rail was being built at this time.

On average, a horse-drawn carriage can travel between **10-30 miles** a day. The distance will depend on factors such as terrain, weather, horse, and weight of the carriage.

The speed of coaches in this period rose from around 6 miles per hour (9.7 km/h) (including stops for provisioning) to a maximum of **8 miles per hour (13 km/h)** and greatly increased the level of mobility in the country, both for people and for mail.

How Fast Does a Horse-Drawn Carriage Go?

At a trot, a horse-drawn carriage will go around **8-10 MPH**. At a walk, a horse-drawn carriage will go about 2-4 MPH. The speed of a carriage depends on the weather, terrain, horse, and other factors.

Summary of the 5 Fastest Animals in the World:

1. Peregrine Falcon 242 mph
2. Mexican Free-tailed Bat 99mph
3. Black Marlin 80mph
4. Cheetah 64mph
5. American Antelope 55mph

The cheetah (Acinonyx jubatus) is the quickest animal on land. With documented top speeds of **64 mph (103 km/h)**, the cheetah easily surpasses other swift animals, like racehorses, to take the title of world's fastest land animal.

The top speed at which the world's fastest equine sprinter, the Quarter Horse, has been clocked is **55 mph**. The fastest recorded race time for a Thoroughbred is 44 mph. The average equine gallop clocks in at about 27 mph.

How fast did steamboats travel?

The steamboats could travel at a speed of **up to 5 miles per hour** and quickly revolutionized river travel and trade, dominating the waterways.

https://www.exploros.com/summary/Steamboats-of-the-1800s

Music/Dance:

https://www.musicalpubcrawl.com/instruments

Traditional Irish instruments:

Banjo, Button Accordion, Irish Uilleann Pipe, Bodran, Harp

Even though the harp is Ireland's national symbol, **the fiddle is the most commonly played instrument in traditional Irish music**. Its ornamental melodies are more relaxed than the classical violin and improvisation is encouraged.

The Gallopade, 1829:

https://www.youtube.com/watch?v=sgcUhQyAJlo

Rings for Weddings:

The groom did not wear a wedding ring. Engagement rings as we know them were not in vogue, although a ring could be given as a symbol of affection—by men and women, particularly in the case of a lengthy engagement. In Jane Austen's "Sense and Sensibility", Edward wears a ring made of his fiancée's hair.

Victorian-era (1837-1901) wedding rings in the United States and Europe typically were made of gold and often featured such gemstones as sapphires, rubies, amethyst, garnet, chalcedony, topaz, pearls, Brilliant Earth says.

The Marriage Act (1753)

Hardwicke's Marriage Act of 1753 stated that all marriages in England had to take place in an Anglican parish church or chapel to be legally binding. **Clergymen who disobeyed the law were liable for 14 years transportation**. The law did not apply to members of the royal family or to Jews and Quakers.

If a Catholic bride wished to be married in her church, the Anglican ceremony had to PRECEDE it (be FIRST).

In addition the banns had to be read, **unless under special license**. A common license was available from a bishop or archbishop and their offices.

Runaway marriages

Hardwicke's Marriage Act did not apply in Scotland where underage couples could be married without the consent of parents or guardians. Hence elopements to Gretna Green.

It should be noted that getting married in Gretna Green had a terrible social stigma associated with it, was a scandal of the first order, and could ruin any sibling's chance of a good match. This is one reason why, in so many books, the relatives are racing to stop the marriage before it takes place!

"The scandal also engulfed the family. It was a sign of 'bad blood'; it made anyone else in the family a much poorer marriage prospect, and the family might well find themselves shunned." – Abigail Reynolds

http://historicalbellesandbeaus.blogspot.com/2011/04/guest-abigail-reynolds-scandal-of.html

https://janeaustensworld.com/tag/marriage-licence-in-regency-england/

Most people got married with banns: the no-cost option. The couple had to notify the parish clergyman a week in advance of the first announcement. They told him their full names, places of residence, and intention to marry. Then the parson announced the banns three Sundays in a row.

The Marriage Act of 1836 allowed non-conformists and Catholics to be married in their own places of worship.

LIVERPOOL IN THE 18TH CENTURY

In the early 1700s, the writer Daniel Defoe also commented on Liverpool's booming trade. He said: 'Liverpool has an opulent, flourishing and increasing trade to Virginia and English colonies in America. They trade around the whole island (of Great Britain), send ships to Norway, to Hamburg, and to the Baltic as also to Holland and Flanders (roughly modern Belgium).'

Georgian Liverpool grew rapidly. By the early 18th century it had probably reached a population of 5,000. By 1750 the population of Liverpool had reached 20,000 and by 1801 77,000. Many of the inhabitants were immigrants. In 1795 a writer spoke about 'the great influx of Irish and Welsh of whom the majority of the inhabitants at present consist'.

Many of the poor in Liverpool lived in dreadful conditions. Their houses were overcrowded and the streets were dirty. There were no sewers only cesspits. The worst houses were the cellar dwellings. The poorest people lived in cellars under buildings. Often they slept on piles of straw because they could not afford beds.

The first dock in Liverpool was built in 1715. Previously ships were simply tied up by the shore but as the port grew busier this was no longer adequate. Four more docks were built in the 18th century. Liverpool grew to be the third-largest port in the country behind London and Bristol. Liverpool benefited from the growth of industries in Manchester; nearby port goods from Manchester were exported through Liverpool.

From about 1730 the merchants of Liverpool made huge profits from the slave trade. The trade formed a triangle. Goods from Manchester were given to the Africans in return for slaves. The slaves were transported across the Atlantic to the West Indies and sugar was brought back from there to Liverpool. At the end of the century, a famous actor visited Liverpool. When he was booed he told the audience that every brick of their town was 'cemented with the blood of an African'.

In the 18th-century **sugar refining** became an important industry in Liverpool. **Shipbuilding** also became a flourishing industry. **Rope-making** also prospered. (Rope was, obviously, needed in large amounts by ships). In Liverpool, there was also some manufacturing industry such as **ironworking, watchmaking, and pottery**.

Meanwhile in the 18th-century rivers were deepened to make it easier for ships to sail on them. The **Mersey** and **Irwell** were deepened in 1720 and the Sankey Brook in 1755. From 1748 night watchmen patrolled the streets of Liverpool at night and in 1778 a dispensary was opened in John Street where the poor could obtain free medicines.

The American **War of Independence began in 1776**. At first, it disrupted trade from Liverpool. Obviously, it ended trade with the colonies themselves but it also meant American ships attacked English merchant shipping trading with the West Indies. They captured the ships and took their cargoes.

In 1778 France, Spain and Holland declared war on Britain. That meant ships from Liverpool could attack French, Spanish, and Dutch ships and take their cargoes.

(and, possibly, vice-versa)

LIVERPOOL IN THE 19TH CENTURY

In 1801 the population of Liverpool was about 77,000 and by 1821 the population had reached 118,000.

The port of Liverpool boomed in the 1800s and many new docks were built. By the middle of the century, Liverpool was second only to London. The Manchester ship canal was completed in 1894. **Although the docks dominated Liverpool there were other industries such as shipbuilding, iron foundries, glass manufacture, and soap making**.

However, like all towns in the 19th century, Liverpool was unsanitary. **In 1832 there was a cholera epidemic in Liverpool**. Another epidemic followed in 1849.

Yet during the 19th-century amenities in Liverpool improved. In 1799 and 1802 private companies began to supply piped water to Liverpool. But it was expensive and poor people could not afford it. They relied on barrels or wells. However, a municipal water supply was begun in Liverpool in 1857.

The **Philharmonic Hall was** built in 1849. It burned in 1933 but it was rebuilt. **The Central Library** was built in 1852 and St George's Hall was built in 1854. William Brown library was built in 1860. Picton Reading Room was built in 1879.

In the 19th-century amenities in Liverpool continued to improve. The Royal Southern Hospital opened in 1814. An eye hospital opened in 1820. The Northern Hospital followed in 1834. Stanley Hospital opened in 1867. The Walker Art Gallery opened in 1877. **Stanley Park was laid out in 1870** and Sefton Park was opened in 1872. The Palm House was built in 1896.

Meanwhile from 1830 **horse-drawn buses** ran in Liverpool and from 1865 **horse-drawn trams** ran in the streets. The trams were converted to electricity in 1898-1901.

Liverpool officially became a city in 1880 and by 1881 its population had reached 611,00. In 1895 the boundaries of Liverpool were extended to include Wavertree, Walton, and parts of Toxteth and West Derby.

- Wikipedia

VAUXHALL:

The Vauxhall area is more famously known as the "Scottie Road area" due to the history of Scotland Road running through it.

Scotland Road was created in the 1770s as a turnpike road to Preston via Walton and Burscough. It became part of a stagecoach route to Scotland, hence its name. It was partly widened in 1803 and streets of working-class housing laid out either side as Liverpool expanded.

Scotland Road was the centre of working class life in north Liverpool. Home to most of Liverpool's migrant communities, Scotland Road was almost "a city within a city but by far the largest community was Irish Catholic following a massive influx of refugees fleeing the famine of 1847/48 It was a place close to both the back end of the city centre and the docks. It could be a place of both romantic nostalgia and brutal hardship. Community was at the centre of Scotland Road and a shared distinctly Liverpool -Irish identity evolved through the nineteenth and early twentieth century.

I have no idea how rowdy any of these saloons actually were.
  Liverpool saloons:
  https://confidentials.com/liverpool/ten-best-irish-pubs-bars-liverpool
  * Shenanigans
  * Molly Malones
  * Flanagan's Apple (original pub)

https://www.liverpoolecho.co.uk/whats-on/food-drink-news/14-old-school-liverpool-pubs-12293593
  * The Slaughter house on Fenwick Street, Liverpool, since early 1800s

Housing

VICTORIAN ERA

The 1891 census reported that outside of London, Liverpool had the highest number of dwellings and among the highest levels of over-crowding in major cities.

Police Constables:

After becoming home secretary in the British government, between 1825 and 1830 Robert Peel undertook a comprehensive consolidation and reform of criminal laws. At the time, policing in London and else-where in Britain was largely carried out by **constables**, who reported to local magistrates.

The Royal Irish Constabulary was the police force in Ireland from 1822 until 1922, when all of the country was part of the United Kingdom.

The irony was that the Royal Irish Constabulary was more successful than the British police system!

"Following the success of the Royal Irish Constabulary" it became obvious that something similar was needed in London, so in 1829 when Sir Robert was Home Secretary in Lord Liverpool's Tory Cabinet, the Metropolitan Police Act was passed, providing permanently appointed and paid Constables to protect the capital as part of the Metropolitan Police Force.

Sir Robert Peel and his 'bobbies' - Historic UK

https://www.historic-uk.com/HistoryUK/HistoryofEngland/Sir-Robert-Peel/

When was the police service as we know it established?

The date for the beginning of the police in Britain is often given as 1829, when the Metropolitan Police first took to the streets of London. The Scots and the Northern Irish can dispute this, pointing to their earlier institutions. **Evidence from the Old Bailey, for example, reveals the presence of a number of courageous watchmen and constables**; these were typically former soldiers, under the age of 40, who knew the laws of the land. In some parishes, these watchmen wore

numbers painted on the back of their overcoats so that they were iden-
tifiable.

Sir Robert Peel and his 'bobbies' - Historic UK

https://www.historic-uk.com/HistoryUK/HistoryofEngland/Sir-
Robert-Peel/

Sir Robert Peel

By Ben Johnson

In Britain today all policemen are commonly referred to as 'Bobbies'.
Originally though, they were known as 'Peelers' in reference to one Sir
Robert Peel (1788 – 1850).

Today it is hard to believe that Britain in the 18th century did not
have a professional police force. Scotland had established a number of
police forces following the introduction of the City of Glasgow Police in
1800 and the Royal Irish Constabulary was established in 1822, in large
part because of the Peace Preservation Act of 1814 which Peel was
heavily involved with. However, London was sadly lacking in any form
of protective presence and crime prevention for its people as they
entered the 19th century.

Following the success of the **Royal Irish Constabulary** it became
obvious that something similar was needed in London, so in 1829 when
Sir Robert was Home Secretary in Lord Liverpool's Tory Cabinet, the
Metropolitan Police Act was passed, providing permanently appointed
and paid Constables to protect the capital as part of the Metropolitan
Police Force.

The first thousand of Peel's police, dressed in blue tail-coats and top
hats, began to patrol the streets of London on 29th September 1829. The
uniform was carefully selected to make the 'Peelers' look more like ordinary citizens, rather than a red-coated soldier with a helmet.

The 'Peelers' were issued with a wooden truncheon carried in a long
pocket in the tail of their coat, a pair of handcuffs and a wooden rattle to
raise the alarm. By the 1880s this rattle had been replaced by a whistle.

To be a 'Peeler' the rules were quite strict. You had to be aged 20 –
27, at least 5' 7" tall (or as near as possible), fit, literate and have no
history of any wrong-doings.

These men became the model for the creation of all the provincial
forces; at first in the London Boroughs, and then into the counties and

towns, after the passing of the County Police Act in 1839. An ironic point however; the Lancashire town of Bury, birthplace of Sir Robert, was the only major town which elected not to have its own separate police force. The town remained part of the Lancashire Constabulary until 1974.

Early Victorian police worked seven days a week, with only five days unpaid holiday a year for which they received the grand sum of £1 per week. Their lives were strictly controlled; they were not allowed to vote in elections and required permission to get married and even to share a meal with a civilian. To allay the public's suspicion of being spied upon, officers were required to wear their uniforms both on and off duty.

Sir Robert Peel

In spite of the huge success of his 'Bobbies', Peel was not a well liked man. Queen Victoria is said to have found him 'a cold, unfeeling, disagreeable man'. They had many personal conflicts over the years, and when he spoke against awarding her 'darling' Prince Albert an annual income of £50,000, he did little to endear himself to the Queen.

When Peel was Prime Minister, he and the Queen had a further disagreement over her 'Ladies of the Bedchamber'. Peel insisted that she accepted some 'Tory' ladies in preference to her 'Whig' ladies.

Although Peel was a skillful politician, and had a long and distinguished career, he had few social graces and had a reserved, off-putting manner.

The Liverpool Mercury

was an English newspaper that originated in Liverpool, England. As well as focusing on local news, the paper also reported on both national and international news allowing it to circulate in Lancashire, Wales, Isle of Man and London.

Founded by Egerton Smith in 1811 the newspaper cost 7d and was published weekly, covering news relating to the city's busy port. By 1858 the newspaper switched from being a weekly paper to a daily, with an extended edition published on Fridays. The paper's second edition was claimed to be 72 columns long, making it one of the largest newspapers in the world. During the early 1900s the *Mercury* merged with rival paper *Liverpool Daily Post* to become the *Liverpool Daily Post and the Liverpool Mercury* whose first edition was published on 14 November 1904.

Those newspapers were very different to the ones we see today. In the 18th century, Liverpool newspapers included some local news but it was mostly centered on the port's shipping.

But 1811, and the inception of the Mercury, was to be the start of 200 years of coverage of Liverpool news by what is the current Trinity Mirror group.

The eight-page Liverpool Mercury, founded by Egerton Smith, cost 7d and was first published as a weekly, covering the thriving port and commercial town.

On January 1, 1850 the proprietors described their long-term aim as **'continual and peaceful progress', and it was these serious, reformist and Liberal principles that guided the Mercury throughout the century.**

Following the death of its founder in 1841, the newspaper passed into the hands of his widow and son.

The newspaper gradually expanded. In 1858 it began to be published daily, with a larger edition published on Fridays, and by 1880 it claimed the weekly 2d edition of the paper contained '72 long columns making it one of the largest newspapers in the world'.

The newspaper was circulated not just in Liverpool, Lancashire and Cheshire, but also in Wales, the Isle of Man and even in London.

And while the Mercury reported national and international news, it was particularly strong on its coverage of Liverpool and its social issues such as poor housing and poverty.

The Mercury was a staunch campaigning newspaper fighting for better housing and public health, and for moral reform, in Liverpool.

In August 1819, the then editor John Smith was one of the journalists on the platform at Manchester's St Peter's Field, later writing a critical report of the behavior of soldiers at what became known as the **Peterloo Massacre.**

And it was on May 1, 1829, that the Liverpool & Manchester Railway ran an advertisement in the paper inviting "engineers and iron founders" to submit plans for locomotives to compete for the winning design.

The rest is, as they say, history.

CHILD LABOR

How Children Earned Money in this Era:
https://victorianchildren.org/victorian-child-labor/
* coal mines
* Chimney Sweep
* Factory Worker
* Laundry for pay
* Scare the birds from the fields
* Farm worker
* Rat catcher
* Ship Yard
* Seller in the Streets
* Domestic Servant
* Pottery making
* Textile Mill
* Pick pocket
* Hat making
* Prostitution

Child labor laws:
https://victorianchildren.org/victorian-child-labor/

1815 Sir Humphrey Davy invented the miners' safety lamp.

1825 Between 1825 and 1831, three more factory acts were passed. The first of these, the **Cotton Mills Regulation Act** (1825), ruled that workers under 16 should be allowed an hour and a half for meals within set time periods and that children should only work for a maximum of 9 h on Saturdays.

1833 Factory Act, this banned children from working in textile factories under the age of nine. From nine to thirteen they were limited to nine hours a day and 48 hours a week.

1836 Registration of Births, Deaths and Marriages, this enabled factory inspectors to check the ages of children working in factories (only applicable in England and Wales).

1842 Publication of the 'First Report of the Children's Employment Commissioners: Mines and Collieries', which had been prepared by Lord Ashley (later Lord Shaftesbury).

1842 Mines Act, this banned the employment underground of boys under the age of ten and all women and girls. No one under the age of fifteen was to be in charge of machinery.

1844 Factory Act, this classed women as young persons under the age of eighteen and limited the hours of both groups to twelve on weekdays and nine on Saturdays.

1847 The Ten Hour Act, this cut the hours of women and the under-eighteens to ten a day and 58 a week.

1850 The Ten Hour Act, this set the working day for all workers at ten and a half hours. 1867 Factory Act, the legislation was extended to all workshops with more than 50 workers.

The **Children's Employment Commission Report** is the second report created by the Royal Commissioners. The Royal Commission of Inquiry was championed by **Lord Ashley, Earl of Shaftesbury**, to investigate the condition and treatment of child workers. Sub-commissioners travelled across Great Britain and Ireland interviewing children and young adults, as well as parents, adult employees, educators, medical professionals, and clergymen. The segments that dealt directly with the condition of workers in Ireland have been published separately on Findmypast as Ireland, Children's Employment Commission.

The first report focused on the working conditions within the mines and led to reform through the **1842 Coal Mines Act**. The second report, found here, covered a variety of trades: textiles (including weaving, stitching, bleaching, and dying), printing, tobacco production, and more. The report shed light on the harsh reality faced by child labourers.

The report documented the hours child labourers worked, their ages, and the dangerous nature of some of their work such as being exposed to high temperatures for long periods of time, over-crowded spaces, and lack of safety procedures.

The report caused a shift in public opinion and lead to the **Factory Act of 1844**, which reduced the number of hours children worked in a day **from up to thirteen hours to six and a half**. After reading the report, **Charles Dickens** was inspired to write *A Christmas Carol*. The story offered commentary on greed, wealth, and power, wrapped in an unsuspecting Christmas narrative.

Haberdasher - Wikipedia

In British English, *a haberdasher* is a business or person who sells small articles for sewing, dressmaking and knitting, such as buttons, ribbons, ...

Dressmakers, mantua-makers, or seamstresses/sempstresses, (and sometimes also called **needle-women** as were the lower class workers), were those catering to the upper classes and learned their trade through an apprenticeship.

Comparative salaries:

A skilled London coach-maker could earn up to five guineas (£5, five shillings) a week – considerably more than most middle class clerks. This was the top of the working class pyramid. The railways generated employment for porters and cab-drivers. The London omnibuses needed 16,000 drivers and conductors, by 1861. Conductors were allowed to keep four shillings a day out of the fares they collected, and drivers could count on 34 shillings a week, for a working day beginning at 7.45 and ending often past midnight. A labourer's average wage was between 20 and 30 shillings a week in London, probably less in the provinces. This would just cover his rent, and a very sparse diet for him and his family.

https://www.bl.uk/victorian-britain/articles/the-working-classes-and-the-poor

20 shillings in a pound.

Jane Austen's World

https://janeaustensworld.com › *tag*

The Dress Maker and the Seamstress in Regency England

https://janeaustensworld.com/tag/19th-century-seamstress/

Over a century ago, Douglas Jerrold asked:

Is there a more helpless, a more forlorn and unprotected, creature than, in nine cases out of ten, the Dress Maker's Girl – the Daily Seamstress; pushed prematurely from the parental hearth, or rather no hearth, to win her miserable crust by aching fingers?

Imagine that it is the Season in London and young ladies and their mamas are ordering dresses by the dozens for balls and visits. In an age when all sewing and embroidery were done by hand, when lighting was poor and wages were so low that they barely paid for room and board, pity the poor seamstress hunched over her sewing assignments, racing against time to meet a series of deadlines that seem endless, and complying with the exacting standards of a boss and clients who cared not a whit for her comfort.

Fingers numb, backs aching, eyes straining to focus on mind numbingly repetitive work meant that burning the midnight oil was no mere phrase. For embroiderers who continued to work well past dusk, lamps were devised that amplified light. Those who sat closest to its source benefited the most. The poor women who sat in the outer circle scarcely benefited from the amplification of lacemaker lamps:

"The three legged stool (candle-block, candle-stool or pole-board are alternative names) upon which the candle and the water filled "magnifying" flasks are fitted, is placed in the middle of the room. The lace-workers then arrange themselves around the light in an orderly manner that allows each person to have at least some of the light. The best lace-makers use the highest stools and are nearest the light source. They have what is known as the "first-light" then the graded workers arrange themselves according to ability to have the "second-light" and the "third light". Whiting tells us that in this way 18 lacemakers can be accommodated around the candle-stool.

From my own experiments with this form of lighting, I find it hard to understand how any maker who was in the third light, or even the second light come to that, could make lace from that single source of illumination!" – Brian Lemin

Mr. Jerrod's prose is purply, like much of the writing during the Victorian era, but one gets the gist of what life must have been like for a lowly little seamstress toiling in a garret room with other seamstresses. The hours were long, and sometimes unpredictable:

Our little Dress Maker has arrived at the work room, After two or three hours she takes her bread and butter and warm adulterated water denominated tea. Breakfast hurriedly over, she works under the rigid scrutinizing eye of a task mistress some four hours more, and then proceeds to the important work of dinner. A scanty slice of meat, perhaps an egg, is produced from her basket; she dines and sews again till five. Then comes again the fluid of the morning and again the needle until eight.

Hark, yes, that's eight now striking. "Thank heaven," thinks our heroine, as she rises to put by her work, the task for the day is done.

At this moment a thundering knock is heard at the door: — The Duchess of Daffodils must have her robe by four to morrow!

Again the Dress Maker's apprentice is made to take her place — again, she resumes her thread and needle, and perhaps the clock is "beating one", as she again, jaded and half dead with work, creeps to her lodging, and goes to bed, still haunted with the thought that as the work "is very back", she must be up by five to-morrow.

Pity the woman who was born to luxury who lost a father before she was comfortably married and, because of his debts or other hardship, had to work for a living. Preferred jobs included governess, chaperone, or a ladies companion, but they often led to a woman living a life of limbo. Neither servant nor family member, they spent lonely lives of servitude, fitting in nowhere. If a woman could not obtain employment in those positions, she could always turn to sewing as either an independent dressmaker or seamstress. Jane Austen's friend, Mary Lamb, made her living as a mantua maker, sewing garments for women and men in her own home, and taking up mending. In *Persuasion*, Mrs. Smith knitted small souvenir objects, which Nurse Rooke sold for her.

Dressmaker in 1840

These women, accustomed to luxury in their earlier years, were exposed to sumptuous homes and surroundings as they visited their clients for fittings. Yet their earnings of twelve or fifteen shillings per week (1840 quote) were hardly sufficient to provide for adequate food and lodging. Independent dressmakers had to look neat and presentable, yet they could barely afford their upkeep. Her life could even turn for the worse if she never married. She would then be fated to grow old in a world that was harsh for single women. Barely able to scrape a living together while she was young and healthy, she was fated to lose her excellent eyesight due to the strain of her work.

The Children's Employment Commission in 1842 estimated that there were some 1000 millinery and dressmaking businesses in London (millinery is here equivalent to dressmaking; the word was not confined to hat makers until the end of the century), and Nicola Phillips estimates that 95 per cent of these were run by women. It is a common mistake to confuse one needlewoman with another, but as Kay points out, 'the businesswoman milliner is a different creature to the jobbing seamstress': one designed and made or had made individual garments; the other worked by the piece, either for a milliner or stitching pre-cut ready-made clothes – (*The Foundations of Female Entrepreneurship*, Alison Kay, p. 48).

Owning a shop was no guarantee of economic stability, for many wealthy women failed to pay their bills on time, if at all. In the 18th century, the enterprising Hannah Glasse ran a dressmaker's shop in London with her daughter, which eventually went bankrupt. She went on to write one of the most popular cookbooks of her era, but in this venture she too lost money.

As the century progressed and with the advent of the sewing machine, life did not automatically become easier for seamstresses and dressmakers, who still worked long hours in cramped conditions, their backs bent over sewing machines in factories and piece work shops. Clothing had become more affordable. The rising middle class was purchasing more items than ever, and etiquette dictated that wealthy ladies were required to change their clothes for different functions throughout the day. Thus demand for new and fashionable clothes remained high.

The Whigs:

The **Whigs** merged into the Liberal Party with the Peelites and Radicals in the 1850s. Many Whigs left the Liberal Party in 1886 to form the Liberal Unionist Party, which merged into the Conservative Party in 1912.

A **Tory** is a person who holds a political philosophy known as Toryism, based on a British version of *traditionalism and conservatism.*

It was only the House of Commons which elected officials. The House of Lords was hereditary. In addition to this intrinsic undemocratic representation, very few citizens were allowed the vote.

A hilarious depiction of rotten boroughs is in BBCs **Blackadder "Dish and Dishonesty"** (Season 3 series 1). Hugh Laurie plays George III, the Prince Regent, and Rowan Atkinson his butler "Blackadder".

Popular Politics in the 18th century, by Dr. Matthew White

https://www.bl.uk/restoration-18th-century-literature/articles/popular-politics-in-the-18th-century

Throughout the Georgian period the political rights of ordinary men and women were extremely limited. Only those men with substantial property or wealth were entitled to vote – this amounted to around **200,000 individuals**, which was only a tiny fraction of the population. Many Members of Parliament were elected to represent 'rotten boroughs' – these were boroughs in which just a handful of voters enjoyed totally disproportionate representation in Parliament. Many large towns such as Manchester, on the other hand, which were expanding quickly as a result of migration and industrialization, had no representation at Westminster at all until the passing of the first Reform Act in 1832.

Though exaggerated for comic effect, such scenes were often common at election time during the 18th century owing to the relatively small and exclusive electorate responsible for casting parliamentary votes. The property qualification to vote stood at 40 shillings freehold value during the century, meaning that only those of means could have any influence on the outcome of elections. Prior to election day lengthy canvassing took place, with agents of candidates approaching voters in person in an attempt to ascertain their political preferences. Many freeholders were offered free transport and alcohol on polling day in order to directly influence their voting decisions.

Political opinion was also expressed in a more direct manner. Rioting was a familiar feature of daily life in both towns and the countryside, and many people came to fear the power of the 'mob'. Crowd action was particularly strong in London, where people regularly threw stones at the carriages of leading politicians or booed unpopular ministers. Crowds sometimes forced householders to light their windows in celebration of political or military victories, and massive mobs formed around their political heroes. In 1780, after the government passed legislation giving more political rights to Catholics, thousands of people rioted for a week in London in protest. Catholics were attacked, and Catholic property smashed up. All of London's major prisons were burnt to the ground, and the Bank of England came under attack. King George III was forced to call in the Army in order to restore order, and over 200 people were killed in the ensuing violence. The incident became known as the Gordon Riots.

The **Gordon Riots of June 1780** are considered by some historians to be the closest Britain has ever come to a full-blown revolution. Following legislation passed permitting Catholics greater freedom in society (such as being allowed to join the army) a huge petition seeking repeal of these Acts was drawn up the Protestant Association, under the leadership of the enigmatic **Lord George Gordon**. On the morning of 2 June a huge crowd nearly 50,000 strong marched to parliament to present the petition to parliament. Events descended into chaos. Members of the Commons and Lords were met with a barrage of abuse and physical violence, with the crowd only successfully dispersed once troops were called to the scene. For a week thereafter violence raged across the capital. Catholic houses and chapels were pulled down by angry crowds, the Bank of England came under attack and prisoners were released from London's principal prisons. 15,000 troops poured into London to quell the disturbances and nearly 300 rioters were shot dead by soldiers.

In 1793, Britain – in coalition with other European states – was drawn into war with France. For most of the following 22 years Britain was in an almost constant state of war, resulting in severe strains on her national economy. A threat of invasion by French forces in the south created a sense of panic throughout the nation and was responsible for a wave of anti-French sentiment sweeping the country. In villages and towns up and down the country thousands of men were called to arms, and dozens of amateur volunteer forces were formed. By the end of the century nearly 400,000 men were in readiness for an imminent French invasion – more than twice the size of the standing Army. These impressive lines of national defense would remain in place until Napoleon's eventual defeat in 1815.

The success of the **French Revolution**, culminating in the **execution of Louis XVI in 1793**, caused increasing consternation among the British Whig government. With the achievements of the working people of Paris on show to the world, many politicians feared that similar revolutionary movements would be stirred at home.

Such concerns were well-founded. Several radical movements such as the **London Corresponding Society** emerged during the 1790s calling for parliamentary reform and petitioning for greater rights for the working population. Despite their rising popularity, these movements were gradually driven underground by a raft of increasingly repressive legislation implemented by the government of **Prime Minister William Pitt**. With France declaring war on Great Britain in 1793 and food riots breaking out across the country, stricter measures were imposed to safeguard the political order. The issuing of seditious words and holding of reform meetings were outlawed (part of the so-called 'gagging acts') and political radicals were imprisoned for treason following the suspension of habeas corpus.

--**Dr Matthew White**, a Research Fellow in History at the University of Hertfordshire where he specializes in the social history of London during the 18th and 19th centuries.

The Rise of Cities in Georgian England by Matthew White:

https://www.bl.uk/georgian-britain/articles/the-rise-of-cities-in-the-18th-century

Life in the 18th-century city would have provoked a dazzling mixture of sensations: terror and exhilaration, menace and bliss, awe and pity.

In the hand-written diary of Francis Place: in it, Place describes his pleasure at the bustling trade of London as seen from his bedroom morning on a fine sunny day in 1827.

Place lived his whole life in and around the Strand and Charing Cross in the capital, being first apprenticed as a leather breeches maker and later embarking on a successful career as a master tailor. Place is best remembered though as a political radical who strongly supported a range of issues considered controversial in the early 19th century: the freedom to vote, for example, education for all and the right to form trade unions.

Pillory punishments were an every-day feature of life in Georgian Britain, employed by the magistracy to punish a variety of crimes deemed worthy of public criticism: forgery and arson, for example, or crimes of sexual deviancy. In this extract from Francis Place's memoirs we see in detail just how raucous the punishments could be.: "Convicted criminals were placed in an upright position with their head and hands locked into a wooden board, and for an hour were pelted by the surrounding crowds with all manner of filth and rubbish: dead animals, horse manure and rotten vegetables."

Pillory punishments became increasingly rare by 1800, mainly as a result of growing concerns with how unpredictable the events could be. Crowds could be extremely violent towards certain offenders and in some cases criminals were literally stoned to death by the mob. Alternatively, pilloried men and women judged to have been hard-treated by the criminal justice system were protected by the crowd. Umbrellas were sometimes held over their heads to protect them from the sun, while others were offered refreshments or showered with flowers during their allotted hour in the device.

Crowds and people

Rises in population added to the sense of confusion in many British cities. Crowds swarmed in every thoroughfare. Scores of street sellers 'cried' merchandise from place to place, advertising the wealth of goods and services on offer. Milkmaids, orange sellers, fishwives and piemen, for example, all walked the streets offering their various wares for sale, while knife grinders and the menders of broken chairs and furniture could be found on street corners.

The Itinerant Traders of London

People crowded around the windows of print shops displaying the latest satirical cartoons, or waited outside lottery offices for the results to be drawn. Others gathered to watch politicians make speeches at election time, or to watch bare-knuckle boxing matches. House fires, accidents, fights and public executions, amongst an array of other urban spectacles, all drew huge audiences whenever they occurred, and added to the sense of excitement that was part of daily city life.

If you believe that people of all time periods are the same and have the same values, compare the music of 1820-1829 to today's music.

Music 1820-1829:

https://www.loc.gov/collections/american-sheet-music-1820-to-1860/articles-and-essays/greatest-hits-1820-60-variety-music-cavalcade/1820-to-1829/

Hail to the Chief. w., Sir Walter Scott. m., James Sanderson. E. Riley [ca. 1820]. (The song was published earlier in London. The words are from Scott's narrative poem *The Lady of the Lake*, published in 1810. The composer was a self-taught English violinist and the conductor of the Surrey Theatre, London, who wrote many songs for local theatrical productions during the 1790s and the early years of the nineteenth century.)

Buy a Broom? w., m., anon. Firth & Hall [ca. 1825]. (The song is an adaptation of the German "O Du Lieber Augustin." According to Wulf Stratowa, *Oesterreichische Lyrik aus Neun Jahrhunderten*, [Vienna, 1848], p. 355, Augustin was an itinerant bagpiper, probably one Marx Augustin, who is said to have survived the plague in 1679 and the Turkish occupation of Vienna in 1683, and died on an Austrian highway, Oct. 10, 1705.)

https://www.youtube.com/watch?v=_u6HPRWR7rc

Love's Eyes (The Forest Rose). w., Samuel Woodworth. m., Scottish air: "Roy's Wife," arr. by John Davies. (*The Forest Rose* was a ballad opera produced in New York at the Chatham Theatre, Oct. 7, 1825, and enjoyed a considerable vogue both in its original form and later in a dramatic version. The words and the tune are reprinted in Grenville Vernon, *Yankee Doodle-Doo*, [New York, 1927], p. 112-13.)

The Dashing White Sergeant. w., General Burgoyne. m., Sir Henry Rowley Bishop. (Composed in 1826.)

I'd Be a Butterfly. w., m., Thomas Haynes Bayly. (The song was written and composed in Chessel, England, in 1826. An American edition was published by E. Riley, New York, during the 1820s.)

Meet Me by Moonlight Alone. w., m., Joseph Augustine Wade. London: F. T. Latour [1826]. (The song was popularized by the celebrated Mme. Lucia Elizabeth Vestris.)

Oh! No, We Never Mention Her., 1828 (Taylor)) w., m., Thomas Haynes Bayly, E. Riley [1828]. (Published earlier in London. The tune and the words were later reprinted under the title "O No, I Never Mention Her" in a small song collection *The Musical Carcanet*, [Collins & Hanay, New York, 1832], p. 11.)

Love's Ritornella (The Brigand). w., J[ames] R[obinson] Planché. m., T[homas Simpson] Cooke. London: Chappell & Co. [1829.] (*The Brigand* was a musical play, produced at Covent Garden Theatre, London, 1829. The above song, also known as "Gentle Zitella," was reviewed in the musical journal *The Harmonicon*, London, 1830, p. 90. Planché was an English playwright and author of French descent, and the librettist of Weber's famous opera *Oberon*, produced in London, 1826. The song immediately became popular in England, and was reprinted in America.)

Crinoline:

So far as I know, there was no actual crinoline fire at the Rainhill Trials. There were a lot of sparks caused by the locomotives.

Crinoline was first used in 1829, so the woman in the novel would have been wealthy and ahead of fashion.

Originally the crinoline, a stiff fabric made of **horsehair and cotton or linen**, was used to make underskirts and as a dress lining. The stiffened or structured petticoat was designed to hold out the woman's skirt and by the 1850s, the ladies wore it up in order the widen skirts to achieve the illusion of a tiny waist.Feb 14, 2020

By the mid-1860s, the crinoline had already begun to be replaced by the bustle. **As city living became more common and women spent more time in public, the crinoline was simply not feasible.**

For starters, **they were a serious fire hazard.** Made often of cotton or gauze and swaying to and fro with grace and vigor, they easily caught on fire. It is estimated that around 3,000 crinoline-fire deaths took place between 1850 and 1860.

https://thecowkeeperswish.com/2018/08/06/the-crinoline-fires/

1869 *Cassell's Household Guide to Every Department of Practical Life*, there is an intriguing recipe "To Render Ladies' Dresses Incombustible." Mixing your whitening with starch, you could make "lace, net, muslin, gauze, or any other light stuff, perfectly inflammable. As white dresses are much worn at evening parties, where fires are often kept in the grates, and numerous ladies have been burnt to death by means of their dresses catching light whilst dancing, it is hoped this useful receipt will not be forgotten by any lady in the habit of attending balls and parties."

Thank you for reading my book, "The Race to Rainhill". You are so appreciated. I love my intelligent, curious, and insightful readers!

First publication August 2024.

Imprint: Traditional Historical Romance

"Romancing the Rails" series

Cover Design by Clint Hollingsworth

https://www.amazon.com/Clint-Hollingsworth

This book would not be possible without my wonderful husband, Clint Hollingsworth, who is an exceptional editor/artist/writer and an award-winning author.

PUBLISHER'S NOTE:

So what is real and what is not? That is the question for the ages.

Printed in U.S.A.

Publisher: Icicle Ridge Graphics

Ebook ISBN: 978-1-960216-07-6

Print book ISBN: 978-1-960216-08-3

Hardback book ISBN: 978-1-960216-09-0

❀ Created with Vellum